R.N.F. (RICHARD) SKINNER has published several poetry collections; composed lyrics for a range of songs, including a musical; and written a clutch of published short stories. He has a degree in Natural Sciences from Cambridge University, where, as well as being a member of the famous Footlights club, he co-founded and performed with the cabaret-revue team Headlights. He continues to write and perform sketch-based comedy.

A south-east Londoner by upbringing, he moved to Devon in 1975 to pursue his writing while working in a variety of jobs, mainly in the mental health sector. In 2012 he was awarded a doctorate from Exeter University for his thesis on religion and evolutionary theory. He lives in Exeter with his wife, four hens and, until recently, two cats.

Still Crazy... is his first published novel. To find out more please visit www.richardskinner.org

Poetry published as Richard Skinner

Leaping & Staggering (Dilettante 1988/1996)
In the Stillness: based on Julian of Norwich (Dilettante 1990/2013)
The Melting Woman (Blue Button 1993)
Still Staggering (Dilettante 1995)
Echoes of Eckhart (Cairns/Arthur James 1998)
The Logic of Whistling (Cairns 2002)
Invocations (Wild Goose 2005)
Colliding With God (Wild Goose 2016)
A brief poetry of time (Oversteps 2017)

Still Crazy …

R. N. F. SKINNER

Published in 2020 by SilverWood Books

SilverWood Books Ltd
14 Small Street, Bristol, BS1 1DE, United Kingdom
www.silverwoodbooks.co.uk

'I deem not profitless…' (p.144) from *The Prelude* by William Wordsworth
'come not single spies…' (p.179) from *Hamlet* by William Shakespeare
'wears man's smudge' (p.194) from 'God's Grandeur' by Gerard Manley Hopkins

ISBN 978-1-78132-991-7 (paperback)
ISBN 978-1-80042-037-3 (ebook)

British Library Cataloguing in Publication Data
A CIP catalogue record for this book is
available from the British Library

Page design and typesetting by SilverWood Books

Acknowledgements

Several friends read the first draft and made many helpful comments, and Sam Jordison gave a lengthy critique under the aegis of The Literary Consultancy. I am very grateful to them all.

Extra thanks to David Thompson who not only read the second, penultimate draft as well as the first draft, but also enthusiastically discussed my characters and their affairs over many glasses of wine and cups of coffee, his suggestions resulting in considerable improvements.

Double extra thanks to my wife, Betsy Allen, for reading both drafts, listening to my ramblings, giving unfailing sympathetic encouragement, and living with the characters almost as much as I have for the past few years.

The team at SilverWood have displayed excellent midwifery skills in bringing to birth Melanie, Phil, their friends, their acquaintances and their antagonists. I look forward to further collaborations with them.

Prologue

Loch Lomond, Scotland: July 1958

Melanie looked through the picnic basket in the hope of finding something else to eat, but could only find fragments of cheese that had fallen out of the sandwiches. They were too small to pick up; she licked a finger and dabbed at them to transfer them to her mouth. Not very satisfactory. She stood up and looked round, wondering what to do next. Her parents were still on their little collapsible chairs, Mummy reading a book and Daddy dozing over a newspaper. Her brother Mikey had gone off on his own, probably looking for more things to add to the broken skull of some animal he'd already found and balanced on a piece of jutting rock near where they were picnicking. Melanie thought it looked horrible.

She wandered down to the loch's edge a few feet away and gazed across the great expanse of water, wondering if a monster like Nessie were lurking in its depths. She'd been looking hard while they had had their picnic, but there had been no sign of anything remotely monster-like. Now she stood as close to the water's edge as she dared without getting her sandals wet, gazing over the loch, seeing the surface ruffled by the wind, trying to remember her father's explanation about why there were proper waves on the sea but not on a loch. The moon came into it, but surely the moon shone on a loch at night as much as it did on the sea?

The water surface was glittering, and she stared and stared, hoping a monster would rear its head and scatter the glittering. With her mind's eye she could see a great grey head rearing up, water cascading from it, flashing from it like countless sparklers on Bonfire Night being whirled around, and a gaping mouth with rows of sharp teeth, and huge staring eyes. Behind the head a series of grey arches also flashed with scattered water, and at the end of them a wildly thrashing tail... But no, with her real eyes she could see no monster.

Yet as she stared and stared, a curious sensation developed that she was somehow part of the loch itself – not simply as though she were *on* the water or *in* the water, but the sensation of actually *being* the water, and not just the water but also the mountains and pebbles and trees and the little islands in the loch. She could see, or she seemed to see, a vast network of lines of dancing golden fire.

Mikey had recently told her the difference between millions, billions and trillions, and she felt sure there were *trillions* of these lines connecting everything to everything, like the huge spiders' webs she sometimes saw in the garden at home in the early morning sun when there was rain or dew on them, only stupendously bigger. These trillions of lines ran between the tiniest pebbles and the hugest mountains, between every leaf on every tree to every leaf on every other tree, between the distant birds in the sky and a little boat moving along near the opposite shore.

She looked at her hands. Golden fire glowed from them. When she turned to look at her family she could see each one radiating the same goldenness. Mummy still reading, Daddy dozing, and Mikey further off holding up some trophy; the car-rug spread on the ground and the open picnic basket; the toppled-over thermos flasks and the old tennis rackets: all were shimmering. Even the skull on the rock shimmered. Threads of golden fire connected it with trees and leaves and pebbles and water and people and everything.

Never before in her eight years had she had this feeling, this reassurance, that *all is well*. It felt wonderful, a trillion times wonderful. She stretched out her arms to embrace it as her ability or desire to think about it and puzzle over it and try to describe it to herself faded away, like seawater when the waves can go no further up a beach sinking into invisibility in the sand.

How long did it last? she wondered later. Although time had seemed to vanish, the trillions of threads of golden fire had begun to fade, slowly fade. Like the dying of the sparklers on Bonfire Night, when no matter how hard you keep whirling them they become just crispy grey ash on lengths of thin wire. The golden fiery threads died away as her everyday way of seeing the world and feeling her feelings reasserted itself.

Chapter 1

Melanie

Exeter: January 1997

How extraordinary. I saw Phil yesterday. Met him. Talked with him. Spent the evening with him. Or rather, I spent the evening in his company with others.

It's over twenty-four years since I last saw him. I can't say 'he hasn't changed a bit', because his hair is definitely shorter and tidier (and in places a bit grey). He was dressed slightly smarter than he used to be (albeit not much), but his voice and speech are unchanged with that odd mixture of fluency and hesitancy, and his laugh and that grin are pure Phil as I remember him. His eyes too, which every so often widen, and he gives a burst of rapid blinking, almost fluttering his eyelashes like a beauty queen.

This was at Charlotte and Jimmy's. They'd originally invited us to come and see in the New Year with them and others, but I'd told Simon I wasn't up to that – my energy levels are still not good enough for me to risk a very long evening and into a late night, in the company of mainly strangers. Far too exhausting. They'd then been kind enough to ask us to what Charlotte promised would be a much quieter, smaller dinner party a couple of weeks later. Actually, I didn't want to go even to that and told Simon when we got the invitation that I felt I wouldn't be up to it.

"I think we ought to go," he said. "It'll look rude if we keep saying no."

"We don't keep saying no. We've been out with them several times, and we were round there a few weeks ago."

"That was months ago, back in September," he said, puffing out his cheeks in the way he has. "Come on, Melanie. We don't have to stay late. You've said you want to meet more people. This'll be a good chance. Have a good rest in the afternoon and you'll be all right."

I capitulated, mainly because I didn't have the energy to stand my ground. However, it's true that I've been desperate to get out more, be more sociable. We've been here in Exeter eight months now, and Charlotte is the only proper friend I've made down here, and that was not originally on my own account but because she's married to Jimmy. Simon's lucky. Jimmy was a real blast from the past for him, finding they're working on the same project. Simon joined Jimmy's chess club, too.

Charlotte and Jimmy live on the outskirts of Teignford village. Simon drove as usual, though I'm looking forward to the time when I can get behind the wheel again without feeling exhausted after five minutes. I wonder if we can afford two cars? I don't like Simon's because of the modified controls; it's fine for him, prosthetic leg and all.

Jimmy opened the door. With his tuft of black beard and narrow moustache he looks very Mephistophelian, and I wonder if he cultivates the diabolic look to make himself appear more interesting. He welcomed us in his best infernal manner, saying, "Come in, come in! Good to see you!" slapping Simon on the forearm, offering me a kiss, and asking, "How are you both?" twice.

"We're fine!" Simon announced cheerfully.

"Pleased to hear it! To hear it!"

He tried ushering us towards the sitting room. I couldn't face meeting other people right away and said I needed to go upstairs. I used the 'facilities', as Mummy would put it, urged my reflection in the mirror to be sociable, and was just summoning up the courage to head back downstairs when I heard Simon calling out, "Come on, Melanie! Where are you?" in his 'just making sure you're all right' infantilising tone of voice. I lingered another minute or two.

When I did emerge and went back down, Simon was no longer in the hallway. He had evidently gone into the sitting room where I could hear general chatter coming from. I followed clattering noises to the kitchen, where I found a harassed-looking Charlotte, glasses steamed up, worrying over the contents of a large glass casserole. She kissed me hello, saying how pleased she was to see me though with a catch in her voice, and as her glasses cleared I could see her eyes were looking a little red and puffy.

I asked if she was all right.

"It's nothing," she said quickly in an artificially bright tone, "just Jimmy. I'm fine. How are you?"

"I'm doing all right, thanks. Touch wood. Energy levels slowly increasing!"

"Good. You were wise to give our New Year's Eve do a miss. It was fun but full on. It's nice you could come tonight," she continued in a normal voice. "A much more civilised affair, but if it gets too much for you, you can always retreat upstairs to the spare room. Oh, what do you want?"

Jimmy had come into the kitchen and was gesturing at us.

"Drinkies!" he said. "Drinkypoos!"

"Oh, all right," Charlotte said.

"Sherry for you, Charlie, I know. What do you want, Melanie? Name your poison! Your *poison!*"

Gin and tonic for me, and as he started fixing the drinks Charlotte guided me along to the sitting room, saying, "You know the Roths."

"I don't think so."

"Simon certainly knows Patrick."

As we went in, I had one of those disconcerting moments when you see someone out of context and know you ought to know them but can't think why. Patrick Roth is unmistakable, being tall and with handsomely craggy features. Early sixties at a guess. I couldn't place him until he spoke, or boomed, rather, when I remembered him singing with a chamber choir at Christmas. He speaks as he sings, in a hall-filling rich baritone, even in a domestic sitting room. Very formal, very courteous, very correct in shaking hands with me, and booming, "Delighted to meet you, Melanie! I know Simon already – the mighty Dragon! Chess," he added, "the Lord has brought us together over the chequered board, and Simon is a fine exponent of the Dragon Variation." He looked at our blank faces and explained, "Sicilian Defence."

His wife, Rita, a rather greyish-looking woman with rounded shoulders, gave a little sigh as if despairing of him, and said, "I think, dear, you're…it's, well, we're all baffled even more."

"Not important!" Patrick boomed, and started talking with Simon about some chess event.

Rita gave another little sigh and said to me, "I've bumped into Simon once or twice, but I don't think we've met."

"I've seen you both with the chamber choir," I said.

"Oh, that's nice!" She gave a little smile which briefly banished her greyness. "Do you sing, by any chance?"

Before I could answer, Charlotte broke in to say apropos of nothing in particular, "Melanie took her degree at Cambridge, then did a PhD, so strictly speaking she's *Dr* Ward."

Although I'd realised there were others in the room behind me, I hadn't seen who they were, and it came as a shock when a new but familiar voice added, "She publishes under her maiden name – Dr Mason. At least, she used to."

I felt I'd been thumped in the chest. I swung round, and there was Phil, levering himself out of a chair, grinning and fluttering his eyelashes.

"Hi Mel," he said casually, as though we'd last seen each other only one or two days ago. "How're you doing?"

Chapter 2

Melanie

Exeter: January 1997

Phil put his hands on my upper arms, kissed me on the cheek and said, "Hey, it's lovely to see you!" and Charlotte said, "Oh! You know each other?" Phil kissed me again and said, "Never seen her before in my life!"

For a few seconds I felt I were in a private bubble with him. He said he'd been wondering if it'd turn out to be me because Jimmy had told him that someone called Simon he worked with would be coming with his wife Melanie. "I thought *funny!*" – he put on a Peter Cook voice – "Melanie and Simon, *funny!* Where have I heard those two names together before? *Funny!*" Abandoning Peter Cook, he said he'd remembered that Simon, like Jimmy, was into engineering. "I took a wild stab at a guess that 'Simon and Melanie' referred to you and Simon. Only the other way round."

"How do you know each other?" I heard Charlotte ask as Phil let his hands drop.

I was smiling at his convoluted explanation.

"University," Simon said from the opposite side of the room. "They were both at Cambridge."

"You did science, Phil," Charlotte said, rather unnecessarily.

"Of the natural variety," he said. "Ah, reinforcements!"

Jimmy had entered with a trayful of glasses. He muttered something to Charlotte, who dashed out of the room with a little cry as he handed round the drinks. Phil had stepped away from me and was indicating someone else behind him. A woman, rather petite, my age or a little younger, with long reddish hair, probably hennaed.

"This is Sam. Sam, Melanie. Melanie, Sam."

"Melanie?" Sam said. "That's a name from the past." She raised a hand in greeting and said, "Hi!" but she wasn't smiling.

"Hi!" I said. Well, well! Cousin Sam. He'd often mentioned her.

Phil gave me a grin. "Lovely to see you. You well?"

"Well enough," I said. "You?"

"Yeah. Yeah! Even better now!"

"Sit down, coz, will you?" Sam said to him. "You're right in front of me."

"Catch up later," Phil said, sitting down.

I went to sit next to Simon, who reached out to take my hand rather proprietorially.

There was a brief silence, then Patrick leaned forward and asked loudly when did we think John Major would get round to announcing the date of the general election "so that the Lord's will might be done," and soon the others were arguing politics in a terribly polite, middle-class way, and equally politely avoiding further mention of 'the Lord'. I remembered Simon telling me that Patrick Roth's nickname is the Roth of God.

Somehow the conversation moved on to Jimmy as chair of the local parish council, and the current campaign against closing Teignford's post office, where Charlotte is the postmistress. I was in agony – all I wanted was to talk with Phil. I glanced at him several times – and every time he seemed to be looking at me and grinning. Sam beside him was frowning, almost scowling, and I had the uncomfortable feeling she'd taken a dislike to me.

Charlotte called us through to the dining room, where she sat Phil and me next to each other with the command, "You two must do some catching up," but that had to be put on hold as Patrick announced, "We must give thanks to the Lord!" and launched into an unnecessarily long grace.

Phil and I couldn't talk privately while there was general conversation, but when it swung back to the coming election we took the opportunity to opt out. He asked what I'm up to these days, and how come I'm down here 'in sunny Devon'.

I told him we'd moved here last summer because of Simon's work on the major roads project. "He's a small bridge designer," I said.

Phil looked across at Simon. "Looks average size to me."

"Idiot!" I said. "I mean he's a designer—"

"Of small bridges!" Phil nodded.

"Still as quick as ever!"

"Sorry. Go ahead."

"He made a name for himself with some designs in Surrey, and was headhunted for this big project to do with the south-west road network, where he's responsible for, well, as you might guess…"

"The small bridges?"

"That's right."

"Impressive. I'll think of him every time I go over one. Or under one. But what about you?" Phil tapped my arm. "Are you at the university?"

Although I don't like talking about my health I wanted him to know what had been going on, and told him I'd been unwell for the past few years.

"Hey, hard luck! What's been wrong?"

"I've had ME. I'm doing pretty well now, but for a long time it was awful. ME is a pig of a condition."

"Yeah, I gather. That's rough. What caused it?"

"I can't say. There are competing theories about it in general. It might be viral, but if it is, no one's isolated the virus. Or it might be psychosomatic, but the evidence is ambiguous. It's probably a combination of both, plus genetics and sheer bad luck. But I'm coming through."

"Hey, sorry it's been bad, Mel," he said sympathetically. "That's lousy for you."

No one else calls me Mel. The way he used the abbreviation, and in the company of others although they weren't listening, came as a sharp stab of intimacy.

"The point is," I said, hoping I was maintaining my composure, "I didn't have to change jobs in order to come down here with Simon, because I'd already stopped working. Couldn't hack it any longer. I got so wiped out. I was a social worker up till then, you see."

I felt him staring at me in wonderment. "A social worker? Since when? You went into academia. Saw a review of your book on, um, mysterious women!"

He knew about my book! I felt a sudden glow invade me. "Mysterious women!" I tried to sound indignant though he was obviously being facetious. "It was—"

"*Transcending Gender,*" he interrupted me. "With the subtitle, 'Heresy, Women Mystics' – told you mysterious women came into it – 'and Mediaeval Society'. Right?"

"Right," I said, amazed. He even knows the title!

"What happened, then? How come the social work?"

I told him it had felt right – how, although I loved academia, I'd increasingly felt I needed to do something more people-oriented; and how I'd worked mainly with young children. "Which is slightly ironic," I said, "since I don't have children of my own."

"No? I'd've thought you'd be a great mother."

"It never happened. What about you?"

He shook his head. "Nah! I'd've been a dreadful mother! But I'm not a bad dad. Two kids."

"Girls? Boys? One of each?"

"Two daughters. Lem and Amy."

At least, I think that's what he said, but before I could ask him to say it again we were interrupted by Patrick loudly asking Phil where his cross would be going.

"My cross?" Phil laughed. "That sounds a spot too religious for my liking."

"Voting cross, not religious," said Jimmy. "Voting. We're talking about the election, when it comes. The election."

"Ah," said Phil. "Well, I'm a Green."

"Thought as much," said Charlotte triumphantly. She'd taken her glasses off, and her harassed look had gone.

"If I were in Exeter," Phil added, "I'd vote Labour to get rid of the Tories. Out here it's true-blue land and won't change, so I can vote with the heart, and that means Green."

"Me too," Sam said in a rather truculent tone. "I've joined the Greens."

"I must say," Charlotte said, "I rather like John Major. He's a real gentleman. Tony Blair is all right, but I don't like that Gordon Brown. He's Scottish."

There was one of those brief, embarrassed silences you sometimes get when no one knows how to respond to a particularly inept remark.

Then Phil held up his glass, saying, "Nice wine, Jimmy. Jimmy's our local wine buff," he added for my benefit. "Famous for his amazing wine cellar. Not that it's a real cellar as such. It's a scullery in disguise."

"Lovely little number. Lovely," Jimmy said, launching into a long description full of the usual guff about 'a hint of blackberry' and 'oaked' and 'velvety'.

Charlotte, who'd slipped away, returned with the dessert and cheeseboard, over which Phil and Patrick started an argument about science and religion. Charlotte had asked Patrick something or other, and he said that 'the Lord' had been doing 'marvellous things' at the church he's involved with.

Phil gave a stifled laugh, and Patrick told him in a ticking-off tone of voice, "You may well mock."

"Thanks, I will!" Phil said.

"What's your problem, exactly?"

"Just about everything," Phil said. "Don't like the way religion claims to know the truth just because it says so in a book written thousands of years ago. It's not a sustainable claim."

"Millions of people throughout the world and throughout history have experienced the truth of the Bible!"

"Millions of Muslims and Hindus and Buddhists would say the same about their so-called sacred books," said Phil. "Who's to say which is correct, if any of them is, which I rather doubt!"

"Jesus," Patrick said, "is the one true revelation of God. He is fully God, and salvation is only, *only*, through him!"

Phil tapped his knife on a piece of cheddar. "Hard cheese for all Muslims and Hindus and others who've never even heard of Jesus? Sorry Patrick, it strikes me as a crazy system. If Christianity is true, the Almighty seems to have made an almighty cock-up in allowing innumerable other religions to strut their stuff."

"God has implanted in the human soul the desire to know him," Patrick said, quoting Augustine's line about the heart being restless until it finds its rest in God. "Other religions are fumbling attempts to respond to that desire, whereas Jesus is the true fulfilment of it. We should base our lives on the revelation of God in Christ! What do you base your life on? Eh?"

"Don't know about 'base my life'," Phil said. "But I do know that science offers a vastly better explanatory system of how the universe works."

"*How*, not *why*," Patrick said. "The trouble with scientists is that they seem to think that understanding *how* some aspect of the universe works is sufficient, ignoring meaning, purpose and value. Science is not equipped to deal with the sacred. The sacred can't be encapsulated in a neat equation or formula."

That was when Rita put in her pennyworth. She's quite a surprise. With her wobbly lower lip which makes it look like she might crumble into tears at any moment, and her feeble voice, you wouldn't think she'd be able to express an opinion, but she shut Patrick up, murmuring, "Now then, Paddy, you're not... this isn't...you're not in a lecture hall or a pulpit now!" and shaking his arm.

"Going on too much again, am I?" Patrick responded in an abashed tone of voice which I found rather endearing. "My apologies, everybody."

"The trouble with religion," Phil was already saying, "is that it *claims* to give explanations, which don't actually explain anything."

Patrick opened his mouth to continue sparring, but Charlotte cut in quickly. "We still haven't got a vicar here, you know! Giles left over two years ago, and no one else has been appointed."

"Not to worry," Jimmy leaped in on cue. "Sonia's on the case with the Church authorities. On the case. She's dealing with it."

"Who's Sonia, coz?" Sam stage-whispered across the table at Phil.

Sonia, according to Charlotte, is some kind of wonder-woman who moved to the village a few years ago when her husband died, and recently became the parish secretary.

"She's a real breath of fresh air on the council. Fresh air," Jimmy added, practically twirling his moustaches. "Very popular, and still in her prime. Her prime."

"A merry widow?" Patrick boomed heartily.

"Very merry," said Charlotte. "Though she is between men at present."

"I wonder which particular men she likes to be between?" Phil whispered to me.

When we returned to the sitting room Sam manoeuvred Phil away from me – or is that just incipient paranoia on my part? – and I ended up on the sofa next to Charlotte. I was just telling her about having had Simon's parents with us for Christmas when I overheard Rita asking Phil and Sam how long they'd been together. I had a horrible lurching of the heart.

"We're not!" Sam gave a shrill laugh. "Are we, coz?"

"Oh, I'm sorry, I thought…" Rita sighed apologetically.

"Sam's just staying with me for a few days while Tom's off doing m[illegible] bonding stuff with their two sons," Phil said. "Her husband."

I tried not to react, but Charlotte asked anxiously if I were all right, and I had to say I was fine but needed to go upstairs. In the bathroom I splashed water on my face and sat on the edge of the bath to calm myself down. Phil and Sam weren't an item. Just cousins, not 'kissing cousins'.

On my way back down I heard a burst of laughter. I discovered Phil was talking about a revue.

"Revue?" I said, staring at him. "What revue?"

"Treading the boards again!" he said breezily.

"Are you? Really? When? Where?"

"Couple of nights in March for Red Nose Day."

"Bit of a laugh!" Jimmy put in. "Always fancied doing that sort of thing myself! A laugh!"

"Splendid!" Patrick announced simultaneously. "Laughter is one of the Lord's greatest gifts to mankind."

I heard Rita correct him with a sigh, "*Hu*mankind."

"Have you seen Phil doing his comedy?" Charlotte asked me.

"Once or twice," I said, and saw Phil suppress a smile at this understatement. Sam was scowling.

"Out with it," Charlotte turned to Simon. "What's he like?"

Poor old Simon was taken aback by Charlotte's question and he stuttered a little before explaining that he'd never seen Phil perform.

"This is the first time we've met," he said. "We didn't know each other before." He spoke with a cheerful tone, but I knew from experience it was fake: it was just that he didn't do not-cheerful in company. "You'll have to ask Melanie," he said. "She's the expert on it."

"It'll be fantastic," I announced firmly to everyone. "Honestly! It'll be really funny! It'll be absolutely…" I paused, "transuranic!"

Chapter 3

Phil

Cambridge: October 1971

After the applause had died down, not to mention the cheering, the whistles and the good-natured catcalls, Alex, Rob and I packed up our gear and stashed it in a side room, all the while whooping and laughing and capering about and congratulating each other.

"Excellent! Superb!" Alex said.

"A cabaret of no mean accomplishment!" Rob said.

"Absolutely transuranic!" I said, and we whooped some more as Gerry, unmistakable in his over-the-top scarlet cummerbund, joined us, swaying and grinning maniacally, saying how good we'd been.

The party was taking place in St John's College, although the three of us, and Gerry himself, along with many of the guests, were from Pembroke. Gerry had seen us perform cabaret earlier in the year, and had asked if we could provide an entertainment for this bash, celebrating his twenty-first birthday and the twenty-second birthday of a St John's friend.

We returned to the main room, and I went to get in the first round. As I pushed my way through to the makeshift bar, several people gave me the thumbs up or a congratulatory slap on the back or said, "Great show! Really funny!" and the like, and I was silently agreeing with them – it'd been the best cabaret to date for Air Raid Precautions.

The bar was in fact a trestle table covered with a green plastic cloth, covered in turn by glasses and spilt drink. As I tried to catch the eye of a bartender, someone pushed into me from behind making me lurch into a girl in front. She turned round.

"Sorry!" I said. "Just trying to get a drink!"

"Oh hi!" she said. "You deserve one! You were great! That was really funny! I haven't laughed like that for ages 'n' ages!"

"Thanks! Good to hear!"

"No, really!" she insisted, as though I'd contradicted her. "It was brilliant. I don't think I stopped laughing the whole time!"

"Your turn," I said, pointing to where a barman had become available.

"Oh right." She turned quickly and asked for a white wine, then turned back to me. "What would you like?"

"It's okay. I'm getting the order for all of us."

"No, come on, it's my treat. As a thank you!"

She bought the drinks, and as we pushed our way back I learned that she was Melanie, from Girton.

"Cheers, man!" said Alex as I handed him his beer.

"Courtesy of Melanie," I said, indicating where she was giving Rob his wine. Alex raised first his glass and then his eyebrows, the former to Melanie by way of thanks, the latter, accompanied by a tilt of the head, to me by way of enquiry.

"One satisfied member of the audience," I said.

"Satisfied, eh?" repeated Alex salaciously.

I rejoined Melanie. "Let's find some seats," I said, taking her by the elbow and guiding her away.

On the way across the room she broke free to head for a table scattered with the remnants of a buffet, returning after a minute or two clutching a paper plate piled with food. We claimed a couple of chairs near French doors that opened onto a grassy court.

"D'you do a lot of performing?" she asked, raising her voice as 'Jumpin' Jack Flash' started pounding through the speakers. "Want one?"

I accepted a sausage. She resumed wolfing down the food at an impressive rate. "Yeah," I said, "we do quite a bit. Started back in Jan. Had a dozen or so gigs since then. This was our third this term, and another couple booked."

"Are you always as good as tonight?"

I laughed. "Wish I could say yes. Reckon we're usually good enough, but tonight was easily our best."

She started on the cake. "When someone said there was going to be a cabaret," she said, spitting crumbs. "Sorry... I thought oh no, the usual undergraduate stuff, full of in-jokes and clever vulgarity. But it wasn't like that at all."

"You mean it was full of *stupid* vulgarity?"

She laughed, putting a hand on my arm. There was a momentary pause. She seemed startlingly vivid, more real than the rest of the party, with her untidy honey-coloured hair, pretty hazel eyes, and a slightly pouty mouth that made me want to moan with desire. 'Jumpin' Jack Flash' ended and 'Get Back' started.

"How did you get into it?" she asked. "Do you write it as well as perform?"

I told her how I'd come to Cambridge to read Natural Sciences but with the main ambition of joining the Footlights. This I'd done in my first term, being invited to join the club after I'd written and performed a sketch in the first of the twice-termly 'smoking' concerts.

"Wow!" Melanie said.

My subsequent Footlights career had been undistinguished, but a friend, Chris, had suggested I help him mount a cabaret for a New Year's Eve party to see in 1971. Inviting Rob and Alex and a girl Chris knew called Fran to join us, we called ourselves the Headlights to parody the Footlights, and together we'd written and presented a half-hour show. People liked us. We were asked to perform at other parties and social events. Chris had graduated in the summer and was no longer at Cambridge, Fran dropped out because of time pressure, and Rob, Alex and I continued under the collective name of Air Raid Precautions: ARP for short, the initials also standing for Alex, Rob and me, Phil.

Melanie gave a tiny laugh and her eyes flicked up. She had one arm across her stomach, supporting her other arm at the elbow. The attitude emphasised her breasts. Round her neck she wore a thin gold chain with a little cross dangling from it.

"What's up?" I asked.

"I was just thinking. When you write, is it all earnest seriousness, or are you falling about laughing all the time?"

As I told her that it's a mixture of the two, I continued looking at her: frothy hair, those lovely eyes with their long lashes, an appealing smile. She's not exactly slim, I realised, but not not slim either – halfway between the two. Definitely cuddly.

"Don't you get at all nervous, doing it?" she asked. "I know I would!"

"Terrified!" I said.

"You all looked totally relaxed, and and and," she stuttered, "really enjoying yourselves."

"Ah, well, once you get going, it's no problem. The nerves just vanish. But yeah, beforehand the panic and terror quotients are in the high nineties."

"How did we rate as an audience?"

"Ten out of ten! You know, there's something amazingly powerful about having a whole roomful of people laughing away. A few weeks before I came up to Cambridge," I continued, "I went to the Edinburgh Festival specifically to see the Footlights. It was a late-night revue, and the place was packed. They were superb! Total genius. It wasn't just that it was all incredibly funny, there was a kind of joy that enveloped everyone in that hall and bonded us for the hour and whatever that it lasted. As I went back to the place where I was staying, I still felt this intense joy, and I'm sure everyone else in the audience must have felt it as well, though I didn't know any of them. Amazing."

"Sounds wonderful!"

"But also, I have to say, when I got back to my digs and went to bed, I felt a sort of sense of dismay as well."

"Dismay?" Melanie sounded puzzled. "Why on earth did you feel that?"

"Couldn't help thinking that to do something like they'd done, getting that sort of response, was something I'd never be able to do. It was way beyond me. They'd set the bar impossibly high."

"What about tonight? Didn't you do that tonight? You had a fantastic response. Everyone was falling about, weren't they? We were wetting ourselves!"

She was right. It had been fantastic, and now the evening had another fantastic element with this immensely desirable woman, whose desirability increased even further as she kissed me on the cheek.

I reckoned I'd been banging on about myself far too much. As I started to ask her about herself she leaped up at the opening chords of 'Ride a White Swan', pulling me to my feet. "I love this! Come on! Let's dance!"

I jiggled around in my usual unrhythmical fashion, as self-conscious as ever at my utter lack of ability in the dance department, feeling I cut a poor figure compared with, say, Edward, another Pembroke friend, who was dancing with his girlfriend in his rather stylish way, like a piece of precision machinery. My style, by contrast, tended to mimic machinery after the spanner has been thrown in but before it grinds to a complete halt.

Melanie's dancing was neither machine-like nor disjointed. She swayed in a dreamy manner that I found uncomfortably erotic, and she appeared to be totally unselfconscious. She caught my eye and smiled. Something surged through me, a mixture of desire and nervousness and exhilaration. Perhaps my luck was changing at last. During the first two years at Cambridge my love life had bordered on the non-existent, but this girl, this Melanie – she was amazing. The look in her eyes and the shape of her face and the froth of her hair tumbling over her shoulders – the whole sheer invitingness of her person. I grinned in what I intended to be a secret manner, but she caught the grin and leaned forward and, with her mouth almost touching my ear, asked what the joke was.

"No joke!"

"You were laughing – what at?"

"Just a thought!"

She drew back slightly, matching my grin with one of her own. I felt exultant. She must have known what I was grinning about.

'A Whiter Shade of Pale' started up. We both hesitated, then moved closer, and she rested her hands on my shoulders as I put mine on her waist. Alex, dancing nearby, gave me an exaggerated wink, followed by a thumbs up. I couldn't tell whether he was silently commenting on me and Melanie or himself and the girl he was dancing with.

I slipped my hands fully round Melanie's waist and clasped them, pulling her closer to me. She turned her head to the side, her right cheek resting on my chest. We were swaying not quite in time with the music, and I hoped she didn't realise I was having to control a tremble. Dear God, holding her like that was unbelievable. I risked tightening my hold briefly, I thought perhaps imperceptibly, and was rewarded by her pressing harder into my chest, snuggling up against me. I wondered if I would faint with desire.

I'd hoped we'd keep dancing like that for some time, but as the record ended she removed her hands from my shoulders. I relaxed my hold and she stepped back, making a motion with her head in the direction of our drinks.

Reclaiming our glasses, I got the impression she'd become rather distant. She kept glancing round the room and standing in an ungainly way, face and body partly twisted away from me like someone contending with head-on driving rain. I had that ghastly sinking sensation in my guts I'd known several times before as an incipient romance curls up and dies. Had I said something wrong? Shouldn't I have had my arms round her? Did my armpits smell? Was she standing there thinking me an absolute prat?

The French doors had been opened. I feigned great interest in the people wandering about outside, thinking, *oh bollocks!* Things had been going so well, but I appeared somehow to have ballsed it up. As usual.

It all changed again as she turned to me and said abruptly, "Phil, let's go outside. If you don't mind."

If I don't mind? If I don't *mind!*

I took her hand, and we stepped outside.

Chapter 4

Emhalt, south-east London: May 1967

"Finally, but, uh, most importantly," Old Brillo, the leader of the boys' section of the Followers, said in his diffident voice which emerged from behind the thicket of black, wiry facial hair which gave rise to his nickname, "our forty-fifth anniversary service which as you know takes place on, erm, um, ah..."

"June the eighteenth," Madam Skull said sharply.

"...as you know takes place on June the eighteenth..." Old Brillo repeated.

"*He* didn't know!" Anne whispered sniggeringly to Melanie.

"...and I have both, erm, uh, good news and bad news, as they, uh, say. The bad news is that unfortunately Mr Cliff Richards..."

"Richard," murmured Melanie.

"...is unable to be our, erm, guest speaker this year after all, um, thanks to a slight muddle over dates, *mea* um *culpa*. The very good, erm, news is that we have procured the services at short notice, as you might, erm, say, of the Reverend Derek Cranbrook, of whom you have, ah, no doubt heard?"

He looked enquiringly around the hall of young people before him who either had not heard of the Reverend Derek Cranbrook or had no intention of admitting it. Only Simon Ward, Melanie saw, nodded.

"Who did he say?" Anne was whispering to Melanie.

"He's that spiritual leader," Melanie whispered back. She was about to say more but was pre-empted by Madam Skull, leader of the girls' section and known more formally as Mrs Armitage, rising to her feet and advancing to the front of the little podium where she and Old Brillo, real name Mr Griffen, were sitting.

"The Reverend Derek Cranbrook," she stated, "is the leader of the 'Movement of the Spirit' Church in this country. They have been called to bring the good news of Jesus and the gift of the Holy Spirit to those who still walk in the dark. We are greatly blessed," she continued imperiously, "that he has chosen to accept our invitation. He is an excellent preacher and will touch the hearts of many."

"Ah, yes," resumed Old Brillo as Madam Skull retreated to her chair. "That's at, erm, St Barnabas' church hall, where the girls usually meet, at, uh, two o'clock on the, um, eighteenth. Now, do invite your family to come along, and any friends are, ah, very welcome to join the, erm, the, erm, the merriment."

"Merriment!" Anne's yelp of laughter was unguarded. Melanie jabbed her elbow into Anne's side as Madam Skull turned her gaze away from Old Brillo for his use of the word 'merriment' and onto the two girls, whose faces instantly straightened.

Old Brillo announced the final hymn – 'By blue Galilee Jesus walked of old' – which Kenny, one of the senior boys, hammered through on the piano at breakneck speed as the sixty or more Followers present sang with varying degrees, or in some instances complete absence, of enthusiasm, tunefulness and understanding.

Melanie gazed around, hardly singing at all, aware that over the past few months her feelings towards the Followers had undergone a marked change. Not towards the people, not towards her friends like Anne and Sarah, and the boys she knew like Kenny, but towards what she, as a Follower, was expected to believe about God and Jesus, the words she was expected to say, the prayers she was expected to pray, the books she was expected to read. When she had first started attending Followers years ago, sent along by her mother who had grown exasperated by her constant questions about God, she had been eager to attend, hoping to understand better the Loch Lomond experience she had treasured for years. Initially it had helped and reassured her that there really was *something* that had touched her, that she wasn't just making it up, and it had given her a language to use. It had never been totally satisfactory. The language never really matched the experience, and for months now, ever since the Aberfan disaster last October, the dissatisfaction had been growing.

She fingered the little gold cross which hung round her neck: the Loch Lomond experience, or 'moment' as she'd come to think of it, was still deep in her, at the centre of her being; while what went on at Followers increasingly diverged from the reality of her having walked, not by blue Galilee, but by that chilly Scottish loch glittering in the afternoon sun when she was eight years old.

Chapter 5

Phil

Cambridge: October 1971

"History," Melanie said, when I asked her what subject she was reading, as we headed across the grass towards a low wall.

"Not exactly my favourite subject, I'm afraid," I admitted, adding ruefully, "I was never much good at it at school. One damned date after another."

She gave her tiny laugh again at my tone. "It sounds like you suffered."

"Certainly did. Only managed to get the O level by memorising a whole series of model answers about, you know, 'everything you always didn't know about the American War of Independence and were too bored to ask'."

We sat on the wall. Melanie shivered. I wanted to use her shivering as a pretext for putting my arm round her, but not wanting to risk rejection I kept my hands to myself, my shoulder pressed to hers, hoping she'd make some encouraging movement. Pathetic: there I was, fine about making a fool of myself in front of cabaret audiences, lacking the courage to do what any other bloke would do in such a situation, namely, viz. and to wit, put his arm round the girl. All the same, I felt marvellous.

"Any ideas what you want to do with your degree when you've got it?" I asked. A tediously predictable question to keep us talking.

She shrugged. "Not sure yet. I would like to do some research. There are one or two areas that really interest me, particularly to do with the mediaeval Church and heresy and the like."

"Oh, right." My heart sank a little at the mention of church and heresy, along with her wearing a cross. As a scientist I was definitely non-religious.

Melanie laughed. "You don't sound gripped by the idea! I find it fascinating."

"Yeah?"

"Yeah! How different belief systems can give rise to immense hostility from the powers that be."

I touched the little cross she wore. "You're a God-botherer?"

She laughed again and removed my hand from the cross. "It's the other way round."

"Yer what?"

"It's more that sometimes God bothers me. God is a Melanie-botherer!"

"Oh. Does he often do that?"

"Just occasionally. I take it that it's not your scene?"

"Don't see the point of religion, to be honest."

"Hmm. Well, I suspect God doesn't see the point of religion, either, so you're in good company."

"If there is a God. Which I doubt. Where's the evidence?"

A third laugh. "God isn't a scientific hypothesis, you know! 'God' is simply the name we give to the deepest reality. The depth of everything."

"Sounds a bit too deep for me," I said.

"Well, what would you suggest we talk about?" she asked, her tone teasing. Emboldened, I did now put my arm round her waist and looked at her face. She's gazing at me quizzically. Her lips part. This is the encouragement I need and my heart, putting on hold its preparations to sink, now begins to pound away excitedly. A moment later we're kissing.

This is no fantasy. I'm actually…she's actually…dear God! I put my hand up to her breast and let it rest there for a couple of seconds before removing it, but she takes my hand and replaces it on her breast as we kiss harder. Don't balls it up, Phil lad, for God's sake don't mess it up; then wordless images stream through my head as I fondle her breast and she makes little whimpering sounds.

We draw apart. I kiss her forehead. "God, you're lovely. Wasn't exactly expecting this."

She doesn't say anything but continues to gaze at me as though I'm an ancient document written in unknown hieroglyphics and she's the historian charged with interpreting it.

"Came here to do the cabaret, have a few drinks, get a dance or two," I continue. "End up sitting on a wall…looking…kissing…"

I stop talking, not because I can't think of what to say but because further speech is rendered impossible by my mouth being occupied by and with Melanie. This time no images, no internal speech, go through my head.

There came the interrupting sound of voices and laughter, and the definite smell of a joint. We broke our clinch and looked round. I knew one of the trio approaching us – the wonderfully named Tristan Edyvean, who had a room in the same college hostel as me.

"Evening, old boy!" he said cheerfully. "Good show, that!" He took the joint from one of the others and offered it to us. "Fancy a blow?"

I held up a hand to refuse and Melanie shook her head, her hair swirling about.

"Already high on success, eh?" Tristan and the other two continued on their way, smoking.

The moment was lost. She was tugging at a lock of her hair, while I scraped my fingernails at some lichen on the wall. She gave what sounded like a sigh of annoyance, followed by a sniff.

"What's wrong?" I asked.

She sighed again. "I'm – I'm sorry. I shouldn't've."

"Shouldn't what?"

"Kissed you."

"Oh yes you should!" I angled my head to kiss her again, but she averted her face.

"I hardly know you," she mumbled. "You hardly know me. Besides…" She broke off.

Her cheeks were wet. She sniffed again and raised a hand to wipe them. I took the hand as she lowered it.

"What's the matter? What's wrong? Melanie?"

"Oh dear!" She put her free hand up to my neck and kissed me briefly. "You are sweet."

"Why the tears?"

"It's all right. I'm all right. I'm just being silly." She again shivered. "I'm getting cold. Can we go back in?"

I tried not to feel too disappointed as, still holding hands, we headed back for the room. As we got to the French doors, she removed her hand from mine and swept back her hair. "Let's get another drink." She sounded and looked mournful.

A few minutes later we stood, drinks in hand, at the side of the room, watching the dancers. Melanie was again emanating feelings of distance.

Rob came bounding up, looking like a manic cherub, his fair curly hair forming a substitute halo. "Hello there! Found you! I've been looking for you."

"Been outside," I said.

"Aha! Hence the non-presence in the room!" He turned to Melanie. "Greetings again, fair lady!" He gave her an ironic half-bow.

She smiled. "You're Rob, aren't you? You were very good, all of you. Very funny! I liked your songs."

"Thank you kindly. We do our best."

"That shooting one, how d'you keep a straight face?"

"Years of practice!" said Rob.

"I nearly jumped out of my skin when the gun went off!"

"Me too," said Rob, "and I'm expecting it!"

They were referring to a mime called 'Russian Roulette'. Rob and Alex stand side by side, facing the audience, Rob holding a gun. He rotates the chamber, then suavely and silently raises the gun to his temple and pulls the trigger. Click. He hands it to a terrified Alex, who goes through the same procedure. Click. They alternate: click, click, click... the smooth coolness of Rob contrasting with the increasing terror of Alex. The pay-off is that finally Alex, gun to temple, pulls the trigger as I fire a starting pistol behind the screen. Alex sways – is going to collapse – only it's Rob who falls to the ground – the bullet has passed through Alex's head and into Rob's. On paper the script looks pathetic, but Rob and Alex invariably get good laughs because of their changing facial expressions, and the final surprise of Rob keeling over and lying on the ground with legs and arms in the air like a dead sheep got a belter of a laugh this evening, and sustained applause.

"It was really funny," Melanie said.

"Thank you kindly," Rob repeated. "I'm afraid I must grab Phil."

"I saw him first," she pouted.

"There's a fellow from Downing," he told me, then paused, frowning. "That's 'fellow' as in 'person of the male gender', not 'fellow' as in 'don'..."

"Get on with it."

"Well, this non-don fellow wants to book us for a gig."

"Oh, right. Excellent! Sorry," I turned to Melanie. "Won't be a minute. Don't want to miss out on a booking."

"Okay!" She gave her mournful smile.

"Sorry to drag you away," said Rob as we headed across the room to where Alex was talking with a bloke sporting an apology for a Zapata moustache. "Not cramping your style, I hope? But he's wanting to fix it up before he heads off."

Mr Zapata Moustache informed me at length that we, the cabaret team, were "very, y'know, funny", quoting mangled versions of our best lines to prove it, and that he was putting on "this, y'know, happening at the end of, y'know, term" and that "a bit of the, y'know, funnies would go down well."

After some haggling, he booked us for one set lasting, y'know, thirty minutes. "Groovy," he said, and left.

"How's it going, man?" said Alex.

"Nice lady," I said. "Melanie. Girton."

"You're doing all right?"

"Reckon!"

"We won't expect you back at SG tonight! You'd better get back to her. Don't do anything I wouldn't do."

It had all taken longer than I'd expected with Zapata Moustache and I'd been feeling increasingly anxious about Melanie. I hurried to where I'd left her. Not there. I scouted around inside and outside. No luck.

Gerry, scarlet cummerbund now ludicrously draped round his shoulders and bow tie dangling from his left ear, was standing nearby with a small group of Pembroke men, laughing uproariously at something. I grabbed him by the arm and swung him round. He staggered and nearly fell, beaming the beam of someone with diminishing amounts of blood in his alcohol stream. "Gerry! Have you seen Melanie? She was here a few minutes ago."

He flicked at me with the end of his cummerbund. "Who?"

"Melanie."

"Who'sh Melanie?"

"The girl I was with."

"I don't know any Melaniesh."

"Girton. Longish hair, dark blonde-ish. Long skirt – blue-ish. Knockout attractive."

"Colour of eyesh?"

"Hazel, if you must know."

"That'sh very impresshive! But shorry – sorry – can't help you, old man. There sheem to be quite a lot of people here I don't know. It'sh only my party – you can't exshpect me to know the people here. What'sh happened to thish Melody?"

"Fuckin' Ada – it's *Melanie*, you cretin! *Melanie!* She's disappeared!"

"That'sh a clever trick! Are you going to put it in your nexsht cabaret? The amazshing dishappearing Melissa?"

"Oh, forget it!"

I gave him up as a bad job and began meandering around the room again in search of her, then back outside again. Still no luck. Melanie had gone. Her non-presence, to use Rob's expression, was total.

Chapter 6

Melanie

Exeter: January 1997

At the end when everyone was milling around saying goodbye and thanks for a wonderful evening, lovely to meet you, Phil gave me a farewell hug. "It's been great to see you."

"You too," I said. "Really lovely."

"Shall we get together sometime? We've nearly twenty-five years of catching up to do. Over half a lifetime."

"That'd be lovely!"

"*Transuranic,* you mean!" he said, fluttering his eyelashes.

"Are you ready, coz?" Sam pulled him away. "Nice to meet you, Melanie," she said unconvincingly. Her hair had definitely been hennaed.

"Likewise," I lied, and we air-kissed.

Phil and Patrick shook hands and said something to each other that seemed very friendly, and Rita murmured to me that she'd give me a ring sometime because, "There's something...would you mind? I'll phone you."

"I'm intrigued!"

I asked Phil where he lives as he and Sam headed down the path in front of us.

"Just the other side of the village! That's how I know those two."

I found it rather painful to see him leaving with Sam.

Simon as ever was over-solicitous, saying as we drove off that he hoped I hadn't overdone it, he'd been ready to leave much earlier if I'd indicated. I told him I was fine – tired, yes, but not the debilitating exhaustion I would once have been suffering from.

"You're really making progress, aren't you?" he said. "That's good." He fell silent as he negotiated a particularly winding part of the road. No streetlights here, and with a cloudy sky the only light came from the headlights. *Headlights.* That, I remembered Phil telling me when we first met, had been the original name of his cabaret team.

"Strange that Phil was there tonight," Simon said. "Did you know he lived out this way?"

"I knew he was brought up somewhere in the depths of Devon, but I didn't know what he did or where he went after Cambridge." Other than go and get married, I added silently, looking at my reflection in the side window. That, I knew, had been barely a year later.

"Ah," said Simon. "Odd that I should meet him now, for the first time."

"Yes. Odd."

As Simon fell silent, I slipped into replaying scenes from the dinner party, especially finding out he's going to do a revue, *treading the boards again*. And my daring – I felt it was daring – in using that ridiculous word he used to like – *transuranic!* – which no one else would understand – and they didn't. It was private to us.

Arriving home, I struggled to get out of the car. Simon came to help, supporting me into the house and up the stairs despite his own physical difficulties. "Hot choccy?" he asked as I slumped onto the bed, hunched myself forward, and started to remove my shoes.

What, I wondered, not stirring as Simon limped back downstairs, half-whistling to himself, what did Phil make of the evening? He used to think that I could fizz like a shaken can of Coke, as he said. Did he see any fizziness tonight? Well, maybe. Just a hint. I hope I didn't bore him with my health stuff – I had tried to downplay it. Then, as vivid as a landscape lit briefly by a flash of lightning, again I saw him, again I heard him refer to my book, quoting its full title. I had to keep hold of that truth – *that* is who I am, *that* is what I am capable of, *that* is who was beginning to emerge all those years ago in the Melanie – the Mel – he knew. I'm still here, emerging from a long tunnel.

What was Phil himself right now thinking? Thinking of me? Was he shaking his head and saying to himself poor old Mel? Or even poor old Simon? Or was he not thinking anything of the sort, but, despite his claim of their mere cousinship, was he in bed with Sam, naked with her, on top of her, doing it?

Chapter 7

Phil

Cambridge: October 1971

I woke late feeling heavy-headed. After finally accepting that Melanie had left the party, I'd sneaked away and spent an hour or two wandering around the city before finally heading for the college hostel in Selwyn Gardens, where I had a room as did Alex, Rob, Edward and several other Pembroke undergraduates.

Now, still half-asleep, I staggered out to the toilet, where I nearly tripped over Tristan, who had a room upstairs but was curled up on the toilet floor. He scrambled to his feet and pushed past me muttering, "Hey, sorry old boy, heavy trip," in his posh voice. No need to smoke grass when Tristan was around, all you had to do was stand downwind and inhale.

Back in my room I made myself a mug of tea using the kettle I kept there, and in lieu of fresh milk I sprinkled in some of the dried variety, which formed a spiral galaxy on top of the rotating fluid before slowly merging with it to produce a grey concoction with a patina of scum. Using a pencil I squashed some of the remaining lumps of milk against the side of the mug: it was like squashing maggots.

Sitting on the edge of the bed drinking the alleged tea, I again thought of the events of the previous evening. The cabaret? Superb! Melanie? Gorgeous! My chances? Fantastic! What had gone wrong? I could still feel my arms round her as we danced; I could still see her face, her lips, her eyes – that look in her eyes! I could still hear her voice and her laugh…

I abandoned the tea halfway through drinking it, reminiscent as it was in taste, texture, smell and visual aspect of a particularly vile end product of some organic chemistry practical. Organic chemistry – hell! I was going to have to get down to some work during the day. Supervision the next day, and I had done zero work for it. Doing organic chemistry was not my idea of a fun Sunday, but then, organic chemistry was not my idea of a fun anything these days.

As I dressed, I thought I heard a noise from the adjoining room. "Hi man!" I called out experimentally, hoping Alex was in. Our rooms on the ground floor had evidently been a single room at some point in the house's history, which had been split into two with an acoustically transparent plasterboard partition. Alex's room was a square, my space was an L-shape around it – in effect a corridor, albeit with cupboards, leading to a decent-sized room looking out onto the garden.

"You there, man?" I repeated the experiment. We'd started facetiously calling each other 'man' following a sketch we'd written parodying hippies. Facetiousness had solidified into habit.

No answer. I went up to Rob's room on the top floor. He too was out. I returned to my own room, sat reluctantly at my desk and opened a file of lecture notes.

About an hour later I heard the front door opening and closing, and the sound of familiar voices. A moment later the owner of one of the voices rapped on my door, and Alex called out, "Hi man!" as the door was opened.

"Hi man!" I echoed. Two sets of footsteps sounded along the short corridor, and Alex entered with Edward, both in sports gear and swishing squash racquets.

"How's tricks?" asked Alex, winking, waggling his eyebrows meaningfully, and making a nudge-nudge gesture with his elbow, as Edward greeted me with a cheery, "Morning, Philippe!" Edward always looked in good shape – squash player, rugby player, keen cyclist.

"Afternoon," I said, stressing the word. It had just gone twelve.

"Pedant!" Edward said. "But thank you, Philippe, we will! Milk, no sugar, and a slice of Fitzbillies' best." He took the only armchair, and Alex the window seat. I had swung round on my swivel chair.

"No milk," I said, "and no cake. Sorry. I can do you a black coffee and a chocolate digestive."

"Splendid! Make it two biscuits and that'll do fine. A good workout gives one an appetite. I've just given Alex a good thrashing."

"Thought you were playing squash."

"Naughty," said Edward reprovingly, pointing the handle of his racquet at me.

Alex was making great play of peering round the room. "I give up," he said. "Where have you hidden her?"

"Ah yes. We're agog to hear all about your latest conquest," Edward agreed.

"His *only* conquest," Alex amended.

"Spill the beans," said Edward. "She looked really nice."

"Not a lot of beans to spill," I admitted. "In fact, the beans are notable by their unspillable absence. This is a bean-free zone."

"You speak in riddles," said Edward. "Don't prevaricate. Kindly translate, or interpret."

As I made coffee and dug out the biscuits, I gave them an edited account of what had happened – and what hadn't happened – the previous evening: the mysterious affair of the vanishing lady.

"Damned shame," said Alex, as Edward banged his racquet on the floor and clicked his tongue in sympathy, saying, "That's a bit of a bummer."

"I thought things looked really promising. All systems go," said Alex.

"You've no idea where she went?" asked Edward.

"Nope. Back to Girton, I imagine."

"Or why?"

"Nope. Bloody women."

"Bloody women," Alex agreed.

"Not all of them. Young Liz for instance," objected Edward, referring to his girlfriend at Newnham. He finished his coffee and stood up. "Speaking of which, or rather of whom, I must go, chaps. Quick shower, then meeting said Liz for an outing somewhere. Destination to be decided. Thanks for coffee, Phil. Sorry about what's happened."

"No luck?" said Alex. It was late afternoon. I had returned from a Melanie hunt at Girton – a tiring ride on my wreck of a bicycle – and drifted into Alex's room. He was immersed in a French essay, but abandoned it on my arrival.

"Nope. The porter was useless, so I went round banging on doors at random to try to flush her out, but nobody seems to have heard of her – not that many were in, mind you. Got rather embarrassed about it after a while. Afraid I was going to get reported for loitering with intent. Or within Girton."

"Don't give up hope," Alex urged, picking up his pipe and refilling it. "That's the main thing. You never know, she may just appear out of the blue again. She can't have vanished off the face of the earth."

"Beginning to think she must have. It seems incredible that nobody knows her. She appears mysteriously at Gerry's party – he has no idea who she is – and then simply dematerialises."

"You could put an ad in *Varsity*."

"Hadn't thought of that."

"It might be worth a try." He struck a match, applied it to the bowl of the pipe and gave two or three expertly timed sucks.

I summoned up the memory of kissing Melanie, and moaned. "She was amazing, man, really amazing. If only we can get it together, things would be fantastic. Honestly, I could strangle the bitch for putting me through this!"

Alex puffed on his pipe and assumed a professorial manner. "As our old friend La Rochefoucauld says," he pronounced, "if one judges love by the majority of its effects, it's more like hatred than like friendship."

"He said that, did he?" I responded. "Well, next time you see the old bugger, you can kick him in the goolies, tell him it's with my love, and let him judge the majority of its effects."

"You'll be shocked to hear that he is in fact dead." Alex pursed his lips, expelling a thin jet of sweet-smelling smoke.

"Good," I said, and I meant it.

Chapter 8

Melanie

Exeter: January 1997

I've dug out *Transcending Gender* from the box in the attic and put it on the sitting room bookshelves. I'm proud of it.

Predictably I was prostrate with exhaustion on Sunday after the evening at C&J's, and I spent most of Sunday and Monday either in bed or stretched out on the sofa. No regrets, and I've enjoyed replaying the events of that evening, the surprise of seeing Phil, his evidently being pleased to see me, our snatches of conversation. They amounted to not very much, but that 'not very much' means a lot to me; and I'd been thinking about my PhD too, and the book. Is it any good? Does it read well? Is it cogent and insightful? The reviewers at the time thought so, but they could have been wrong.

Anyway, when I woke up this morning I felt recovered enough to retrieve it from the attic. *Transcending Gender: Heresy, Women Mystics and Mediaeval Society* in my hands again. A hefty tome. I've been sitting with a mug of coffee, flipping through the pages, reading the occasional paragraph. It *is* good, and there's been this little voice whispering in my ear, asking why did I give up academia? Why don't I resume it? I could, couldn't I? What's to stop me? After all, *TG* elicited a lot of responses and developments and criticisms and critiques, and I know there are parts of the arguments I put forward which could do with revising, expanding, and even refuting. I could plunge deeper into Marguerite Porete, say, or the works of Hildegard. Just the idea, the thought of doing that, gives me a thrill.

A couple of phone calls as well. Rita first, who started off by going, "oh, um, ah, er," in a very muffled voice. "Why I've rung you," she finally said with her distinctive little sigh, "is because I was wondering if you would be interested at all. You must say if you wouldn't be or if you're too busy. If you could it would be splendid."

"Sorry Rita," I had to say, "I haven't got what you're talking about."

"Talc. T-A-L-C," she said faintly, sighing again. "The Adult Literacy Class. It's a literacy class I help with. It's...for adults and they...well, it's to do with giving them more confidence and encouraging them, they're all, or most of them at least, doing some training and we...what they're learning... we give, well, supplementary input."

She said more in her convoluted sighing style, but what it boils down to is that there's this weekly class staffed by volunteers for encouraging adult literacy, especially for those who are slow learners and never got a good grounding at school.

"I was hoping," she sighed, "if you could, well, it's a couple of hours a week. You're probably, like all of us, so much on our, in our, diaries..."

"I'd be really interested in doing it," I said quickly.

"Oh would you? That'd be...that's splendid!"

"I must warn you my health's still dodgy and I wouldn't want to let you down."

"Oh, we'd be grateful...anything you could...whatever."

There's an induction session next week for new volunteers I've said I'll go to, and I'll just have to be very careful about pacing myself. But once a week? Come on, surely I can manage that.

That was followed by a slightly odd phone call from Charlotte. Ostensibly she rang to ask how I was after the dinner party, which was kindly meant, but once she'd established that I was all right and really had enjoyed the time as much as I'd said on the card I'd sent, she mentioned Phil.

"How amazing you knew each other at Cambridge!" she said. "I'm so pleased to have reunited old friends!" Then she started digging (not very subtly) to find out *exactly* how well we'd known each other. I think she's a bit put out that I know him; or rather, she's put out by the fact that she hadn't known beforehand that we knew each other.

Well, I wasn't going to give her chapter and verse about our relationship. But it's difficult to fend off questions like, "Did you see a lot of each other? Did you go out together? Did you have a fling?" She was keen to get across that *she* has known Phil since they were children – though I'm slightly hazy about details, all to do with Phil's aunt and uncle and cousin Sam living in what is now Phil's cottage. However, I did admit that Phil and I had gone out together 'two or three times', and got a bit of a shock with her response.

"Phil was sweet on me, you know," she said with a coy laugh. "When we were teenagers. Well, I was a teenager, he was twenty or twenty-one. We went out several times, but it never came to anything. He took me to a disco once."

Annoyingly, all this has made me feel jealous. Sad, isn't it? Phil was sweet on her, was he? That was years ago, and he was a lot more than just 'sweet' on me. Not that I was going to give Charlotte details. Especially as

I got the distinct impression that she was wanting to know if I still harboured feelings for him, whether I still fancied him, but she couldn't bring herself to ask anything like that outright, and I wasn't going to help her.

"I had been hoping," Charlotte said, "that Phil would bring Sonia along on Saturday. I'm sure there's a bit of a spark between them."

Sonia? Sonia? It took me a few seconds to recall that Sonia had been part of Charlotte's diversionary tactic when Phil and Patrick had been arguing about religion. "She is a bit of a merry widow as Patrick put it," Charlotte continued. "She lives just down the lane from us. Great fun. She's definitely in the market. Very attractive and heaps of energy."

I didn't particularly want to hear about Sonia the merry widow. I nipped that topic in the bud by saying how impressed I'd been by Jimmy's wine cellar. Good move. She groaned theatrically and said it was the bane of her life, a perfectly good storage area which she had plenty of other uses for. "Jimmy hijacked it when we got married, the day he moved in – and he's claimed it ever since for his bottle collection."

It's stirred me up. All these women: a teenage Charlotte, cousin Sam, Sonia the merry widow, Phil's ex-wife… I've got an unsettling image of Phil with a composite woman and I don't like it. I don't want to be part of any composite woman; it makes me realise that I still want to be *the* woman.

Chapter 9

Emhalt: May 1967

Kenny was playing 'Paint It Black' on the piano, just audible above the buzz of conversation and laughter which had broken out immediately after the final 'Amen' of the service. Anne was talking with one of the boys, Jeremy, who had a Beatles haircut and invariably wore cords – dark blue today – and desert boots, and Melanie was heading towards the twins Sarah and Rose who had called her over when Simon intercepted her with a "Hi Melanie!" in his over-bright voice.

Melanie sighed. Although she liked Simon – her age, friendly, kind and bright – she didn't fancy him, not in the girlfriend-boyfriend way, though it had become increasingly evident that he fancied her. At the end of the Sunday afternoon joint Followers classes, he would come up and engage her in chat when she wanted to be with the other girls. When there were special events for the older Followers, ten-pin bowling or a theatre trip or a Saturday evening barbecue, he was always wanting to know if she'd be attending, and then at the event itself, there he was, by her side, making conversation, being helpful.

"Hi Simon!" She forced a smile.

"How are you?"

"Pretty groovy!"

"How are your exams going?"

"All right, thanks. They're not really all that important, are they? How are yours?"

"Not bad, thanks." He puffed out his cheeks, a little mannerism which suggested he was trying to blow out invisible candles. He still sported a short-back-and-sides haircut, and with his smart, old-fashioned jacket and trousers, neat tie and polished black shoes he looked like he belonged to an earlier era, not that of the so-called Swinging Sixties. In his right hand he clutched a Followers' Bible and a small book with a red and grey cover full of the choruses which featured in every Followers' service. "What are you going to do when exams are over?" he asked.

"I don't know," Melanie replied, glancing to where Anne was now laughing loudly with Jeremy. "Why?"

"It's just that a chap at school is going to have a 'rave-up'," Simon said. He put 'rave-up' in audible inverted commas. "I was wondering..." He puffed out his cheeks again, and Melanie felt paralysed. She was about to be asked out. She didn't want to be asked out. Not by Simon. She'd say no, she had to say no. But a rave-up? She'd love to go to a rave-up. Though she wasn't quite sure what a rave-up actually entailed.

"...if you would like to go with me," Simon concluded in a rush. A tinge of red had appeared on his usually pale cheeks, and he had shifted his stance, supporting himself by holding onto the back of a chair while rubbing the toecap of his left shoe against the back of his right trouser leg, as if it required an emergency polishing.

"That's very kind of you, Simon," Melanie said, desperately trying to trawl up some excuse. "When is it?"

"First Saturday in June."

"Oh, um, I'm not sure. I'll have to check when I get home. I think I might have something on."

"I hope you can come. What are you doing tonight?"

"Revising," Melanie said quickly.

"Yes, me too!"

Melanie felt trapped, feeling she couldn't just walk away, but fearing Simon was going to suggest another date for him to take her out. She stared over his shoulder at the picture on the wall immediately behind him, hoping to pluck inspiration from a Caucasian Jesus in a white robe, holding a compliant lamb; but rescue came in the form of Old Brillo.

"Pardon me for, ah, intruding," he laid a hand on Simon's shoulder. "Could I ask a, erm, a favour of you, young Simon? Excuse me," he added ponderously to Melanie, his thick black beard waggling alarmingly, "I, um, need the services of this young man. Simon," he steered him away, "about the, erm, the anniversary service. We were, ah, rather hoping that you could, erm..."

Simon turned and was trying to mouth something to Melanie, but she had already joined Sarah and Rose.

Chapter 10

Phil

Cambridge: November 1971

"*Voilà! La salle de bal de* Dorothy," announced Rob, waving his guitar in the air. He pushed open the door, and the sound of dance music, already audible in Hobson Street, leaped in volume. We paused in the entrance lobby, Alex and I putting our bags down before lowering to the floor the screen we'd been painfully carrying between us from Selwyn Gardens. As well as his guitar, Rob had various props in a rucksack.

A doorman or bouncer – black-bearded, wearing black jeans, a black tee-shirt and wrap-around sunglasses – appeared through a swing door.

"Whaddya want?" was his merry greeting.

"We're the cabaret," I said.

He looked unimpressed.

"Damien booked us," added Alex.

Still unimpressed.

"Chap with a Zapata moustache," I said.

He grunted something along the lines of, "Oh yeah, that cretin," and lumbered back to his lair.

"I'll go and investigate," said Alex.

It was the last Saturday of term, and the cabaret in question, due to take place in the Dorothy Ballroom, was the one we'd been booked for at Gerry's party a few weeks earlier. I hadn't seen Melanie since then. Over the following couple of weeks I'd returned to Girton several times, creaking along the Huntingdon Road on my bike, knocking on doors and generally haunting the place in my search for the missing Melanie; and every day, going into Pembroke, I'd asked at the porters' lodge if anyone had been asking for me. On one such occasion, head porter Mr Scrimshaw had divined that it concerned a girl.

"Dangerous things, sir, affairs of the heart," he observed. "I'd stick to your studies if I were you."

"Would you now?"

"I would indeed, sir. Young ladies are very flighty."

"All of them? A touch of overgeneralisation there, wouldn't you say?"

"I wouldn't take it too hard if I was you, sir," he'd persisted, ignoring my remarks. "When the time is right there'll be plenty of other fish in the sea."

Being a Cambridge undergraduate, I'd spotted the flaw in his argument immediately. "The future availability of amorous fish is hardly relevant, seeing as I myself am not, for instance, a mackerel or a haddock."

"Indeed you're not, sir," he'd rejoined stiffly. "Mackerel and haddock would not be allowed to become members of the college."

The notice I'd placed in *Varsity* asking 'Melanie of Girton' to contact 'Phil of Pembroke' had drawn a blank, and as the days went by I'd begun to distract myself by getting down to more work. I had, since coming to Cambridge, struggled academically – whereas at school I'd been top in chemistry and near the top in physics and maths, here I was at best average, and it felt like too much effort to try to rise higher so I'd drifted along, every now and then doing the academic equivalent of doggy-paddle to ensure I didn't sink completely. I'd attended lectures with moderate regularity, bought and even dipped into the recommended textbooks, struggled through the work set by my supervisors, attended the occasional debate at the Union, gone to various discos and parties, tried punting in the summer, and increasingly directed my energies to writing sketches and performing cabarets – but for the past few weeks I'd turned my attention more seriously back to *The Fundamentals of Organic Chemistry* and other scientifically mystical writings.

Alex returned with the information that Damien Zapata Moustache was currently throwing up in the bogs.

"Oh terrific," I said. "Very helpful."

"Let's take this lot in and get set up," said Rob.

The ballroom was full of people intermittently illuminated by flickering and flashing lights of vivid red and green and blue, and the music was belting out from two great banks of speakers. A disc jockey, even more heavily bearded than the doorman, and sporting a Led Zeppelin tee-shirt, was operating an array of turntables. As we shoved our way through the liquid mass of humanity with our gear, his distorted voice announced it was time for the greatest band in the history of rock. A moment later the riffs of 'Whole Lotta Love' started testing the structural integrity of the building.

We staked out an area at the far end of the room with chairs, erected our screen, and commandeered a small table for our props. Alex started pacing up and down, frowning and muttering to himself as he ran through a solo sketch. Rob was sitting on a chair tuning his twelve-string. He had a look of benign puzzlement on his face.

I studied the running order pinned to the screen, still trying to memorise it – we had included some new items. Alex came up.

"How're you doing, man?"

"Shitting bricks," I said.

"Me too."

"Forgotten your lines?" I asked, indicating the script he had in his hand.

"A temporary touch of amnesia. *Hamjambo wanachi wote*," he broke into Swahili. He had lived for many years in Kenya, and had written a sketch in which a television presenter reads a bizarre version of the news consisting of strings of random Swahili words punctuated by ludicrous phrases in English. He'd performed it for the first time a couple of weeks earlier at a cabaret for the local chapter of Mensa, where it had gone down well with the intelligentsia, and he'd worked on refining it for this performance.

Rob joined us, guitar tuning completed. He was biting at the skin round his fingernails. He clapped his hands and beamed his cherubic beam. "Are we all prepared? Nerves all steady? Pulse rate normal?"

"Brick-shitting," said Alex.

"No change there, then."

Alex went off on another search, returning with the news that Zapata had forgotten we were coming but we could do, "some, y'know, funnies at, y'know, ten o'clock". It was now nine thirty.

I ducked, and the pint glass bounced off the screen and fell onto the floor. The sound it made suggested it was not glass but plastic, a fact I couldn't have realised as I saw it sailing through the air towards me from the middle of a restive audience. My immediate impulse was to get the hell out of it in case the next missile wasn't quite as innocent, but I still had about two-thirds of the sketch to go and didn't want to abandon it straight away as there were a couple of lines coming up which always got a belter of a laugh and could conceivably drag us back from the brink of comedic oblivion. I speeded up my delivery to get to them and tripped over the lead-in line, mangling it such that the pay-off line didn't make sense. A loud voice from the audience yelled "ha-fucking-ha!" which got more laughs than my script, and what might have been incipient applause developed instead into a slow handclap, faint but unmistakable.

We were about ten minutes into our thirty-minute set, and the problem we faced was that most of the audience counted as audience only in name and not in reality. We'd found enough chairs to make three rows and these were all occupied, but everyone else – and there was an awful lot of everyone else – had to stand. Most of the standees couldn't see us – there was no stage – so were talking or, indeed, shouting, which negated the 'audi-' element of 'audience'. Increasingly the shouting was aimed at us, with "ha-fucking-ha!", along with "what a load of crap!" and "wankers!", exemplifying the type of inventive linguistic skills that could be acquired and honed by attendance at one of the premier universities in the country.

"This is bad, this is really bad," I mutter to Alex as, having finished the sketch at top speed, I retreat to safety behind the screen while Rob ventures out with his guitar and cherubic features.

"Morons," says Alex, and hidden by the screen we relieve our feelings by making furious V-signs in the general direction of the audience.

"And now," we hear Rob announce, raising his voice to a near shout, "a little ditty accompanied by my trusty twelve-string guitar." He plays a chord. "Eleven-string guitar," he amends. The twelfth, he superfluously tells us later, had just snapped. More sallies of searing intellectual wit emerge from the audience in response, and the slow handclap is spreading.

When Rob comes off at the end of his song, he's perspiring freely. "The natives are restless tonight," he pants.

Alex goes on and performs a shortened version of his Swahili sketch which elicits cries of, "Speak English, you knobhead!" and, "A pox on both your tongues!" which does at least sound wittily Shakespearean; then on I go for another solo sketch to yells such as, "Not this tosser again!" and, "Why didn't your father take precautions?"

Now it's the turn of Alex and Rob in Russian Roulette, and the slow handclap dies down. The sketch follows the pattern of its predecessors in getting next to no laughs as it moves to the pay-off when, with Alex holding the gun to his temple and his finger on the trigger, behind the screen I fire the starting pistol.

Click.

I fire again.

Click.

And again.

Click. Click.

Oh *sod it!* I'd forgotten to load the pistol with blanks.

"*Bang!*" I shout.

Alex sways...and sways...and Rob falls to the ground, doing his dead sheep impersonation.

Not a titter. Totally titterless.

"One down, two to go!" someone yells. Others cheer.

Alex exits to behind the screen, and Rob gets up.

"Shit! He's still alive!" the same voice yells. Retreating, Rob beats by a short head a second plastic glass which bounces off his guitar on its stand, making a distinctive boinging noise at which someone calls out, "*Ten*-string!", and the slow handclap has resumed at a livelier tempo.

We cut straight to the final item, a song with all three of us. Give a perfunctory bow. "Thank you kindly for being such a unique audience!" Rob calls out, just as a blast of 'Strange Brew' blisters the paintwork.

⋆

It was as we were packing up our things, having cowered out of sight for a few minutes while the party resumed its former, pre-ARP aspect, that the tenor of the evening changed. Alex was the one to spot her.

"Hey man," he said, "have you seen?"

"Seen what?"

"Over there. The girl you got off with at Gerry's party."

"What, Melanie? Where?"

"Over there." He pointed. All I could see was a mass of people milling about, some dancing, some drinking, some laughing loudly. "She's by the wall," Alex continued. "Hey, look, there she is."

The crowd, operating in accordance with the arcane laws which underlie the ebb and flow of people at a party, momentarily parted, and I saw her. She was standing against the wood panelling, head tilted back like someone examining the ceiling, then she lowered her head and looked in my direction, but before I could tell whether or not she'd seen me staring at her, the sea of people had flowed back and she was once more hidden.

"Go on," Alex was urging. "Now's your chance. Go on!"

He said something else I didn't catch. It was irrelevant. I'd already started pushing my way through the partygoers towards the elusive Melanie.

Chapter 11

Melanie

Exeter: January 1997

I've written to Phil.

I've been thinking about him a lot since meeting him at C&J's, hoping he'd get in touch, but as he hasn't I've risked taking the initiative. Thanks to Anne, really. I rang her this afternoon, and when she'd finished telling me her news I took the plunge and told her about meeting Phil again. She and Phil never met, but I'd talked with her about him loads when it was all going on, so she knows him by proxy.

"Well, well! What was that like, seeing him again?" she demanded. "How did it go?"

"It was great. It was lovely to see him and talk with him."

"No hard feelings?"

"None at all. We're twenty-five years older. Not necessarily twenty-five years *wiser!*"

"Is he still as gorgeous as you always thought he was?"

Although I only paused briefly, Anne was onto it straight away before I could answer. "Oh! Is there something you need to tell your Auntie Anne? Come on, out with it! *Is* he still gorgeous?"

"Sort of," I said.

"Sort of? What sort of gorgeousness is that? Come on, 'fess up. I reckon you've never been out of love with him, have you?"

"No," I had to admit. "I don't think I have. But I'm married, Anne."

"Doesn't stop you being in love!"

We talked and talked and talked; and as a result, I've written to him.

I know I could simply ring him up, but that really doesn't feel right. I don't want to intrude into his life – well, yes, I do want to intrude, of course I do, but not in a way that could back him into a corner and cause him to resent me. I'd find that intensely painful, knowing or believing he resented me, and I need to ensure that if he doesn't want our chance reacquaintance to develop into a renewed friendship he can simply allow further contact to fizzle out.

I'm not going to tell Simon. I might in time; not straight away. He wouldn't be comfortable about it, however much he managed to maintain his habitual stance of Mr Cheerfulness. That's understandable – after all, would I be comfortable if he resumed a friendship with, say, Olivia? Actually, now I think about it, the answer to that is 'yes', I would be comfortable. Then again his involvement with her was only in reaction to my involvement with Phil; the two relationships aren't comparable.

The bottom line is that I want to see Phil again, and I've written to him. It was a brief note, saying how lovely it was talking with him, I really would like to have that catch-up, how about meeting for a coffee; and I suggested a couple of possible dates. I wasn't sure how to sign it, settling on 'love, Mel', without an 'x'.

There are a couple of P. Ellises in the local phone book, only one at Teignford: 'Rose Cottage'. Dropping the letter into the postbox, I had the scary sense of taking an irrevocable step.

Chapter 12

Phil

Cambridge: November 1971

"This is amazing! You're so lovely!" I said for approximately the millionth time, give or take a few.

Melanie, pressed up against me, gave inarticulate murmurs of agreement. We were in Hobson Street, outside the Dorothy.

At the glimpse of her I'd barged through the heaving crowd, afraid I'd been the victim of a passing hallucination, but there she was, leaning against the wall, hand up to her throat, looking like some strange goddess with psychedelic patterns in reds and greens and oranges of the light show flickering across her body and flashing in her eyes. She was breathing rapidly, her breasts rising and falling with quick, jerky movements as though she were choking or sobbing. Her lips were parted, her hair in chaos. I grabbed her hand and led her without speaking round the sides of the room. We skirted the mass of revellers, gained the door into the lobby area, then through the lobby into the street and the night air.

We stayed hugging each other for some minutes until a blast of music hit us as a group of party-leavers emerged. We moved on.

"How come you were there this evening?" I asked as we headed down the street. "And what happened to you at Gerry's party? Where did you get to? I tried to find you, then kept going out to Girton, banging on doors..."

"Did you? Did you really?" she demanded eagerly.

"Course I did! Trouble is, I don't know your surname or what year you're in or anything..."

"Mason, second year. Did you really come looking for me?"

"Loads of times. But you'd done the vanishing lady act."

"Oh, I'm so sorry, Phil. I'm so sorry! I really messed things up."

"Hey, hey, hey," I stopped and put my arms round her again. "Now's the time to un-mess them." I held her tight, then released her. "Come on, I don't know about you, but I need a drink – let's go to the Union."

"Don't you want to go back to the Dorothy?"

"God no! Terrible party! Terrible cabaret! Where did they dig that lot up from?"

"Well, it wasn't just luck I was there tonight," Melanie said as we sat in the Union bar. I was on beer, she had a gin and tonic. "A friend of mine, Sarah, said she was going to this party and she'd heard that Air Raid Precautions were performing. You're getting quite a reputation, you know."

"Which is down the plughole after tonight," I grunted.

"Don't be silly – no it's not – it was just not the right occasion. It was like a message from God when she told me. I knew I had to see you again, even if it came to nothing. I had to try. I wangled my way in with Sarah and her boyfriend and a couple of others."

"Glad you did," I said. "But what did happen to you at Gerry's party?"

"Um, well, everything was happening so quickly, between us. I didn't believe it could last." She was frowning as she spoke. "I thought you were probably on a high from your performance, you know, and and and you went off and you didn't come back..."

"I was fixing up for tonight's cabaret!" I interjected. "You knew I was..."

"Yes, yes, yes," she said hurriedly. "You were gone for so long I thought, well, you were using it as a way of getting rid of me. I felt awful."

I tilted my head back and gave what was, though I say it myself, an impressive impersonation of a wolf baying at the moon.

"Get rid of you?" I cried as the echoes died away. "How could you think that? It was just that the prat who was booking us for tonight's gig has a brain that a nematode worm would be ashamed to admit to, and he took an entire geological era to make up what passes for his mind what he wanted. I got back to where you were, or rather where you weren't, as soon as poss, but you'd vanished, fled, evaporated, disappeared."

"I thought," she continued mournfully, "I really did think, that that was that. All over. A lovely half-hour or however long, then thank you and goodnight. I couldn't bear to stay. I couldn't bear the thought of seeing you a bit later on dancing with some other girl and ignoring me. I had to go. Afterwards, the next day really, I did wonder if I'd got it all wrong. I didn't know what to do. I did think about going to ask at Pembroke but was too frightened that if I did find you you'd be angry with me."

I encored my baying wolf impersonation. Other users of the bar looked at me, no doubt wondering if they could hire me by the hour, but I ignored them.

"I know that's unfair," she hurriedly added. "That's what I was afraid of. I thought... I thought if you did want to see me again, you'd get in contact. You'd find a way of finding me."

A third baying wolf. "Christ Almighty!" I groaned. "I tried!"

"I know, I know! Are you angry?"

"I'm not, honestly, I'm not. Just frustrated that between us we managed to get it completely cocked up."

"Well, I've been pretty much in anguish all term since then, but when I heard you were going to be at the Dorothy tonight, I knew I had to see you again, talk to you again...kiss you again if I possibly could."

To suit the action to the words she stopped talking and kissed me, then I kissed her, then we kissed each other.

I said I'd walk her back to Girton. After I'd nipped into the gents we left the Union and soon were on the Huntingdon Road.

It took twice the usual time to get to her college as we regularly stopped to kiss and fondle each other. I felt I was somehow flouting all the laws of the known universe, and some of the unknown universe as well. I half-expected to feel the tap of a cosmic finger on my shoulder from one of fate's messengers sent to inform me that there'd been some sort of cosmic cock-up, and that according to the decrees of fate I wasn't scheduled to be in said company of said woman after all, would I please instantly resume my true place in the scheme of things, namely, viz. and to wit, being permanently womanless and hereby consigned to an onanistic future. Then again, had such a messenger arrived, I would have had no option but to tell him, her or it to piss off double quick.

We arrived at the entrance to Girton College.

"Would you like to come in for some...coffee?" Melanie asked.

"I'd like to come in," I said.

Chapter 13

Melanie

Exeter: February 1997

I've just got back from seeing Phil and I'm buzzing. When I wrote to him I was hoping we'd rekindle a friendship, but expecting it'd come to very little, that it'd be at a very superficial level. His reply came by return, saying yes, that would be great – *transuranic!* – let's get together, and the first date I'd suggested (i.e. today) was fine for him.

I was really nervous about meeting him, and doubly nervous about being late, so it was well before ten as I headed across Cathedral Green to Leofric's, but he'd beaten me to it, and I saw him sitting hunched up on the little wall that surrounds the Green, his back towards me. He had on a brown leather jacket, his hair overlapping the collar, and his hands thrust into its upper pockets, causing his elbows to jut out as though he were about to flap them like chicken's wings. A few feet away from him I paused, heart pounding, mouth going dry, legs shaking and a light airy sensation in my head. I slowed my breathing, deepened each breath, then resumed walking.

"Hi!" I said when I was just about within touching range.

He jumped up and spun round, pulling his hands from his pockets. "Mel! Hi! Great! Fantastic!" he virtually yelped, and I felt myself flush at his delight. We stood staring at each other for a couple of seconds, his eyes wide and bright; then he jumped over the little wall and, just as he had done at Charlotte and Jimmy's, grabbed my upper arms and kissed me on the cheek.

"Well, you're here," he said, letting his hands drop and taking a step back, colliding with the wall and almost having to sit on it. "You've turned up! Not a rerun of the Friar House!"

I lowered my eyes. "All right! I know I haven't got a good track record for turning up! But here I am."

"Here you are! Come on – let's celebrate!"

As we stepped over the wall he took my arm to steady me, a gesture that triggered a quick thrill in me, and he led the way into the cafe. We ordered coffees and took a table by the window.

He stuck his elbows on the table, tugged up the neck of his jersey in the mannerism I remembered, interlinked the fingers of his two hands, rested his chin on them and stared at me. I felt under scrutiny. He said how lovely it was to see me and that I was looking really good. That can't have been true – the second bit that is – because I know I look rather pale these days, but not of the 'pale and interesting' variety, and my eyes, or eye sockets really, are rather darker than they should be because of lack of sleep. Also I'm at least a size bigger than I used to be – or want to be. I've never exactly been slim.

I said something crass about what a shock it'd been to see him at Charlotte and Jimmy's.

"A nasty shock?" he asked, I don't know how seriously.

"Oh no," I said. "A lovely shock. I'm *so* pleased to see you."

"And me you," he said.

There could have been an awkward silence but the coffee arrived and we both busied ourselves with that, exchanging some trivial comments about the cathedral and all the scaffolding on the west front before I finally said, "Well, you heard a tiny bit about me the other evening. Now it's your turn."

He fluttered his eyelashes. "What d'you want to know?"

"Everything!" I said. "What do you *do*, for a start? How come you're able to be here on a weekday morning?"

"The joys of self-employment. I have, as they say," he put on a pompous voice, "a portfolio of interests!"

I laughed. "Do you now! What's in this portfolio?"

"Oh, a bit of this and a bit of that."

The 'bit of this' turns out to be private tuition, principally for A level students. Maths mainly, he said, with some chemistry and physics. The 'bit of that' is freelance editing of scientific articles which, if I've understood properly, are mainly translations from other languages into "pretty ghastly English", as he put it, from which he has to produce something that makes both scientific and grammatical sense. "Guess what my specialist subject is," he said.

I was stumped for a moment, before remembering his particular hate at Cambridge. "Not the dreaded?" I said.

He nodded. "Organic chemistry!" and we both laughed slightly more loudly than was natural. Nervous, both of us.

"Do you do any regular performing?" I asked cautiously. He had been so hopeful about entering the world of entertainment. He shook his head.

"Nah. Never happened. I've done the occasional sketch here and there when there's been some social event and people have wanted party pieces, but nothing, you know..." he shrugged. "This Red Nose revue is the first thing like that for years."

"I'm really looking forward to it."

"You might just recognise one or two of the sketches!"

"I'd love it!" I said. "But what of other things? I know you've been married."

"Um, yes. Still am, strictly speaking." He fiddled with his coffee cup, then looked at me ruefully. "If you want the gory details, Ros and I got married in '73, and separated in '89. My fault. I made a fool of myself with the mother of one of my pupils, and ended up hurting Ros rather badly. She didn't exactly chuck me out, but made distinct chucking-out noises, and I sort of self-chucked. We were living in Kent, where she still is, but my uncle, you see, used to live in Teignford, and as it happened he'd just moved out to go and live with Sam, my cousin Sam, you met her, up near Barnstaple, so I came back down here to rent the cottage from him. I knew the place from childhood. Our families were close and we often visited. We were at Silveridge. Mum and Dad still live there."

"That's how you knew Charlotte?"

"Oh yeah. She went to the same school as Sam."

"She told me you used to be sweet on her."

The look Phil gave me was of pure horror, and he held up his hands, making a cross with his fingers to ward off evil. "Back! Back I conjure thee! Me? Sweet on her? Nah! I was keen on her older sister, Penny, who was Sam's best friend. Charlotte kept getting in the way. If anything, *she* had a crush on *me*. Mad girl. I was eighteen when I really fancied Penny, and Charlotte must have been about fourteen or fifteen at the time."

"Did this Penny fancy you?"

"Ha! Not one little bit. Quite the opposite. Gathered later that she thought I was a 'pest', so that was that. I never had a thing for Charlotte. Ah, hang on, I've just remembered. Christmas vac, 1971. I did sort of go out with her a couple of times."

This shook me. He took her out while he was still seeing me? But I realised that he was referring to the Christmas vac following the Friar House fiasco. "Hadn't heard from you," he said. "Thought it was all over between us. I went to see Sam and talk stuff over, and went for a drink with her and her then boyfriend, and with Penny and *her* boyfriend, and Charlotte found out and tagged along, acting as if she was my girlfriend. Nothing happened though!"

"Did she want something to happen?"

"Nah. Think she just wanted to be seen with someone. Then I discovered I was taking her to a Christmas disco in the village hall. That was all. Highlight of the year, I don't think. She lost interest after that, thank God. Give Charlotte her due, when I moved back down to the cottage in '89 she was incredibly helpful in rallying round and using her contacts to get me some pupils. I'm very grateful to her. She's a good sort."

"When you got married," I said cautiously, wondering if I was about to venture into a quicksand, "it wasn't that long after you and me had...well, it was Sarah told me, via Alex, you'd married. They were still an item then. I was wondering..." I couldn't finish the sentence and left it hanging in the air.

"Ah, yes." He was silent for some time, wondering, I suppose, whether to give me the details. "There's a touch of irony in how Ros and I met," he eventually said, tugging at the neck of his jersey again. "That day I came down to see you. That park we met in."

"The Tarn."

"The Tarn, that's it. Well, Ros and I were in the same compartment on the train to London, and to cut a long story short she'd mislaid her purse and I lent her some money."

"Sweet of you, but I suppose she was very attractive?" I said teasingly.

Phil winced. "She did have sexy legs," he admitted.

"Oh."

"But otherwise, nah!" he added quickly. "Nothing like as sexy as you!"

"That is the right response! And what happened about this money you lent her of the sexy legs, then?"

"She was meant to send me a cheque, but she went and lost my address. Then months later she found it, and as she was coming down to Devon in any case to visit some friend somewhere, she came to Silveridge – I was still living there – to give the money back in person. It sort of took off from there." He gave a shrug. "We got on pretty well, I went to visit her, and one thing led to another and, er, how can I put this?"

"Put what?"

"The inevitable. She went and got pregnant."

"Oh," I repeated.

"Wasn't exactly planned," he shrugged again, "but these things happen. Ros wanted to get married, and I thought 'why not?' so we did. I moved down her way, to Kent, because she'd already started up her own business. She's a hairdresser. A hair*stylist*, rather. She runs her own salon and...what?"

He broke off and stared at me, and I'm not surprised. My jaw must have hit the floor. I was, to stay in cliché mode, gobsmacked. Phil, with his perpetual dragged-backwards-through-a-hedge mane; Phil, who thinks that 'brush and comb' is some girlie affectation... Phil married to a *hairstylist*?

Something deep inside me opened up. Starting deeper than the solar plexus, it rose up through my body, my chest, into my throat and exploded into laughter. It was unstoppable. I know I've got a loud laugh at the best of times – Phil used to tell me that when I was in the audience of his cabarets, my laughing was better than ten ordinary members of the audience combined, but in Leofric's this morning I must have outdone an entire audience. My eyes went all blurry as I simply howled with laughter. I couldn't get my breath properly. My side hurt. I remember stabbing the air repeatedly with a finger, pointing at him and gasping, "You...you...you..." though I'm not sure what I was trying to say. I became aware that he was grinning, then laughing, then he too was howling with laughter. He grabbed my hands across the table again and we simply rocked.

"I can't believe it, I simply can't believe it," I finally managed to gasp. "Did she see you as the ultimate challenge? Thinking if she could tame this," I reached up and ruffled his already more-than-ruffled hair, "she could tackle anything?"

"She did a good job," he protested self-mockingly. "I looked great. Real smooth."

"Oh my God!" I burst out, and within seconds we were both weeping with laughter again.

We were still laughing when we realised another customer had come to a halt by our table. Patrick. The Roth of God. He was towering over us, looking severe, which I think is his default expression. Although we weren't holding hands at that point, I felt myself redden. Phil carried it off perfectly, stifling his laughter, raising a hand in greeting and cheerily saying, "Patrick, my man! How're you doing? Still on the trail of unrepentant sinners?" and standing up to shake hands with him.

"Philip!" Patrick boomed, "We all have much to be repentant of! But a good coffee is pleasing unto the nostrils of the Lord! Melanie, how do you do? How are you?"

"Very well, thank you."

"Good! I enjoyed an excellent game with the Dragon last night!"

"Simon said it'd been a fierce battle."

"You were having a mighty laugh just now," Patrick continued. "Is the joke repeatable, I wonder?"

"Too long to explain," Phil said. "Concerning the length of my hair."

"Hmm, I see. Well, there's a good precedent. Our Lord would not have had a short-back-and-sides. I must say, Philip, I enjoyed our verbal tussle the other evening. Sharpens the wits, keeps me on my toes. We must have a return match sometime!"

"Epistles at dawn?" Phil said, pronouncing it 'e-pistols'.

Patrick laughed loudly but briefly. "I prefer the gospel," he said.

He moved on after that and we heard him ordering a coffee and croissant, and we watched in silence as he went and sat at a table on the far side of the cafe. Tact? Or fearing defilement?

I said, "Whoops!" and Phil said, "That was close!" He fluttered his eyelashes at me and added, "Oh Mel, you are great! You are the best."

"Still crazy after all these years?" I quoted Paul Simon.

"Fifty ways to leave your lover," he quoted back, and we both fell silent, simply gazing at each other.

All my anxiety had vanished and I felt utterly at ease with him. That intense laughing together had shifted something, like the action of a fierce paint stripper which rips through multiple layers of years-old paint covering, smothering and completely jamming a door to a secret room, a door that now swung open. We'd reconnected at a deep level. Patrick's interruption had the effect of binding us together as conspirators.

There's a passage in a Hardy novel – one of the minor ones, I think – about two lovers who part, and when they're reunited years later the time that they'd been separated just falls away, the gap closes up and it's as if they'd never parted. That's exactly the feeling. We've linked back over the intervening twenty-five years.

I wanted to know more. There was so much about him I didn't know, and so much he didn't know about me. I was greedy, I wanted to know everything now.

His daughters – what of his daughters? He was going to tell me about them at C&J's when we'd been interrupted.

"Lem and Amy," he said when I asked.

"Lem?"

"Lem."

"Unusual name. Short for something?"

"In a way. It's more of a sort of nickname."

He was silent for a while, and I had to ask if he was going to explain. He seemed reluctant, but the story emerged slowly. When the second daughter, Amy, started to speak, she couldn't manage her sister's name and it came out garbled and the wrong way round. She called her sister 'Lemony', which got shortened to 'Lemon' and then 'Lem', and the nickname Lem had stuck.

"What's her real name?" I asked.

Across the table, he took both my hands and pulled me towards himself. His eyes were wide.

"Melanie," he said.

"Yes?" I said, holding his gaze.

He shook his head. "I mean," he said, and just before he explained I realised what was coming, "that's what she's called. Melanie. Her real name is Melanie. My eldest daughter," he articulated the words slowly, "is called Melanie."

Chapter 14

Emhalt: May 1967

"Guess what!" said Melanie as she walked along the road with Anne, gaily swinging her bag. "Guess what's just happened to me!"

"Madam Skull's told you that you're her illegitimate daughter?" Anne suggested.

"Idiot!"

"You've decided to become a nun?"

"It's Simon."

"What about him?"

"He's asked me out."

"Simon *Ward*? Asked you out?"

"Just now. After the service."

"He's a complete doppo! What did he do? Did he look you soulfully in the eyes and say, 'Melanie my darling'," Anne adopted a deep voice, "'I can't live without you. My heart throbs with desire. If you do not accept me, I'll batter meself to death with a copy of the CSSM chorus book'!"

The girls doubled up with laughter.

"Well," said Anne, "I think that's absolutely..." she left a slight pause, then the two girls chanted in unison, "Fantastic!...amazing!...incredible!... boring!" The first three words had a rising intonation, with a sudden, sing-song drop on the word 'boring'. They had developed the chant recently, and used it on all possible occasions.

"You can't talk," said Melanie accusingly. "What's happening with you and Jeremy?"

"Oh, him? He's all right, I s'ppose." Anne affected indifference, but her face told a different story.

"All right? It looked more than that to me! You fancy him!"

"What if I do? I'm not saying I do, but if I did?"

"Oh, *if* you did! Well I think you do! *And* I think he fancies you, too."

"Who do *you* fancy?"

Melanie considered. "Kenny's nice, isn't he? He's really good on the piano. Almost as good as Daddy."

"I bet your dad doesn't play the Rolling Stones!"

They continued on their way, bantering with each other as to who fancied whom among their friends, until their routes divided. Anne headed for her home on the council estate, and Melanie continued to her own home near the little park called the Tarn.

She pushed open the gate and went along the right-hand fork of the path to the front door. The left-hand fork led to her father's surgery. As she opened the door, she could hear the piano being played. Bach. Anne was right, Daddy wasn't a fan of pop music.

"Hello, Daddy!"

Her father stopped playing as she went into the front room. "Hello, angel! Had a good afternoon? Now, are you going to join me? Your mother's only just got in. Tea will be some time yet. Your flute's here."

"What shall we play?" she asked, opening the instrument case.

"Well *done*, angel," her father said later as they triumphantly completed a complicated piece they'd been working on for some while. "Your fingering has really come on a treat. Angel fingers!"

Melanie flushed with pleasure. She enjoyed the praise of her father and the way he called her 'angel'. He had done this for years, ever since she had been told that one of her great-grandmothers had been called Mary Anne Angel.

"What a lovely name!" she had exclaimed. "I wish I was called that. I'd love to be an angel!"

"You are!" her father had said. "You must be – you're descended from the angels!"

When it was explained to her what 'being descended from' meant, she had run around the house gleefully exclaiming, "I'm an angel! I'm an angel!" until her mother told her to stop making such a racket.

Chapter 15

Melanie

Exeter: February 1997

Phil's daughter is called Melanie. As he told me this, I felt an immense calm descend on me, like a boat entering a harbour from a wild sea, and as it goes over the harbour bar into the shelter of cliffs the wind drops, the sails drop, the water is completely still, and there's no sound at all except a gentle reassuring swishing as the boat's forward momentum slowly peters out.

"Melanie?" I made the name a question, and he returned it as a statement. "Melanie."

"I suppose," I said, deliberately adopting a puzzled tone of voice, pretending ignorance, wanting to extend the moment, wanting to tease Phil, "that's the name of your wife's mother? You named your daughter after her?"

Phil shook his head slowly. "She's named after you – and only you."

The ship in the harbour was now completely becalmed. Pure serenity. My eyes were again blurred with tears, and I felt him dab my cheeks with a serviette. "Shall we go?" he asked.

We headed for the quay, saying nothing, and were soon walking along the path by the river, now arm in arm. I had on my thick winter coat, fur-lined boots, thick gloves, and my faithful Cossack hat, about the seventh or eighth I've had since Cambridge, but the main protection against the cold had to be the small thermonuclear device that had detonated inside me causing a wonderful glow to spread throughout my body.

Eventually I broke the silence. "When you called your daughter Melanie, did you tell your wife about me? About why the name?"

"No," he said. "I didn't."

"She didn't suspect?"

He shook his head, his hair flapping. "What happened was that one of the names she came up with was 'Melinda', after some American friend of hers. I felt it was too good an opportunity to miss, so I said yes, I like 'Melinda', but how about 'Melanie'? Added something about it having a softer sound, and she bit – said it was a lovely name, she liked it. 'Melanie' it was." He took my hand, though both of us had gloves on, and continued, "I had one of those nanosecond choices: do I tell her that Melanie happened to be the name of my, um, girlfriend..."

"Girlfriend?" I queried.

"Well, could hardly say lover, could I?"

"Perhaps not."

"My girlfriend at Cambridge, or don't I? Tell her, that is. In that nanosecond I decided not to tell her, and having not told her, I couldn't tell her later on."

"D'you wish you had told her?"

He said, "Nope!" decisively. "If I'd told her, I bet we'd've been looking for another name straight away."

"I'm glad you didn't tell her." We'd paused at a weir to watch a heron. "I'm glad your daughter's named after me. It's lovely." I took my hand from his, pulled off my glove and offered my hand again. He tugged off his glove too, and we held hands, resting our wrists on top of the railing. It was so cold, thermonuclear devices notwithstanding, that after a little while he pulled my hand inside his coat pocket. We resumed our walk.

"Tell me about your daughters. What are they doing? Are they at university?"

"Amy is. At Kent, studying English. I don't think she quite knows what she'll do with her degree. Lem on the other hand knows exactly what she's doing. Handmade jewellery. She's done her City and Guilds and had an apprenticeship, and now has her own business, which started in the back bedroom, and she's on the verge of renting premises which'll be a shop as well as a workshop. Exciting times for her. 'Melanie Ellis Jewellery'."

"Wow," I said, "fantastic!" I was thinking that 'Melanie Ellis' could have been my name. Then abruptly Sam came to mind. I had to be sure. "What about your cousin, Sam?"

"What about her?"

"You two seem pretty close."

"We are. Always have been. Lots of family holidays, and Christmases and stuff, and hanging out together in school holidays. Yeah, we're close."

"What about her husband?" I asked, feeling I might be venturing onto thin ice.

"Oh, is that it?" Phil tipped back his head and laughed at the sky. "No, no, no, nothing naughty is going on between us. She's very happily married to Tom. He's a mate. Good bloke. He'll be doing the lighting for the revue. You'll really like Sam when you get to know her."

"That'd be nice," I said cautiously, "but I rather got the impression that for some reason she took an instant dislike to me."

"Ah," Phil said, and looked awkward. "Sorry about that. My fault in a way. When you and I went our separate ways all those years ago and I told her about it, Sam decided you must be pretty awful even though I said, no, not at all. She'll change her mind about you soon enough. Honest!"

Our time together was limited as he had to get to a couple of his pupils. While we were still reasonably alone – there were only a few other people walking dogs or cycling along the path – we stopped again and put our arms round each other. He kissed me on the lips – very chaste, but also very exciting. Then he said he had a problem.

"Which is what?" I asked.

"Want to see you again."

"Why's that a problem?"

"Because I want to see you lots. Lots and lots. I'd like to see you every day, but I don't think that's possible, is it? Or right. You're a respectable married woman."

"So are you. Married."

"But not respectable. And separated. Somewhat different. Have you told Simon you're meeting me today?"

"No, I decided not to."

"Will you?"

"I don't know. No, not today. Sometime maybe."

He tapped his foot, as I remember he always used to do when he had something awkward to say. I don't know if he knows he does it. "I'll find it difficult if I can't see you at least sometimes."

As a respectable married woman, I should have backed away at that point, and said something neutral. What I actually said was, "I'd like that. Really. I want to see you."

We looked at each other for several seconds, then kissed again. This time, not very chastely. Actually, not chastely at all.

Chapter 16

Phil

Cambridge: November 1971

"Great stuff, man!" Alex exclaimed, adding, "As the actress said to the bishop! What next? When are you seeing her again?"

"Tuesday. She's coming round for tea."

"Tuesday, eh? Excellent!"

Late Sunday afternoon, in Alex's room, drinking coffee, and I'd just given him an expurgated version of the events of the previous evening following my precipitate departure from the Dorothy with Melanie.

There was a bang on the door and Edward strode in carrying his sports bag. "Afternoon all! Dear oh dear, slouching around again, are we? Come on, Alex, it's time for squash!" He turned to me and grinned knowingly. "How are you, Philippe? Are you doing all right?"

"Doing all right!" I said.

"He's doing all right!" Alex confirmed, grabbing his sports gear.

"No need of any more exercise for the time being, then?" Edward said.

As they went off I returned to my own room, where I sat in the armchair, clasped my hands behind my head, and drifted into a reverie, replaying what had happened at Girton.

Her room was larger than mine but equally untidy, if not more so. "Sorry about the mess!" she said airily. "I'm the world's worst cleaner-upper of rooms! Now then Mr Cabaret Man," she put her arms round me and smiled up at my face, "what would you like?"

"You!"

"I was talking about something to drink. Coffee? Tea? Hot chocolate? Or I've got some cheapo vino."

We settled on coffee. As she headed for the communal kitchen, I wandered around her room. Two armchairs were submerged beneath a mound of jumbled-up clothes, books, papers and ring binders. On the floor by a record deck was a scatter of LPs, pop, rock and classical. She had an impressive range of books, too. The expected history books along with poetry, art, several Russian novels as well as a range of English classics. A number of them, I discovered, were several years' worth of school prizes for history, English and Latin. There were also two or three philosophy books of the popular introduction type, and a number with religious titles. There were two Bibles, one of which I pulled out and opened. On the inside front cover a bookplate in the shape of a Christian cross proclaimed that 'Emhalt Followers' had awarded 'the Word of God' to Melanie Mason 'for attendance'.

The top of a dressing table was hidden under a whole clutter of things, including several cards. I picked up one with an angel on it. The message written inside said, "Our darling daughter. We know you'll work hard, but do enjoy your Cambridge career as well! Remember: you're descended from the angels! Much love, M & D xx". There was a framed photo of a younger Melanie in school uniform with a gangly older boy looking stony-faced in a blazer.

The allegedly angelic descendant returned. "That's my brother Mikey," she said. "He couldn't stand wearing school uniform, but that's the best photo I have of him."

"Are you close?"

"We look out for each other."

We sat on the bed, drinking coffee from a Marc Bolan mug (her) and a Paul McCartney mug (me), and talking about where our homes were, what our families were like, what we'd done between our third year sixth and coming up to Cambridge – at least, I told her what I'd done in those few months. She was less forthcoming.

"Worked for my father quite a bit," she said. "He's a doctor. Helping the receptionist. That's about it. Went shopping!"

"Boyfriend?" I asked. "Or friends? Bet you had 'em queueing up to ask you out."

She gave an awkward laugh. "I've got friends who are boys, but not, you know... Anyway, I don't want to talk about boyfriends, Phil. I'm here with you."

I put my mug down and stroked the side of her head, running a finger over her cheek, and tracing the contours of her jaw and the shape of her lips. She kissed my fingers, then lay with her head on my lap, looking up at me, hair spread out like Ophelia's where she's floating in the river. I leaned down and kissed her.

A few minutes later I turned on a bedside lamp as she went to switch off the main light. Soon we were lying together on the bed. Her skirt was rumpled up around her waist, and as she had already removed her tights, her knickers were fully exposed. Lying on my left side, I had my right hand resting on her leg. We continued to kiss hard, and I felt certain everything was about to happen, especially when she murmured, "I think we're overdressed."

As I stripped off, she removed her skirt and top, but kept on her bra and knickers. Her little gold cross dangled on its chain.

"Shall I?" I offered, reaching round to undo the bra fastening at the back.

"No!" she said quickly, putting her hands up to her breasts before the bra could come off. "I… I'll keep it on."

"Come on, sweetheart."

"No, Phil, please. I prefer to keep it on. It's just that my boobs aren't my best feature."

"They look more than all right from where I'm sitting!"

"Well, they're rather odd."

I counted them, touching in turn the hand which was shielding each breast. "One, two! Nope, definitely two of them, not one, not three – that means you've got even boobs, not odd ones!"

She giggled. "Idiot! You know what I mean!"

"No, I don't! In what way are they 'odd'?"

"D'you really want to know?"

"What I really want is to see them, and fondle them, and kiss them."

She looked at me coyly. "All right, you smooth operator! Don't say I didn't warn you."

She took her hands away and allowed her bra to slide off. I pretended to examine her breasts critically, then put my hands on them, before kissing them in turn. They were round and firm, slightly freckled.

"What's so odd about them?" I asked. "I think they look fantastic."

"Can't you see? I've got inverted nipples."

"Yer what?"

"Inverted nipples. They don't, well, stick out, they're sort of inside out."

"See what you mean," I said, though my experience to date of women's nipples – in the flesh, as it were, rather than in girlie magazines – provided only a very limited basis for comparison. "But so what? I think…" and she gracefully yielded as I gently pushed her back onto the bed, "…I think they're fantastic." I kissed each breast again in turn.

She still had her knickers on, and as we lay on the bed, kissing and fondling each other, my hand, now between her legs, was frantic to explore what those knickers were concealing. I started pulling them down, but she stopped me. Put a hand between her legs as a barrier.

"No?" I said, startled.

"No…don't go on."

"Want to make love with you, Mel. Come on, we've got this far."

"No, please. I'm sorry."

"Oh, come on."

"Please don't get grumpy."

"Don't tell me you think your pussy is odd as well?"

"It's not that."

"What is it?"

"I'm scared. Oh, don't get me wrong, darling. I would love to have you in me. I want you so much. I can't help it – I'm scared."

"It's okay, I've brought some johnnies."

I started to scramble off the bed to retrieve from my trousers the packet I'd got from the slot machine at the Union. Melanie caught me by the arm, saying, "No, it's not that. Not just that."

"What is it?"

She sighed. The earlier glow of her face had vanished. "What it all implies. I've, well, I've been a bit of an idiot in the past, and I'm scared of making an idiot of myself again. I don't think I'm ready, that's all. I do love you, Phil, honestly. Please don't think it means I don't."

"I love you too," I said quickly.

"Oh!" she wailed, "You must think I'm an awful prick-teaser."

"No I don't!" I assured her, but since my prick had never been teased to quite this extent ever before, she was, strictly speaking, not an awful prick-teaser but an extremely accomplished one. "I'd love to make love with you, but if it doesn't feel right, well, then it doesn't."

"I didn't know this was going to happen!" she continued to wail. "I thought it'd be wonderful to make love with you! I want to, I really want to...but my body won't let me."

"That's okay. Don't worry about it! I understand...well, no," I amended, "I don't really understand. But it's no big deal. I can cope. It's just lovely being with you and kissing you and holding you."

"Is it? Is that all right?"

"Sure, fine." I swallowed my disappointment, hoping that if I didn't press her, she'd be more likely to change her mind.

"You are sweet. Kiss me, please kiss me."

I kissed her, and she said that if I wanted she'd bring me off on her stomach, but I said no, I'd prefer it if we just cuddled – so we lay on the bed, holding each other, kissing gently, and soon we got under the bed covers where she fell asleep in my arms. I remained awake a while longer.

Chapter 17

Emhalt: May 1967

"Melanie!" Her mother's voice sounded up the stairs. "Telephone!"

Melanie jumped up from behind the desk in her bedroom. She had heard the phone but had assumed it would be a patient needing to talk with her father out of hours. A call for her was welcome – she had had enough of revising. Although, as she had told Simon, the school exams were not particularly important – she'd gained a cluster of A grades in last year's O level exams and knew she was expected to get all A grades for her A levels the next summer – she still wanted to do well in these intermediate exams and had been revising hard. She knew everyone assumed she would again win the history prize, and that she would probably win the English prize as well. After that it would be full steam ahead for A levels, followed by the Cambridge entrance. A scholarship might be beckoning. High hopes, Melanie, her teachers had started saying; we have high hopes of you.

"Who is it?" She clattered down the stairs to where her mother was standing in the hallway holding out the receiver. "Anyone exciting?"

"It's a boy," Mrs Mason announced with an uncertain smile. "Now don't go hogging the phone all evening. Your father will probably need it."

Puzzled, Melanie took the phone and waited until her mother had, lingeringly, retreated to the sitting room and closed the door.

"Hi?" she said.

"Melanie? Hello! It's Simon here."

She turned her eyes ceilingwards and leaned against the wall. "Oh, hi Simon," she said heavily, sliding down until she was slumped on the floor.

"How are you?" he asked puffingly.

"I'm still okay."

"I hope I haven't interrupted anything."

"British foreign policy between the wars."

"Jolly good. I hope you don't mind, I thought I'd give you a ring about the 'rave-up'." Again the inverted commas. Melanie wished he wouldn't use the expression; it sounded like a parent trying to be groovy and failing by a mile. "Sorry about this afternoon," he continued. "Mr Griffen collared me for quite some time about the anniversary, and you'd gone by the time... anyway," he interrupted himself, exhaling noisily, "have you checked? Will you be able to come?"

"Where is it?" was all she could think of to say.

"It's at Bill's. Chap from school. He lives just round the corner from me. It should be a good rave-up. His parents won't be there."

"In June, you said?"

"The third. Saturday the third."

Melanie took a deep breath, put her hand up to her cross, and decided to sacrifice the opportunity of finding out what made a rave-up a rave-up. "I'm afraid I can't," she said. "I'm doing something else."

"Oh. I see." Simon's voice had lost some of its brightness. "That's a pity."

The sitting room door opened and her mother re-emerged. "Do you want some tea?" she mouthed silently at Melanie, who shook her head impatiently. Her mother had clearly chosen this precise moment to go and make tea so that she could monitor the phone call.

"I'm sorry about that, Simon," she said rather loudly down the phone as her mother went through to the kitchen.

"Not to worry," said Simon, his tone belying his words. "Anything interesting you're doing?"

"Oh, nothing much. It's a family thing. We've got this family get-together," she improvised.

The sitting room door had opened again, and Mikey came shambling out. At twenty, just over three years older than Melanie herself, he was tall and skinny, and the medication he took gave him a perpetually dry mouth such that unpleasant sticky sounds accompanied his speech. He stood in front of Melanie and stared down at her in his disconcerting fashion. She gave him a little wave.

"Sis, can you help me? I've got cancer," Mikey whined.

Melanie put her hand over the phone. "No, Mikey, you haven't," she said patiently.

"I have. There's this article in the *Reader's Digest* about it."

"Mikey, you have not got cancer." Still she was patient. "Ask Daddy, he'll tell you. Please, I'm on the phone."

"Is it your boyfriend?"

"Are you all right?" Melanie heard Simon asking.

"Mikey! Are you going up to your room? Why don't you go and play some music? I'll come and have a chat with you in a minute. Be a dear."

Mikey pushed past her and slouched his way upstairs. Melanie turned and watched him sadly.

"Are you all right?" Simon was repeating anxiously when she returned to the phone call.

"It's Mikey, he's – you know how he is."

"It can't be easy."

"No, it's not. Look, I must go." Loud rock music had started pounding away upstairs. Mikey always left his bedroom door open when playing records. "I need to spend some time with him."

"You're very good to him," said Simon. "I like that about you."

"Oh, well, thank you," said Melanie in some confusion. "You'd do the same if he was your brother."

"I hope I would."

The phone call ending with the conventional "see you soon" from both of them, Melanie felt bad for lying to Simon, and realised gloomily that she had merely postponed the time when she would have to be direct with him, because he would probably ask again.

"What family thing?" her mother asked, emerging from the kitchen. "We haven't got anything arranged. What are you up to?" Then she called up the stairs, "Mikey! Close your door please!"

Melanie struggled to her feet. "It's all right, I'm going to go and spend a bit of time with him," she said, and disappeared up the stairs, leaving her mother unanswered.

Chapter 18

Melanie

Exeter: February 1997

Mummy rang this morning about Mikey. Not good news.

I'd been rather enjoying myself until then, back up in the attic with the boxes containing bits of my past – school reports and old history essays, and a couple of those long school photos rolled into cylinders, with us all looking like a cross between St Trinian's and Roedean; my Mark Bolan mug, slightly chipped; and my Followers' badge along with my scripture-reading certificates. In the CSSM chorus book I found a photo of Anne and Rose and Sarah all trying to look sexy and sophisticated, with only Sarah succeeding. There's the letter from Girton as well, offering me a scholarship, and my flute along with a sheaf of music, including Gluck's 'Dance of the Blessed Spirits'.

I was really looking for my Phil memorabilia, which turned up in a carrier bag from Heffers. There's the key ring he put on my finger after he'd proposed; photos of our Lake District holiday; the *Best Love Poems Ever* book he gave me there which is full of romantic slush; and the tee-shirt I bought him which I later pinched from his room after one of the May Balls. I used to give myself a lot of masochistic pain during my final year by burying my face in it when I was in bed, conjuring up his presence; but not surprisingly his scent has now vanished.

I was hugging the tee-shirt to me, remembering the Lake District, when the phone rang.

"It's Mikey," Mummy said. She doesn't do the "how are you?" type of stuff. "I've had a letter from Oaklands. They say they need to move him on."

"Oh no. Why?"

"They say, and I quote, 'the demands he puts on the staff have become unsustainable'. They mean," she added, "he's soiling himself so much that they've had enough. Quite frankly I can't blame them."

"No, me neither. What are they suggesting instead?"

"They've asked me to a meeting to discuss his future, but it's all getting too much for me at my age. I was hoping, dear," and her voice dropped in volume, as though she were finding it hard to speak, and I couldn't catch the rest of the sentence.

I asked, "What was that, Mummy?"

She raised her voice. "I said I'd like you to go with me. But," sarcastically, "if it's too much bother…"

"Yes, yes. I'll come. When is it?"

"Good," in a more conciliatory tone. "Your professional experience will come in handy. What was that?"

"Nothing." I'd given a brief laugh at her reference to my 'professional experience', she's never before conceded that social work is a profession. That concession and calling me 'dear' had caught me off guard. "I was thinking," I said, "that Simon would want to come if possible."

"Would he?" Mummy immediately sounded brighter. "That would be extremely helpful. He'll know what to do."

I came away from the phone feeling sad. Dear Mikey. I've always been fond of my big brother. I remember how comic we sometimes found his odd statements before he was diagnosed, but it wasn't really funny – his obsession with all things to do with death, like his horrible collection of old bones and sheep skulls and things. Then there was that dreadful period when he tried living on his own in a flat, with Daddy paying the rent, and his self-neglect was awful. It shook us pretty badly when he was sectioned, but I can't see what else could have been done, he really had become a danger to himself.

It's been rough on Mummy, too, for years. It's a pity that when Daddy died Simon and I couldn't persuade her that I should be the effective next of kin for social services and the like to contact, but she chose to retain that role. That was fair enough at the time, but now she's in her eighties it really has all got too much for her.

Remembering how Mikey had liked Phil the only time they'd met, I went back up to the attic to pack away the memorabilia, except the Marc Bolan mug which is now in the kitchen.

Chapter 19

Phil

Cambridge: November 1971

Melanie came for tea on Tuesday afternoon, the last day in November. It was raining, and she arrived wet and dishevelled. "Hello, gorgeous," I said. "Did you cycle?"

"Might have been a mistake, this weather, but I've got a good bike."

She came into the hallway where Tristan the resident dopehead was slumped on the floor, holding the telephone receiver the wrong way round. He looked as spaced out as ever.

"Doesn't work," he muttered, waving the receiver in the air.

Melanie took it from him, turned it round and gave it back, putting the earpiece to his ear and the mouthpiece to his mouth.

"Hey, right on," Tristan mumbled. "Where d'you learn that?"

"Girton," she said. "First thing we privileged classes are taught is how to use a telephone in the absence of servants."

"Right on."

As Tristan examined the telephone, she shrugged off her waterproof and asked me where to put it. I showed her the downstairs lav.

When she returned, she'd dried herself off and brushed her hair, which now lapped enticingly over her shoulders. Wearing blue jeans and a thick, fluffy sweater of a lighter blue, she looked intensely desirable. We stepped over Tristan, who now appeared to have gone to sleep on the floor, and went into my room.

"You look fantastic," I said, gazing at her, my hands on her waist.

"Fantastic!" she echoed, then chanted, "Amazing! Incredible! Boring!"

"Yer what?"

She laughed. "Oh, nothing. Just something Anne and I used to say. School friend," she added. She looked around the room. "Hmm, you don't win any housekeeping prizes either, do you?"

"He's an untidy bugger!" Alex's disembodied voice pronounced from the adjoining room.

"Who's that?" Melanie looked round. "What's that?"

"I am the ghost of Selwyn Gardens," the voice continued, followed by a maniacal cackle.

"Stop mucking about and come in here. Meet Melanie properly," I told him through the wall.

"Hello, Melanie Properly," Alex said, entering a few seconds later. "I'm Alex."

"Hello! I've seen you performing with Phil and the other one with the guitar."

"Rob," said Alex. "He's our music maker. Hey, man," he turned to me, "I don't want to intrude if you two have, how shall I put it, *intimate* things you want to say to each other," he waggled his eyebrows, "so I'll get back to my room...and listen from there – oh, what a giveaway!"

Melanie giggled.

"'S all right," I said, "stay and have a spot of tea if you like."

I switched on the kettle and dug out the cake I'd bought from Fitzbillies. It was one of their specials. All their cakes are special.

Melanie and Alex started talking to each other about their respective subjects of history and French; I put the Beatles on the turntable; the kettle came to the boil; I made the tea – I'd bought fresh milk – and sliced up the cake; there was a loud knock at the door and Rob's voice called out, "Hello there!" as he came down the corridor to the room.

"Hello, all!" he amended on entering. "Aha!" He pointed at the sliced-up cake and struck a dramatic pose. "Is this a cake I see before me, its chocolate icing before my mouth? Come, let me bite thee! I taste thee not yet I see thee still. I was," he reverted to his normal tone of voice, "just thinking to myself as I walked along, a nice slice of a Fitzbillies' cake would go down a treat, and blow me down with a feather, I walk in here and see one straight away." He turned and addressed Melanie, "It's my uncanny psychic powers!"

"It's your uncanny being with me when I bought it," I pointed out. "Plus I told you Melanie was coming round this afternoon."

"Not so much *un*canny psychic powers as canny ones," said Alex.

A few minutes later, more inmates of the Selwyn Gardens asylum turned up: Edward and Ewan, the two E's. Edward, another scientist, had a room on the top floor; Ewan, a tall, quietly-spoken classicist, occupied another of the ground-floor rooms. They had with them a box of Fitzbillies' Chelsea buns.

"Excellent!" said Rob enthusiastically.

"Hear, hear!" said Melanie.

"Transuranic!" I said, eliciting loud groans and eyeball-rolling from all but Melanie.

"What's that mean?" Melanie asked.

"Phil has this loony idea of getting the word 'transuranic' into common usage as a way of expressing approval," Ewan explained.

"What does it really mean?"

"No idea."

"It's chemistry," said Edward. "In the periodic table of elements, uranium is the last one that occurs naturally. Other elements have been created artificially, and their place in the table is beyond uranium, hence they are 'transuranic'."

"Meaning 'beyond what is natural'," I said, "or 'extraordinary'. I rather like it."

"We don't," said Edward.

"It's rather clever," said Melanie, sounding doubtful.

"Don't encourage him," Ewan warned. "If it catches on he could become insufferable!"

"I'll suffer him!" Melanie put her arm round me. "Now, please can I suffer some more cake?"

Although I'd been expecting to have tea alone with Melanie, I was pleased Rob and Alex and the two E's were also there. It established her as part of my world. I wanted them to like her and her to like them, and they were getting on extremely well. She was chatty, engaging, attentive, and very pretty. I thought of us lying on her bed, me holding her, stroking her, fingering her knickers... I had to distract myself as images arising before my mind's eye were evoking the inevitable response in my body.

I got up and put on the other side of the record.

"You missed a good laugh this afternoon," Ewan was saying. "The JCR meeting was a right fiasco."

The meeting he referred to had been called at short notice for members of Pembroke Junior Common Room to discuss whether the bank account should be removed from Barclays because of their connections with apartheid South Africa.

"It all got rather heated," Ewan continued, "until someone stood up and asked how much money we had in the account and it turned out that we have a permanent overdraft, so he said I see, you're proposing that we go along to Barclays and tell them that if they're not good little boys, we'll take our overdraft elsewhere. Big laugh. There were a load of amendments and counter-amendments, and counter-counter-amendments, and counter-counter-counter..."

"We get the picture," said Alex.

"Well, it turned out that the meeting wasn't constitutional in any case so no resolution could have been implemented. It's all been deferred until a scheduled meeting next term, when facts and figures can be circulated beforehand."

"It's the principle of the thing, isn't it?" Melanie put in. She'd been enthusiastically eating the cake, leaving traces of chocolate around her lips, which she wiped with the back of her hand. "It's right to make a stand, whether or not there's much money in the account. It shows you care. Don't you think?"

"Not sure how much good it'd do," I said. "It's not likely to have any effect on their South African policy if we take the overdraft elsewhere. Is it?"

"I don't know so much," she answered. "If enough people and institutions did the same, it would have an effect, and even if it didn't have a direct effect you could sort of measure, it's important to act on the principle of the thing. We ought to do whatever we can. It's because people don't do what they could do because they don't think it'll help is why things like apartheid get their power. If we don't do something then we're colluding with it."

"Hear, hear," said Alex.

"Sorry," Melanie added. "I'm preaching, aren't I? I just feel strongly about it." She finished the slice of cake on her plate.

"I think you're right about the danger of collusion," said Rob. "He who is not with me is against me, and all that."

"Matthew 12:30," said Melanie.

All this while, Edward had been doing something to one of his eyes. "Sorry about this," he said, blinking rapidly. "I've got a bit of a problem with the lens." Pulling an odd face, he removed the contact lens from his right eye, squinted at it, put it in his mouth and took it out again, then transferred it to the tip of a finger to reinsert it.

"Don't sneeze," said Alex as the lens-tipped finger approached Edward's eye.

"Wrong eye," I warned mendaciously.

Ignoring us, Edward successfully replaced the lens. A new conversation started about the Christmas vac due to begin in a few days' time, and what plans for it, if any, everyone had. I made a fresh pot of tea, along with a mental note to turn Edward's experience of contact lenses into a sketch.

"I didn't make a fool of myself, did I?" Melanie said anxiously, after the others had left. "About the bank account thing."

"God no! I thought it was great what you said. It sounded like it came straight from the heart."

"It did," she nodded.

"How come you knew where that Bible quote's from – or did you just make it up?"

"Oh no, I know masses of verses from the Bible off by heart. I used to go to a Bible class for years. Followers. We had to learn all these verses."

"You *were* a God-botherer!"

"I don't think I bothered God very much. As I told you, he tends to bother me. I used to be very religious in that I believed everything in the Bible was absolutely true, that Jesus died to save my sins, and that if I didn't believe in him I'd go to hell. All that sort of thing."

"That's not what you believe now, is it?"

"Well, yes and no. It depends what you mean by 'believe'. I believe that something is *there* at a transcendent level of things, as it were. But I don't believe the Jesus-in-a-nightie, bash-you-over-the-head-with-the-Bible, get-up-out-of-your-seats-and-come-to-the-front, Billy Graham sort of thing. D'you know what I mean?"

"I'm a fully paid-up atheist, thank God. But what happened to you? Why did your beliefs change?"

"A mixture of things. The real biggie for me was Aberfan."

"Ah, right. That was ghastly," I said, and told her I remembered watching the news with Mum and Dad, with the appalling pictures of the school and homes wiped out by some slag heap which had slid down the hill onto the Welsh village. "Who cares whether anyone is religious or non-religious. It was mind-blowingly awful whoever or whatever you are."

"It shook up everything I believed in," Melanie said. "Up till then I'd gone along with what they kept saying at Followers that God loves you and if you trust him everything will be all right, but if you do various things he doesn't approve of you get punished and all that sort of thing. I'd just taken it as read that if bad things happened to me it must be because I'm a bad person and didn't love Jesus enough, and all that."

"Crazy," I said, adding hurriedly, "Don't mean you personally, I mean that sort of religion that's peddled by the Church."

"What kind of God would let children be killed like that?" she demanded. "Suffering as a consequence of our own actions, that's bad enough and painful enough, but at least it makes sense that if I do something stupid things are likely to turn out badly for me and I'll be hurt – and maybe you could call it punishment, in a way. But it's ludicrous to think there's a God who punishes children, however naughty they might've been, by pushing a slag heap on top of them. It seemed to me that the simplistic 'God's in charge of everything' idea just isn't good enough when you're trying to make sense of what happens in the real world."

"You still wear a cross."

"That's because I still think the cross is important. I think Jesus was the supreme example of compassion in action and not betraying your principles whatever the cost. As for God *planning* the death of Jesus as part of some great salvation plan, well..." she shrugged dismissively. "Have you ever believed in God? Did you ever go to Sunday school or anything like that?"

I shook my head. "Bunch of heathens, my family. Me included. It doesn't worry you that I'm not the tiniest bit religious?"

"No, why should it? It's you as you I love."

Later, there was the sound of Alex returning to his room, and I put a finger to Melanie's lips. We were lying on my bed, where we had been fondling each other. I slowly swung myself round until I was sitting up, but despite my care the bed creaked loudly. Melanie only half-managed to suppress a snort of laughter. I coughed over-loudly and started clumping around the room as Melanie got off the bed and pulled her jeans back on. I asked if she'd like a coffee or something.

She shook her head. "I'd better get back. It's rather late."

"Okay. See you on Thursday? Fancy going to the Friar House for a bite?"

"Great."

We fixed a time, then stood in the middle of the room, holding each other tightly.

"I love you, Phil," she said eventually.

"I love you too," I said.

"Whey hey hey!" said Alex, on the other side of the shared partition.

Chapter 20

Melanie

Exeter: February 1997

Phil rang last night. "Take it Simon's at chess?" he said.

"Suppose you'd been wrong and he had answered?"

"Don't worry. Had a cunning plan all prepared. I'd've invited you both to a dinner party."

"Do you *do* dinner parties?"

He paused. "I can make porridge. That's oat cuisine."

"Oh ha, ha," I said. "Have you rung me up just to make bad jokes?"

"Rung you up because I want to see you."

I caught my breath. "I want to see you too."

"Good. When?"

It turned out that for various reasons we can't realistically see each other again until after I get back from the visit to Mikey. Maybe that's for the best – not seeing him for some time. I long to see him, but at the same time I'm a respectable, married woman. Dare I allow myself to see him frequently?

He tells me he's acquired a cat. "More precisely, he's acquired me. Or adopted me. I'm calling him Erwin."

"Erwin? What kind of name is that?"

"After Erwin Schrödinger. Schrödinger's cat? Yes?"

"If you say so."

"I both say so and don't say so. Ah, now then, how about, 'automatic cat feeder'!"

"What?"

"Automatic cat feeder," he repeated.

I was baffled. "What are you talking about?"

"I was in the pet shop and I saw this automatic cat feeder." He repeated, with a different emphasis, "Automatic-cat…feeder. Hello, I thought, just the thing if you have an automatic cat that needs feeding!"

"Oh, very good!"

"It's a sketch I'm working on, and it's all your doing," he said.

"How?"

"You told me that Simon is a 'small bridge designer' which got me going. There are loads of ambiguous things like that. At least, I think there are. 'Real estate agent' is another. To distinguish themselves from fake estate agents? And Mum told me the other day that she's had a letter inviting her to make an appointment with a mobile breast clinic!"

"Oh dear! Is there something wrong with her?"

"No, you don't get it!" He sounded slightly exasperated. "'Mobile breast clinic' – is that a clinic for mobile breasts? 'Allo darlin', 'ave you got *mobile breasts*, eh? eh?"

He added others about an electric trouser press being a press for electric trousers, and what do occasional tables turn into on the occasions when they aren't tables? I tried to think of one myself, but nothing came. My brain just doesn't work that way. That's one of the things I love about Phil: he makes me laugh with his ability to see strange connections, and it's the speed at which he can do it. He's constantly seeing patterns in words I can't see. At least I can take credit for giving him the idea in the first place.

We couldn't talk for much longer as Simon would be back before long, but we'll see each other again as soon as we can. I'm going to get a mobile phone. It'll make contacting each other so much easier. Not to mention safer.

Chapter 21

Phil

Cambridge: December 1971

"Make your balls swing!" I said.

"Put life into your balls!" said Alex.

"Always take precautions!" said Rob.

"Very good, chaps," I said. "Which do we use?"

"I like Alex's," said Rob.

"Me too," I agreed. "I think it's the best."

"Excellent!" said Alex. "You're both very discerning!"

'Put life into your Balls', it was. We continued eating our toasted sandwiches while batting around more ideas. Thursday lunchtime in the Hat and Feathers, and we were trying to compose an advert to put in *Varsity* next term, and something longer to send to May Ball committees. We were hoping to drum up more bookings for Air Raid Precautions in June when the May Balls take place, Cambridge University existing in a different, and superior, time frame from the rest of the universe.

I hadn't been able to see Melanie on Wednesday, the day after she'd come round for tea. She had a history essay to complete for her final supervision of term, and I'd had a couple of tricky supervision sessions myself, on organic chemistry and pharmacology, with each supervisor, unsurprisingly, strongly recommending several topics I should work on during the Christmas vac. I'd mentally shelved any thought of more academic work until Monday at the earliest, when I'd be back home. Before that, in these final couple of days, with just one more lecture to miss, I needed to focus on much more interesting matters such as Air Raid Precautions and, supremely, Melanie. I'd be seeing her in only a few hours' time for a meal at the Friar House.

By the time we'd finished lunch and left the pub, we'd finalised the newspaper ad which began, 'Put life into your Balls/with cabaret-revue team/Air Raid Precautions'. Rob undertook devising a flyer to send round to May Ball committees in the new year.

We headed back to Selwyn Gardens, where Rob disappeared upstairs to his room to work on a speech he was going to deliver the following week to the Lower Sixth at our old school, and Alex had to finish packing for Kenya where he would be rejoining his expat family. I settled down at my typewriter to work on a new sketch we had recently devised, a commentary on a fight between Shakespeare and Dickens.

In time the random noises of packing from Alex's room gave way to the kind of loud exclamations and grunts you make when forcing an overfull suitcase to submit to being closed.

"Excellent!" Alex's voice came through the plasterboard wall loud and clear.

"How're you doing?"

"Put the kettle on! I've got something for you."

He came into my room a few minutes later and handed me a half-full bottle of port. "There you go, man! Hope the lovely Melanie likes port as well. If she doesn't I'm sure you can manage it!"

"Cheers! Very acceptable. Thought for a moment you were going to give me something else!"

"You get your own supplies of them!" he responded.

I made some tea, and Alex lit his pipe. We talked of what we'd each be doing during the Christmas vac – he'd be on the Kenyan coast much of the time, "while I'll probably be snowbound on Dartmoor!" I said. "Send us a postcard saying wish you were here!"

"Will do," he puffed contentedly. "With any luck I'll be picking up from where I left off with Jilly. Her last letter was very promising! Will you get to see Melanie much? Or will it all have to be at the end of the phone?"

"Hope we can see each other at least a couple of times. It'd be great if she could come down for the new year cabaret." Alex would not be with us when Rob and I put on a short entertainment at Rob's home.

"It's great it's going well," Alex said, "but don't forget La Rochefoucauld!"

"Thought he might have something to say! What gem this time?"

"'The intellect is always fooled by the heart'," Alex offered sagely.

"So much the worse for Rochefuckup," I said. "Reckon the heart happens to be a better judge in these matters."

Alex drew on his pipe and released a cloud of aromatic smoke. "To be honest, I'm inclined to agree with you. You've got to follow your heart, and it's a good thing the heart does triumph over the intellect. The heart has its reasons et cetera, et cetera."

Shortly after this, Alex's taxi arrived and spirited him away. I had a bath and spruced myself up, and though there were still a couple of hours to go before I was due to meet Melanie, I wanted to get under way, as if walking into college now would speed up the passage of time. My knees and, despite the layer of thermal insulation provided by my hair, my ears attested to the fact that the weather had turned bitingly cold, the wind sweeping in – as people insisted on telling me – all the way from the Russian steppes. I hunched myself inside the old fireman's coat I'd bought from a charity shop. It was thick and heavy, with metal buttons each embossed with the letters NFS standing for 'National Fire Service'. Ridiculous really – I have the height but not the shoulders to carry it off, and it was rather cumbersome.

I reached Pembroke to find Mr Scrimshaw, the head porter, standing outside the porters' lodge, hands on hips, examining the sky as if for snow. He was a thickset man, and the jacket of his dark suit perpetually looked on the brink of either splitting up the back or having buttons ping off the front, the latter possibility now tending towards probability by virtue of his fabric-straining stance. There was always a pachydermous air about the man.

"Afternoon, Scrimmers!"

"Good evening, sir!" You couldn't fault Mr Scrimshaw on the degree of courtesy he displayed towards the 'young gentlemen' of the college, yet he always managed to convey a faint sense of mockery towards us. There was a note or undercurrent of scepticism in his voice which was absent when you heard him talking with the dons and college officials.

"May I enquire where the fire is, sir?" he added.

"Sorry?"

"The fire, sir. I see you are attired in the apparel of a fire service, albeit one that was decommissioned many years ago."

"Don't you like the coat, Scrimmers? I got it at a charity shop."

"I take it that *they* donated it to *you*, sir? Being unable to sell it. Doubtless you wear it, sir, to deter the young ladies? Very effective!"

He gave me a bleak smile, tipped his bowler hat and retreated to his porters' lodge lair. I sensed that I'd come off second best in that encounter.

It was barely seven when I left college again for the Friar House, which was only five minutes' walk away, if that. I wanted to make sure I was there, at the restaurant, when Melanie arrived.

Impatient for the time to pass, I wandered up and down the street deliberately slowly, stopping myself from looking at my watch until I had got to this corner, or to that building. I started to execute a series of small jumps and hops on and off the kerb, then tried balancing on the extreme edge of the kerb on just my toes. Then I used the kerb as a tightrope, heel-and-toeing my way along it for several yards, arms outstretched, before attempting an elegant about-turn, and failing.

Seven thirty finally came. Still no Melanie. Seven thirty-five. Seven forty. I began to get anxious. Where was she? Where the hell was she? Don't do this to me, Mel.

Her non-presence – Rob's expression came forcibly to mind – was again total. A heavy dismay settled on me. I no longer paced up and down, but leaned against the wall of the restaurant, not caring too much about the cold. Hell. Oh hell. Hell and damnation! It was always possible that after I'd left Selwyn Gardens Melanie had rung there to warn me that she'd be late for some reason or other, and that right at this very moment she could be pedalling madly along, hair streaming out behind her, desperately hoping I'd still be waiting for her – which indeed I was. Always possible that she was on her way, but though my intellect could accept the proposition in that it didn't run counter to the laws of nature, my heart feared otherwise.

Alex's port back at Selwyn Gardens, it seemed certain, was not after all destined to be drunk jointly by Melanie and me. By ten past eight and counting, my returning and knocking back the lot in a solo effort had become the bookies' favourite.

I abandoned the restaurant and headed into college. I had the number of the phone in Girton nearest to Melanie's room. It rang interminably. I couldn't bring myself to replace the receiver.

Suddenly the insistent "brr brr" gave way to a scratchy voice. I pressed the button and jerked the receiver to my ear.

"Hullo, hullo?" a girl's voice was saying.

"Hi. I'm trying to get hold of Melanie. Could you see if she's in please? Melanie Mason."

"Hang on."

I entered suspended animation until there was the clatter of the phone being picked up again. "No, sorry. No one there. Can I take a message?"

"No, that's all right. Thanks."

I ran back to SG just in case, just in impossible case, she'd gone there.

She hadn't.

I uncorked the bottle of port and swallowed a mouthful – it felt both fiery and soothing going down – before clumping the bottle back onto the desk, then ran out of the room again, out of the front door, grabbed my bicycle, swung my leg over and began to pedal furiously. Maybe Melanie had by now returned to her room.

Despite the cold, the cumbersome nature of my coat, and the inherent dangers of the deathtrap bike – the saddle had a tendency to swivel without warning about both the vertical and horizontal axes, and the pedals wobbled so much on their connecting shaft that having thrust down on one pedal I had to hook my foot underneath it to bring it back to the top while simultaneously thrusting down on the other pedal – I made it to Girton in a world record time. Lungs heaving and legs shaky, I belted along to Melanie's room, at the door of which I spent a painful few seconds bent double, fighting an urge to throw up. Then, at last, I knocked.

No answer.

I knocked again, louder, and called her name. Still no answer.

I tried the door. Locked.

I banged hard on the door and yelled.

A door opened, two or three rooms away, and an Indian-looking girl looked out. She had a red dot on her forehead.

"Could you please stop doing that?" she said quietly.

"Sorry! Melanie, I'm looking for Melanie," I gasped. "D'you know where she is?"

She looked at her watch. "She should be home by now, I would think."

"What?"

"She left this afternoon. Going home."

"She can't be. She's supposed to be at the Friar House. With me!"

"I cannot help that. I am so sorry. I think it was a sudden decision."

"Why? What did she say? Was there some emergency or something?"

She shook her head slowly. "I do not know. Just that she is not here."

"Did she leave a message for me? Phil."

The girl shook her head again. "I am sorry," she said sadly. "Not with me."

As I turned the corner and achingly pedalled the last stretch to the college hostel, I saw Ewan opening the front door and entering, and when I went in he was standing outside his ground-floor room, looking in puzzlement at a piece of white card in his hand.

"MI5 must be having a recruiting drive!" He waved the card at me. "This has been stuck under my door. Solve the cryptic message and become a spy! What do you reckon?"

He gave it to me. I looked at the single line of handwriting scrawled there and felt myself tremble. "Melissa rang," the note said, "can't make Fr H. will write asap."

Evidently another incumbent of the Selwyn Gardens penitentiary – I didn't recognise the handwriting but there was a small piece torn from the card, about the size which when rolled into a cylinder would fit into the end of a joint, so I could guess who the culprit was – had taken a phone message and mistaken Ewan's room for mine.

"It's okay, Ewan," I said groaningly. "It's meant for me. From Melanie."

"Ah," he said. "Hard luck."

"I'll survive," I said, and headed for the rest of the port.

Chapter 22

Melanie

Exeter: February 1997

Well, Simon is full of surprises. Did he mean it about inviting Phil round? He must have – it's not the sort of thing he'd joke about. He repeated it this morning as he dashed off to work, saying we'll look at dates this evening, so it wasn't an aberration brought on by all the driving and seeing Mikey and general weariness over the past couple of days.

It's not exactly the best time of the year to drive to London and beyond, but there was no point going by rail as we needed the car for picking up Mummy and taking her to Oaklands.

"I'll drive," Simon had said.

"I'll do my bit," I said.

"No, no. It's a long way."

"That's why I'll do my bit."

"You don't like driving this car. It's all right, I'll do it."

A year or two back I would have given in at this point. Let him drive if he insists. Not this time. "I said, I'll do my bit," I said firmly. "In fact, I'll do the first bit." I took the car keys from him.

He remained apparently cheerful, puffing out his cheeks and saying, "Okay, okay," but I could tell he was put out by my insisting.

We stayed at Monica and Alan's Wednesday night. It works well for Simon, being able to see them without great expectations of our staying long. Alan, as ever, was friendly, asked about my health and how is Exeter treating me and have I explored Dartmoor yet? Monica remains Monica. Absolutely fine, except on the topic of children – or grandchildren, rather. She no longer actually refers outright to the fact that Simon and I are childless, but over dinner, under the guise of catching Simon up on people he knows or at least knows of, she did talk a lot about friends and neighbours who enjoy time with their grandchildren. I'm not sure which is preferable – her current tangential allusions to the matter, or how she used to be in asking directly when were we planning to start a family. Simon would never tell her to mind her own business, and more than once, years back, I almost reached eruption point of shouting at her, "You don't have any grandchildren and you're not going to have any because *your son doesn't fuck me!*" Maybe I should have let rip, although it wouldn't have been completely true: we did have sex in the first year or two of our marriage, but I can't say I enjoyed it much, and I reckon that for him it was done more out of duty than pleasure, and after a while the whole sexual charade died away.

We picked up Mummy yesterday morning. It's helpful that she's always got on well with Simon. He chatted away to her in the car and she put on a good impression of her abiding passion being road networks and bridge design. She's much livelier with him than with me.

We arrived at Oaklands early enough to spend time with Mikey before the meeting. He was in the smaller of the two day rooms – the designated 'smoking room' – sitting in an armchair and staring at the ceiling.

He looked reasonably presentable in the black jeans and sweater I'd bought him for Christmas a year ago, though his beard could do with the attentions of a hedge trimmer. His first remark to us came as no surprise: "Have you got any cigarettes?" I produced the pack I'd brought. He lit up immediately.

Mummy asked how he was, and he said in his monotone, "I think I've been a naughty boy."

"Oh, have you?" Mummy responded.

"I've been shitting myself."

"Why do you do it?" Simon asked, as I thought he would. It does no good, but Simon just doesn't *get* psychosis. He's known Mikey for years and he still tries to argue Mikey out of psychotic thought patterns.

"Dunno," Mikey said. "I shitted myself to death. Dunno why I did it. Wasn't very clever, was it?"

"It's good to see you, Mikey," I said. "I'm really sorry I haven't been for ages."

"You haven't been well, sis, have you?" he interrupted. "How are you now?"

"I'm fine, doing fine now." I smiled and took his hand. His fingers seem to be more nicotine-stained every time we see him.

"You're my little sis, aren't you?" he said. "I should look after you, but I can't. You can't do that when you're dead."

I felt tears pricking in my eyes at that. As kids he'd always looked out for me, called me 'little sis', and however weird he's become I've always been his 'little sis' and always will be. That's one thing he's not deluded about.

I held his hand as we talked, seemingly at random, for quite a while, with Mummy making the occasional comment, and Simon frozen in discomfort. The food, his sleeping, the other residents, the television, his medication – they all evoked much the same response, "all right, yeah, all right," dotted with allusions to being dead, having shitted himself to death. Mummy has become inured, or just indifferent, to this expression. Once upon a time she would have hit the roof if Mikey or I used 'bad language'.

Simon still gets offended for her sake when Mikey talks about shitting himself. It's something he's unable to retain his cheerfulness about – being in the presence of Mikey, or any of the other residents, freaks him out. At one point he butted in again to demand, "Why do you keep saying you're dead? You're alive and breathing and smoking and talking to us. You're not dead, are you?" Mikey just stared around the room, then told me he'd been watching a programme about African predators.

A staff member came to say that Dr Sepamla would like to see him, and Mikey went off, and after ten or fifteen minutes Mummy and I were invited along. Mikey himself decided not to stay, saying he was going to smoke another cigarette and, "you decide for me, sis. You know what's best."

The social worker was also present as well as the manager of the unit. It turned out reasonably well in the end – I can quite see why the staff feel that it's no longer the appropriate place for Mikey: his soiling hasn't quite reached epidemic proportions, but it's getting there, and it's increasingly unfair on the other residents. After all, it is their home.

It helps that they know I've been a social worker, and also that I am, technically, Dr Ward – they're aware it's not a medical qualification, but it still seems to give me status in their eyes. Dr Sepamla said they were intending to move Mikey back to an assessment unit – better staff-patient ratio – more active input – develop a behavioural programme to manage his soiling – assess and review medication. It sounded promising, but when the social worker chipped in about a unit where she'd already checked a bed was available, I had to point out that the place was even further away, making it much more difficult for Mummy to visit. How about the Maidstone unit, where he's stayed before? There's a residential home associated with it. Dr Sepamla said a bed wasn't currently available there, but I pushed them saying that the turnover at these places is usually such that a bed would probably become available before too long, and in the end they agreed they'd wait for that. I went to check with Mikey how he felt about it, and as I expected he simply said, "Yeah, whatever sis, whatever." That, then, is what'll happen.

On the way back to Exeter I spotted an 'ambiguous adjective' for Phil: on the M4, there was inevitably a stretch where a lane had been closed and the speed limit reduced to fifty. A sign warned us of 'Average Speed Cameras'. I pointed it out to Simon, who was driving at the time and cheerfully humming something I couldn't recognise.

"Why don't they use *good* speed cameras?" I said.

"What?"

"It said 'average speed cameras'." I stressed it as, '*Average*...speed-cameras'. "Why don't they use '*good*...speed-cameras' instead? Why only average ones?"

"That's not what it means," he said, rather didactically. "It doesn't mean the *cameras* are average. It means they've got cameras at each end of the stretch which can calculate your average *speed*, so you can't go..."

"Yes, yes!" I had to interrupt him. "I do understand that."

"I'm not with you then!" he said cheerfully.

I said it didn't matter.

It was some time later – after we'd joined the M5 – that he came out with the surprise of the century. I'd taken over the driving and had given one of those abrupt yawns you sometimes get, as though you've forgotten to breathe for a minute or two and an emergency corrective mechanism kicks in. Simon immediately said he'd do the driving again.

"No," I said, "I'm fine."

"All right. I must say you do seem to be much better these days," he acknowledged. "Your stamina. And how you made your point at the meeting – that was impressive."

"Thank you."

Another pause, then he said, "I've been thinking, we could start asking people round for a meal now and again."

"Good idea. Got anyone in particular in mind?"

"Jimmy and Charlotte for starters."

I must have been hyped up by having spotted the 'average speed camera' sign, and replied to Simon's suggestion with, "Wouldn't prawn cocktail or avocado vinaigrette be preferable as a starter?" which I think was quite clever.

"First on the guest list," he said condescendingly. "We've been to them more than once. How about Patrick and Rita as well?"

"The Roth of God? He's a bit heavy going, isn't he? When he gets onto his high religious horse."

"I think we should. You're getting to know Rita, aren't you? At the adult literacy club thing you do. Who would you suggest?"

There, I'm afraid, he had me. That's the problem – I still haven't really got a circle to call on or make suggestions about. Rita is fine, it would be nice to see her outside the TALC sessions, so I said all right, let's invite them; and it was after that he tossed in his stun grenade – well, it stunned me.

"I was also wondering," he said, "if you'd like us to invite Phil. Careful!"

The 'careful!' was because I'd jerked in surprise and the car had swerved. I said, "That'd be nice," hoping he didn't put two and two together. "I'll ring him."

"Have you got his number, then?"

"I can get it from Charlotte," I said, even though I do already have it.

"Ask him to bring his cousin."

"Tricky," I said, telling him Sam was married and had simply been on a visit to Phil when they'd been at Charlotte and Jimmy's. Simon was clearly disconcerted by this, making tutting sounds then muttering something about the numbers being uneven.

I'm not sure I was safe to drive for the next few minutes, as I continued to think of Phil. He'll be coming here for a meal, and after that I won't feel I'll have to keep secret *all* my contacts with Phil.

Only most of them.

Chapter 23

Emhalt: June 1967

Air shimmered above the bonnets and roofs of parked cars, and the tarmac looked in places to be on the point of melting as Melanie meandered along the road towards St Barnabas', where the Followers' anniversary service was being held in the church hall.

Her head ached. She had a dull throbbing at the back, and a more acute stabbing in her temples. She had been feeling generally washed out since the end of the exams.

The anniversary service did not really interest her, and she was only coming out of a sense of duty. Her parents knew of the event but had not asked to come and she had not specifically invited them. Mikey, having said he would like to come, decided at the last minute to stay at home playing records. Typical Mikey.

As she neared the hall, a car pulled up at the kerb and a moment later Anne got out, followed by her parents. Anne was wearing a green and brown skirt and pixie boots Melanie hadn't seen before. She gave a little skip as she came alongside Melanie. "Hello, sweetie! Dig my boots?"

"They're fab. Where d'you get them?"

"Got them up town. Me and Mum had a day out at the shops!"

"Lucky you! They look great!"

When Anne's parents had gone ahead to claim seats, Melanie said to her in a pleading voice, "Do us a favour, will you? Go in and see where Simon is and let me know."

Anne made a great play of looking up at the sky and spreading out her hands in a gesture of disbelief. "You're not still avoiding him?" she said. "Honestly, Melanie, what are you scared of? All you've got to do is say no next time he asks you, *if* he asks you. He hasn't asked you again, has he?"

"No," Melanie admitted. "But he might today. I just feel it. I don't want to go in there and him to be sort of, you know, waiting for me."

"All right! You owe me!" Anne laughed, and trotted into the hall while Melanie waited outside.

Other Followers were arriving: twin sisters Sarah and Rose who waived gaily at her; Kenny the pianist striding along in the manner of someone who should have arrived much earlier; Jeremy in startlingly red cords and his clumping desert boots. More cars arrived, more girls, more boys; and more parents, most of whom Melanie did not recognise.

She had assumed Simon was already in the hall, conscientiously arriving early to run through whatever he had been detailed to do. Although since his phone call he had not rung her again, and although he had talked to her on the intervening Followers' joint service without again broaching the subject of asking her out, she nevertheless feared it was just a matter of time: there was a definite brittle brightness about him in her company, as though he were gearing himself up for a repeat attempt. Like an exam resit.

She did not want to go out with him, yet shrank from the prospect of saying anything that would hurt his feelings. Not simply because they would be *his* feelings being hurt, but because in rejecting him she knew she herself would also feel the pain of rejection. She wished she could conjure up a way of ensuring he didn't ask again, sparing them both from possible hurt.

Chapter 24

Melanie

Exeter: March 1997

Damn! Damn, damn, damn! If I weren't so refined and ladylike, I'd add *fuck!*

As agreed, Simon had settled with Charlotte and Jimmy, and Patrick and Rita, for them all to come for a meal next Saturday, and I'd rung Phil quite openly to invite him, and that's fine for him too. Simon's been fretting about having unbalanced numbers, and a few days ago he suggested asking Sonia the merry widow as well because he'd been talking with Jimmy, and, "According to the local bush telegraph, aka Charlotte – that's Jimmy's description by the way, not mine – there might already be something going on between Phil and this Sonia."

There'd better not be, I thought, as he asked, "Did Phil mention her when you rang him?"

"No. I think he's footloose and fancy-free."

"Then I don't think it's appropriate to invite her as neither of us know her."

I agreed, but didn't have time to feel relieved because he went on to say, "I could see if Chloe can come. It's short notice, but worth a try."

"Chloe? I don't know any Chloe."

"Yes, you do. You know Chloe."

"I don't know Chloe."

"Yes, you do know Chloe," he insisted.

"Remind me who she is."

"She goes to the cathedral."

"I don't."

"Yes, you do."

"No, I don't. Not for services."

"You go to choral evensong sometimes, which she goes to, and we go for concerts, don't we? She was at the Bach last month. Sitting behind us. Lipstick."

"Oh, her. I didn't know she was called Chloe."

"I introduced you."

"That doesn't mean I know her."

"*I* know her."

It gets tiring when Simon knows that he's right even when he isn't, and I felt wrong-footed: he knows her, therefore I must know her. "You're going to invite her?" I said.

"It's worth trying, to make up the numbers. You'll like her."

An image had come to mind of long, thick, glossy, chestnut hair and very red lipstick. Mid-thirties? Very attractive. I'd rather she didn't come.

"It doesn't matter about making up numbers," I said. "These days you don't have to worry about having equal numbers of men and women."

"I don't want the seating at the dinner table to be lopsided," he returned, rather as if he were talking about a design for one of his bridges. "Also," he added, "I reckon Phil would get on well with her. She's separated as well – or divorced, one or the other. Phil's divorced, isn't he?"

"Being separated or divorced hardly counts as having an interest in common," I said.

"It means they're both without a partner."

"Is she?"

"I believe so."

I can't see the fact that they're both without a partner as much of a basis for compatibility, but I felt I couldn't object any more, and anyway I hoped she would have something else already planned. However, he came back from this morning's service and said, yes, she can come. Oh great.

I'm already feeling jealous. Suppose Phil gets on well with her, and asks her out, and she says yes, and they really get it together, and, and, and…? The thought of even the possibility of it hurts.

Why shouldn't he ask her out? I'm out of bounds for him, even though we've seen each other several times now for coffee or lunch or a walk. If he did get involved in another relationship, that might make it easier for me since I shouldn't feel the way towards him that I do feel, and if he were to get really involved elsewhere that would at least remove temptation from me. Oh, who the hell am I trying to kid? I don't want temptation removed, do I?

I do sometimes wonder who Simon would have married if he hadn't married me. There was Olivia he went out with for some time at Bristol – that could have got serious if he hadn't been, as it were, pining for me. We – or rather, he – had Christmas cards from her for several years, always signed with varying numbers of 'x's. In thinking all this I know I'm falling into the romantic trap of the modern, Western era – wishing for or expecting romance rather than the pragmatic, economic, utilitarian considerations which marriage has been about for most of human history and, presumably, prehistory. But then, what pragmatic, economic, utilitarian considerations are there regarding *our* marriage?

I'm sure that the happiness I feel when I'm with Phil isn't about the thrill of having an illicit relationship, because what's happened between us feels like the continuation of a relationship after a gap of many years that Hardy writes about. Whereas, if I were having a relationship with Joe Bloggs who I'd just met, that probably would be simply a reaction to being in a dull marriage. The thrill would be in the illicitness. But my feelings for Phil are what they've always been – now revived, renewed, resuscitated by meeting him again. Almost a homecoming. Why do I qualify that with the word 'almost'? It *is* a homecoming. The times I've been spending with Phil are just that: coming home to what should be.

Simon is downstairs doing something useful in the sitting room with the curtains. I only had to mention in passing that the cords you pull to open and close them keep snagging, and he's right there, toolbox out, dismantling and fixing and screwing and putting it all together again. Doing all that, while I'm up here having sexy thoughts, though admittedly not about him. For all he knows I could be having sexy thoughts about him…hmm, perhaps not. He clearly never has sexy thoughts about me. In the entire course of our marriage he hasn't once come storming upstairs with his toolbox open, pulled down my knickers and done a whole lot of screwing. I can imagine Phil doing it. Frequently. Phil frequently doing it I mean, as well as me frequently imagining him doing it.

I've tried phoning Phil a couple of times, wanting to tell him of Simon's Chloe-intrigue – the mobile phone makes it much easier. No reply. He's probably at some meeting or rehearsals to do with the Red Nose Day revue – he said last Monday when we had lunch at the Double Locks that the pressure was building and he was spending a lot of time honing the sketches. It's lovely to see him excited and happy to be doing revue again.

That makes me think yet again of my aspirations. My health is much better these days – admittedly I'd been improving for quite some time, so maybe my immune system has been readjusting, but I can't help feeling that a major factor is that there's a buzz in my life now which counteracts the immense fatigue that's crippled me for a long time. Part of the buzz, too, is that realising I could approach the university, to offer some teaching, tutoring, supervising, anything. There are several possibilities arising from *Transcending Gender* I'd love to pursue – perhaps I could develop my chapter on Hildegard into a book. We shall see.

Another thing: when I brought Phil up to date about Mikey, he listened without making simplistic suggestions, then offered an interesting thought. "I wonder if there's any connection," he said, "between the sorts of delusions he suffers from, and comedy?"

"His delusions aren't exactly funny," I pointed out.

"No, I get that. But he seems to be – and I'm guessing here – interpreting experiences he has in a way that's very different from how the rest of us might interpret them – he's using a different framework. A lot of comedy is like that, based on seeing something in a different way – maybe only slightly differently, maybe in a big way."

"How d'you mean?" I said. "Give us an example."

He went all thoughtful and swirled his beer around. He usually has a pint when we have lunch together. Then he said, "Okay. Like you describing Simon as a 'small bridge designer'. You intended it to mean that he's a designer of small bridges, but it can also be understood to mean that he's a bridge designer who is small. The same words interpreted differently. That's the basis of a lot of comedy – interpretations of a situation, or seeing things in a situation, that are different from the norm. A shifted perspective." He shrugged. "Just wonder if your brother's delusions are a bit like that, only scary rather than funny? Wonder if delusions and comedy are close cousins?"

He didn't develop this thought but asked more about what was going to happen to Mikey. I think I see what he means. His words could also apply to my Loch Lomond moment and the other ones since then: it's years since I last had one, but they remain within me – ordinary things which, briefly, intensely, I experienced in a different, heightened, deepened way. Maybe that's another cousin to delusions and comedy, only not dark and frightening like Mikey's delusions, or funny like Phil's comedy, but joyful and reassuring.

Chapter 25

Phil

Cambridge: February 1972

The rattle of Alex's typewriter, which had been sounding through the wall for most of the morning, ceased, and there was the "zzzzp!" of a sheet of paper being pulled from the machine.

"How're you doing, man?" I called out. I was sitting at my desk, tackling a sequence of reactions as detailed in *The Synthesis of Natural Products*. It was proving slightly – only slightly – more comprehensible than I'd expected. Perhaps I'd absorbed more of the lectures than I'd realised.

"Another Bovarian analysis completed," Alex responded.

'Good, is it?"

"World-shattering. It'll revolutionise Flaubertian studies. Or possibly not."

"Going to trot along into college in a mo. I need to give a supervisor a heart attack by dropping off some work on time."

"I'll come with you. I must collect some things – followed by a squashing of Edward." Their rivalry at squash had been steadily mounting.

We were well into the Lent term, and since my return to Cambridge after the Christmas break I'd been working moderately hard, all the while consciously trying not to think of Melanie – which turned out to be much the same as thinking about her non-stop. Christmas had been dire, redeemed only marginally by a successful New Year's Eve cabaret with Rob at his home, where we'd been joined by our former fellow performer Chris. I'd also spent a couple of days with the Teignford gang, hanging out with Sam for a bit, and got roped into going to the village disco with Charlotte who seems to like me but talks too much. I didn't intend it to come to anything and it didn't. All I wanted was to go into romantic hibernation.

Melanie. I'd received a brief note from her a few days after my return home, redirected from Pembroke. The card itself was of a Pre-Raphaelite picture called *The Beguiling of Merlin*, with the not-very-reassuring message scribbled on the back: "I'm so, so sorry. Everything's all too complicated to explain at the moment. Please forgive me. Please. M." She hadn't put her address. Nor love. Nor an 'x'.

I hadn't sent a card or anything in response. I did start writing a letter, but soon abandoned it – in a way I wanted to punish her by remaining silent, though I think I was hurting myself more. My hope, fuelled by desire, was that she'd write again at greater length, explaining that 'everything' – whatever 'everything' referred to – had been resolved and let's get it together now.

No further missive arrived.

Since returning to Cambridge, the intense desire to shoot round to Girton to see her had been counterbalanced by an equally intense fear of precipitating an irretrievable ending of our relationship – as though by *not* taking the risk that the worst would be revealed kept alive the possibility that all would ultimately work out. Moreover, I really did have to get down to some serious study.

I forced myself to work. Extraordinary that once upon a time I'd felt keen and eager and all fired up by the symbols and equations and concepts of the scientist; I'd seen myself as a great research chemist of the future, pushing back the frontiers of knowledge with the best of them, perhaps even becoming the best of them. Laughable that I used to think of myself along those lines – or did I? Was it me who'd had those thoughts and expectations? Those pre-A level aspirations seemed to belong to a different person, not simply to a younger me. If I were a different person, presumably a different future awaited me for when I left university.

But what future? Others in my year had started assiduously trotting along to the Appointments Board to arrange meetings with prospective employers, or were investigating the possibilities of postgrad research at this or another university, or were making plans to work abroad for a year or two in a voluntary capacity, or were plotting their next step in a master plan to become supreme ruler of the universe or at the very least the next prime minister but three. I'd been, and still was, equally assiduous in doing nothing whatsoever along any of those lines. They held no attraction. What was attractive was the possibility of ARP taking a show to the Edinburgh Festival Fringe – but even if that idea were to be realised, so what? There'd then be the question of whither, post-Edinburgh?

Alex and I reached Pembroke to find the head porter again standing outside the porters' lodge, again hands on hips, and scowling.

"Morning Scrimmers!" Alex greeted him. "Nice day!"

"Look at them, sir, look at them!" Mr Scrimshaw expostulated.

"Look at what?" I asked.

"Them ducks, sir, them ducks!" He gesticulated towards the central lawn of Old Court, where three ducks were waddling slowly across it, away from the porters' lodge and towards the dining hall. He was practically frothing with head-porterly indignation.

"What about them?"

"What about them, sir?" His 'sir' took in both of us as his voice rose querulously. "What about them? They're walking on the grass, sir! Walking on the grass! Only dons are allowed to walk on the grass!" With a "Hey! Hey!" accompanied by a clapping of the hands, he suddenly lumbered forward towards the ducks, which started waddling faster.

"Mr Scrimshaw!" Alex called, warningly. "You're walking on the grass!"

"No, he's running," I said, as the head porter's efforts paid off and the three ducks flapped into the air. He plodded back like a disgruntled rhino, muttering anti-duck sentiments.

After a quick diversion to deliver my supervision work, I continued to the JCR where Alex was already checking his pigeonhole. There was a square white envelope in mine, with just my name and college on it in handwriting that was disturbingly familiar. I had difficulty in tearing it open, partly because the flap had been well stuck down, but mainly because my hands had started to shake.

"God almighty," I said, finally getting the envelope open.

"Anything interesting?"

"It's from Melanie."

Alex gave a brief, low whistle of surprise. "I thought that was all off."

"Me too."

"What does she say?"

I gazed at the single sheet of paper, on which she had written on both sides. "Think I'll..." I started to say, then indicated the nearby television room. "You get going, man."

"Right. See you later, then. I hope it's...well, whatever you'd like it to be."

I nodded.

As Alex headed off, I went into the deserted room and sat down near the window. For several seconds I couldn't bring myself to read the letter – I don't have to read it, I thought. Why should I read it? Could go along to the bog and flush it away. Why the hell has she got back in touch? Why can't she...

Abruptly I started reading:

Dear Phil,

I've been wanting to write to you for ages, but it never seemed the right time until now, and even now I wonder whether I should, or whether it would be unfair on you – I realise you might have put it all behind you, thinking me hopeless, but I can't put it behind me and I don't want to put it behind me. I hope when I've finished writing this I'll find the courage to send it – I've told Anne what I'm doing, and she'll probably nag me until I do (sorry – you don't know Anne. Lovely friend from home. My confidante).

I really am very very sorry for letting you down at the end of last term, not turning up at the Friar House, and not getting in contact afterwards. Well, I did send that card. Please forgive me. It's been a rather traumatic time for me, the last two months, and I didn't know what to do for the best. I am so sorry if I've hurt you and upset you, but there's stuff been going on in my life for quite some time now (years, actually) and it all suddenly reared its head without me expecting it – my own fault, I know, but still traumatic. I don't feel I can go into details in writing, but I really would like to be able to explain it to you and hope you will understand and be able to forgive me.

I know it's asking a bit much, expecting you to say yes, but can we meet? Can I tell you what it's all about? I've been really miserable not seeing you, and feeling I couldn't – or rather shouldn't – get into contact with you, but the situation has again changed. I don't mean it's all resolved and hunky-dory but at least it's not as ~~difficult~~ intractable as it once looked.

Are you free tomorrow afternoon? Wednesday, that is. I'll be at the Whim about four, after a supervision. Can you be there? Will you? I'll understand if you don't come. I know you might not be able to come then even if you wanted to, so if you'd like to meet but can't make tomorrow, let me know when you can make it.

I'm sorry I can't explain more in this letter, but it does feel complicated, though I think it's more complicated to write than to explain. If that makes sense.

I do hope you'll come.

Melanie x x

My head felt to be full of sherbet fizzing away as I finished the letter. I reread it a couple of times. She wanted to see me; did I want to see her? Yes, no question. Would I be at the Whim tomorrow, come what may? *Yes!* Definitely yes. What would she say? What was all this 'stuff' going on in her life? She was *miserable* at not seeing me! I felt a supressed excitement trying to force its way out. How would I survive until Wednesday?

Wednesday? But today is Wednesday! She'd written and sent the letter yesterday – and there's the confirmation at the top of the letter: Tues 1st Feb.

It's four o'clock now. Just on.

I grab my coat and bolt out of the TV room, out of the JCR, along the side of Ivy Court, through the archway, past the duck-defiled lawn of Old Court, past the porters' lodge, through the college entrance, and out into Trumpington Street. I swing to the right, dash over Pembroke Street and go charging along, not letting up until, lungs on fire, a pain in my right side, I reach Trinity Street. Here I just have to stop a minute, gasping frantically. When I feel able to continue, it's on trembling legs that I approach the Whim.

There she is, standing outside the tea shop, waiting.

Chapter 26

Melanie

Exeter: March 1997

It's three in the morning. The crack-up hour, according to Scott Fitzgerald. I don't think I'm actually in danger of cracking up, but I can't sleep because everything is whirling around in my head after our dinner party. I keep telling myself that it's nothing to worry about, it's absolutely fine with Phil, I'm reading far too much into the situation, but the trouble with fears and anxieties is that you can't reason yourself out of them. Like the impossibility of Simon arguing Mikey out of his delusions.

Simon had gone off to sleep straight away and is sleeping the sleep of the just. He was very happy at the way the evening went – and quite right too, it did go very well. The only problem is how I've been left feeling desperate for reassurance because of Chloe. Rita and Patrick had already arrived when she turned up, as had Phil, who came with Charlotte and Jimmy.

I'd told Phil on the phone yesterday (to be more accurate, the day before yesterday, Friday) about Simon's thoughts of pairing him off with Chloe, and we'd had a good laugh about it. When it came to it, it was no laughing matter, not for me at least. She made quite an entrance: all red cloak and floppy, velvety hat. Her lipstick was as red as I remembered, and she was wearing – once the cloak had been disposed of with the sort of gesture which is both carefree and graceful – a long dark burgundy dress, perfectly plain except for an elaborate belt affair with a very fancy buckle. Stunning, I have to admit, as is her figure and her gorgeous mane of chestnut-coloured hair. Contrary to what I expected given her appearance, she came across as genuinely charming and friendly, presenting me with a posy of flowers and saying how lovely it had been to get the invitation, what a treat, she was so grateful.

"I don't get out as much as I'd like to," she said. "It's my own fault, I know. Maybe I'm too choosy!"

"Why choose us?" I laughed.

"Simon asked! We've had two or three interesting conversations after Sunday services. To be honest, you see, I'm not very religious, but I love the aesthetics of ritual. Not too sure about the actual content!" she added in a confiding voice which everyone could hear. "I'm one of the many who mime saying the creed, or say it with fingers crossed."

She gave a rather throaty laugh of self-mockery which made me warm to her, but my goodness she's one hell of a flirt! Several times during the evening (even at the dinner table) she took out a little mirror and a lipstick from her tiny, red leather evening bag and touched up her lips, which inevitably drew attention to them. She also has this habit of putting her hand on the arm of whoever she's talking to, and being just marginally in your personal space, and smiling at you winningly, as though you're the most important person in her universe. The fact that she does it openly with everyone should reassure me, but every time I saw her doing it with Phil I had this jab of intense jealousy. It wasn't helped by the fact that Phil, sitting next to her, seemed to enjoy it.

Phil was on good form. At one stage we were talking about the joys and horrors of flying and Patrick boomed out how he always pays for a seat "with extra leg room". That look immediately came onto Phil's face – he keeps quite still, head tilted slightly to one side, not a suspicion of a smile – which tells me some clever comment is coming.

"Extra leg room?" he said in his mock-professorial voice. "That's just what you need for your...extra leg?"

Everyone laughed, and Chloe put her hand on his arm and said, "Wicked!" in a sultry tone.

Jimmy said, "Aha! Jake the Peg, with the extra leg! Extra leg!" and he started to do a terrible Rolf Harris impression, singing, "I'm Jake the Peg", as Simon disappeared from the room and returned with his spare prosthetic, which he brandished like a war trophy.

"*My* extra leg!" he announced, and did a three-legged walk round the room, while Jimmy continued Rolf Harris-ing. It's not like Simon to be funny, but he did do it perfectly. Patrick threw back his head, almost trumpeting with laughter; Charlotte had to take off her glasses and wipe her eyes, she was laughing that hard; and Rita gave a series of little laughs like sighs, although I got the impression she didn't really see the joke. Phil was banging the table in admiration and exclaiming, "Brilliant! Brilliant!" as Chloe leaned into him, pressing herself against his side and whispering something to him. He nodded and whispered something back, and she laughed again and squeezed his arm. Even as I was still laughing at Simon and his leg I felt the dagger of jealousy jabbing away at me.

This all led to Phil being asked about the revue, and he launched into an explanation of his 'ambiguous adjectives' sketch. With 'automatic cat feeder' and 'mobile breast clinic' Chloe's admiration clearly went up by several notches, as did her arm-squeezing. "Come on!" she breathed (she doesn't speak so much as *breathe* her words). "Tell us some more!"

"You'll have to come to the show," Phil said. "Next Friday and Saturday at the Barnfield."

"I'd love to come," she cried. "Is everyone else going?"

"We're going on Friday," Simon said. "I'm off up to Bristol on the Saturday for a university reunion."

"How do I get a ticket?" Chloe demanded, hand still on Phil's arm.

"Send you one," said Phil, and the dagger really jabbed away at me.

Everyone started making other suggestions for his sketch, most of them rather feeble, before Chloe clapped her hands and said excitedly, "I've got one! I've got one! Did you know I work in Boots? That's the chemist, before you ask, not a fashion statement – I'm a pharmacist there. The other day I saw on the shelves an 'electronic head lice comb'. Isn't that good?"

"Oh yes!" said Phil, "I like that! Electronic head lice comb! Have *you* got electronic head lice? Or even an electronic head? I'll work it in somehow!" Then he gave her a hug.

He. Gave. Her. A. Hug.

A rather brief, awkward one, admittedly, as we were all still sitting at the table, but a hug nonetheless. She lapped it up.

I felt really wound up by all of that, which probably explains to some extent why I got onto my high horse later in the sitting room when Charlotte filled in a pause in the conversation by announcing that a woman priest is about to be appointed to the church at Teignford. The fact that Charlotte isn't a churchgoer doesn't stop her having an opinion on the matter, namely that it was about time too, what on earth had taken the church so long to get round to it, isn't it obvious that a woman is just as capable as a man at doing the job.

That's when there came a gravelly throat-clearing noise from the direction of Patrick, which turned out to be the prelude to his begging to disagree since the decision of the Church of England to appoint women priests was a grave mistake, going against both tradition and scripture as it did, and stalling any progress in developing unity with the Catholic Church.

"What's the Catholic Church got to do with it?" Charlotte said, rather indignantly. "I'm talking about the Anglican Church."

This triggered a rather long explanation from Patrick, who turns out to be a fully paid-up member of Forward in Faith.

"What I don't understand," Jimmy managed to interject when Patrick paused, "don't understand is why chaps like you, Patrick, stay in the Anglican Church if you disagree with it. Why not join the other lot? Other lot."

Another long explanation followed. Rita put a hand on his arm and shook it to shut him up, unsuccessfully on this occasion. Simon added his opinion, backing Charlotte and Jimmy, as did Chloe. I hadn't said anything at this point – still feeling raw over the intimacy developing between Chloe and Phil – and neither had Phil himself. Then in a lull Chloe asked what Phil thought of it.

"Come on," she said, nudging him this time with her elbow. "You've had plenty to say until now. Why the sudden silence?"

Phil laughed. "Keeping out of it," he said. "It sounds like a family row to me, and I'm not a member of the family."

"It's more than a family row, Phil," I said. "I know what you mean, but the anti-women priests view is a good example of how our society has always viewed the contribution of women, and seeks to downgrade it or dismiss it unless it accords with the male view of where authority lies." In about three minutes flat I went on to summarise one of my lines of argument in *Transcending Gender*!

When I'd finished, Phil said to the others, "You should listen to her, you know, 'cos she's descended from the angels!" No one picked up on my family joke.

Patrick had been nodding solemnly. "You make good points," he told me, "and I'm aware this is your field of expertise, but nevertheless," here he wagged a finger, "what matters is discerning the will of the Lord, and for that we must understand how the matter was understood by Paul and the early Church. To begin with..."

Rita's arm-shaking had intensified. "I think that's...you've said enough dear," she sighed, smiling a very wobbly smile. "We don't need...I don't think we want a sermon on it. If anyone wants to know...I'm sure they...want to know your views they can read your letters to the *Church Times*."

"Overdoing it again, am I?" Patrick said with a rueful smile.

"I rather think you...yes, you are, dear." As she often does, she seemed to be addressing the carpet. "I think we can agree...can't we agree?...that different people have different things they can...different talents to offer, whether they're male or female..."

"Or gay?" said Phil, and Patrick, instead of saying anything, made a zipping motion across his own mouth.

"Or whether they're gay, yes," Rita sighed. "We all have our...we've been given different...things we can do. Now I know you disagree with me about...about the gay issue, Paddy, and...what the Church says, well, you know my opinion."

Chloe said, "Surely it's irrelevant whether someone's gay or straight or bi or whatever. Shouldn't the Church accept them all equally?"

"Jimmy used to work for a boss who was gay, didn't you?" Charlotte said.

"He was, he was!" Jimmy gave his diabolic look.

"Not that Jimmy's got anything against gay men," she added hurriedly.

"And he fully intends to keep it that way," said Phil.

I've made myself a camomile tea, then I need to get back to bed in a minute and try for some sleep – in the spare room, I think.

I hate to admit that I do need reassurance from Phil. Dammit! After all I claim to believe about women's strength and validity and everything! But reassurance is a human need, not exclusive to women. The real issue about wanting reassurance is more to do with the fact that the source of any reassurance I might need ought to come from Simon. But I can hardly seek reassurance from Simon that Phil loves me, can I?

We'd agreed on the phone that during the evening we had to be careful to behave towards each other just as good friends; so strictly speaking it was a good thing that Chloe was flirting with him, and he seemed to be attracted to her. He was just acting, wasn't he? He's a good actor. He gave no hint to me, even when it would have been safe, that I was anything special to him. I wish he had. A chaste kiss on the cheek when he arrived with Charlotte and Jimmy was about the sum of it, and a rather formal enquiry after my health, but almost, it seemed, an avoidance of me on occasions – deliberate, I hope, to make sure there was no possible suspicion of anything going on between us.

Not that I have broken my marriage vows, not in the technical sense, that is, but here I am, in the small hours, needing sleep, thinking about lovemaking with him. Though not so much about lovemaking as about curling up with him and drifting off to sleep in his arms. That's what I'll be doing in my imagination when I get back upstairs – I'll replay those times when I would fall asleep in his arms...usually after the most sublime sex.

Chapter 27

Phil

Cambridge: February 1972

Melanie had on a thick, dark coat, a Cossack's hat from which her hair bulged out untidily, and a scarf wrapped around her throat and over her mouth. She reminded me of Julie Christie in *Dr Zhivago*. She had her hands in her pockets, and one leg was partly thrust forward as if frozen in the act of running away.

I had the advantage of her, looking at her for some time without her having seen me. As I approached her, apprehension lunged at my heart like a rugger player diving over the line. Turning her head, she saw me. She drew her leg back, adopting a more upright posture, and raising a hand she pulled the scarf away from her mouth. I could see her breath.

"Hi!" I raised a hand as I went up to her.

"Hello, Phil." She gave a quick, uncertain half-smile with her eyes partly closed. Her eyelashes quivered. "Shall we go in?"

"Why not?"

It was less crowded than I'd been expecting, and we claimed a small table for two in a corner. As she sat down I noticed her hair was shorter than before and shaped differently, allowing her ears to be glimpsed. She was wearing dangly green earrings.

There was a tentativeness about her movements, and she sat at the table looking anxiously about the tea room, running her tongue along her lips which looked chapped. She'd taken off her hat and was repeatedly twisting a lock of hair between her fingers.

A waitress appeared, little notebook and pencil at the ready. She was nodding rapidly, as though her neck were a powerful spring and her head had just received a severe blow. She asked what we'd like.

"Oh, I don't know. Tea for me," I said.

"Tea for two," Melanie added.

And me for you, I thought.

"Anything to eat?" asked the waitress, her head continuing to oscillate. She indicated the bill of fare.

We settled on toasted teacakes.

As the waitress noddingly departed, I studied Melanie's face, expecting to see her looking pale, but she looked robust enough. She briefly displayed her pouty look before giving a half-smile.

"I'm glad you've come," she said.

"Why shouldn't I have?"

She sighed, tugging again on a lock of hair. "I thought that probably you wouldn't want to see me again. I was afraid you wouldn't even read my letter when you realised who it was from."

"Only picked it up this afternoon."

"Did it..." She bit her lower lip. "Did it come as a surprise?"

"You could say that. In fact, I will say that. It came as a complete surprise. Why didn't you phone?" I asked heatedly. "You've got the number."

"I was going to, before I lost my nerve. I was scared to ring, I thought it'd be easier to write. I thought it'd be easier for you, too, not having to respond on the phone."

"Suppose you're right," I conceded. "If you'd rung you might've found yourself speaking to Ewan or one of the others, which could've been awkward."

"What was Christmas like?" she asked abruptly.

"Crap," I said.

"I'm sorry. Why was that?"

I could feel a band of tension round my head getting ever tighter. "Are you serious in asking that?" I muttered thickly. "Can't you guess?"

When she failed to answer, I looked up and saw that a deep flush had permeated her face.

"It was crap," I repeated, adding with intentional brutality, "because of you."

She lowered her eyes. "I'm so sorry."

"D'you know what I did for the entire Christmas bloody vac?" I continued. I didn't care that we were in a public place. I didn't care that others might hear what I said. In fact, I rather wanted them to. I needed to deal with this terrible pain that had been both within me and surrounding me for the past God knows how long. "The only thing I did was think of you. Over and over again. You, you, you."

"Oh Phil..."

"I wasn't able to do anything but you were there, going round and round in my head like some sodding stuck record. All I could think of was you. Wondering where you were, what you were doing, who you were with. Kept replaying the times we'd been together, what we'd said to each other, kissing you, holding you. I wanted to see you and hold you, but I couldn't, could I?"

Melanie was staring at me, her hazel eyes wide and shiny, her delicate lashes curling above and below like tiny, immaculate portcullises.

"Phil, I am sorry. I am *so* sorry," she said miserably.

"Sorry! My God!" I burst out. "D'you know what you've put me through? I just haven't known what's been happening to me! Hell – it even drove me to doing some studying!"

Melanie gave a brief laugh, then stopped, looking mortified. "I'm sorry, I shouldn't laugh."

I waved a hand dismissively. "Just being...y'know. It got me down."

"Oh Phil, Phil!" She was squirming on her chair. "The last thing I wanted was to do that to you. I didn't want to hurt you or upset you. I've been so confused and everything, not knowing what to do for the best."

"Waited for ages outside that damned place," I said, "then phoned you at Girton and was told you weren't there. I still went pedalling out on the off-chance I could find you, nearly committing auto-castration in the process, only to discover you'd gone home. Gone home!" I repeated incredulously.

Melanie indicated with her eyes something behind me. It was she of the oscillating head with our tea and toasted teacakes.

"Don't you dare say 'shall I be mother?'" I muttered as the waitress withdrew, still nodding.

This drew a faint smile from her. "Why not?"

"Can't stand it when people say that."

She put milk into the cups, and I poured a small amount of tea into one. It was still very weak, looking like another end product of one of my failed organic chemistry practicals.

"I like mine strong," said Melanie.

"Yeah. Me too." I replaced the teapot on its stand.

I took a teacake and very slowly began to spread butter over it, thinking all the while, God almighty, this is awful. I watched the butter melt, and smeared on some more. If I were a dam, I thought, they'd be wildly tolling the church bells by now to warn the local inhabitants that I was about to burst.

"Phil, believe me, I was trying to do what I thought was right. I'd got this letter that morning, the Friar House day, that threw me into a complete spin, and I knew I had to get back home as soon as possible to sort things out."

"What letter? Meanwhile, forgetting about me?"

"No! Not at all! How could you say that? I did ring you, you weren't in. I left a message – didn't you get it?"

"Got a message when I came back from the Friar House that you wouldn't be able to make it – no, it was after that, it was after I'd been out to Girton and back. Whoever had taken it had shoved it under the wrong door, Ewan's door, instead of mine. It didn't say much though."

"I left quite an explanation – which was probably unfair on whoever it was I was talking to. He did sound distracted. He kept saying 'Right on!'"

"Tristan," I said. "Thought it must be him. Hopeless. He's out of his head ninety per cent of the time. Always on the weed. All he'd scribbled was that you'd rung and you couldn't make the Friar House. He got your name wrong, too," I remembered.

"Oh dear, I'd said a lot more. I'm *sooo* sorry, Phil." With a shaking hand she poured out the tea. We both drank some.

"I was hoping you'd write after that," I said. "Why didn't you write to me? Tell me what was going on?"

"I know – I wanted to write a really long letter, but everything had got so complicated that I couldn't do it – all I could manage was that card I sent you. You never wrote back," she added accusingly.

"No! Right! I was waiting for a proper explanation from you!"

"I didn't know you'd got my card."

"It didn't exactly tell me anything, did it?"

"Does it matter now? I'm really sorry, I should have written again and told you more. If it's any consolation to you, I don't know how I got through Christmas either. You said yours was crap, well mine was..." She hesitated.

"Crap squared?" I offered.

"That about sums it up."

I sighed and shook my head. "Well, it's not any consolation, because I'm sorry if your Christmas was ghastly as well. Look, we did both get through it and we're here, now. Can we move on?"

"Can we do that literally?" Melanie asked. "I need to get outside."

"You haven't eaten your teacake thing."

"Neither have you."

We got the bill from the head oscillator, paid it, and left, with the teacakes concealed in some serviettes.

Chapter 28

Melanie

Exeter: March 1997

I've been trying to get hold of Phil all day. He's not answering his phone, and he hasn't rung me. I'm trying not to worry. Twice our landline's rung, and I've dived for it despite knowing it wouldn't be him.

The first time, just after I'd managed to struggle out of bed having had a rotten night, was Charlotte to say how much she and Jimmy had enjoyed yesterday evening and hoping it hadn't taken too much out of me. "Wasn't Simon a hoot with his artificial leg!" she added. "I didn't realise he could be that funny. He's usually so serious."

"Once in a blue moon," I admitted. "I think making fun of having an artificial leg is one of the ways he's coped with it over the years."

"And having a good woman behind him!" Charlotte said chirpily. "Like Jimmy! We're the unsung heroes, you and me."

"Or heroines."

Inevitably, I could feel it coming, she started to talk about Chloe. "I thought I knew her from somewhere when she arrived," she said. "I've seen her in Boots. She seems very nice, very friendly and outgoing." I waited for the qualification, and it came. "A little too glamorous, I thought. There's no need to be quite that chic. This isn't Paris, is it? Still, there you are. She and Phil were getting on very well together, weren't they?"

"They seemed to be."

"I think they'd be rather good together, don't you?"

No, I thought, clenching my free hand. This was *not* what I wanted to hear, thank you very much. "Didn't you have plans to marry him off to the merry widow Sonia?" I said.

"Oh, that was just a thought I'd had! I've decided it wouldn't work, Sonia's too frivolous. Not that she isn't a very efficient council secretary, but there's no real depth to her. No, from what I saw I'd say Phil and Chloe would be a much better match. After all he did science at university, didn't he? She's a chemist, so they've got a lot in common."

I drew in my breath and said, "Yeees," at length to register scepticism.

Charlotte took no notice and continued, "He was very quiet in the car on the way back, so I did probe him a little, in a very subtle way. I asked him what he thought of Chloe. Did he like her?"

"Oh, very subtle," I said.

"I thought so too, and it did work."

"Why, what did he say?"

"He said something about she's very nice."

Nice? That's not a Phil word, except when he's being sarcastic.

"I'm sure he likes her," Charlotte continued. "In fact, I think he's definitely attracted. He said she seems like good fun. What about you, did you like her?"

"She's very lively," I said. The nails in my clenched fist were digging into the palm. I forced myself to unclench before I drew blood.

I finally diverted her, after a few more comments about the mutual suitability of Phil and Chloe to the extent that I was surprised she hadn't booked the register office for them and ordered the vol-au-vents, by abruptly asking her advice on hanging baskets. They're one of her specialities, and she took the bait by giving me masses of suggestions.

I'd hardly got off the phone to her when it rang again, and of all people it was Chloe herself. I recognised her voice straight away from that slightly husky, sultry intonation.

"I want to say what a lovely evening it was," she said. "Thank you so much. I really enjoyed it, and it was kind of you to invite me despite not knowing me before."

"You knew Simon."

"Yes, but not the both of you, so thanks. I hadn't really met Rita and Patrick before, not properly. I've seen him at concerts in the cathedral. He's quite something, isn't he!"

"He rather got to me," I admitted, "as you might have noticed!"

She gave her throaty laugh. "That was great fun!" she said. "Theology isn't often a spectator sport! I wanted to ask you, what did he mean when he referred to your 'field of expertise'?"

When I explained about my PhD and book, she became very animated, asking questions and making several perceptive comments. "I'd love to do some more studying myself sometime," she said.

"Why don't you?"

"I'm not sure how to go about it. Or what subject to go for."

Despite myself I was really warming to her, and suggested meeting for coffee on Tuesday, her day off. To my relief she didn't mention Phil once. Because there's no attraction there, despite my anxieties? Or low cunning on her part?

Chapter 29

Phil

Cambridge: February 1972

We left the Whim and, holding hands, made our way onto the Backs. We didn't speak for some while, relieved – at least, I was relieved – simply to be with each other again. It was already getting dark, and the cold was intensifying.

"I would like to explain," she eventually said as we paused by the water's edge. "Is that all right? I'm afraid it's rather involved."

"I've gathered that."

"You see, I've found it very difficult over the past few weeks to do what I've thought is the right thing, and I don't know if I've made a very good job of it. The trouble is half the time I haven't known at all what *is* the right thing, so it's all been muddled."

"Well, I'd like to know what happened," I said, feeling as I've felt before in a number of situations: wishing I could know something without having to go through the tedious business of having to endure the recitation of a linear sequence of salient and not-so-salient facts.

"When we met at that party," she said, "where you did your cabaret…"

"Gerry's."

"Well, actually, at the time – oh dear, I do feel bad about this – at the time I wasn't really a free agent."

I felt ambushed. "You weren't a free agent – meaning what, exactly?" We'd resumed walking.

"Meaning I'd been sort of going out with someone, on and off really, for, oh, about three years. Simon. His name's Simon."

"Fuckin' Ada, Melanie! Why didn't you tell me?"

"I'm telling you now, aren't I?"

"Okay, okay. Go on."

"I've known him for years. He's a member of Followers – you know, the Bible class I used to go to. That's how I know him."

"You're still with him?"

"No. I never was really 'with him'. At least, I never thought of it that way. Just that we sometimes went out together, that's how it started. Sorry if this sounds like I'm boasting, but he was dead keen on me, and I liked him but I wasn't *keen* on him. It was nice to have someone to go out with, though, 'specially when, you know, a group of us went out together to a film or something. We'd go with Anne – my friend Anne – and usually Jeremy, unless they'd had a row. Quite often a bunch of us would go out together to, well, wherever."

"Fair enough," I shrugged.

"The thing is, when I was sixteen, sixteen and seventeen, I went through a bad time. Really bad. It was grim."

Her voice had faltered, and we stopped walking. I let go of her hand and put my arm round her shoulder. As she snuggled into me I put my other arm round her to hold her tight.

"'S nice," she murmured, and I could feel her body shuddering against mine. After a while she pulled away and we resumed walking. "Simon was very kind and supportive and a good friend during this period," she said mournfully, "and he took me out two or three times when I was feeling so low you wouldn't believe it, and everyone else just assumed we were going out together. He'd asked me out before all that and I'd said no, and I'd been involved with someone else, which all went horribly wrong, and Simon was sort of picking up the pieces. I felt I couldn't just say no after I started feeling better, because I'd feel that I'd just been using him, which wouldn't have been fair."

"Uh-huh," I said cautiously, having lost the thread of what she was saying. So much for it being a linear sequence of facts.

"I felt under an obligation, really, expecting that after he'd started at Bristol – he's doing engineering – it'd fizzle out and he'd get a girlfriend up there. However, he kept writing to me, and in the vacs there he was, all ready to take me out again. When I came here I just hoped that'd be that, but I was wrong. He came up and stayed over a weekend during my first term, and, well, it just continued."

"He stayed in your room?" I was appalled at the thought.

"No, silly! Whenever he came up he booked into a B & B, the same one every time. Last summer I tried to break it off, but couldn't go through with it, though I was feeling more and more trapped. And, well, he'd come up again to see me that weekend of the party."

"You mean – he was up here? In Cambridge? When we met?" I didn't try to keep the incredulity out of my voice. I kicked moodily at a passing stone.

"I hadn't wanted him to come," she said hurriedly. "I'd already told him I'd be out on the Saturday, but he still came. He didn't want to go to the party, saying he wanted a romantic meal together, puke, puke. I said I was going to the party and that was that. We didn't row – Simon doesn't do rows, he just sulks – and I went on my own, which is what I wanted. Well, I went with Amirah, and Sarah and her fellow. I was determined to enjoy myself. Then I met you."

"And didn't enjoy yourself!"

"Idiot! Course I did."

We moved on and found a decaying bench underneath a massive oak. We sat, Melanie unwrapping the serviette she'd put in her pocket and offering me a cold toasted teacake. It looked on the manky side and I declined, but she bit into it voraciously. She was not a delicate eater.

"Okay," I said, "while we were dancing together and, um, getting to know each other, and, um..."

"Enjoying each other," she mumbled with her mouth full.

"Enjoying each other, this Simon was...where? Back in the B & B?"

She nodded. "I'm embarrassed to say it, but yes. That's why I disappeared when I did. You'd gone off, and I suddenly felt very guilty. When I'd been with you, everything was wonderful, so lovely, and I sort of forgot about him! When you went I suddenly thought, what am I doing? It's not fair on Simon, it's not fair on you, it's not fair on me. It all felt wrong, and I was cross with myself, and I sneaked away, back to Girton.

"He came round on the Sunday morning, and we had another non-row. He wanted us to go to church which I vetoed, so he went on his own and then back to Bristol, leaving me feeling really bad and miserable."

"That was the end of it, was it? You two properly split up after that?"

"No, not right away. That's the problem."

"Why on earth not?"

"He wrote to me hoping I was all right as I'd seemed 'out of sorts' as he put it. I wrote to Anne – she's at Birmingham – and she sent back this lovely letter saying I was being an idiot and I shouldn't allow Simon to have a hold over me, that I had to make up my mind and I'd be an idiot to decide in favour of Simon when there was Mr Wonderful gagging for me. That's you, in case you hadn't guessed."

"It's not what I usually get called."

"I still dithered for weeks. Then Sarah told me about that party at the Dorothy, and that Air Raid Precautions would be there, and that's when I finally got the courage to write to Simon. I tried to be as nice as I could, basically saying I couldn't be his girlfriend anymore. He wasn't to think of me in that way."

"A 'Dear John' letter?"

"When I posted it I felt at last I was free to really be with you. If you'd still have me."

"If I'd still have you? Of course I would. I will!"

There was the sound of several voices, shouting and laughing, somewhere in the vicinity. They started singing a ragged version of 'Four and Twenty Virgins'.

"Okay, I'm with you so far, I think," I said. "You come to the Dorothy, we meet again, et cetera, et cetera. We make a date to eat at the Friar House, and only fifty per cent of us turns up, namely, viz. and to wit, me. What happened to the other fifty per cent? Namely, viz. and to wit, you?"

The owners of the singing, shouting and laughing voices had been approaching and were now upon us, disclosed as a group of rugger buggers, all dressed in muddy striped shirts, shorts and cleated boots. They were throwing a rugby ball between them. They made to walk past us, only the one who had been singing the loudest stopped his singing and came to a halt in front of us.

"Hello, darlin'," he said cheerfully.

"Hello, gorgeous," I responded, possibly unwisely.

"Not you, faceache."

Melanie stood up. I jumped up beside her.

"You I mean, sweetheart!" the rugger bugger said.

"Well, *I* am neither your sweetheart, nor your darling!" she announced firmly. "Got that?"

"Oooh!" The rugger bugger put on a camp tone.

"Come on Geoff, don't be a pillock," another of them urged, taking him by the arm and pulling him back. "Sorry about this," he apologised. "He's a pillock and he's completely pissed. Not that that makes much difference – he's a pillock even when he's sober."

"Bog off, Henry," the rugger bugger pillock said, jerking himself free and again taking a step closer to Melanie. "You're surely not having it off with this specimen?" he demanded of her, waving his hand towards me to eliminate any possible misunderstanding as to whom or what the designation 'this specimen' applied. "You need a real man!"

He reached out towards Melanie.

There was a sudden, violent movement, and a second or two later the rugger bugger pillock had assumed a position on the ground, face down, groaning, writhing and acquiring more mud in the process, and Melanie, still standing, was slapping her hands together in satisfaction at the success of her throw. The others cheered and laughed. One of them bounced the rugby ball on the head of their overthrown colleague.

"Brilliant!" cried the one called Henry. "Well done! He had it coming!"

"Sodding hell," grumbled the grounded pillock, rolling over and getting into a sitting position. He was rubbing his shoulder. "How did you do that?"

"Just a little thing I picked up in the course of life," said Melanie nonchalantly.

"You don't play for the 'Quins by any chance? Give us a hand, someone."

He was helped to his feet and led away by the others, who were still laughing, the one called Henry turning to us as they went and mouthing another apology.

"That was impressive," I said as they disappeared into the gloom. "See I'm going to have to watch my step!"

"I did self-defence classes a few years ago," said Melanie, "and then some judo. That's the first time I've used it for real! Just you watch your p's and q's from now on, Philip Ellis!"

I held up my hands in mock surrender.

Chapter 30

Melanie

Exeter: March 1997

I really do warm to Chloe.

We met for coffee at the little canal-side cafe, near the lock where the river and canal meet. A large dog with a shaggy coat was in the entrance lobby when I went in.

"That's Baxter," Chloe said when she turned up. "He's an impressive snapper-upper of unconsidered cake crumbs."

We sat with our coffees on tall stools at the window, looking out to the canal and, just beyond it, the river. Chloe pointed to a newish block of apartments on the far side of the river and a little downstream. "That's where I live," she said.

"Looks lovely. Great location."

"I was pleased to get it. Pricey, but my ex had just been paid for a big commission he'd done – he's an artist – and he helped me out. I moved in just about this time last year. You must come round sometime. If you'd like."

"I'd like," I said.

Chloe's an intriguing combination of the glamorous and the down to earth: her make-up was as immaculate as it had been on Saturday evening, and several times while we were there she had a quick check in her little mirror of her lipstick (bright red again, which you'd think would be too much, but she carries it off perfectly) and repaired some invisible lippy flaw. Her hair is really profuse and a gorgeous shade of dark chestnut (its real colour, I'm sure); and she was just as well dressed for coffee in an unpretentious cafe as she would have been in Claridge's. Although the immediate impression she gives is one of elegant sophistication, she comes across as very genuine, and that's also despite her immensely flirty manner (most of the time she had her hand on my arm, and often when talking she swayed towards me as though she wanted to kiss me).

After chit-chatting for a bit, which was very easy to do with her, she said she really appreciated that I'd suggested we meet, because, "I'd love to hear more about what you were saying the other evening – but it's more that, well, I felt in general you're very *simpatica*. I wanted to get to know you. I hope that's all right."

I found myself telling her more about my years in academia, and my decision to leave that world and train as a social worker – all the things about wanting to make a practical difference to people's lives.

"For what it's worth," she said, having listened intently, "I'd say that the type of research you've done *does* make a difference to people's lives. I think it helps us understand where we are now, and why things are as they are, and it can shed light onto how to change things which need changing."

As this is pretty much the argument I've made in the past, justifying my research to one or two people who've thought it was all ivory tower nonsense (Mummy, step forward), no wonder I warmed to her. "I think you're right," I said, "provided you do look for ways of translating your research into the everyday world."

"Did you?"

"That was part of the problem," I had to admit. "I could see that it *ought* to translate, but I'm not convinced it did. Whereas in social work you know that what you do, recommendations you make, decisions you implement – all that does make an immediate difference. The trouble there is whether the difference is positive or negative in the long term. You can't always be sure."

"I suppose I did my pharmacist training for similar reasons," she said. "I know what I do makes a difference. *And* it's really fascinating. The very idea that small amounts of this chemical or that can have a huge impact on people's lives – well, it's staggering! Now I'm hankering for another challenge! An intellectual one. The problem is time. Oh, and money!"

"Why not do some short courses?" I said. "You don't necessarily have to go for a degree course, do you?"

"That's what I'm wondering. However, I'm a bit of a duffer at knowing what the possibilities are."

We got into discussing all sorts of ideas, and getting rather excited about it, the upshot being that she's going to check out Exeter University for possible non-degree courses, maybe in women's studies; and I've said if she gets on a course and wants some sort of discussion partner, I'd be happy to be there for her. That was when she *did* hug me and kiss me!

Talking with her has had its effect on me, too. I've just contacted the university myself to ask about the possibility of doing some lecturing, and bingo! The Head of Department turns out to know my work because she attended a couple of conferences where I gave papers – Birmingham '74, we decided one of them must have been, and probably Liverpool '76 was the other. Though that was years ago she still includes *TG* on her recommended reading list for students. Anyway, I'm going in to see her at the end of the week.

★

Phil rang. He'd had to shoot off to Kent first thing Sunday morning, which is why he hasn't rung before. Ros had phoned him in a panic about Amy being picked up by the police on suspicion of possessing drugs, and in the hurry he'd managed to leave his mobile behind.

"Sorry Mel," he sighed, "afraid I don't know your phone number off the top of my head. I couldn't let you know what was going on."

"It's not engraved on your heart?" I asked, to which he retorted, "Do you know mine?" and I had to admit I didn't.

"All the same, I'm sorry I couldn't get a message to you until I got back," he said. "Hope you didn't think I was ignoring you."

Though I would have liked a lot more reassurance from him, I simply said that was okay, but what's happening to Amy?

"Panic over," he said. "As it happens she was clean, more by luck than judgement I reckon. I'm fairly sure she does speed from time to time. Her boyfriend turned out to be clean as well, but some of the others are being charged. The club they were at apparently has a dodgy reputation, and the police chose the night they were there to have a crackdown – ha! Perhaps not the best expression to use! She was released Sunday morning, when I was already on my way. Mind you, would still have gone even if I'd known she wasn't being charged."

"Is she all right? Quite a scare for her."

"All right enough, I'd say. Rather shaken. Glad I could get there and spend some time with her. She acts tough at times. Underneath she can be very vulnerable – it was great to spend yesterday with her."

He needed to talk more about her, and as I listened I became conscious of a glow developing throughout my body – I don't think I've ever heard Phil be quite that open before – the love he has for his daughters is completely unconditional.

"Well, I'm glad it's turned out better than you thought," I said when he ran out of steam. "It must've been worrying for you. Kids, eh? We *never* worried our parents, did we?"

"Paragons of virtue," he agreed. There was a brief silence – I wonder if he was thinking what I was thinking, about my teenage stupidity.

"I'm really glad you're back," I said. "I did wonder where you'd got to. Can we meet soon?"

He said he'd love to, but he has several tutoring sessions, and there's the grand revue fast approaching, demanding most of his time and energy. Fair enough; all the same I was starting to feel that I only came third on the list (or fourth if you count his daughters, which is as it should be) when he said, "To hell with that, let's have lunch tomorrow" – which has made me feel a lot happier.

Even happier-making is this: he asked what I'd been doing since Saturday, and when I told him I'd had coffee with Chloe he said great, he thought I'd get on well with her, and I said that he'd seemed to be getting on *extremely* well with her on Saturday evening. There must have been something in my tone of voice, because he said, "Hello! Do I detect a touch of the green-eyed monster?"

"She's rather gorgeous," I pointed out.

"Too right, I could see that. Yeah, reckon she's good fun, lovely person. But you haven't twigged?"

"Twigged what?"

"Ah. I'm fairly sure she's gay."

"No, she isn't!"

"Might not be, I agree, but I think she is."

"You know she's been married and has a son?"

"Yeah. Doesn't mean she's not gay."

"True," I conceded. "What makes you think she's gay? Oh hang on," I started laughing. "Don't tell me you felt she doesn't fancy you so you conclude she must be gay? You are *so* conceited!"

"With much to be conceited about," he said quickly. "No," he went on, "it's just the way that when we were talking she said she'd been in a couple of relationships since her marriage ended, and she referred to those partners as 'she'."

"Okay," I acknowledged, "that would be a definite clue, but..."

"...but it doesn't matter one way or the other," Phil said firmly. "I got on well with her, which was lucky, because I found it incredibly difficult on Saturday not to spend any time with you – I hated that bit of it. I was concentrating on Chloe to make sure I wouldn't be giving any sort of hint of how I feel about you."

"How *do* you feel about me?"

He gave a sigh. "This is dangerous territory. I don't want to make it difficult for you."

"It won't."

But he refused to elaborate.

Chapter 31

Phil

Cambridge: February 1972

Melanie put her hand on my knee. "Hey you, I've been thinking."

"Don't overdo it."

"No, listen. For Easter, what will you be doing over the Easter vac?"

"Nothing planned," I said. Easter lay a few weeks in the future. "Suppose I'll have to buckle down and do a load of revision for the old finals. Trouble is, in my case it tends be a matter of vision rather than *re*vision. Subtle difference."

"You can't tell me you'll be spending the whole vac sweating over your books."

"True, true. I'll probably do a concentrated burst about twenty-four hours before next term starts. Or twenty-four minutes."

"I was thinking – why don't we go away together somewhere? Just for a short time – I'll have loads of work to do as well, but surely we can manage a few days away. It wouldn't work for you to come and stay in London, the Mason household is not the most relaxed. There's Mikey, for a start. He's not easy."

"Your brother?"

"He has...problems. He tends to freak people out sometimes by his behaviour and odd things he says. Mainly about death."

"Cheery. You could come and stay with me, in the wilds of Devon. Mum and Dad get on with anyone."

"Including me? I'd prefer it to be just the two of us. What d'you think?"

"I think," I said, swirling the beer around in my glass, watching as it mounted the sides like a wall-of-death rider, "I think you are gorgeous and that's a brilliant idea. Where shall we go? It'll have to be somewhere cheap. I'm practically skint – my bank must be on the verge of writing to suggest I revert to banking with them rather than the other way round."

"How about the Lake District? It doesn't have to cost much – we can go B & B, or even camp. How about that?"

"I'm not camping around for anyone, ducky," I said.

"B & B then. Let's fix dates and I'll find a place and book."

Saturday evening in the sweating cellars of the Union building, with hammering music, flickering lights and a wide range of piss artists in evidence. We were the first of our group to arrive, and had bagged a table in one of the odd-shaped alcoves away from the main area. Warty candles stuck wonkily in wax-encrusted bottles dripped onto the table.

Edward joined us, looking very flash in a high-necked red jersey. "How are the lovebirds?" he asked cheerily, sitting down.

"Tweet, tweet," said Melanie.

"I interpret that to mean," Edward addressed her, "that you continue to labour under the peculiar belief that Philippe, this horse-lover, is worthy of being your heart's desire?"

"Horse-lover? That sounds weird," Melanie said, laughing.

"From 'philo' meaning love, and 'hippo' meaning horse," said Edward sententiously. "There you go."

"What does my name mean?"

Edward pondered. "'Melano' must mean black, as in melanin, which makes you a black lady – Shakespeare's dark lady I'd say. A mysterious, romantic figure!"

Melanie liked that and laughed again. When she laughed, her tongue protruded a little – it was incredibly sexy. She seemed to be exuding gaiety, there was a vibrancy about her.

"You hear that?" she said, snuggling up to me. "I'm mysterious and romantic."

I gave her a long kiss, and Edward groaned. "If you two are going to behave like that, I want my money back," he said, adding, "Talking of money, someone from Darwin rang this afternoon, asking for you. He wants to book you lot for their May Ball. I've got his details back at SG."

Excellent. That made it two May Balls ARP would be performing at. Our advertisements and leaflets were doing their work.

Others arrived. Drinks were bought. The air soon grew thick with jokes and badinage. As our table became an island of hilarity I felt that everything was very right with the world. Here I was in the company of good friends. People I trusted, people I was at ease with, people I could laugh with, people I could talk seriously with. I felt I was part of something that was important and fine and good, something that should be preserved as a permanent part of my life.

What had brought on this feeling? Not only the beer, though I certainly liked sinking a pint or two; not only the cushioned – some would say privileged – existence of university life, though I liked the freedom and diversity it offered; not only the jokes and wisecracking, though there's something luxurious about sustained laughter. No, more than these things. It's Alex, Rob, the two E's, and a bunch of other guys and girls, and Melanie, oh God yes, Melanie.

It's being with these people, being a part of these people, having a part in their lives and they all having a part in my life. What convoluted sequence of events in all of our lives had resulted in our being there, that evening, drinking and talking and laughing together? The outcome of innumerable decisions and contingencies and unpredictable confluences and random occurrences, involving not only us but a whole raft of unknown others, the tracking of which and whom was impossible. How strange that my being there, that evening, with Melanie, was almost infinitely improbable. Yet there I was. There she was.

What of the future? What of five years' time? Ten, twenty years? Where will Alex be? What will Rob be doing? Will we still be in contact? One thing's for sure – we won't be here, not all three of us, even if one or both of the other two stay on to do research, I won't be here. This is all ephemeral, passing, unpindownable. The desired permanence is so precarious. How the hell can it be that all this, which feels intensely real – one of Melanie's favourite words, I've noticed – will disappear? It's disappearing even now, every single second it's vanishing, tick, tick, tick. I don't want it to vanish; I don't want the present to become the past. I want it to be a permanent present. And Melanie, oh Melanie – in ten years' time, twenty years' time, what of us? Will I return one day to Cambridge as a visitor and think, oh yes, when I was at university here, I went out with a girl called...what was her name? Oh yes, Melanie. That was it. Melanie.

"Hey," her voice broke in, and with relief I found myself back in the cellars with music, laughter, drink, friends...and Melanie poking me in the ribs. "You're miles away. Sorry if I'm boring company! Come on," she added, standing up, "let's dance."

Melanie was on good form. She danced energetically, crazily, sexily, throwing herself about. These Saturday evening discos were rendered slightly bizarre by the fact that at the same time as the music pounded away in the cellars, the Christian Union held its weekly meeting, what they called a Bible Reading, in the debating chamber above. You paid your money and you took your choice: descend to the depths for drink, dancing and debauchery, or ascend to the empyrean for spiritual exhortation. Melanie had confessed that in her first year she'd come to the Bible Readings – which sounded suspiciously like they were extended sermons – several times, stoutly maintaining in the face of my cynical comments that it had usually been very good and thought-provoking.

"If you mock me about it any more," she'd said, herself in mock threatening mode, "I'll deal with you like I dealt with that rugby moron and dump you on the ground."

"Promises, promises," I'd said.

Now as we danced she yelled, "I agree it's much better down here than..." she pointed to the ceiling, then put her hands together in the standard prayer position to refer to the pure and applied God-bothering under way up in the Union's debating chamber. I gave her a thumbs up, and she grabbed my hand and started kissing the thumb erotically. I did not want to continue dancing. I wanted to leave with her. I wanted to make love with her.

It was only three days since our long conversation on the Backs, when she'd told me about Simon, her old boyfriend, or whatever designation he should be given, a conversation which had ended memorably with her executing a perfect judo throw on the rugger bugger.

On our way back to Girton that evening she'd continued with her account of the complications over Simon. After she'd written to him on the morning of the Dorothy Ballroom party, saying she wasn't going to be his girlfriend anymore, she'd received his letter in response on the Thursday morning, the very day we'd arranged to meet at the Friar House in the evening. His letter, in her words, had made her feel, "*sooo* guilty! He wrote how I meant everything to him, and how I was the centre of his life and how precious I was, and what we'd been through together and how we'd grown together and all that sort of stuff, and how he needed me and wanted us to be married one day so he could cherish me for ever and and and – and yuk! It was all rather sickening."

"Must remember not to say those sorts of things," I'd said.

"Oh no!" she'd cried out. "I'd love *you* to say them! It's just I didn't want *him* to. I knew I had to sort it out immediately, face to face, before I saw you again."

So she'd gone back home early and on up to Bristol to see Simon where he was at university. Try as she did, she hadn't been able to get through to him how she felt. She'd told him about me, how we'd met and fallen in love, but he simply didn't take it on board, saying she was fooling herself, and all through the Christmas holidays the situation had remained unresolved.

"It only changed," she'd concluded, "when Anne stepped in. She went round to see him, I discovered, and she must have given him a huge piece of her mind, which is saying something, because I didn't see him or hear from him again until after I got back here. I was still all messed up over it. The first couple of weeks of term I was really low, I thought I was going to crash again. Then he wrote what I must say was the kindest letter imaginable. I don't know what had brought about the change – well, maybe I do, because he put in it that he'd been praying hard about it and had been guided – that's how he put it – to let me go my own way."

"How magnanimous of him!"

"There's no need to be like that," she'd said sharply. "He wished me well and said he only wanted what is best for me. He even put in his letter that he'd like to meet you sometime."

"To kick me in the goolies?" I'd asked, but that apparently was not the case. It was just that, "he thinks you're a very lucky person," Melanie had said reprovingly, "and, well, maybe he wants to make sure you're not some kind of sex fiend!"

"Oh, but I am!" I'd told her.

"Goody!" she'd laughed.

The letter had had the effect of making her feel released, which was when she'd felt able to write to me, asking to meet at the Whim.

I wasn't sure I'd followed it all exactly, this on-off business with Simon whatever-his-name-was. Nevertheless the central message came through loud and clear, and it was the message I'd wanted to hear. Whatever entanglements she'd previously been in, Melanie now felt free of them. Free for us to be together. Free for her to love me and me to love her.

Aware of all this as we danced in the Union Cellar on a Saturday night to Slade, the Stones, Jeff Beck and other great music, I felt exultant. Who knows what sort of degree I was going to get, whether or not Air Raid Precautions could continue post-Cambridge, how I would earn a living – but one thing was certain: I'd have Melanie, and she'd have me.

We returned to the table after a long dance to find Alex talking with a girl who had very long, very straight blonde hair and pale lips. There was something Scandinavian about her features, and she was nodding vigorously at some remark of Alex's. I wondered if he had just unleashed one of La Rochefoucauld's bon mots.

"Hiya, Sarah! Thought you weren't coming!" Melanie greeted her.

"Hiya, Melanie. In the end I decided, why not?" Her accent, far from being Scandinavian, was similar to Melanie's south-east London, only slightly posher. "Just because Dave's a complete jerk doesn't mean I can't come and enjoy myself and make new friends. Which I'm doing. Aren't I?" She addressed her rhetorical question to Alex.

"She's a Flaubert aficionado!" Alex offered. "At Newnham."

"Ah, learning from the expert," I said.

"She certainly is," agreed Alex.

"It was *you* I was speaking to," I said.

Sarah gave an abrupt laugh and said, "You got it!" She resumed talking with Alex, who looked completely captivated.

We had several more dances in between more rounds of drink, badinage and bad jokes with the others, then as the others started to leave, Alex and Sarah together, we too took our departure.

On the way back to Girton I told her I was crazy about her and that I'd never felt that way before. She asked me why I loved her. I said that I couldn't quite say, I didn't have a checklist that I'd ticked things off against and she'd scored ninety-nine point nine per cent or something. I loved her because I loved her and because she was who she was.

We'd stopped walking, and despite it being cold I was feeling randy, and I put my hand inside her coat and fondled her breasts through her clothes, and she started sighing and gasping, and saying that what I did to her was unbelievable. We were pressed up against each other, and under the cover of our coats she unzipped me and took me in hand, almost making me come on the spot.

"I want this inside me," she whispered.

We hurried back to Girton as quickly as the arousing circumstances allowed, and she sneaked me into the college, and along to her room, where we stripped off and tumbled into bed. A few seconds later I tumbled out of bed again to retrieve the packet of johnnies from my trousers, and soon afterwards I was, at last, as fully inside her as it's possible to be.

Chapter 32

Emhalt: June 1967

"He's at the front with Old Brillo and some others," Anne announced, suddenly reappearing and startling Melanie. "To be on the safe side, why don't you put some boot polish on your face and tear off a bit of that bush and disguise yourself as a tree? Birnam Wood to St Barnabas hath come."

"Idiot," said Melanie. "But thanks. You go back in first."

"Follow me," said Anne.

As they entered, two of the junior Followers competed to hand them a service sheet, a hymn book and a hated chorus book. Melanie took a service sheet from one of the juniors, a hymn book from the other, and a chorus book from each of them.

The main body of the hall was filled with rows and rows of tubular-framed chairs with green canvas seats and backs, and behind them several rows of collapsible wooden chairs. Many of the green chairs were occupied, only a few of the wooden ones were. Groups of Followers and adults were standing around, and the whole place was loud with talk and laughter and shouts punctuated by crashes and twangs from an amplified guitar. A knot of figures, in which Melanie could see Simon, had formed near the front, and on the platform, above which hung a banner announcing with blatant possessive inaccuracy, "EMHALT & DISTRICT FOLLOWER'S 45th ANNIVERSARY", Madam Skull and Old Brillo were talking with a tall, elegantly dressed man in his thirties whose beard, unlike Old Brillo's, clung tightly to his chin, cheeks and upper lip. Melanie recognised him from newspaper photographs as the Reverend Derek Cranbrook, spiritual leader of the 'Movement of the Spirit' and today's guest speaker. Kenny was at the piano, practising.

Melanie and Anne joined a small group of their friends at the side of the hall, talking about the charts and what might be on *Pick of the Pops* later.

A few minutes later a crashing sound from the PA system made them all jump, then Old Brillo's amplified and distorted voice echoed round the hall.

"Hello, hello? Testing, er, ah, testing."

"Why do they always say 'testing, testing'?" Anne complained. "Why can't anyone think of anything more original?"

"Could you, um, be seated please, everyone. We are, er, starting in five... Oh, what's happened?" His voice had suddenly dropped to an unamplified level. "Hello?" Several bangs came over the PA as he tapped the microphone with a fingernail. "Can, er, you hear me? Ah, um, that's better. We are going to start in, er, five minutes, could, er, you please take your seats."

"And put them on the chairs provided," said Anne. Melanie recognised the line from a radio comedy show.

There was a general movement towards sitting down, and the small group made its collective way to a row of the tubular-framed chairs.

Madam Skull and Old Brillo were up on the platform with the guest speaker. After a few more minutes as latecomers found seats, Old Brillo stood up and advanced to the front of the platform where he blew his nose. The sound was amplified by the PA system, and several people laughed. Mrs Armitage frowned. Old Brillo pocketed his handkerchief and held up his hands in a restraining gesture. The hubbub in the hall died down to an expectant hush. The hymn tune which Kenny had been continuing to play softly now drifted into silence.

"I would like to, ah, welcome you all in the name of our Lord, um, Jesus Christ to this special anniversary, er, service," Old Brillo announced, leaning forward into the microphone, his voice making a series of little plosive sounds. "Shall we all bow our, um, heads to ask his blessings on, er, these proceedings. Let us, er, pray."

Chapter 33

Phil

Cambridge: March 1972

At the end of term Melanie's father came to collect her. Knowing he'd arrive sometime, I wasn't surprised when he knocked on the open door of her room and walked in. I was surprised, however, by his baggy trousers, highly chromatic pullover and tennis shoes. My idea of a GP wore a sober suit and brogues. Behind him was an incredibly thin chap with dishevelled carroty hair and the beginnings of a pale beard. He was wearing jeans and a bomber jacket. I recognised him from the framed photo in the room as her brother.

"Anyone at home?" Chromatic Pullover asked. "Oh, hello! Any daughter of mine around?"

"Melanie? She's just returning some books to the library."

"Right. Good. I'm her father."

"I gathered."

"Ah!" he said genially, extending a hand to shake. "The benefits of a Cambridge education! Call me Roger."

"Phil."

"No, Roger! Ha, ha! This is Mikey. He's come along for the ride."

"Are you her boyfriend?" Mikey asked. He had a slightly whiny voice and looked incredibly grumpy, with Melanie's pout magnified ten times.

"Yep!" I nodded.

"Does Simon know about him?" he whined at his father. He had his hands thrust into his jacket pockets and was rocking backwards and forwards on his heels as though preparing for a hazardous standing jump.

"More to the point, does her mother know?" Melanie's father grinned at me. "Which college are you at, Phil?"

"Pembroke."

"Excellent choice! I'm a Pembroke man myself."

"Great!"

"Pembroke, Oxford, that is!"

"Oh, hard luck."

"I was going to say the same to you!" He gave me a gentle punch on the shoulder. "What are you reading?"

"Nat. Sci. Third year."

"Good for you. Hope you're enjoying it. Now where has that daughter of mine got to?"

"Right behind you," said Melanie. "Hello, Daddy!"

They hugged, then she hugged Mikey and said it was lovely he'd come as well, and he stopped looking grumpy. She turned to me and put a hand on my arm.

"Phil, would you mind making us all some coffee while I finish packing?"

"Yeah, sure."

"Mikey, can you help Phil?"

As we went along the corridor to the kitchen, Mikey said, "Aren't you afraid Simon might kill you?"

"What?"

"You know Simon?"

"Of him. Never met him. Why would he want to kill me?"

"'Cause he's in love with my sis as well. That's what you do when you both love the same woman. You have to fight to the death. Whoever kills the other one gets the girl."

"Don't think it's obligatory! Doesn't the girl get a say?"

"Or you have to kill yourself, like Romeo and Juliet. They kill themselves, don't they? You have to enter the dark realms."

I'd put the kettle on and was taking coffee and mugs from Melanie's cupboard, wondering what the hell to say to all this.

"I've been in the dark realms," he announced.

"Yeah?"

"Yeah."

"Died a few times myself," I said.

"Hey, wow! Have you?" His whining completely vanished and he sounded unnecessarily enthusiastic. "You've died? Fantastic! Wow!"

"On stage," I said. "When I've been performing."

"You're dead? You've died and you're dead? That's fantastic. I'm dead as well. I have been all my life."

"On *stage*," I emphasised. "Died on stage. It's a saying. It means I didn't get the laughs I thought I would. It doesn't mean I've shuffled off this mortal whatsit. I'm not an ex-parrot."

"Hey! I like you!" Mikey said. "You know what it means to be dead. I like you."

As we went back with the coffee, Mikey kept chuntering on about death and dying. "He's dead as well," he announced gleefully, re-entering the room. Melanie and her father both looked startled.

"Just said I've died a few times on stage," I explained. "That's all."

"Whoops," said Melanie.

"He knows what it means. I like him!" Mikey continued chuntering.

"Not to worry," Melanie's father said to me, then to Mikey, "Come on old chap. Why don't we drink up. You and I can go for a walk in the grounds, and let Melanie finish her packing in peace, and these two can make their goodbyes in private. All right, angel?"

"Thanks, Daddy. It won't take long."

"Sorry about that," I said when they'd gone. "Have I put my foot in it?"

"No, it's all right. You weren't to know. I should've warned you, but I didn't know he was coming. I expect my mother insisted."

"What's with this death fixation?"

Melanie was distractedly walking round the room, picking up things and putting them at random into a couple of suitcases. "He's always been a bit weird," she said. "He's had this obsession with death for years."

"What started it?"

"No one really knows. Ever since I can remember he's collected things like sheep skulls or skeletons of birds, which my mother always makes him throw away." She sat next to me on the bed. "He now keeps some in the garden shed. I love him dearly, my big bruv, and I get worried about him. He's been on anti-psychotics for a while now."

"Sounds heavy."

"He seems to have taken to you, which is nice."

"He has good taste!"

"Big-head!"

"Big something."

"I'd better finish my packing," she said a little while later. "They'll be back soon."

Chapter 34

Melanie

Exeter: March 1997

I've just dropped Simon off at the station. Whew. Time to reflect on last night.

The revue was amazing! The theatre was full, and well done Charlotte because she'd really rounded up the troops, with quite a contingent from Teignford, who know Phil in any case, but she'd also evidently issued a three-line whip to lots of her other contacts and they'd turned out in force.

The set resembled a cross between an old-time music hall and a sleazy nightclub, fronted by an androgynous-looking female MC in a tuxedo, with dreadlocks and stylised eyelash markings in white painted onto the skin below her eyes. The whole get-up looked louche and slightly menacing. The programme had the performer down as Natasha Nkomo. She oozed confidence as she delivered her lines (several of which I recognised as Phil's work), and when she'd finished her opening routine Chloe muttered, "Wow!"

For me, my heart could have burst with joy when Phil first came on and launched into his football commentator monologue of old, and he didn't disappoint! He was in practically every other item, except (thank goodness!) for the songs, and although all the cast were good, he was just great – I would say that, wouldn't I? There were several sketches from Cambridge days and a number of new ones, including 'Ambiguous Adjectives' which he delivered straight, and it went down a riot. He played the audience, as they say. One of the sketches by the Natasha woman was semi-familiar: it both was and wasn't the solo sketch I'd seen Phil's friend Alex perform several times, in which he'd interwoven sentences in Swahili with ludicrous English phrases. She was doing similar in what I guessed to be her mother tongue. Her delivery was faultless.

The other performers were also very slick, though one of them who was also the producer did mangle his lines sometimes – and even the mangling was funny in its way because he had a very resonant delivery, making it sound like a send-up of one of Shakespeare's more incomprehensible speeches.

During the interval Chloe and I were in the bar laughing together at the show so far when Phil appeared at the far end, spoke briefly with henna-haired cousin Sam, saw us, gave a double thumbs up which I reciprocated, and disappeared again.

"He's looking good," Chloe said. "Don't you think?"

"You might be amused to know," I said, "that Simon thought you and Phil might hit it off."

"Romantically?"

"Mmm. That's one reason you were invited the other week."

"Is that what was going on?" she said very slowly. "I must say I was picking up very mixed messages from him. I wasn't sure whether he was genuinely interested in me, or whether it was for show because...well, just because. I can't see him being interested in any woman except one." She looked at me meaningfully, putting her hand on my arm. "You don't have to say anything." Her voice dropped right down. "Plead the fifth amendment if you like."

I nodded. "Another time."

"Sure. In case you're wondering, I did drop heavy hints to Phil that he's not my type. Nothing against him, lovely bloke as you'll agree, though he's a bit full of himself, isn't he? But, well, he's male, not my type. If you understand me."

Again I nodded. "Phil told me he'd picked up your hints."

"Good!" Again she looked at me meaningfully. "I didn't think he could miss them." She gave me a dazzling smile, squeezed my arm, and said, in her particularly husky tones, "Don't worry, honey, I'm not hitting on you either! You're also not quite my type!"

"Ditto!" I told her, and we had a quick hug of understanding.

We returned to the auditorium. As Natasha stepped onto the stage to begin the second half, now in the guise of a sullen Goth, looking about nineteen or twenty, Chloe whispered, "Now she's more my type!"

"Bit young for you, isn't she?" I whispered back.

"Appearances can be deceptive! I like a bit of deception!"

At the end of the show there was masses of applause, and as we all filed out of our seats loads of money was going into the collecting buckets. Simon was in very good spirits on top of his habitual cheerfulness; he'd been laughing practically non-stop, and I saw him toss in several fivers. "Very good!" he kept saying. "That was very good!"

"Come on," Charlotte said, organising us, "let's go and find Phil. We must tell him how good it's been!" With others of the Teignford contingent we made our way backstage where there was already a considerable scrum. Phil was with Sam, who had an arm round his waist at the same time as holding the hand of another man. Phil turned and saw us, and disengaged himself from her to push his way through to us. His hair was all over the place and his black shirt had become unbuttoned almost to his waist. We were all congratulating him. Jimmy, who had been chortling non-stop, switched to repeating, "Good show! Good show!" and Simon was puffing out his cheeks and slapping Phil on the back as though they were blood brothers. Charlotte started to do up Phil's shirt buttons, but he backed away and collided with someone who cried out, "Careful, dear boy!" It turned out to be the show's producer who, making a bow to us, enquired of Phil, "Are these your camp followers, dear boy?"

"Not as camp as you, Tredders," Phil said.

"Really Philip, you're such a tease!" Then to us, "You are all very welcome! James Tredwell, author, thespian and producer, at your service!" at which Chloe pushed against me, laughing, and Jimmy switched from "Good show! Good show!" to "Thespian, eh? Know what I mean? Nudge! Nudge!" until Charlotte told him to shut up. At the same time Phil said, "Don't be such an arse, Tredders!" and the Tredwell man responded even more campishly, "I can't think *what* you mean, dear boy!" He didn't quite go, "Whoops, dearie!" and flail a limp wrist, but it was a close-run thing.

"Aren't you going to introduce me to these beautiful creatures?" he demanded, so Phil elaborately introduced us in turn (Chloe, however, had slipped away and was heading to where Natasha, now dressed in blue jeans and a check shirt, was leaning against a wall, looking rather amused). Tredders responded with, "Charmed!", "Delighted!", "Enchanted!" and the like. He asked how we knew Phil, "Our drama king – you don't object to being called a drama king, do you dear boy?"

"We live in the same village," Charlotte said before Phil could respond.

Tredders gave a theatrical gasp, clapped his hands and said, "*Such* a concentration of beauty in one village! I'm amazed it hasn't exploded!"

"We don't live there," I said. "Simon and I live in Heavitree."

"Through what arcane channels have you come to be acquainted with our esteemed scribe?" Tredders asked.

"Cambridge," Phil said. "While I was hacking my way to a lower second, Melanie was serenely sailing to a starred first."

Tredders bowed again to me, saying, "Brains as well as beauty! A potent combination! Just as well I am happily spoken for. However, my dears, I must move on. People to see, hands to shake, plays to produce." After reminding us of future productions he went off to greet other 'dear boys' and 'dear ladies'.

"Is he always like that?" demanded Charlotte.

"Only when he's doing theatre," Phil said. "Don't be fooled by all that 'dear boy' stuff – it's all an act to go with the role of actor-producer. He claims it makes him feel the part better. I think he just likes poncing about."

Jimmy asked if he were a professional actor, and Phil laughed. "God no! In real life he's an estate agent. Put him in a theatre and he becomes battier than a batty bat from Batchester, but he's a damned good producer. Now, come on everyone, don't be shy – did you like this evening's offering?" and we all chorused that we had.

"What was that black woman on about?" Charlotte said. "The thing she did in the first half. The gibberish thing."

"Natasha? It's not gibberish, it's Xhosa," Phil said, clicking his tongue. "She's South African."

"Quite funny," Jimmy said. "Funny in its way. Its way. Did you like it, Charlie? Like it?"

"My favourite," Charlotte said, "was Phil losing a contact lens. What a hoot!"

I longed to be able to talk with Phil on his own, which wasn't really possible with everyone milling around; but as we were leaving through the stage door into Barnfield Road, I managed to slip back inside, making up something about having left my water bottle behind. There were still a lot of people around, including Chloe talking with Natasha – she had her hand on Natasha's arm. Natasha seemed to be enjoying the attention, smiling and biting her lip and writhing in the way you do when you're not good at receiving compliments. Phil was up on the stage again with Sam and some others.

Sam gave an impish smile as I joined them, then took me totally by surprise by kissing me. "I gather you're taking good care of my coz," she whispered.

"I think he can take care of himself," I said.

She looked doubtful. "Most of the time. He has his moments. Don't you, coz?"

"It has been known," Phil said.

"Anyway," Sam turned back to me, "what did you think of the show?"

"Brilliant!" I said. "Wonderful!"

"How did it compare with other times you've seen him?"

"He's as good as I remember," I said. "Even better, perhaps. How about you – have you seen him perform before?"

Sam gave a sardonic laugh. "He was always the joker at family gatherings. And you sometimes did turns at our village entertainments, didn't you?" She nudged him. "This," she told me, "was vastly better. Right, I'm going to make a noise like a bee and buzz off, leaving you two to say goodbye. Bye Melanie. See you tomorrow, coz."

"Bye," I said. I turned back to Phil. "Tomorrow?"

"Cheers, Sam. Yeah, Tom has to be here. Her husband. He's the gaffer. Chief electrician. She's coming with him for a second dose."

"Me too," I said. "You know Simon'll be away at his reunion?"

"Yeah," he nodded slowly. "I hadn't forgotten. I was hoping you'd be able to come again. You know there'll be an aftershow party? Here, backstage. A bit of a booze-up and celebration."

"Sounds good."

"It will be if you're there. Will you come as my partner?"

"I'd love to!" I said.

Chapter 35

Phil

Keswick: March 1972

"Fantastic," Melanie sighed as, bags safely stowed away, we flopped down on seats in a sparsely occupied carriage. "We made it!"

"Piece of cake," I said nonchalantly. "With time to spare."

"Ha! About two minutes!"

"Two and a half minutes," I corrected her solemnly but inaccurately.

"Pedant!"

"Strictly speaking, pedant means…oof!"

Melanie, having slapped me, giggled. "Sorry, did that hurt?"

"Not at all."

"Pity, it was meant to!"

The train gathered speed. We were on our way to the Lake District, and we talked idly for a little while about what we might do that evening, and where we might go the next day, knowing that all plans were as flexible as we wished. When we eventually fell silent, we simultaneously took out our books.

"What you got?" Melanie asked.

I showed her John Wyndham's *The Chrysalids* and a book containing the scripts of *Beyond the Fringe.* Also in my bags were a couple of pharmacology textbooks, the contents of which I planned to assimilate by a process of intellectual osmosis.

"You?" I asked. She held up Hermann Hesse's *Siddhartha.* "Plus I've got *Revelations of Divine Love,*" she added.

"Lucky old you," I said. "Hope they're good ones."

"It's a book! Julian of Norwich. A mediaeval mystic. She had a series of revelations about Christ on the cross."

"*She?*"

"A woman. Took her name from the church her cell was attached to."

"Think I'll stick with John Wyndham."

We settled down to read. Soon I was gazing unseeingly out of the window, thinking about Melanie. She was amazing: fun, attractive, sexy, intelligent, sweet, sensitive – with one bit that didn't click for me. Her involvement with religion. Not that she was heavy about it; she wasn't terribly pious or Bible-bashing, and I didn't know if she still went to church or to her college chapel – I was fairly sure she didn't, at least not regularly. On the other hand, she clearly liked to read about it, serious stuff too.

My involvement with matters religious began and ended with school assemblies and scripture lessons. Sure, I knew what everybody knows about the basic Christmas story, angels and wise men and all that; and I also knew the gist of what the Church claims happened at Easter – but really! How could anyone believe it these days as having happened in the way the Bible says? Despite not being a very good scientist, I had no doubt that the scientific way of working out how and why the universe works as it does is the correct way. Old-style religious explanations from the pre-scientific era just don't hold water. God, the devil, angels, people walking on water, miracles, a dead man coming back to life – no, sorry, how could any rational person believe that? But Melanie, I assumed, believed something along those lines, and she wasn't stupid. Far from it. What exactly did she believe? She rejected the label God-botherer, saying it was the other way round, and though she was serious and thoughtful about it, it didn't stop her being fun and fun-loving, at least with me.

Would our differences affect what we had between us? No, why should they? There'd never been any indication that she would try to convert me; and atheist though I was, it didn't bother me that she was religious. It just slightly bemused me.

I returned to John Wyndham.

"Two single rooms," pronounced the middle-aged landlady of Roselea Guest House as she closed the front door and bustled us into the dining room, all stripy wallpaper and Formica-topped tables, where she took what turned out to be a register from a desk drawer and opened it. I didn't know her name. A small woman with a big nose, and dressed in bright green clothes, the appellation 'Mrs Parakeet' would suit her. Her resemblance to the bird was intensified by her tilting her head slightly to one side when she spoke. Regrettably she didn't squawk.

"Name of Mason?" she asked.

"That's right," Melanie confirmed.

"And Mr?" She turned her beak and beady eye on me.

"Ellis. Phil Ellis."

"Well, Miss Mason, Mr Ellis, your rooms are ready. If you could both just sign in, I'll take you up. You're on the first floor."

Rooms, plural: Melanie had made the arrangements for our time away, confessing to me afterwards that she'd booked two single rooms, though we'd agreed we'd have a double.

"I felt uncomfortable when I rang about it," she'd explained over a drink in the Union bar, "sort of half-expecting that if I'd asked for a double room, I would've been cross-questioned about whether we were married and all that."

"None of anyone else's business."

"I know. It's daft. I just felt that way, and I would've stammered and gone all, you know, and I would've felt really guilty."

"Ah," I'd teased her, wagging a finger. "The pernicious effects of religion. Makes you feel guilty whatever you do. Whoa, sinner! Thou shalt be cast into the everlasting pit of the damned!"

"Don't, Phil!" she'd said. I didn't pursue it.

We followed Mrs Parakeet up a staircase, its walls laden with paintings and photos of the lakes. At the turn of the stairs she pointed at a mighty stuffed perch mounted in a glass case.

"My husband," she said, which sounded biologically implausible until I realised she'd indicated a little brass plaque attached to the glass case enlightening the casual but curious passer-by as to the where, when and by whom the perch had been outwitted. Bassenthwaite featured in the information.

"Many people staying at the moment?" Melanie asked.

"Indeed yes, my dear. We're full at present." Mrs Parakeet, or possibly Bassenthwaite, stopped on reaching the first-floor landing, panting slightly. "Now, we do have a slight problem. It's nothing to worry about, dear. We've had to close off one of the single rooms – problems with a little bit of damp."

"Not surprising with all these lakes around," I offered. Melanie turned to shush me, but Mrs Parakeet-Bassenthwaite didn't seem to have heard as she went to a door and opened it.

"Here you are, this is one of them." She beckoned us along. "It's quite a nice little room."

I looked in over Melanie's shoulder, putting my hand on her bottom at the same time. She pressed back onto it.

'Quite a nice little room' was a reasonably accurate description: it was indubitably a room, it was nice in that it was not positively nasty, and it was certainly little. Verging on the epitome of littleness. Squeezed into it were a bed (single), a dressing table (Hornby 00 size) and a wardrobe (ditto) with a long mirror on its door. There was so little space in which to turn or manoeuvre that anyone entering the room facing away from the bed would presumably have to sleep standing up in the wardrobe. My heart sank. If the other room were similar, we'd have to do a lot of sneaky furniture reorganisation – mattresses on the floor in one room, everything else stashed in the other. Melanie wriggled her bottom against my hand, which I interpreted as a sign of dismay.

"Right, thanks," she said in a neutral voice.

"This is the other one I've put you in," Mrs P-B said, going further along the landing and opening another door. "I'm afraid," she added apologetically, head tilted right over, "it's a double. The other single you were to have had is the one that we've had to close off, and I don't have another single available, but I'll not charge you any more for a double. Just for two singles, like you booked."

We looked in. A total contrast to the other room. Large and decorated in light, cheerful colours, with items of furniture dotted about, a small washbasin in one corner, and a great expansive view of hills through the large window. Best of all was the bed. It was decidedly, beyond all possibility of gainsaying, double. Verging on triple. It had a fancy headboard, a fancy footboard, and fancy frills round the edges of the mattress. A valance, Melanie told me later.

My hand was back on Melanie's bottom. This time her quick wriggle conveyed delight.

"It's lovely," Melanie said faintly.

"Excellent!" I said, following her into the room. "Totally transuranic!"

Mrs P-B smiled uncertainly, handed over room and front door keys, told us where to find the bathroom, gave us the times between which breakfast would be served, adding, somewhat superfluously, "in the morning", and left us to it.

Melanie clapped her hands and started pirouetting around, her hair swirling out in an aureole. She was really fizzing; being with her was like opening a shaken-up bottle of Coke. Her eyes were shining. "This is wonderful, and I have you all to myself for a whole week. No lectures, supervisions, cabarets – just us!"

She threw her arms round my neck and we lurched crazily around the room before toppling onto the bed.

"It's a brilliant room," I panted, lying half on top of her. I unhooked her arms from behind my neck, and held her down on the bed by the wrists. She gave a perfunctory wriggle. "With a simply transuranic bed!" We kissed.

"I think," she gasped on resurfacing from the kiss, "it needs road-testing. The bed. Just to make sure it can take the strain." She rolled free from me, pushed me onto my back and started fumbling at the belt of my trousers. "I couldn't stop thinking about doing this for most of the journey!" she added, giving one of her raucous snorts of laughter.

"I might not be called Julian," I warned her as she struggled to free me from my underpants, "but stand by for another revelation."

"Divine!" she giggled as she succeeded.

Chapter 36

Melanie

Exeter: March 1997

The best thing in the entire world must surely be waking up slowly after a long deep sleep, with your lover snuggled up to you, holding you and kissing the top of your shoulders. I didn't even go through a period of having to remember I was in bed with Phil; I knew it even as I started to move out of sleep, as though the one constant in my life has been to wake up every morning with him beside me.

He murmured something I didn't quite catch, and a moment later his hand had come beneath my arm and cupped my right breast, and I felt him pressing against my bottom. I don't know how long we stayed snuggled like that, with me drifting along in that languid state where you think you're awake but begin to realise you're floating through some dreamscape and the thoughts you're having are totally Alice-in-Wonderland-ish. I'd been on a stage with Chloe in a vast arena singing sixties hits for an indeterminate period when I heard the word 'tea' coming from a great distance, and I slowly realised I wasn't headlining a 1960s pop concert but was still in bed with Phil who'd asked me something.

I shifted onto my back and made the kind of noise of enquiry you make when you don't feel like formulating actual words.

"Shall I make some tea?" he muttered, evidently not for the first time. I still couldn't work out how to speak. I made a noise of assent, and he kissed me on the lips before sliding out of bed. He was naked, and speech came back to me as he took from the back of the door the reddish-brown dressing gown that Simon never wears which is why it's in the spare room, but nevertheless it is Simon's and I didn't want to see Phil in it. I managed to mumble, "No, not that one. Get mine from the main bedroom."

I could track his movements by various sounds – in and out of the other bedroom, down the stairs, the creak of the kitchen door, the noise of the kettle being filled. The next sound I became aware of was the clunk of a mug being placed on the bedside table.

"Hello, beautiful," Phil said.

He climbed back into bed. I struggled to a sitting position, with him propping up pillows behind me. We drank our tea slowly and in silence.

"It was wonderful last night," I finally said.

"The revue?" he asked. "Or the post-revue party? Or the post-post-revue-party-fun-and-games?"

"All of them," I said. "Especially the last!"

Seeing the revue a second time, but on my own, had been really special. Watching it I could imagine being back at Cambridge that first time I saw Phil performing with Alex and Rob at some party. All so long ago – yet here I was, watching him performing once more, and fancying him like mad. Still crazy...

Afterwards, at the aftershow party "to celebrate the end of a truly stupendous run of theatrical and comedic brilliance" (to quote the utterly mad but rather fun James Tredwell, or 'Tredders' as he insists on being called, complete in a ludicrous Cavalier-style floppy hat with half a dozen pheasant feathers sticking up from it. "Don't mind me, dear lady, I'm a pheasant plucker and a Spoonerist to boot," he informed me at one stage, stroking the feathers suggestively, then he did say, "Whoops!" and flapped a bent wrist. Which, as Phil said, proves without doubt that he isn't in the slightest bit gay). So there I was, at the party, drinking champers (well, some cheapo substitute), laughing and chatting with people I'd never met before, taken by them as being Phil's partner, and me being bold enough (after three glasses) to slip my arm through Phil's. Risky I suppose, but I reckoned there was no one there who knew Simon.

At one point there was a terrific shriek, and we all looked round to see Natasha in the doorway of a changing room. She appeared not to have many clothes on, giving rise to a loud – mainly male – cheer, which Phil joined in with along the lines of "Whoar!" I had to tell him to stop being a dirty old man and put his tongue back in his mouth. "Just window shopping," he said. Men! She reappeared fully dressed a few minutes later, looking unconcerned, and again wearing jeans and a cowboy shirt.

Tredders proposed toasts to all the members of the cast and backstage staff in turn, including a specific toast, "to Phil our august, nay inimitable, wordsmith and his delightful and pulchritudinous muse," at which I must have turned beetroot as they all cheered and roared and whooped, and Phil gave me a very sexy lingering kiss (in front of everyone), and Sam, her hair now falling loose on her back, put her fingers in her mouth and gave a piercing whistle. Then Tredders congratulated everyone for raising thousands for Comic Relief, followed by more drink, and while going through the best bits of the show Tredders banged Phil on the back and gasped, "Christ, dear boy, I almost died when you fed me the wrong fucking line in the aubergine number." He and Phil clung onto each other laughing helplessly.

Sam, standing next to me at the time, whispered, "You will handle him with care, won't you? He's very precious."

He's gone back to the theatre to help with the clear-up, and then he'll head back to Teignford. I must record something of what we talked about as we sat up in bed drinking yet more tea this morning. He asked what I'd normally be doing on a Sunday morning, and I said it could be anything from pottering around doing house things, working in the garden, reading, making phone calls, going for a walk...and that Simon normally goes to the cathedral for the service.

"Not you?"

"I rarely go," I told him. "I like choral evensong, and go quite a lot to that, but not to Sunday services. I don't like the liturgy."

He touched my cross. "You still wear this? Why?"

"Because it's important to me."

He repeated, "Why?"

It's always difficult to explain that simply, so I told him it's because it symbolises that this life is just a part of a much deeper existence, and holding on to that awareness is the most important thing I know. He nodded and said, "Possible sublimity?"

"You remembered?" I said.

"How could I forget?"

"It's not all about possible sublimity," I said. "It's a mistake to think that religion and spirituality are just about private experiences. What's *really* important is how you are in the world. The people dimension."

"What d'you mean?"

"You know Rita? Rita Roth? She got me into doing TALC, the adult literacy thing."

"What about her?"

"She's really impressive. She doesn't make a song and dance about it, but I gather that as well as doing TALC once a week, she's a prison visitor, and she helps with a refuge for homeless young women. It's a practical spirituality."

"You don't have to believe in God to do that sort of stuff!" Phil protested.

"Of course you don't. But anyone who does is doing God-work, even if they don't know it! It's far more important than having nice private spiritual experiences or claiming you've got a direct line to God."

"Okay, what about the other religious stuff?" Phil asked. "Like life after death. Is that something you believe in?"

"I believe there must be something beyond this life, yes, but don't ask me to describe it because I can't. Nobody can."

"Why believe it? What's the evidence?"

"It's not a scientific theory, you know. It's not something you can test by experiment to prove or disprove. It's more an attitude to life, to do with accepting the continuing connections between all things, past, present and future."

I told him about my archipelago image, that all our separate individual consciousnesses are connected in the same way that all the islands of an archipelago like Polynesia are connected, but because of the sea we see them as individual islands. If the sea level were to fall, we'd see that all the islands are simply peaks rising from the same land mass. I have this sense that death is like the sea level falling, and in death we discover that every single spark of consciousness in the world is simply a part of a vast continent of consciousness.

Phil picked up on the obvious, that death is the *end* of consciousness, to which all I could say was that I believed some aspect of us endures, our fragment of the underlying continent. The ground of being. It goes beyond words, that's the problem. Only partial metaphors will do. It's also, as I pointed out to him, what the mystics of all ages and all religions have struggled to articulate.

I don't think I explained it very well, and Phil kept asking, "Where's the evidence?" which rather misses the point because it assumes that the scientific approach can be applied to everything. As I said to him, science by definition can only deal with *physical* reality – any claim that science can disprove religion and spirituality is invalid, because it's a presupposition of science that it deals with the material aspects of existence. It can't deal with spirituality, ethics, meaning, purpose. The important stuff.

He hit me with a pillow and called me a religious fanatic, and I hit him back with another pillow and called him a scientific pedant, then we made love again which, we agreed afterwards, clearly demonstrated that science and religion are perfectly compatible.

Chapter 37

Phil

Keswick: March 1972

"Skiddaw," Melanie said in answer to my question as to what we should do that day. Opening a little guidebook she read out, "'The ascent of Skiddaw from Keswick is easy, and…' de dum de dum… 'Skiddaw is and undoubtedly always will be one of the favourite mountain ascents in the country'."

"Okay, if it's not too strenuous, I'm willing to give it a bash," I said.

"Give it a bash!" Melanie cried, hitting me with the book and exaggerating her London accent. "What sort of way is that to talk? This is yer actual Romantic country, mate! Yer don't think Wordsworth said to Dorothy, c'mon gal, let's give Skiddaw *a bash* today, do yah?"

"Melanie, sweet, I thee implore," I declaimed, "to bash me not, we'll climb Skiddaw! Anyway," I added, "it'll be good to stretch my legs. Make a change from stretching another part of my anatomy."

It was the fourth or fifth morning of our holiday and we were at a late breakfast in the dining room. On the previous days we'd strolled around Keswick, gone to Grasmere, had lakeside walks, visited the pubs. There were also long periods when we were silent together, reading, or just sitting by the edge of a lake and gazing across the water. I loved simply watching Melanie: the changing expressions in her eyes, the curve of her fingers at rest, the inviting swell of her breasts, the way she stroked her hair as if it needed reassuring. I was aware that she watched me as I sat, knees drawn up and arms wrapped around them, gazing into the middle distance as was my habit, or as I lay on my stomach reading or watching ants and beetles going about their mysterious insectile ways.

I felt we'd been abstracted from the linear course of time. We'd scrambled out of its rushing stream onto a large boulder, where we could rest or dance or sit or muse, and could look with astonishment at the tumult and turbulence from which we'd emerged. Or maybe we were still in the stream but had entered a vast looping slow-moving oxbow backwater of time in which we were gently floating at a totally different tempo. Time was not passing in the sense of our tramping along at an unvarying pace along the edge of some one-dimensional temporal ruler with marked divisions; it felt more like an exploration of an entire two-dimensional surface.

We stuffed our day-bags with rolls and cheese and tomatoes and fruit and biscuits and chocolate bars and cans of drink, and set off for Skiddaw. After about twenty minutes we began the ascent proper. A steep climb to begin with, we kept up a good pace. There was a piercing clarity to the air; the stillness of a world holding its breath, as Melanie put it.

"Look," she said, stopping and turning round. "Isn't that wonderful?"

I turned to look back the way we'd come. We could see down into Keswick, and just beyond it a glittering lake.

"Derwentwater," said Melanie.

I took her hand. She looked at me and smiled. "I don't know about you, but I feel a real sense of connection."

"What with?"

"Everything. The lake, this mountain, that bush," she pointed. "You too!"

We continued to climb, and of a sudden we entered a cloud or possibly a bank of mist. The transition from bright sun was surprisingly sharp; no gentle phasing in but a distinct boundary which could have been plotted to the nearest centimetre. It had also instantly become bitterly cold.

Curiously, a strong wind had sprung up which seemed to make no difference to the cloud. As we continued, the wind kept switching direction, one moment opposing our progress with a ferocity which threatened to blow us off our feet, and the next moment it'd swung round and seemed intent on carrying us to the summit of its own accord.

"You said the ascent of Skiddaw is easy," I gasped after a while. "Thank God it's not a difficult one."

"I didn't say it was easy. The book did."

"Who wrote it? Sisyphus?"

After we'd been climbing for what seemed like ages, the cloud fleetingly thinned, and looking down to our left we could make out another stretch of water.

"Bassenthwaite, I think," Melanie said.

"Where once swam the mighty perch," I said. "Our landlady's—"

"Look! Not far to go," she interrupted excitedly, pointing ahead. The top of Skiddaw had briefly emerged from the cloud, only to disappear the moment I glimpsed it.

We tramped on to the summit, cheered loudly on achieving it, then simultaneously groaned as, through the cloud cover, we could see ahead another, higher rising of the ground. We'd arrived at a false summit. We had to descend again for a while before re-ascending to what must be the real summit. Only, when we got there, it wasn't, but yet another illusion. And another one after that.

Because of the cloud there seemed to be a whole series of illusory summits before we finally reached the real one, where the cloud was at its densest and coldest. We peered suspiciously ahead for some while before accepting we'd arrived. "Well," said Melanie, guidebook in hand, "you'll be pleased to know that we can see Scotland and the Isle of Man from here."

"Provided you have X-ray vision and an active imagination," I said.

"Which in our case, we have not got," Melanie said dreamily.

"Let's go down," I said.

We half-walked, half-ran down the path, skidding and sliding on the scree, laughing and shouting, until we emerged from the cloud as abruptly as we had originally entered it.

"I'm hungry!" Melanie cried out.

"Me too!"

Clinging on to each other, still skidding and sliding, we veered off the scree, onto a patch of grass, and collapsed. Now we were out of the cloud, the sun dazzled.

"Time for a spot of culture," Melanie said after we'd eaten, fishing a book from her day-bag. "As we're in the Lake District, I've brought some Wordsworth."

"The only Wordsworth I remember from school is, er..."

"Don't tell me! 'Daffodils'?"

"Correct."

"Only that's not its proper title. And 'Intimations of Immortality'?"

"Don't know it."

"You must! 'Trailing clouds of glory' and all that."

"Oh, is that him?"

"Now listen to this." She'd found the page she wanted. "It comes from *The Prelude*. Do something with my hair, will you?"

"'Do something with my hair,'" I echoed, brushing back the tresses which kept flopping forward. "That's not very poetic." I kept my hand on the back of her neck, trapping her hair.

"Are you sitting comfortably?" she asked. "Then I'll begin." She began to recite in her clear, slightly over-articulated way:

> "I deem not profitless those fleeting moods
> Of shadowy exultation: not for this,
> That they are kindred to our purer mind
> And intellectual life; but that the soul,
> Remembering how she felt, but what she felt
> Remembering not, retains an obscure sense
> Of possible sublimity, to which,
> With growing faculties she doth aspire..."

She stopped reading and twisted round to look at me, repeating, "'An obscure sense of possible sublimity.' When I first read that, I had this incredible feeling that Wordsworth was talking straight to me. I felt – yes! That's it! 'Possible sublimity' – awareness of those tiny little moments which strike you from time to time when everything seems to be in harmony. Then," she sighed, "it goes again. You know it's been there, and it will be there again, sometime, if you're lucky, but you can't force it, can you?"

"Dunno. Not really sure what you mean."

She'd put down her book and was now lying on her back, shading her eyes. "It's a way of acknowledging...well, something important, the sense that there's an inner reality to things that every so often breaks through and we can have a brief glimpse, a brief experience, of, well, real reality, how all things are connected and and and there's a deep unity."

"Is that what you're saying you felt when we were looking across to Derwentwater?"

"Not quite. What I've said, this experience, is something that happens very rarely to me. I was feeling how lovely it was, and how peaceful, and there's a general sense that this real reality is *there* even though you're not fully experiencing it right now. It's a *possible* sublimity."

"Well," I said slowly, "I can look at something like that and feel peaceful, and see how lovely it is, and there've been loads of times when I've been out on Dartmoor at night when the sky's clear, and the stars are stunning and I feel wow, that's fantastic. It's even more fantastic when you know what's actually going on in stars, the incredible reactions that are taking place. I think that's what reality is."

"Yeees," she said, clearly meaning, 'no, not really'. "Yes, it is reality, but there's a deeper level. An interconnecting level. It's not just to do with what we automatically think of as beautiful and incredible and awe-inspiring, but everything, however everyday we might think it is. For instance..." she added, "when I was eight, I was on holiday with my family in Scotland, Loch Lomond, and one afternoon we were having a picnic by the loch and I had this immense experience, like a visitation, of suddenly seeing everything connected with everything else by what looked like strands of fire, and a sense of being told that everything would come right, I didn't have to worry. I don't mean I heard a voice in the sky or anything like that, just this inner conviction. A complete certainty. I think it only lasted a few seconds, though I think of it as a 'moment'. A moment out of time. In real time it was a couple of minutes at most, though at the time it felt endless. Then it faded away, but the memory of it has stayed with me."

"Does it mean anything?" I asked.

"I think it does, even if you can't put it fully into words. Anyway, after that I started talking a lot about God and pestering my parents about what God was and heaven and things like that, until they got fed up with me and sent me along to Followers. That became my religious education for several years, along with, you know, school lessons. Not that anything really explained what had happened to me!"

"Was that it? Was that experience a one-off?"

"Not quite. There've been one or two others, not quite as intense. The most recent was about this time last year. Shall I tell you?"

"Yeah, go ahead!"

"Well, I was in Silver Street – I was going to see Sarah in Newnham – and I had this immense sense of an overwhelming joy. It seemed physically to rise up inside me like a huge fountain being turned on, and filling me, or, rather, overfilling me and flooding out over absolutely everything around. This vast flood was somehow drawn up into the air by the sun – it was a warm day – only to fall again as what looked like a rain of liquid gold onto everything: the road, the buildings, trees, even some old black and rusty railings. They were all covered in this golden beauty.

"A minute or two earlier I'd noticed a row of grotty dustbins and had thought how horrible they were and it was a pity they'd been left out, but now they'd become wonderful containers of light, not full of rubbish and waste. They were, well, full of glorious *love* – love, not just light and joy, spilling out of them. That's how I saw them. No, that's how they *were*."

She sighed, and looked at me wistfully. "Again, it was over in just a few seconds, because when everything reverted to being ordinary and everyday, I was only a few steps further along the street, but it had seemed like an eternity while I was in it, and everything felt like a complete unity. Everything..." she brought her cupped hands together to form a rough sphere, "Everything cohered."

"You'd not been taking certain substances?" I asked facetiously. "A touch of the Tristans?"

"No! This wasn't triggered by anything artificial and I didn't engineer it by doing special breathing or fasting or chanting or anything like that. It just happened. It's that awareness that there's sublimity lurking in absolutely anything, even ugly old dustbins full of rubbish, ready to pop out – that's what 'possible sublimity' is. For me, at least. The sublime is possible, but it can't be forced – it just comes...or it doesn't."

"Sounds amazing," I said.

"Just as long as you realise how significant it is for me, and you don't try to dismiss it on scientific grounds. If science tries to dismiss these sorts of experiences, so much the worse for science."

"It never crossed my mind," I assured her, although it had.

Chapter 38

Melanie

Exeter: March 1997

Having got back I don't know whether to laugh, cry, or play with myself!

We went to the Nobody Inn this morning, and it was warm enough to sit outside with our coffee. We talked about this and that, then there was a pause as I thought we were both simply enjoying the quiet and listening to birdsong, but he said in a rather serious voice, "D'you mind if I ask you something?"

"Course not! Go ahead."

"Been spending a lot of time thinking back to our Cambridge days..."

"Me too."

"...and wondering why it didn't work out. I wish it had. Rather regret it didn't."

He hadn't actually asked a question, but I could feel one hovering. I couldn't think how to respond.

"Sorry," he held up a hand. "Maybe I shouldn't have brought it up."

"I wish it'd worked out as well," I admitted, answering the unasked question.

"Sometimes wonder," he said, "if there really are parallel universes with parallel 'me's and parallel 'you's in them, like something out of John Wyndham. And whether some of my parallel selves have got it together with your parallel selves. Lucky parallel bastards. And lucky bloody Simon in this universe."

"We've got each other now," I pointed out.

"Up to a point, Mel. You're still actually with him."

We had one of those long silences as we looked at each other, literally gazing into each other's eyes. Another unasked question hovered.

"It'd really hurt him," I said eventually.

"If...?" he said.

"If."

"Better not go down that route," he said, blinking rapidly. "What say you we get some lunch?"

We went inside, ordered food, a wine for me and beer for him, and took a cosy table near the fire. When a little later I decided not to have a dessert, Phil stared at me and asked if I were feeling all right.

"I'm being good," I said. "I need to lose some weight."

"Who says?"

"I do. Wouldn't you like me to be slim and svelte?"

"Is this a trick question?" he asked suspiciously. "Whatever I answer could get me into trouble. Am I meant to say, 'sweetheart, you're already slim and svelte' and be told I'm a lousy liar, or should I say 'about time too' and get hit?"

"You're supposed to say, 'I love you just the way you are'."

"I love you just the way you are," he said in a Dalek monotone.

"Oh well, in that case I'll have a chocolate mousse with extra clotted cream."

Phil suggested a walk, but I said no, I wanted to see where he lives, and he said what sounded like 'Elysian Fields'.

"It's what we call the cottage," he explained.

"I thought it was Rose Cottage. That's what I wrote to."

"That's its postal address, what the post office recognises. My uncle dubbed it Ellisian Fields, as in his surname, and mine: Ellis. Ellisian Fields. That's what the family call it, and some other people too. Land of the blessèd!"

It's pretty well in the middle of a field, and you have to go through a rickety five-bar gate and drive up a rather rough track. Thatched, with that comical look of the upper windows resembling eyes with bushy eyebrows. It's lovely going inside. I say hello to Erwin the tabby who's curled up on the back of a ponderous settee in the sitting room and allows me to stroke him, then wander around as Phil goes to make some tea. There's a modernish conservatory, all glass, lovely and light and airy, looking out onto a large garden with a fantastic pond, fruit cages, a very ancient-looking double swing in a metal frame, a large wood store and a couple of outhouses. There are several bird-feeders dangling from branches, most of them with nuts and seeds in.

The room has wonderful blackened beams which he's kept free of any ornamentation like horse brasses, an old fireplace with a stove and armchairs either side of it, and rather wonky windows looking out to the front. There's a dining table with four chairs jammed round it; bookshelves crammed with paperbacks; a sound system in one corner of the room, and framed photos of (I guess) his two daughters at different ages covering most of one wall. On the door that leads back into the hallway is a framed poster from Cambridge days advertising Air Raid Precautions. This is Phil. His lair.

When he comes back into the room with the tea, he sits next to me, but I'm not in the mood for tea right now, and a moment later I'm kissing him.

He responds instantly (as does Erwin who jumps down and goes, I suppose, to investigate his food bowl in the kitchen). Soon I'm pulling off my jeans and Phil's hand immediately goes between my legs, touching me, stroking me. I'm trembling already. I unzip his trousers and after some fumbling I take hold of him – I don't know which of us gasps the louder. I can barely speak, I'm so excited; but I do manage to croak, "Bed?"

We strip off in the bedroom, get onto the bed, and he's fiddling with me and saying all the sexy sorts of things I love hearing; and I'm going utterly wild with excitement when the wretched doorbell sounds. Not a discreet "ding, dong!" so much as a horribly loud, extended, jarring jangle. Phil jerks up and says, "Hell!" softly, as I give a loud groan. He puts his hand over my mouth. "Hang on," he whispers.

A few seconds of silence follow. He removes his hand only for another, longer and, it seems, even louder doorbell cacophony to break out, accompanied by the sound of knuckles rapping on the front door. A cat flap also clatters.

We wait, not moving, and when there's no further ringing of the doorbell he kisses me. Our hopes are premature – a moment later we can hear his name being called – from the direction of the back garden, which the bedroom overlooks. The intonation of the voice is very familiar. Phil and I look at each other again and simultaneously groan and say, "Charlotte!"

Phil swings himself off the bed and peers out of the window, keeping himself well away from it. He nods. "Yep. It's her! She's going down to the bottom of the garden – must think I could be lurking down there. She has this belief that I'm a crypto-gardener and vegetable grower just because I have a large garden and that's what she'd do with it. Shit!" he ducks down, "Don't think she saw me," he mutters.

He returns to the bed, keeping his head down and doing a Groucho Marx silly walk. After a few more seconds there's a third shattering of the silence by doorbell and knuckles.

We wait, saying nothing, not moving, for what seems an age though it was probably only a couple of minutes, but there's no repetition from bell or knuckles. "She's gone," Phil eventually says. "We're safe. Wow, that's enough to give you a nervous breakdown! Not *coitus interruptus* but *Charlotte-interrupts-us*!"

"Dreadful bell," I say.

"Been meaning to replace it ever since I moved in."

We're sitting on the edge of the bed, and his erection has vanished. I start touching him again and life begins to twitch back, but I catch sight of his little bedside clock. I remove my hand.

"Don't stop!"

"The time! It's way later than I thought. I ought to get back."

"A quickie?"

"I can't. I won't be able to relax now. I'm really, really sorry! I so wanted to make love with you."

"Tell me about it," he says.

"Will you be all right? There'll be another time. Soon, I promise."

Outside the front door we discover several eggs in a plastic container: a contribution from Charlotte's hens, and Phil comments that he counts as one of her good causes; last week it'd been a batch of flapjack.

He checks that she isn't lurking down the lane, ready to pounce out at us, then drives me back to Heavitree. We agree it'd be best for him not to bring me all the way back. He drops me at the traffic lights and I walk from there.

It's hard to leave him. I want to be with him. My body still aches for him.

Chapter 39

Phil

Keswick: March 1972

"What's up?" I asked on my return from the bathroom.

"Nothing," Melanie said wearily. She was sitting on the edge of the bed, head lowered, curtain of hair hanging down.

"Come on, something's wrong. What is it? Still got a headache?"

"No. That's gone."

"That's something. What are you like this for?"

She mumbled something.

"What?"

"I said leave it, Phil. I'll be all right."

"It doesn't look like it from where I'm standing."

"Phil!" she moaned in distress.

"All right!"

I started to get dressed, feeling mildly aggrieved. The previous evening, after we'd spent the day ascending Helvellyn and braving the perils of Striding Edge, she'd developed a headache, not helped in the evening by the stifling atmosphere in the theatre where we'd gone to see what turned out to be a hilariously bad amateur production of *Loot*. Her fizziness had gone flat, and she'd pronounced herself exhausted by the time we'd returned to the Parakeet-Bassenthwaite establishment. For the first time since we'd arrived in Keswick we'd not made love either during the day or as a prelude to sleep.

When I'd woken up it was clear that all was still not well. Melanie, already out of bed and sitting on its edge in a miserable hunched attitude, responded to my "Morning, sexy!" with only the tiniest of head movements, barely causing her hair to ripple. I said I'd use the bathroom first unless she wanted to, which hadn't elicited even that much of a reaction.

Dressed, I now sat next to her on the bed and put my arm round her. She stiffened; I let my arm drop.

"What's going on, Mel?"

She looked up at me, brushing her hair away from her face. There were traces of tears on her cheeks.

"Hey, sweetheart! Why the tears?"

"I just need some time," she said in a barely audible voice.

"Time for what?"

"Please. Just let me be. Why don't you go and have breakfast?"

"What about you?"

"I'm not up to it."

"What's going on, Mel?" I repeated.

"Please."

I got up and shrugged, feeling rebuffed. "Okay, see you in a bit. Want me to bring you up anything?"

Her head was bowed again, and her curtain of hair briefly shook. I picked up my copy of *Melody Maker* and left.

Breakfast was not much fun. I tried to read about the latest exploits of the Stones and a forthcoming album from Emerson, Lake and Palmer as I tackled the suspiciously liquid scrambled egg, but a mixture of unease and annoyance nagged at me, and I took in little news of the rock world. If Melanie wasn't feeling well, then she wasn't feeling well, and I was sorry; which didn't stop me wishing she could be a bit more forthcoming about it. I felt pushed away. Not wanted on the journey. Surplus to requirements.

I took two cups of coffee and a couple of slices of cold toast and marmalade up to our room. Melanie had moved from the bed and was now standing at the window, the curtains drawn back. She was in her dressing gown. She turned, smiling weakly, and came silently towards me. She took the cups of coffee and plate of toast, put them on the dressing table, then wrapped her arms round me. All she said was, "Hold me."

I held her.

"Are you going to tell me?" I asked.

She was still pressed against me, and I felt her give a tiny shake of the head as she mumbled, "Give me time."

"Was thinking we could take a boat out on one of the lakes today," I said.

She drew away from me. "Um. No. Maybe. No. Don't know."

"Well, what do *you* want to do?" I handed her one of the coffees.

"Nothing. Nothing."

"We've got to do something!" I said, feeling exasperation mount.

"Please, don't push me." She sat on the edge of the bed again and drank some coffee, then reached for the toast. "You're sweet to think of this."

"I'm not pushing you. I just, you know...well, let's do something."

"I've overdone it. That's all. Haven't paced myself. I just need to be on my own for a while. I'm not much company right now."

"Are you going to stay here? All day? Oh come on, Mel!"

"Please. Please don't push. I just need...to be left."

"All right, if that's what you want."

Baffled, I went along to the bathroom to clean my teeth, then returned to put some things in my day-bag. Melanie, toast eaten but coffee only half-drunk, was lying curled in a foetal position on the bed. I sat and looked at her, then brushed her hair away from her eyes which looked swollen.

"Would you like me to stay?"

She gave a tiny noise of dissent.

"Okay. I'm going to explore the bookshops," I said, standing up. "Be back here lunchtime-ish. Yeah?"

She gave a second tiny noise, this time of assent.

"Wouldn't you like to come?"

She gave a third tiny noise. Dissent.

Feeling worried and, if not disconsolate, far from consolate, I left.

When I got back at about one, Melanie, still in her dressing gown, was sitting by the open window, reading. This looked promising.

"How're you doing?" I dropped a bag of books onto the bed.

She nodded and gave a quick smile before resuming her resting expression of a slight pout. "Better."

"Better as in 'improved', or better as in 'fully recovered'?"

"Improved. Coming through."

"That's something."

"I'm really sorry if you feel I've messed you around."

"You haven't," I said, not quite truthfully.

"I still need to take it easy and slowly today," she said. "I'm feeling fragile. What have you been up to?"

"Bought, wrote and sent postcards to Mum and Dad, and to Sam. My cousin. We always send each other cards."

"And bought books?" She indicated the bag. "What did you get?"

I showed her. John Wyndham's *The Seeds of Time*; *Madame Bovary*, which Alex had been urging me to read; and, "For you," I said, handing her a book which claimed to contain *The Best Love Poems Ever.*

"You are *so* sweet," she said. "Thank you. It's lovely." She looked at the contents page. "Hey, there are quite a lot here I don't know. Thank you darling. Will you write in it? Come here..."

She said she'd be up to doing something not too strenuous, so after a pub lunch we made our way to Derwentwater and hired a rowing boat for a couple of hours. I was adamant that she did none of the rowing.

"You lie back, looking glamorous and trailing a languid hand in the water," I told her.

"Yes, O master. Your word is my command."

"I wish."

I started heaving inexpertly on the oars.

"Are we meant to be going round in circles?" she asked presently.

"We're not going round in circles."

"We've already passed that duck three times."

"It must be the duck that's going round in circles," I puffed. "Oh, *rowlocks!*"

Melanie grabbed the recalcitrant oar before it floated out of reach.

I heaved again on the oars but with greater diligence, and finally got the hang of it. We steadily made our way out into the lake, with no particular place to go, and Melanie adopted the required languid-hand-trailing-in-the-water pose. It was all very peaceful.

We'd been on the water for maybe twenty minutes. I'd stopped rowing and we were just gently drifting when she spoke. "I'm really sorry about this morning, Phil. I'm afraid it's something that happens to me from time to time. Especially when I'm physically exhausted."

"What did happen? I don't understand."

She still had a hand in the water. She now lifted it up and examined it, as though expecting to find some aquatic life clinging to it. "Everything seems to go dark for a while and I get this terrible…bleak feeling. I go right down and it feels like I can't do anything, and everything is, well, sucked dry. It's all grey and miserable and, well – you know some ice lollies, if you suck hard at them you can get all the flavour out, and you're left with a lump of boring tasteless ice on a stick? It's a bit like that – it feels that all the meaning's been sucked out of life, and it's just empty."

"Sounds grim. Does it happen often?"

"Not as often as it used to. I'm better nowadays at not getting myself completely debilitated, and there's a blood sugar thing as well. That doesn't always prevent me spiralling down sometimes. It usually diminishes during the day, like today, but it's really horrible when it hits. I went through a long period of it when I was sixteen, and had to drop back a year at school. It was awful, Phil, honestly it was. Relentless dread. Now, when it hits again, there's always the terror that it's come back for good. I just have to retreat into myself, man the barricades and keep telling myself that it'll pass. I'm afraid I'm not much fun to be around when that happens."

"Hell. I'm really sorry."

"It's hardly your fault!" She flicked water at me. "Listen, the best thing you can do if it hits while you're around, is not to ask me loads of questions or make suggestions that are meant to be helpful, which is what my mother does, and makes it worse for me. You just need to leave me, or put your arms round me and hold me, just so I know you're there. Even if I don't respond. That would be lovely."

The boat rocked dangerously as I made my way to the stern, sat beside her and put my arm round her in the prescribed manner. She snuggled up to me.

"I know I come across as all frothy and bouncy," she said. "Unfortunately there's this other side too. Sometimes it comes out and bites you on the bum. And there's something else I want to say."

"What's that?"

"You need to change your shirt. I'm glad we're out in the open!"

"Charming!"

The boat rocked.

On the way back to the B & B we came to a clothing store. "Come on," Melanie said. "I'm going to buy you a shirt."

"Of the tee variety?"

"I can't see you wearing any other type."

There were racks of the blighters: vivid reds and blues and oranges, pale pinks and yellows and greens, black, white, multicoloured, vertically striped, horizontally striped, psychedelic, some with slogans, quotations, witticisms, images of Hendrix, Clapton, Che Guevara, Lennon – all the usual suspects.

Melanie went rummaging. She'd haul a tee-shirt out of a pile, examine it critically, discard it immediately or hold it up against me and make judgement. "Too big!" or "Too small!" or "Too boring!" or "Too silly!", adding each time, "and so's the shirt," before replacing it and hauling out another one. Eventually she found one she liked: light green at the neck grading down to dark green at the hem, it featured the outlines in black of Scafell, Skiddaw and Helvellyn above the legend 'Peak Experiences'.

"It's about your level of joke," she said.

We spent the evening in companionable silence, reading. Melanie seemed restored though her fizziness was still subdued. We looked up at each other and smiled from time to time, blowing kisses. Going to bed, and weary as we both were, we again fell asleep without making love.

Chapter 40

Emhalt: June 1967

Old Brillo prayed a long prayer, free of the hesitations that usually peppered his speech. Melanie had decided some time ago that he was less nervous talking to God than talking to human beings. Unfortunately he had almost immediately forgotten about the microphone and tilted his head back, presumably the better to address God, but it made his large, black, bristly beard stick out almost horizontally like a hirsute shelf, and it kept rubbing against the microphone, sending amplified rustles and scratching sounds round the hall, until Madam Skull crept forward and stealthily moved the microphone out of his beard's sphere of influence.

After Old Brillo's few prayerful minutes of debatable glory, Madam Skull herself, sucking in her cheeks and inadvertently transforming her face into the eponymous skull in the eyes of those who had a vivid imagination, took charge of the afternoon proceedings. She bobbed up and down, announcing each item on the programme, marshalling people on and off the platform, and from time to time conferring with, or giving instructions to, Old Brillo or Kenny at the piano or even the Reverend Derek Cranbrook himself, who smiled courteously all the while, keeping his hands, Melanie noticed, clasped in a prayerful fashion.

A hymn was followed by a brief history of the Followers both nationally and locally, delivered in a nervous manner by one of the younger boys Melanie didn't know, after which came a dramatised Bible reading in which Simon took the part of a cheek-puffing-out Jesus with short-back-and-sides healing a man with a withered arm. At the moment of healing – the boy receiving it shooting his arm out horizontally and almost punching a disciple in the process, eliciting several stifled guffaws from the adults in the congregation – Anne whispered to Melanie, "Fantastic!"

"Amazing!" Melanie whispered back.

"Incredible!" responded Anne.

"Boring!" the two girls whispered in unison.

A parent in the row in front of them half-turned and smiled vacuously.

Sarah went to the front to lead the main prayers in her mildly posh voice, and half a dozen choruses were introduced by Kenny, followed by another senior boy playing guitar and singing two of his own songs, with Kenny on piano and Jeremy on bass.

Madam Skull introduced the guest preacher, the Reverend Derek Cranbrook. "A true servant of the Lord...brought many to the Lord... untiring work...dedicated to spreading the word...example to us all...hand over to him."

He stood, bowed his head in acknowledgement to Mrs Armitage, and advanced to the front of the stage, slowly smoothing down his jacket. He held up his hand like a policeman on point duty, and maintained a dramatic pause, sweeping his gaze across the gathered listeners.

"Let us ask God's blessing," he said in a clear, decisive, authoritative voice, "as I share with you this afternoon some of the many insights and understandings he has seen fit to deliver to his very humble servant, that we may learn how the divine is in all things, and all things are in the divine."

Melanie, having been prepared to daydream through the next however-long, was transfixed.

Chapter 41

Melanie

Exeter: March 1997

I went to Chloe's on Sunday evening for a meal – the first time I'd been there. She has a lovely apartment, right by the river and practically overlooking Trews Weir. Very modern, and beautifully decorated and furnished, but not too scarily neat and tidy. What's very noticeable are the photographs and paintings she has on the walls. In the main room there's a set of drawings of horses' heads, absolutely exquisite, done by her ex. "He's a terrific artist," she said as I admired them. "Pity he was a useless husband! Mind you, I was a useless wife!" and she gave a sad laugh.

"You miss him?" I asked.

"In a way. Once we'd done the sensible thing and said this marriage isn't working, let's call it off, we got on much better!"

"That sounds nice."

"It is. He's now like the older brother I never had – only we'd had sex." She gave another laugh. "Does that count as retro-incest or something?"

"Where is he now?"

"In Greece. The country, not the musical. He went on to find true love with Thea and they now live on Rhodes, while I found – well, I had already found that girls are much more exciting than boys! Ah!" The timer had pinged and she headed for the kitchen, "Why don't you open the wine?"

The food was chicken-based and gorgeous. I'd noticed before that she has quite an elegant way of eating, perhaps as a way of avoiding smudging her lipstick, but it didn't stop her doing a lippy repair partway through. She caught me smiling at her.

"One has to keep up standards!" she said with mock seriousness. "Don't worry, I'm still not hitting on you! You're already accounted for, aren't you?"

The way she looked at me rather quizzically made me think she wasn't simply referring to my being married, and I knew I was starting to blush. "I suppose I am," I said.

She gave me a second look without commenting, and I felt my cheeks burning. "What about you?" I asked to deflect her attention. "Anyone special around for you?"

She shook her head. "Nothing long-term. I've had my moments, mind you, some of them quite long moments, but these days I'm more interested in friendships and affairs than anything requiring commitment. There's always the joys of fantasising!"

"About, for example, Natasha from the revue?"

"Could be!"

"Have you seen her again, since chatting her up backstage?"

"Hey, I wasn't chatting her up! Just telling her how much I'd enjoyed her performance!"

"Yes, right, I believe you!" I said, adding mischievously, "I probably shouldn't tell you this, but I've seen her in her underwear!"

Chloe dropped her fork and had to scrabble about on the floor for it. That's the first time I've seen her flustered.

"What?" she demanded. "When? Where? How?"

"I was at the post-revue party on the Saturday and she was there. She came into the room where we all were, pretty well undressed, took one look at us, gave a shriek and retreated at a rate of knots! It was quite funny really."

"Then what? What happened?"

"Apart from all the men leering? Well, a couple of minutes later she came back in, fully dressed, as cool as anything, and carried on regardless."

"That's ma girl," Chloe drawled like a frontiersman. "Lucky you," she continued in her normal voice, "though I don't suppose you appreciated it as much as I would have. More to the point, what were *you* doing there?"

"You probably know."

"Phil?"

I nodded. Over the rest of the main course I told her how he'd invited me to be his partner at the party. I told her how I've been in love with him for more than twenty-five years; and that he's loved me for twenty-five years. I told her how the original relationship had ended, and how we'd met up again by pure chance and found that nothing has changed in our feelings for each other, and that we've been seeing each other since then without Simon knowing. I told her that after the party we'd made love, and it had been the most utterly wonderful time, being with him again. Still crazy...

"How lovely," Chloe sighed. Then she looked at me with a long, enquiring gaze.

"What?" I said.

"You're still with Simon."

I nodded, looking away.

"I'm not saying you shouldn't be," she continued, "but it does make me kind of wonder. You're very loyal."

"He's been very kind to me, Simon."

"He's kind, he's nice, yes. I don't deny that."

"It's more than that." I took a deep breath and looked back at her. "When I was a teenager I had a very bad experience with a married man and, well, the upshot was that I took an overdose. A serious one."

"Oh my God, I'm so sorry. Me and my big mouth."

"No, it's fine. The thing is, Simon found me in time and, well, he saved my life. Literally. Fingers down the throat to make me sick. Called an ambulance and everything."

Chloe remained silent. I could sense her attention was total.

"I was off school for nearly a year with depression, and he was very supportive and kind and friendly, and we sort of started going out together."

"You went out with him because you felt you ought to? As a thank you?"

I nodded. "I felt it was the right thing to do. He was keen on me in any case, and I hadn't the heart to turn him down. Not after he'd saved my life."

Chloe had taken out her lippy and mirror again, and I realised that doing her lipstick gives her thinking time. "Thanking him included marrying him and staying with him for twenty whatever years?" she said, clicking shut her thinking time. "That's one hell of a long thank you, honey!"

"It's also got to do with the accident he had. When he lost his leg. That was seriously difficult for him, and he relied on me. That's when I agreed to marry him."

"If he hadn't had the accident, you wouldn't have married him even though you were grateful to him? But he did have the accident, and you married him, and you've stayed with him...because you're a good, loyal person?"

"I hate hurting people," I said.

Chloe's comments were triggering something. I tried to ignore it, but couldn't. You could leave, an inner voice was saying. Leave Simon. Leave Simon. Be with Phil.

We'd finished the bottle. Chloe went to find another.

"Where's Phil at the moment?" she asked. "Or would you prefer to talk about something else now? As you'll have gathered, I can be a nosey old cow!"

"It's fine," I repeated. "Phil's in Kent, helping his daughter with her business. He'll be back at the end of the week, and then, well, I don't know. We'll keep seeing each other, but heaven knows if we can keep it a secret, or how we'll find time together when we can, um..."

"Shag?"

"I was going to say 'make love'!"

"They're not mutually exclusive. What's wrong with his place?"

I told her about the Charlotte-Interrupts-Us episode. She nearly choked with laughter.

"Oh dear!" she said when she'd recovered. "That's not going to happen again, is it?"

"It could. Even if it didn't, it'd be pretty hard to keep secret. Charlotte is the local bush telegraph, as Jimmy calls her."

"Your house isn't really on?"

"Hardly. Even when Simon goes away because of work, I don't think it's a good idea for Phil to come there again."

"'Come' being the operative word," Chloe remarked. "I can see that it's not best to have illicit romps in the marital home. Too many unknowns – such as an unexpected return home by marital partner. Whoops apocalypse! Still, that can easily be resolved – why don't I give you a key to this place? You can make use of the spare room whenever you want to. The bed's really comfortable."

I started to protest, but not terribly convincingly or strenuously, and didn't argue when she said she'd get two spare keys, one for each of us.

It was time for dessert, which went by some fancy name but essentially consisted of a base of chocolate surmounted by a chocolate mousse covered with a chocolate sauce and surrounded by a veritable palisade of chocolate. I think chocolate came into it as well, somewhere. For the second time within a week my diet was ambushed by chocolate. What's a girl to do?

After the first helping had disappeared as we talked through the practicalities of Phil and me using her flat, Chloe asked, "More? Or have you had your fill?"

"Oh yes," I said, deliberately misunderstanding her. "I've had my Phil all right. And I want lots more."

Chapter 42

Phil

Cambridge: April 1972

I was getting up a good speed. The narrow, high-pressure tyres hissed over the wet tarmac, the rear one doubtless sending up a spray which was marking out a streak of damp down the centre of the back of my coat. There was the metallic purr of a well-greased chain passing over rapidly turning cogs. The pedals rotated effortlessly on their shaft, the toe clips allowing me to thrust down hard with each stroke. The rain had stopped; the sun embellished the road with patches of dazzling, eye-paining light. The only wind was the illusory one generated by my own speed.

I was on the Huntingdon Road and rapidly approaching Girton College. Sunday afternoon, and Melanie had just rung me at Selwyn Gardens to say she was back. As my bike was out of commission with two flat tyres, I'd borrowed Edward's superb machine.

Faster, faster, I had to go faster. Every moment counted. Something horrible and nameless would happen if I wasted the least part of a second: Melanie would cease to be; I would be struck down by lightning; World War III would break out with unusual severity; the universe would wink out of existence.

The road was almost dead straight, but at any hint of a slight right-hand tendency I was swinging in perilously close to the opposite kerb to cut a few vital centimetres off the distance and save a microsecond or two; on any left-hand tendencies I was leaning so far over that the pedal must have been coming within a hair's breadth of gouging chunks out of the road surface. I was breathing in time with my pedalling, sharp intakes of breath on one downstroke of the right foot, explosive exhalations on the next. My speed was such that a pain which had been trying to develop in my right thigh for some time couldn't keep up – I could sense it charging along behind me like someone chasing a bus. I knew that if I eased off for one second, the pain would jump on board.

Melanie had been due back at Girton on Saturday. I'd arrived at Selwyn Gardens late on the Friday evening to find Rob already ensconced in his room, with no sign of Alex, Ewan or Edward, only the smell of weed wafting out of Tristan's room. I'd expected Melanie to ring me on Saturday around lunchtime to say she was also back, but by the evening no phone call had come. I'd repeatedly rung the payphone near her Girton room. On the fifth or sixth attempt her friend Amirah had answered, telling me that Melanie wasn't back yet. When I tried her home number her father told me that she'd just gone out – she'd tried ringing me and had been unable to get through. There'd been a change of plan, her father added; he'd be bringing her up on Sunday.

Alex and the two E's had arrived back at Selwyn Gardens at different times on Saturday, and we were all in Alex's room having coffee and catching up on the Sunday morning when the phone had rung. I dashed out to the hallway – accompanied by the ironical cheers of the others, who knew I was awaiting Melanie's call – snatched up the phone, yelled "Hi!" into it with unnecessary violence, to be rewarded by hearing Melanie's voice saying she was back, her father had just left, and she'd really *really* like to see me. Having already fixed with Edward to borrow his bike I shouted to him and the others that I was off to Girton, and flung open the front door – again accompanied by a chorus of ironical cheers, catcalls and innuendo.

Swinging into Girton, I attempted to leap agilely and in romantic hero fashion from the machine while it and I were still in motion.

I picked myself up from the gravel path, cursing the toe clips which had foiled the leap, and the pain which had been chasing behind me saw its opportunity to make a much more successful leap onto my right thigh.

I hobbled away. The pain had instantly spread out to the other thigh, and began to colonise my torso, making it feel as though someone had inserted an inflatable rubber dinghy in my chest and pulled the ripcord. I bent over, hands on tremulous knees and tried breathing deeply, an action which brought me close to throwing up. This was becoming too frequent a part of my existence: running or cycling at lunatic speed in order to see Melanie, only to utterly knacker myself in the process.

I reached her room. The door was open but the room was empty – empty of life forms, that is. Otherwise it looked very occupied, with things scattered all over the place. I sat at her desk and tipped forward until my forehead was resting on a book. At least the inflatable dinghy had developed a slow puncture and no longer threatened immediate rupture of the chest wall, but my legs were still trembling violently.

"Phil!"

Melanie's voice revived me. I leaped up.

She was standing in the doorway, clutching her Marc Bolan mug. She looked tired and her hair needed brushing.

"Oh, I'm *sooo* pleased you're here!" She banged down the mug on a small table, causing liquid to slosh out, and came quickly to me across the clothes-strewn floor, arms outstretched. "I wasn't expecting you to get here so quickly."

"Not objecting, I hope?"

"Oh no, no, no!"

"Came the moment I put the phone down. Borrowed Edward's bike. Mine's knackered."

She went to make fresh tea, first giving me a pack of photos she'd taken in the Lake District. They weren't great works of art, and several showed distinct camera-shake because of her tendency to laugh while looking through the viewfinder, but they were good reminders. There were a couple of pictures of her that I'd taken, one which was particularly good: I'd caught her gazing across a lake, with a very Melaniesque look on her face, mischievous and enticing at the same time. The wind blowing through her hair had given her the semblance of an elemental spirit.

"Like this," I said when she came back with the tea. "It's very you. Can I have a copy?"

"Take it. I thought you'd like that one."

"I'd like to send a copy to Sam as well. She's dying to see what you look like." I put it in my coat pocket and went to clear a space on her bed for us to sit. "Missed you," I said. "How come you didn't return yesterday?"

"My father was all ready to bring me back yesterday, but, um, how can I put this? I'd had a phone call earlier in the day."

There was something in her tone of voice and the way she articulated the words 'a phone call' that alerted me, and I asked, "Who from?" strongly suspecting I already knew the answer.

"Give you three guesses," said Melanie.

"Simon, Simon and Simon?"

"Right every time. I really didn't want to speak to him. My mother – she took the call – practically made me. She thinks I ought to be going out with him, you see."

"Why on earth does she...anyway," I interrupted myself. "That's irrelevant...what about old pain in the arse? What did he want?"

"He wanted to talk with me, obviously." She was twisting a lock of her hair. "He said it was important, but didn't want to say what it was about over the phone, and he wanted to take me out for a meal. I said no. He said how about a drink. I said no to that as well. He was insistent, and my mother was standing there mouthing things at me – I don't know if she could hear what Simon was saying but she clearly got the gist, and she was telling me that my father would prefer to bring me back here today in any case, which I don't actually think was true, and I ought to see Simon. In the end I caved in and said all right."

"Bloody hell!"

"I know. All this took place yesterday morning. I wanted to phone you right away to let you know but it had left me with the most dreadful sick headache and I just had to go and crash out. I did ask my mother to ring and tell you I'd ring later."

"She never did. I was in all the time."

"I know she didn't. I found that out later. She claimed she couldn't find the number, which was rubbish. I'd told her exactly where to look. She deliberately didn't want you to know."

"The old cow."

"Don't insult cows," said Melanie. "She can be so manipulative. Anyway, I met Simon in a pub just up the road, and we had a long talk about the past few years and what had been going on. Well, *he* was the one who had a long talk, while I was cast in the role of head-nodder-and-shaker-in-chief."

"What was it all about, for God's sake?"

She sighed. "I'll just give you the short version."

"Which is?"

"Which is that Simon," she said, rocking forward, "asked me..." she took a deep breath, "Simon asked me...to...to..."

She seemed unable to finish the sentence.

"Marry him?" I supplied.

She nodded. "Marry him. He wants me to marry him. Him to marry me. He wants us to get married. There. I've said it. Simon wants us to get married. Him and me. He proposed to me. He even bought me a ring. Well," she added after a pause, turning to gaze at me, "don't just sit there looking like a stuffed penguin. Say something."

Chapter 43

Melanie

Exeter: April 1997

I'm going to do it. This coming weekend, when Simon will be back from his time away on site. First thing on Saturday. Quite how I'll break it to him that I'm leaving, I still don't know, but I must do it.

Ever since last Tuesday at Chloe's her comment has been going round and round in my head that sticking with him for twenty-five years is "one hell of a long thank you, honey." She's right; it's an insanely long time, and there's no getting away from the fact that I married Simon, and have stuck with him for all these years, for what are completely the wrong reasons. Partly out of gratitude, and partly because after his accident he needed me. In a way, I suppose, they're not in themselves bad reasons, but where I've got it wrong has been in thinking that the only legitimate way to express that gratitude was to agree to marry him when he needed me, as he insisted he did. I couldn't see before now that being grateful is not a good basis for a marriage, even if he did 'need' me.

It has struck me that I must have thought, or *felt*, maybe, that it was God's will that I should marry Simon, and it would be a way of doing penance, albeit a totally ludicrous way. Dammit, I don't believe in a God who has that sort of expectations, who operates in that fashion – that's precisely the sort of Followers' God I gave up believing in way back. But the gods of old are like rivers careering back into their original channels given half a chance, and they still have power to carry you along with them without you realising it.

Suppose I could go back in time to give my younger self advice – what would I say? Other than "Don't do it!" which I would almost certainly have ignored. Actually, I don't think *any* advice would have got through to me, because I genuinely believed I was doing the right, moral thing; I was obeying my conscience. The fact that there can be situations in which obeying your conscience turns out to be the wrong thing to do seems highly paradoxical, but clearly it would have been much better for all concerned if I had refused to marry Simon. If I'd gone against my conscience.

Yes, I know he would have been upset, badly hurt even, but he would have got over it, found someone else and been happy with her; I would not have entered a deeply unfulfilling marriage which, at least partly, I'm increasingly convinced, contributed to the hugely debilitating years of ME.

Then there's Phil. What has been happening between us these last few months has been so life-affirming that I can't and mustn't ignore it. How we'll work it all out remains to be seen, but he's been separated from his wife for several years now; and...well, we'll see. The thought that the time will come when we'll be able to be openly in a relationship is, frankly, thrilling.

Chapter 44

Phil

Cambridge: April 1972

"Fuckin' Ada," I said. Simon *proposed* to her? Someone had just struck an enormous gong about three inches away from my ears, setting up a tremendous and persistent ringing. Everything else was completely blotted out. Simultaneously the trembling in my legs induced by the manic cycle ride leaped back into action and broadened its field of operations by invading the whole of my body.

"It sort of did and didn't take me by surprise," said Melanie. "Yes, it did take me by surprise, but it had crossed my mind when he'd said he had something important to say, but I thought no, that's stupid, it can't be that."

I stroked her tangled hair. "Well, it is stupid, isn't it? Isn't it?"

"Not from his point of view, that's the problem, Phil. For him it's not stupid, it's what he feels he has to do. Propose."

"He isn't claiming to have received 'guidance' from God again or some such crap?" I asked.

"He didn't say." She was fingering her cross. "And I wasn't going to ask."

"Did you simply laugh, or what?"

"No I didn't! That would have been unkind. Neither did I say all that Jane Austen stuff about he's done me a great honour in asking me, and I don't deserve it. I simply said no. Or more accurately, I said, 'Thank you, but the answer has to be no' – or something along those lines. Oh Phil!" She stopped fingering her cross and put her hand up to her mouth, looking shocked. "You didn't think I would've said anything else but no, did you?"

"No, of course not. But, hell, it's a bit of a shock. Some other bloke asking you to marry him when I love you and you love me."

"*Do* you love me?" she asked mournfully.

"As much as you love me."

"Oh. Well, that's all right then!" She brightened up. "Anyway, I said no. I also said that he must've known that I'd say no, so why on earth had he asked? That," she shook her head ruefully, "was a mistake."

It had been a mistake because, as she recounted, he'd gone on at great length about how much he missed her, how miserable he felt without her, how he was only keeping going because surely she'd realise she'd made a mistake and would eventually return to him – basically, the same crap he'd laid on her before, only even more so, while she'd kept telling him that she wasn't in love with him, had never been in love with him, and wasn't going to be in love with him.

"He didn't get it?"

"Eventually, but only when I told him..." She broke off and gripped my hand tightly.

"Told him what? Mel? Told him what?"

"Um, I'm sorry, I shouldn't have lied, please forgive me, but I couldn't think what else to say. You see, I told him that...that you and me...that we're engaged, that..." and now the words came out in a rush, "that we're going to get married as soon as I've finished my degree next year."

She fell silent. I was silent. Then, "Fuck*in'* A*da*!" I said.

"I'm sorry, I'm sorry, I'm sorry, I know I shouldn't have said it, but it did the trick, honestly it did."

"Why, what did he say?"

"For a while, nothing at all. He looked stunned. He kept shaking his head, and finally asked if I was sure. Absolutely sure. I said yes, I was sure. He offered me his congratulations, which made me feel awful, and said he hoped I'd be happy with you. He said it in a rather mechanical way, and after a couple more minutes he said perhaps he should be on his way and that was that really. He sort of offered to see me home, but I think he was relieved when I said no. I must admit I was feeling very wobbly."

Simon had looked stunned? That was nothing to what I was feeling. The giant gong had just received another belting. *Married.* Okay, she'd told Simon what she'd told him simply as an expedient, which apparently had fulfilled its purpose, but it didn't really mean anything, did it? It didn't count in the real world of what the future would be for Melanie and me... Only, although it *shouldn't* have meant anything in the real world, as the reverberations of the gong continued it felt very much that it *did* mean something. Something very important.

Another wave function of our relationship was collapsing into a distinct reality from out of several possibilities, a reality called 'getting married'. Married? To Melanie? Well, the possibility was bound to arise for real at some stage – unless we chose to live together without tying the knot, which would still entail a decision, a commitment, an agreement even though not ratified by church and state and all that palaver.

All these considerations seemed to be present in my mind in a single block, not as a developing, linear sequence of thought; and at the same time I had no doubt at all what to do, what I wanted to do.

Aware that I'd be acting out one of the great clichés, I slid off the edge of the bed onto the floor, turning round as I did so, then raised myself on one knee to adopt the time-honoured position. I pulled my hand free from Melanie's grip, took hold of her hand and looked up at her face which had an expression combining surprise, bemusement and wariness.

"Before anyone else comes along and tries to claim you," I said, "it's my turn. Melanie Mason, will you marry me?"

There was a brief pause, then she cried out, "Oh, don't mock me, Phil, please!"

"Not mocking you." I stroked the back of her hand with my thumb. Her other hand was gripping her cross. "I mean it. I want to marry you."

She was now open-mouthed. "Are you proposing to me?"

"Believe that's what it's called. You told Simon we were going to get married, so let's. It'll mean you won't have told him a lie. Just a premature truth!"

"Say it again," she said faintly. Her eyes were glistening. "Ask me again."

"Melanie. I would like to marry you. I would *love* to marry you. Will you marry me?"

"Yes," she said. "Of course I will."

Chapter 45

Melanie

Exeter: April 1997

I don't know what to write, I just don't know what to write. It's all so appalling. I feel utterly sick. The last couple of days have been dreadful, the pits, totally shattering, hellish. Some terrible squid-like creature seems to have wrapped itself around me and is squeezing so hard it's going to crush me. I seem to be sweating and freezing at the same time, and I can't stop shaking.

Simon thinks I've got a fever and I ought to see the doctor, but it's not a doctor thing, is it? I know it's not a doctor thing, because it's Phil. Phil! How could you? How *could* you? What do I do now? What can I do? The stupid thing is I know that this will pass – the question is *when?* Will I survive until then? Yes, no doubt I will – and every now and again there comes a bizarre lull in my feelings, the eye of the hurricane sort of thing, and there I am standing outside myself, looking at what is going on, and calmly telling myself, "this will pass". Then it all rips up again and I rage and rage at such a trite thing to say. All things must pass? Thank you George Harrison, thank you so *very* much.

What a shit! What a shitty thing to do! How dare he mess me around like this. How dare he! Utterly out of the blue. I couldn't begin to imagine it coming. Am I stupid? Is that it? Am I a stupid, brain-dead, idiotic, gullible fool? How *could* I have been taken in? How could I have opened myself up like that to such hurt? How could he have done it? What on earth has been going on in that oh-so-bloody-clever brain of his? Why hadn't he warned me? Why hadn't he *said?*

Oh, I don't know. It makes me sick to think of it, but I can't help thinking of it all the time! I'm not in control of my thoughts. Round and round they go, black and dark and horrible. Sometimes I just can't cry at all, then suddenly it's a whole tidal wave crashing down on me and through me, and I'm crying uncontrollably, and the strange thing is that it's my whole body that's crying.

Thank God I hadn't said anything to Simon about leaving. It's utterly mortifying to think what it would be like if I had told him, then had to go back and say, "Whoops, no! Sorry, my mistake! As you were! Forget I said anything! I'm still here!" That's the one tiny crumb of comfort – unbelievably, it could have been worse.

How dare he! How dare he treat me like this.

Chapter 46

Phil

Cambridge: April 1972

We decided to celebrate our engagement with a meal at the Varsity. Melanie rang to book a table.

"You're not going to pull a Friar House stunt on me?" I asked when she put the phone down.

"Course not! Cross my heart and hope to die!"

We agreed to keep it a secret for the time being, until we'd seen our respective parents and told them; a process which I envisaged would present no problem with my family, other than engendering surprise and, from Sam, hugs, but Melanie was far from sanguine about her parents' reaction.

"Daddy'll be fine," she said, "whereas my mother – you might have to buy a ladder and two tickets to Gretna Green."

I returned to Selwyn Gardens to find Alex in his room sprawled out angularly in his chair, pipe in full smoke, with Rob perched on the window seat, nursing his guitar. After some badinage about my love life, we turned to talking about ARP, tossing around ideas for new sketches and songs. I was not absorbed enough to forget the time, and at six o'clock I levered myself from the chair, announcing that I had to go for a shit, a shower and a shave.

"And a shag?" said Alex.

As I left the room Rob strummed his guitar and sang, "A shit, a shower, a shave and a shag/all wrapped up in a paper bag!" which didn't sound too promising.

I arrived at the restaurant just before seven to find Melanie already waiting. She smiled sweetly at me. "Where have you been?" she asked with mock impatience. "I've been waiting simply...*minutes* for you!"

I woke up around three o'clock needing a slash. As I slid out of bed Melanie shifted her position slightly, without waking. I put on her dressing gown, opened the door and peered out. All clear. I padded along to the lav.

On my return, finding that Melanie had shifted again and now occupied all the bed such that I couldn't slip back into it without disturbing her, I sat in the armchair, thinking.

Sitting opposite my fiancée in the restaurant – my *fiancée!* – had been curiously thrilling. Partway through the meal, I'd announced that I had something for her to mark our engagement in the traditional manner.

"Oooh!" she said. "That sounds exciting!"

For the second time that day I went down onto bended knee, aware that other diners were watching.

"It may not fit," I warned, taking from my pocket the little box that had formerly contained the blank rounds for ARP's starting pistol.

"I don't mind! Oh, let's see!" She was clasping her hands in girlish excitement. "Don't keep me in suspenders!"

I slowly lifted the lid from the box, which I tilted towards her so she could see its contents.

"Oh, it's gorgeous!" she exclaimed, sniggering. "Will you put it on my finger?"

I removed from its cushion of cotton wool the stainless steel split ring from which I had earlier removed my keys and the Volvo fob, and taking her hand I slid the key ring onto her finger.

"It's wonderful," she said, examining it. "Maybe a bit loose."

To demonstrate, she bent her wrist and the ring fell off onto the table.

I picked it up, took her hand again and slid the ring back in place, this time onto two fingers.

"That's better," she said. "It won't fall off now. It must've cost you the earth."

"Dad got it free from a garage," I said.

"I'll always treasure it," she giggled. "You can buy me a proper one when you're rich and famous!"

"Might have a long wait," I said.

"I don't mind."

As I kissed her, there was some ragged clapping from other diners, and a couple of loud whistles. I got up and bowed. Melanie stood up and curtseyed. The waiter brought us a small complimentary bottle of fizz.

Chapter 47

Melanie

Exeter: April 1997

Still dreadful, but at least I feel a little calmer – well, some of the time. I still find it hard to take in. It still feels utterly unreal – a massive dislocation, as though I'm on a train that's jumped onto a different track and is now thundering along in completely the wrong direction and I can't stop it. I feel powerless.

Simon's convinced that it's my ME rearing up again, which I guess is as good an explanation for him as any and I'm not going to tell him the real reason, am I? He's being helpful, being understanding, telling me that, "You've been rather overdoing it recently. You must take it easy, get as much rest as you can," which is all very well, but I feel as restless as anything and can't settle. I can't read for any length of time, or follow anything on television, or listen to the radio or to music. The garden is about the only place where I'm just about okay enough, because there I can be constantly on the move as well as doing something useful – but all the time it's still going round and round in my head: why, why, why?

Charlotte called in. That was almost unendurable. She'd rung up just to have a chat and Simon told her I wasn't well so she came on a visit. She brought me some flowers and some gossip – and the gossip had to be about Phil, and I had to sit and take it.

When she said, "He's getting back together with his wife," I wanted to yell *I know, I know he is! He told me!* I didn't yell anything of course, just sat there and faked a surprised look and drank some more tea and asked how she knew, and she said Phil had told Jimmy.

"I don't know what they've decided," Charlotte said in her pensive way which means she intends to find out as soon as possible, "whether Phil's going to move back to Kent – that's where his wife lives, or whether she'll move down here – unlikely I would have thought. She runs some beauty parlours, doesn't she, which she wouldn't want to give up, whereas Phil works from home and it doesn't really matter where he's based. He'll be a real loss, won't he?"

Chloe on the other hand was lovely when she came round yesterday after I'd rung her (ironically, she assumed I was ringing about Phil and me using her flat). We sat on the settee, and she just let me talk – though much of the time I didn't say anything but stared into space feeling dazed, and she held me and said nothing, which in itself is amazingly eloquent. She simply radiated acceptance, not pestering me with questions. She didn't fall into the trap of criticising Phil, either – I couldn't have borne that. In fact, at one point she suggested that it must be difficult and painful for him as well, and I burst into tears.

I told her that I really do believe him when he says he loves me and that his decision to give his relationship with Ros another go is the hardest thing he's ever done. He was the one who'd broken up the marriage by his affair with whoever she was, and he feels he owes it to Ros as she's asked for another go at the marriage. He wishes she hadn't, but she has, and how can I object to his agreeing? As I told Chloe, when I'm not screaming in pain I do understand why Phil has made the decision he's made.

But it hurts so much.

Chapter 48

Emhalt: June 1967

"...that is where and how you will know," the Reverend Derek Cranbrook concluded emphatically twenty-five minutes or more later, placing his right hand on his chest. "This is where the Spirit dwells. Amen. Let us now bow our heads and close our eyes in prayer."

Melanie did not immediately bow her head or close her eyes, briefly watching as most of those gathered in the hall dutifully obeyed, yet here and there were islands of unbowed heads, unclosed eyes, some of the resistant being Followers themselves, others being a number of the adults present. Then she too closed her eyes and dropped her head as the Reverend Derek began praising and pleading with God.

She had heard many times before at Followers close variants on the evangelical message he had preached – God, Jesus, sin, salvation, justification by faith, love of God, born again, baptism in the Holy Spirit – but the Reverend Derek's words, the tone and rhythm of his voice, had caught her interest, had stirred her up, challenged her, called her. The divine as an ocean in which all are called to bathe had thrilled her, as had the divine indwelling all creation.

At one point in his address, as he had leaned forward to emphasise his words, Madam Skull and Old Brillo, sitting behind him on the platform, had also leaned forward in unison, looking for all the world like sedentary backing singers. Anne had whispered a jokey comment, but Melanie had been oblivious to it. Her headache gone, a warmth had developed within her as the exposition had continued, and she felt captivated. Now, as she listened to his concluding prayers, it occurred to her that she must be in danger of falling away, of 'backsliding' – against which they, the Followers, were regularly warned. To backslide was the verb of all verbs to guard oneself against.

The service continued with a hymn, some notices, an invitation to stay on for tea and cakes, and concluded with a three-part blessing bestowed jointly by Old Brillo, Madam Skull and the Reverend Derek. The service was over.

As Kenny played another hymn tune – rather than the latest from the Beatles or Rolling Stones as he would normally do – people started moving. Followers started folding and stacking the chairs, others brought out tables from a side room, several mothers were carrying in food from the kitchen area.

Melanie was one of the last to rise from her seat.

"Ah, Melanie! Come here a minute, dear," said Mrs Armitage, before Melanie could head for the food. "This is Melanie Mason," she continued, marshalling her into the little group surrounding the Reverend Derek. "She's been a Follower for many years and is one of our most regular attenders."

"I am delighted to meet you, young lady," the Reverend Derek enunciated gravely. He reached out and placed an index finger on the little gold cross around her neck. "You have accepted the Lord Jesus into your heart, I take it? I trust this is not simply an item of jewellery?"

"I assure you that Melanie is fully committed to the faith," Mrs Armitage said firmly.

"You are doing splendid work for the Lord with these young people," the Reverend Derek nodded slightly to Madam Skull and Old Brillo in turn. "I would like to put a suggestion to you. Perhaps you would care to organise an outing to our headquarters after the schools have broken up? We are called to offer guidance and teaching in the name of the Lord, and he will work through us with these young newcomers to the Kingdom and strengthen his work among you here in Emhalt. The Spirit, as I sought to stress, is at work throughout the world, indeed throughout all creation, and we are the channels through which he does his work."

"Ah, erm, indeed, a very good idea," Old Brillo's beard agreed.

"We would need to inform parents and get their permission," added Mrs Armitage immediately. "Any such visit would need to include myself or Mr Griffen and maybe a parent or two."

"Naturally," the Reverend Derek nodded again. "That would be right and proper. We must all pray about it. What do you young people feel about the idea? Would you like to come and share the Lord's work, learn more of his promises?"

"I'd be interested," said Melanie.

"Me too," said Simon.

"I will pray with my colleagues, and get back to you with two or three possible dates," the Reverend Derek said to Mrs Armitage.

"Erm, tea?" put in Old Brillo. "I think we would be, ahem, well advised to get ourselves some tea and, ah, cake before it all disappears. Very healthy, erm, appetites our young people, ah, have."

Chapter 49

Melanie

Exeter: April 1997

Oh dear. Poor Charlotte. Sorrows "come not single spies but in battalions." I am so sorry. She's devastated, and I'm not surprised.

Simon gave me the news when he came in from work a couple of nights ago. "Jimmy's walked out on Charlotte," he said before he'd even taken off his coat.

"You're joking!"

"I wish I was. He's moved in with that Sonia person from their village." Simon made his puffing sound as he started opening his post. "I did have my suspicions something might be going on. I saw Jimmy with her at Honiton station when I was coming back from my reunion. I thought they looked a bit cosy. There have been one or two other little incidents as well."

"Why didn't you tell me before?"

"I couldn't be sure – I might have got hold of the wrong end of the stick. As he's chairman of their parish council and she's the secretary, there was quite possibly an innocent explanation. Council business or something."

"I wonder what'll happen."

"He says he's going to get a divorce on the grounds of unreasonable behaviour."

I was going into the kitchen to get supper, but swung round at this. "What unreasonable behaviour? That's ridiculous."

"He says she talks too much," Simon said.

"Well, if that counts as unreasonable behaviour, so does going round looking like a complete plonker," I retorted.

"I don't think someone's looks can be taken into consideration," Simon said in his explaining-it-to-an-idiot voice. "Besides, I wouldn't say Jimmy looks like a complete plonker."

"No?" I was starting to bang around in the kitchen. "In my opinion they could use his photograph to illustrate the word in a pictorial dictionary. 'Plonker', see 'Jimmy Openshaw'."

★

I rang Charlotte yesterday morning, and she came round for two or three hours. She's all over the place. I managed to take a leaf out of Chloe's book and let her talk and be silent as she chose, and I held her hand and let her cry. She talked a lot, mainly about their marriage over the years and the problems they'd had, and she was sure Sonia wasn't the first.

"As he's chair of the council," she said in between sobs, "and she's the secretary, he's had the ideal alibi for being out of the house with her so much. 'Sorry dear,'" she put on a sneering voice, "'I've got the finance committee this evening' or the parking committee or the something else committee. I'd thought for some time he seemed to be on an awful lot more committees with an awful lot more meetings to go to." Then she spat out, "But he was simply doing his bit of Any Other Business!"

While Charlotte was still here my mobile beeped to say I had a text, which I ignored until she'd left. It was from Phil, asking if we could meet this afternoon to talk things over. One thing about listening to Charlotte is that it puts what's happening in my life into perspective. She's facing the break-up of a marriage that's lasted for I don't know how many years, a break-up she hasn't initiated. Whereas what have I lost? Probably just a ludicrous hope, an unrealistic dream about leaving my own dull marriage because of the rekindling of an old romance.

But it still hurts to think about it – I can't bring myself to write down all the details, just the bare bones of what happened: Phil returned from Kent and we went for a walk up in the woods, me full of happiness to be seeing him again and intending to tell him I was going to leave Simon, him evidently ill at ease, reluctant to hold hands as we walked along the muddy paths. I asked what was wrong, and he dropped the bombshell. He's going back to his wife. Ros had said she wanted them to get back together, have another go at the marriage. He'd agreed. Which meant our times together had to come to an end.

"Just like that?" I demanded, shocked. "She asked out of the blue?"

"It's not the first time," he admitted, "but I've always resisted until now."

"Because of me?" I'd managed to ask.

"No. The previous occasions, just a couple of times, were before we'd met again."

"You said no before? Each time? Why say yes to her now? Why, Phil? It doesn't make sense."

He took my hand and turned me to face him. He was fluttering his eyelashes, and the wind was blowing his hair into his face. I could see the untidy young undergraduate I'd fallen in love with. "Look, Mel," he said, flicking his hair back, though the wind blew it about again, "the situation is that you're married to Simon, and much as I adore our times together, and I adore *you* more than I can say, I know I've been very hurtful to Ros and I respect her for the way she's dealt with it, and I feel she deserves another opportunity to make a go of it. For us, her and me, to make a go of it. It's ironic I know, but being with you, and knowing I can't be with you all the time, has made me realise I must be grateful for what I do have, or could have again, with Ros."

Unable to respond, I looked past him into the wood. I knew I wouldn't tell him I'd been gearing myself up to leave Simon. That twenty-five years of being grateful to Simon was long enough. That I'd wanted to be able to love him, Phil, freely and openly. The time had passed when I could say any of that. I didn't tell him then, and I won't be telling him when we meet this afternoon.

Chapter 50

Phil

Cambridge: May 1972

The heat was intense. A few degrees higher and it would take the form of a material substance, the thermal equivalent, I could imagine, of a vast block of expanded polystyrene. The absence of noise and speech was virtually absolute, with the occasional cough or rustle of a turned page or tread of footsteps doing nothing to disturb, but rather to deepen, the inescapable sense that an all-pervading invisible entity by name of silence had trapped that part of the universe demarcated by the college library like amber entrapping a fly.

I'd come to the conclusion that heat and silence were the true dimensions of existence in which the library and its occupants had their being. The conventional dimensions of space and time had been relegated to a subsidiary role. Going up the spiral stone stairs and through the heavy door was an initiation ceremony, a rite of passage from one universe to another, from that of time and space to that of heat and silence. Since existence was now defined by those dimensions, my existence that afternoon must have been hyperreal, for the heat and silence were profound.

Someone at the far end of the library groaned despairingly, a long slow groan like a heavy oak door on rusty hinges being opened with fatuous slowness in some horror B-movie. The groan ended with a dull thump, not unlike the noise made by an undergraduate forehead hitting a library table, followed by several more thumps suggesting an undergraduate clenched fist, or possibly fists, repeatedly striking the same table top. Someone else, or perhaps the table thumper himself, hissed like a pressure cooker reaching its working temperature.

The silence reasserted itself.

Thank God the exams would soon be upon us, and soon after that would be over, because I couldn't take much more of this. There'd been a time when I'd been led to believe by my alleged elders and betters at school that sitting endless exams and passing them, preferably with high grades and even more preferably with little stars appended, counted as some of the most important and significant events of my life, only marginally less important than my actual birth, and vastly more significant than my first shag. I couldn't remember the former so was not in a position to comment either way, but I could recall the latter with exceptional clarity and could safely assert that it beat doing exams hands down, not to mention anything else down. Even though I couldn't be sure that I would have been awarded anything higher than a third-class pass, if that, by the girl concerned.

These thoughts led unsurprisingly straight to Melanie being present before my inner eyes, though my outer eyes had not rested on her for several long days, our having agreed, after we'd seen each other every day for more than a week since we'd got engaged, that we both really ought to commit ourselves to study and revision. I wondered what she was doing right at that moment – thinking of me? Was she also amazed at how our relationship had dramatically shifted into another phase? Did she also keep replaying our times together and conjuring up future scenes for when we could once again spend a decent amount of time together, talk, laugh, make love? Pondering this, I doodled a mass of large, improbable, molecules vaguely phallic and vaginal in design, constructed from numerous carbon rings with double bonds, and added at random nitrogen and oxygen atoms, before returning to the real life molecules of benzene and phenol derivatives.

The exams arrived. The usual mix of the appalling and the not-so-bad-after-all. Melanie completed her papers – not finals for her – with two days still to go for me before my last ever, and we met briefly that afternoon out at Girton, but I needed to blast on with more last-minute revision and didn't stay long.

Late the following afternoon, with a fairly decent pharmacology paper out of the way and just one more to go the next day, I headed for the Pembroke JCR and started idly flicking through *The Times*. Coming to job adverts, I was about to flick on more rapidly when one ad leaped out at me from the *Media and Entertainment* section: "PRODUCER, LIGHT ENTERTAINMENT, RADIO." It continued, "As a member of a creative group to submit, develop and subsequently to produce original ideas particularly on comedy, both traditional and experimental. Must have experience in the media, or in University revue. £2601 – £3573 p.a." Details followed of where and by when to apply and with what details about oneself.

I instantly had an upsurge of the same mixture of optimism and pessimism which had regularly punctuated my pathetic pre-Melanie love life – intense hope and desire that this would be the one, coupled with a near certainty that it would all be a laughable failure. I had to apply though. I had to apply.

I was tearing out the advertisement when Alex appeared and asked what I was up to. I showed him the ad. He stared at me.

"Is this the Phil Ellis we all know and love? Or has the real one been abducted by aliens and a near-identical copy substituted, correct in every detail except one – applying for a job! What's brought this on, man?"

"Ah, you know – got to earn some money sometime. It's just the idea of working in science that holds no attractions. If I can get paid for writing and performing – well, can't be bad."

"True. Very true." He took out his pipe and started fiddling with it. "I have a message from Melanie for you – she rang SG this afternoon. She's had to go home for a few days." He lit the pipe, continuing to explain between puffs. "It's something to do with her brother. He's in some sort of difficulty and she wants to be on hand to give support and so forth. I gather her mother is taking it badly, whatever 'it' is." His pipe being well lit, he waved his hand to disperse a cloud of smoke. "Keeps the mozzies away," he said.

"There aren't any mosquitoes here."

"Shows how good it is. She'll ring you this evening."

"Right, thanks. No further hints?"

"She didn't sound frantically worried. More exasperated, I'd say. He can't be at death's door. I wouldn't worry. Mind you," he added in professorial mode, "as a certain someone once said, it is always easier to bear the misfortunes of others than the inconveniences of one's own."

"He would say that, wouldn't he?" I said. "Fancy the inconvenience of a pint?"

"My shout," Alex said as we entered the bar.

"Think it's my round," I said.

"Toss you?" he suggested.

"No, thanks," I said. "I can toss myself."

Chapter 51

Melanie

Exeter: April 1997

I arrived early at the canal-side cafe and sat outside, feeling dispossessed and unbelonging. Several earnest canoeists paddled past, an elderly couple walked slowly by with a Golden Retriever on an unnecessary lead, two or three cyclists, more pedestrians, people going into the cafe or coming out, a family group with two small girls and a boy running and jumping about – they all suddenly became very odd: although I could see them I couldn't quite take in what they were. All these strange shapes in motion – lumps of protoplasm – I couldn't grasp that they were people. I *knew* they were, but couldn't *feel* that they were.

How could this random chaotic mass of movement arise out of any sort of purposefulness or consciousness? That's what eluded me: that all around were entities that were conscious, aware of feelings and thoughts and hopes and fears, with plans and ideas and loves and hates all jostling about inside them as they jostled about inside me. I felt so distant from them. I wanted to experience the realness of other people, but sitting outside that cafe with the canal right in front of me and the river only a further few yards beyond, I didn't know how to.

A couple of teenagers walked by, hand in hand. I stared intently at the backs of their heads. If only I could experience directly what was going on inside them, feel their feelings, think their thoughts – all I could see was the colour of their hair, the shape of their heads, the slope of their shoulders, and the fact that they were holding hands.

Phil arrived. We ordered some tea and cake, and went into the little courtyard area round the back, with its rustic tables and benches. No one else had ventured out there; only Baxter the dog who came padding out of his kennel.

Phil looked tired – and I must have as well. He said thanks for coming and I said I'd wanted to come, I wanted to see him, and he looked surprised at this and said he thought that I'd probably never want to see him again.

Unfortunately that set me off – I didn't go into complete meltdown, I simply reached across the table and held his hand while I could feel tears trickling down my cheeks. I didn't dare say anything for a while. I realised that he too was weeping, and we both gave that rueful kind of a smile and a little laugh of acknowledgement.

"It must be the cold weather," he said facetiously, his voice cracking. "Makes the eyes sting."

"Something like that," I agreed. "Nothing to do with our feelings."

As we were wiping our eyes the tea arrived; the waitress one I'd not seen before but who reminded me a little of the one in the Whim at Cambridge who was perpetually nodding. "Do you remember…" Phil started to say as she retreated, and I nodded (appropriately enough) and said, "I was thinking the same!" and we laughed again, very briefly.

He reminded me not to say "I'll be mother" as I poured the tea, then asked how I was and I said well, you know; and I asked how he was and *he* said well, you know. I said no, I didn't know how he was and I really would like to know. How are his plans going? Have he and Ros sorted out details yet?

"We're getting there. There's been more to sort out than either of us had realised."

He seemed to enter a trance, and I had to say, "It must be tricky," to prompt him to continue.

"Yeah. There's the problem of my work. For a while I'm going to be coming back down here for a week at a time, and cram in a load of tutoring, but in time I'll have to get some students in Kent. I don't earn enough from the editing stuff." He's arranging for the cottage to be sublet on behalf of his uncle, and friends in the village have offered to take the cat. "If Erwin agrees," he added. "Charlotte's been really kind, not her usual intrusiveness, just offering helpful suggestions. It helps her too, I guess. Something to focus on."

"What do Lem and Amy think about you two getting back together?"

"Thought they'd be pleased," he admitted, "but I think they're a bit sceptical. Lem rang me the other day and asked if I was sure, she just wanted both me and Ros to be happy, and Ros has told me that Amy asked *her* exactly the same thing."

"You both told them that you're sure?"

"Yeah, we both told them that's what we're going to do."

He asked how am I really, am I okay? I didn't know how to answer although it hardly came as a surprise that he'd ask.

"I'm all right enough," I said. "I hate what's happened, but there it is." I wasn't going to let on how much I'm hurting.

He grabbed my hands again. "I am so sorry, Mel. I'm appalled that I've hurt you, and believe me it hurts me too, but that's irrelevant. I hate hurting you like this. You're very precious to me, you know, and—"

"Don't!" I said quickly. "Don't go there! You'll set me off again and I have no intention of being set off again."

"Sorry. Just hope you can find it in you to forgive me."

"Not yet," I had to tell him. "It'll come."

Who knows how long we would have sat there, getting colder, if a couple of young mothers with three toddlers and two babies between them hadn't come outside and taken one of the other tables, chattering brightly as their offspring shouted, argued and ran around. Phil fluttered his eyelashes at me and jerked his head to indicate, let's go. As we left we gave Baxter the remains of our cake.

"Can I ask," he said as we walked along by the canal, "have you got enough support, or are you keeping it all to yourself?"

"Chloe's being wonderful. We've spent a lot of time together."

"She must think I'm a total shit," he said morosely. "Quite right too."

"She hasn't uttered a word of criticism about you."

"Yeah? How about you? You must think I'm a total shit?"

"Not *total*," I said, which made him smile. Briefly.

We wandered back towards the Maritime Museum in silence.

"I don't think there's anything else to say, is there?" I said.

He shook his head. "Wish there were."

"I hope it works out," I said. "You and Ros."

"Thanks Mel," he said, and he sighed. "What can I say? I'm not allowed to tell you how precious you are to me, so I won't say that. I do want you to know that you're unique, and I'm grateful that you're not making this harder for me than it already is. And if I were at all religious I'd be praying that you find happiness and fulfilment, and I'll be bloody angry with God if you don't."

"That's the loveliest non-prayer possible," I said. I was on the verge of tears again, but determined not to give way to them.

We had a brief embrace, then he went off to find his car, and I turned back to walk along the river, my heart fit to burst.

It was there, a few minutes later, as I was crossing the little suspension bridge, and paused to lean on the metal railing as Phil and I had often done in our hand-in-hand wanderings, that I registered briefly the electric blue flash of a kingfisher, and for the first time in years was struck by sublimity.

Chapter 52

Phil

Cambridge: May 1972

I beat a strangely unstoned Tristan to the phone in a photo finish when Melanie rang just before ten.

"The thing is," she said after we'd done the usual 'How are you, darling? Lovely to hear your voice' bit, "Mikey's been admitted to hospital."

"Christ! What's happened? Some accident?"

"Psychiatric hospital."

"Oh, God! Why?"

"He hasn't been sectioned. It's a voluntary admission – he's in an assessment unit."

"Why?"

"He's been behaving even weirder than ever over Easter, saying he's been contacted by aliens from Andromeda who've told him he's got to sacrifice himself to save Earth. Pretty mad stuff. My father arranged emergency admission to this unit and Mikey's gone there. Without protest, apparently. It's all rather scary."

"I bet. Is there anything you can do?"

"I'll stay for a few days to give my mother some company, and I should be able to visit Mikey. He might be weird but he is my brother and I do love him." She said some more, then suddenly switched tone, asking, "Oh, and how did today's paper go?" I could hear her mother's voice indistinctly in the background.

"Not bad!" I said. "Managed to dredge up some vital knowledge I didn't know I knew. Hey, much more important – listen to this." I read the job ad to her. There was a brief silence before she giggled.

"I don't believe it! You're not going to apply for *a job?*"

"Yeah, why not?"

"Don't get me wrong! I think it sounds wonderful, but I never would've thought – mind you," she changed tack, "it wouldn't be a nine-to-five, would it? Or would it?"

We talked about how it could be just right for me, give me a focus for writing and expanding my comedy, and earn some much-needed money especially during her third year. "Possibly for longer than that," she added. "I'm seriously thinking of doing a PhD after I've graduated. My mother's disappeared again, by the way."

"PhD? Really?"

"My supervisor's all in favour. She's suggested I go in for the Henry Chambers History Prize next year. It's very prestigious – you have to submit a long essay on some aspect of mediaeval history, twelve thousand words I think, and I could do something over the summer on 'Heresy, Women Mystics and Society' – how's that for a theme!"

"Fantastic!" I said. "What the hell does it mean?"

"Er, what it says, really!" She laughed, and I could imagine the facetious look on her face she pulls when mocking me. "If you really don't know, I'll give you a tutorial sometime! Anyway, that's the area I'd like to research for a PhD, so this essay'd be a great start even if I don't win the prize, which is more than likely. Just to go in for it's great. Sorry, you were saying about applying for that job, and I was just thinking well, that would be fantastic, amazing, incredible! – because I might be immersed in academia for another four years at least."

Four years? Four years at least? "What about getting married?" I asked, aware that I must sound rather petulant. "Thought we'd said we'd get married when you graduate. Next summer, or autumn."

"Idiot!" More facetious face-pulling was probably in progress. "We'll get married! Doing a PhD doesn't prevent that! What it does mean is that I won't exactly be earning much, other than doing some tutoring and suchlike."

Light dawned. "You want to be a kept woman? Living off the immoral earnings of a comedy writer?"

"'S right!" she said happily. "You get going with that application so you can wow them at an interview, and start being paid to be creative! Then you can keep me in the manner in which I deserve to be kept."

The final paper the next day was another spasm of pharmacology. Not too bad at all, and after three hours I emerged from the examination room feeling faintly stunned, having expected to be swept along by a tidal wave of relief, exhilaration, joy, rapture and all the rest of it.

I walked slowly down the steps as others were animatedly discussing the paper, arguing the merits and demerits of this question as opposed to that. Someone started bemoaning the fact that the paper was too easy and provided no test of knowledge or understanding at all, but within seconds she was being shouted down by yahooic chanting. Quite right too.

Rob emerged from a different door. He had just completed his final physics paper.

"How was it?" he asked as we swung into step along the pavement.

"Crap, as expected," I said, "but less crappy crap than expected."

We passed two figures attempting to clamber up the same lamp post simultaneously, one of whom was clutching a traffic cone, evidently intending to cap the lamp with it. A feeble prank compared to such legendary exploits as nocturnally winching an Austin Seven onto the Senate House roof.

"Who cares, though," I continued. "They're over! Our finals are finally history, and as someone once said, not even God can undo history. What was your paper like?"

Rob stopped biting at the skin round his fingernails. "Not bad. Who's that?" Someone was shouting Rob's name and then mine.

We looked round to see Gerry hurrying towards us, waving. "Just the chaps I wanted to see!" He was panting like an asthmatic Golden Retriever. "How would you chaps like to do a cabaret at the May Ball?"

"You're somewhat late in asking," Rob pointed out.

"Don't blame me," Gerry held up his hands in defence. "I was pushing for you chaps from the off, but got overruled. The Footlights have now pulled out for some feeble reason, so now's your chance."

"We've already got our tickets," Rob said. "We're all going. Natalie's coming up from London, Alex is taking Sarah, and Phil's with Melanie."

"You'll already be there? Terrific! You can just dip out of the revels for half an hour in order to do your worst!"

"What about the fee?" I said.

"You'll get what we were going to pay the Footlights," said Gerry, "which is quite a fair whack."

"Plus a refund on our tickets?"

"Only for you three, not for your partners as well."

"Come on, Gerry!"

"Sorry, I wouldn't be able to swing it with the others."

"Throw in use of your room in college," Rob said. "It'll give us a base."

That was agreed.

Rob and I headed back to Selwyn Gardens. This extra booking – our third May Ball cabaret – coming on top of the final exam paper *ever* was the icing on the cake, the shot of whisky in the beer, the surge of adrenalin in the bloodstream.

I became more and more exultant, and when, on our getting back to our den of vice, Alex emerged from Ewan's room, followed by Ewan himself, each holding up bottles of what turned out to be champagne, I let out a roar of approval. I told Alex of our Pembroke booking, and he echoed my roar.

My room being the largest, we four gathered in there, and were soon elevated to five by Edward's arrival. Corks popped, fizz fizzed, toasts were drunk, cheers echoed. All of us had completed our exams: Rob and I our finals, the others their Part I's. More corks popped, more fizz fizzed.

Rob dashed upstairs for his guitar, and returned to serenade us with his work in progress on 'A Shit, a Shower, a Shave and a Shag'. We cheered and clapped and shouted that it was genius, a masterwork, out-Beatling the Beatles, out-Rolling the Stones, out-wrecking T. Rex, slaying Slade, and we insisted he sing it again and then again while the rest of us improvised an as-yet-unwritten chorus. Ewan commandeered my free-standing convector heater to use as a drum. Edward started blowing across the top of an empty champagne bottle to make hooting noises. Alex kept singing 'Gotta Whole Lotta Love' and vocally impersonating Led Zeppelin riffs, while I danced around tearing up lecture notes on organic chemistry and scattering them like confetti.

From the guitar strumming, the convector heater banging and the bottle hooting, a new rhythm developed. I abandoned confetti strewing, sat at the typewriter and clattered the keys in rough time; Alex switched to chanting, "Number nine, number nine, number nine..." from the Beatles' 'White Album'; Edward added the rhythmic chinking of bottles to the hooting sounds; Rob played some fancy guitar work; Ewan became more adventurous as he pounded away on the convector heater drum. The volume increased and increased. The pace became more urgent, frenetic. All of us started adding vocal contributions: "Oh yeah, baby!", "Mama's got a brand new bag!", "Get down and get with it!", while Alex intoned, "Number nine, number nine, number nine," in a crescendo, "number nine, number nine, number nine... number ten!" With a final almighty crash, we stopped in unison.

It was cathartic if nothing else.

I rang Melanie later that evening; but it was her mother who answered. I put on my politest manner, despite a distinct, champagne-induced throbbing in the temples.

"Good evening, Mrs Mason. It's Phil here."

"Indeed?" She sounded slightly wary, as though I might be a telephonic Jehovah's Witness. "Are you the young man she went away with before Easter?" Her tone had plunged into a flask of liquid nitrogen.

"We went to the Lake District, yes. That's me. Is Melanie around, please? She is expecting me."

There came a sound which could well have been the gritting or grinding of teeth. "Wait!" she commanded. "Melanie!" I heard her calling. "Telephone! Melanie! For you! I must say," she continued, talking to me again, teeth-gritting or grinding again in evidence, "I was surprised that she went away as she did. You do know she has an understanding with a very nice boy here? Simon? They've been going out together for some years. He comes from a very nice family."

"Know the name," I said, thinking, *that tosser.*

"He helped Melanie through a very difficult time indeed, when she... with the little bit of trouble she had. He was a real tower of strength, and I think that brought them very close."

"How nice," I said, vigorously gesticulating with two fingers of my free hand. This was no idle conversation merely filling in the time before Melanie got to the phone. I reckoned I could expect to find a horse's head on my pillow if I crossed her, and even the pachydermous Mr Scrimshaw could take lessons from her. No ducks would violate *her* lawn without express permission filed in triplicate.

"She does still have a year to go at Cambridge," the wretched woman continued remorselessly, "and Simon graduates this year. We expect to hear good news from them both after she's graduated. I'm sure you wouldn't want to endanger her happiness, would you?"

"I assure you, Mrs Mason, nothing could be further from my thoughts."

"Here she is now," the Mafia matriarch said, adding unconvincingly, "How nice to have had a little chat with you, Bill." There was a clattering sound, and next I heard Melanie's voice.

"Hiya, Melanie here," she said brightly.

"Hi darling, how are you?"

"Oh, hello Phil," she continued in the same bright, slightly artificial tone. "How kind of you to ring!"

"Is your mother listening?"

"Yes, I think that's right! How have you done? Was it your last paper today? I hope you..." Her voice changed abruptly, losing the artificial brightness and sounding weary as she continued, "She's gone! I do wish she wouldn't do that!"

"She's just been banging on about Simon being your boyfriend and threatening to have my goolies for golf balls."

She gave a squeal of irritation. "Oh no! I am *so* sorry! She's obsessed with Simon and can't get it into her head that he and I are not, 'n' 'o' 't' 'not', underlined, in big capitals and italics, *not* an item in any way, sense or form."

"Like Simon himself? Fixated about it?"

"Worse. He at least has moved on. Believe it or not, I heard via Anne that he's going out with someone called Olivia, and and and he met her in the Bristol Christian Union."

"Praise de Lord!" I said.

"Amen!" Melanie said fervently.

That afternoon she'd visited Mikey who had been a little more rational than before; she'd let her supervisor know she would go in for the history essay prize; and before long she'd be returning to Cambridge, well in time for the May Balls.

I headed back to my room in a happier frame of mind, but still in the dark about what it was in Melanie's past that she herself had hinted at some weeks ago and which her mother had just alluded to as the 'very difficult time' and 'little bit of trouble'. It was more, presumably, than simply ordinary adolescent angst, but quite what and how much more I couldn't say.

Chapter 53

Melanie

Exeter: April 1997

'Struck by sublimity' isn't quite the right expression. It suggests a physical force, an abrupt and brutal transition from one state to another, whereas it's more like a musical segue where there's continuity despite a shift in what's being played that's so seamless you don't realise it's changed until it's well under way; or as in a film where there's a dissolve from one scene into the next and when it's done well you feel it's natural and could not be other than it is.

Here the transition was my entering an awareness, an altered state of consciousness which simply felt like an elaboration of my everyday awareness, a deepening or enriching or intensification of how I am. My everyday awareness didn't actually disappear but became its own distillation. It transmuted into an essential oil of itself, until I'd become fully immersed in the deeper awareness which was permeated by a sense of graciousness, as every bit as natural and real as the everyday awareness in which Phil and I had sat in the courtyard of the cafe, talking and holding hands, weeping and saying goodbye, and in which I'd been enveloped by a deep sorrow that was not quite grief, more an abiding ache deeper than physical.

Now I no longer felt sorrow but a profound restfulness. A tranquillity accompanied by a sense of the underlying unity of all that is, a glittering network connecting all with all. A profound recognition, too, that this is where I belong and have always belonged and will always belong, for I've been here before: on the banks of Loch Lomond, in the streets of Cambridge, at a visit to the Royal Academy, on a pew in George Herbert's church. Each and every occasion revealed as the one occasion, unified across time since time has been transcended, unified across place since all places are the one place.

I'd halted on the little suspension bridge across the Exe a few hundred yards downstream from the quay when the kingfisher flashed by. It's odd how you can see the same scene many times and never take in what it consists of, because when Phil and I would meet two or three times a week, often to walk along by the river, we must have stopped a dozen times or more on the Trews Weir bridge, but this was the first time I'd paid any proper attention to what you can see from it. We had always been too wrapped up in each other. The kingfisher had opened my eyes.

Looking back towards the quay you immediately see Trews Weir itself as a ragged line of churned-up water and spray, and on the right-hand bank there are the modern apartment blocks where Chloe lives, the Port Royal pub, and various other buildings dotted along with a church spire visible behind them. Straight ahead you can make out a clutter of buildings including the Custom House on the quay itself along with another church spire beyond. There are various buildings on the left-hand bank too, and the whole scene is not terribly harmonious but busy-looking, all concerned with human activity.

When you turn around and look downstream it's amazing how it changes. The river curves gently to the left as it heads towards Salmon Pool, and there are loads of trees on the banks – willows, sycamores, alder and ash among others – and it looks immensely peaceful, with only an electricity pylon some distance away reminding you that the earth 'wears man's smudge'.

With that before me, the city behind me, I leaned against the rail. The earlier chill had given way to a burst of unclouded sun and I'd taken off my Cossack hat while gazing down at the river to watch the swirls and little vortices and curious creases on the water surface. The wavering shadows cast by the trees on the bank and the peculiar permanence of the ripples and furrows give the surface of the river the look of a vast expanse of carved, polished, living stone: in turn white marble, green marble, ebony; mottled and flecked and exquisitely fashioned. Leaves and flecks of foam on the surface drifted along.

I am neither actively thinking nor actively not thinking; I have no desire for either, I am simply here, a recipient. Sense impressions come and go, flickering in my awareness without my doing anything other than acknowledging briefly to myself that they're there: the pressure on my arms where I'm leaning against the rail, a bird call and a second call in response, the rhythm of breath in my nostrils, the percussion of heavy shoes and a rocking sensation as several young men tramp jauntily across the bridge in step, a snatch of conversation, the breeze ruffling my hair, distant church bells waxing and waning on the wind, the feel of denim against my legs as I shift my stance – all these sensations filtering in and out of my awareness, losing their individual identities until they are without any absolute distinction. As they enter my mind, my mind enters them; I become the swirling water, the metal rail, the bird calls, the denim and the distant church bells; I am the shadows of the trees and the trees themselves, the current-borne leaves and flecks of foam, and the swans that come sailing regally from beneath the bridge.

I become aware of an out-of-the-corner-of-the-eye change in the continuous interplay: dark shapes seemingly at a distance become foreground, reveal themselves as the trees on the river banks, enormous trees now, not simply physically, enormous in their spirit. Huge extrusions of pure existence out of nothingness, ramifying into broad angular branches and thinner spidery branches and manifold twigs and buds and leaves, all charged with a desire to burst through their physical restraints; the shapes I see are repositories of something more than real straining to escape and make itself actual. The trees are in constant interchange with the air and the soil and the sunlight which now bathes them and now withdraws as the shadows of clouds come and go; all boundaries are permeable, transient; they melt and re-form and melt again; they flow, they dissolve.

Another out-of-the-corner-of-the-eye change as I turn my head such that I'm now looking down the length of the rail, and at the hawsers which are wrapped in windings of a thick black tape, curving down from the pier-ends to the centre-point of the bridge where I'm standing, and at the vertical steel struts, silvery in the sun, taking the tension. The rail itself is painted a cream colour, with the suspicion of rusty pockmarks dotting its length – this is what I know, but what I see is a ceaseless interplay of qualities: cream and rustiness, black, pockmarkedness, silveriness, solidity, tensile strength – all transcending any simple specific description as I become the rail and the creaminess, the rust, the pockmarks, the tensile strength – I am no longer the subject experiencing the object but am the object being experienced by the subject, yet subject and object are merged into one as the boundary between me and what I perceive becomes thin and porous. I do not see the interplay, or feel it, or hear it, simply know it as one knows one's body, as one knows one's thoughts. I am part of the interplay while remaining still myself; inside me there floods the awareness that I am separate yet no longer separate.

Another change, and now a sensory constellation develops of sight and sound, a regular pulsing which grows in intensity, a rhythmic beating of wings, a flurry of splashes, a distinct series of quacks as two ducks launch themselves from the river, climb steeply, circling, then descend again onto the river, alighting almost silently. Someone cycles past me on the bridge, tinging their bell; a gust of wind chills my face and whips my hair into my eyes. There are wind-created furrows on the river surface.

The deep awareness is fading. It cannot be captured or rendered permanent. I feel serene and somehow cleansed as I resume my walk across the bridge. On the path, I take the left-hand fork such that I'll pass by Chloe's apartment, by when the moment is over and everyday awareness is with me once more.

Chapter 54

Phil

Cambridge: May 1972

I arrived at the station absurdly early. Even if Melanie's train were on time I had the best part of an hour to survive, which I managed to get through by drinking three coffees, solving four or possibly five clues of *The Times* crossword, and unwillingly concocting fantasies that she'd changed her mind about returning that day or that she'd forgotten all about me in the twelve or thirteen hours since we'd last spoken on the phone, or that bloody Simon had again insinuated his disruptive self into the fabric of her, and therefore also my, existence.

A minute after the train had pulled up only marginally late she was flinging herself into my arms. She had with her a large, flat, rectangular cardboard box as well as a suitcase and her shoulder bag.

"Just something," she said, mysteriously and gaily when I asked what it was. "You'll get to see in due course! Now, what's the plan? I'm dying for a coffee!"

The plan I instantly developed was to gaze adoringly at her, which I was soon able to carry out as we stood at the counter of the cafe I'd patronised earlier. Wearing boots, tights the correct description of which was, I thought, flesh-coloured, an Op-Art mini-skirt rather turquoise-y in colour, a simple plain blue top and a cute blue beret – wearing this ensemble she looked stunningly sexy. I longed to go back to Girton with her, remove or help her remove boots, skirt, top, tights and underwear, and spend the rest of the afternoon in bed. She could always keep her beret on if she wished, for fun.

A few minutes later, as I toyed with a hot chocolate, she was greedily downing a large mug of the brownish muck that passed for coffee in that establishment. Once when I'd asked them for a coffee, saying I was in a hurry and the instant variety would be fine, I had in all seriousness been warned that, "instant takes a little longer".

"How's things with your brother?" I asked.

"Well, they've changed his medication which should damp down his weird thoughts. The trouble is it rather zaps him out."

"That's a bit useless. What happens next?"

"They keep him under observation, as they say, and juggle the medication until he isn't zapped out but it still does its work. It seems to be a bit hit and miss. The unit he's in seems pretty good but depressing. I visited him every day. He's safe, which is the main thing, and my parents are all right enough about it, though I think my mother feels guilty. My father doesn't. His attitude is you have to do what's necessary, so do it."

"And you?"

"I feel, well, sad about it all." She pulled a face. "I don't know what else could be done. I just hope he won't have to be in there long. The idea is when they've got the medication right and he's back to normal – well, *his* normal – he'll be able to come back home. Trouble is, I don't think my mother can cope with much more, at least not all the time. I can do my bit when I'm home over the summer."

Which could mess up our time together, I thought gloomily.

"Hey," her tone lightened, "guess what! Nothing to do with Mikey."

She'd acquired a moustache of coffee. I flourished a serviette and wiped it off.

"What?" I asked.

"What what?"

"You said, guess what."

"Oh yes! Well, last night, as I was going to sleep, I was lying there and had this really exciting thought!"

"I have those as well. Fun, isn't it?"

"Naughty boy! No, listen. This history essay thing I'm going in for – I've got a great title. I'm going to call it 'Transcending Gender' with the subtitle 'Heresy, Women Mystics and Mediaeval Society'. What d'you think?"

Appropriately, I felt mystified.

"Don't you get it?" she asked. "'Transcending gender' has a double meaning: it suggests both that mysticism is something that transcends gender and can't be appropriated by just one section of the Church or society. It's also descriptive of the gender that I am concentrating on – women. Women as a transcending gender. The mediaeval Church, you see, was incredibly suspicious of women who claimed to have direct experience of God, mainly because it undermined the power and authority of the Church which was male-dominated. Still is, for that matter."

"Great," I said, still in the realm of mystification. "You're really going to get on with it this summer?"

"Yes. Now don't worry!" she laughed as it was my turn to pull a face. "I'll find time to fit you in."

There was a momentary pause as we both silently replayed that last statement.

"You're giving me ideas," I said.

"Nah, you've already got 'em," she put on her faux cockney accent.

Coffee finished, we left. I was not able to go to Girton with her thanks to a meeting I'd already fixed with Rob and Alex for a rehearsal in the Old Reader. We agreed that I would drop round to Girton that evening.

The rehearsal went well. The Old Reader is a small performance room which forms a part of the building that houses Pembroke Library. Complete with a little stage and lighting gantry, it has over the years been home to the Pembroke Players, seeing such illustrious alumni of the college as Peter Cook and Tim Brooke-Taylor strut their comedic stuff before their enthusiastic contemporaries. We were hoping to emulate them, or at least pay homage to them, in the first of the three May Balls at which we'd be appearing. Over the previous few days we'd worked up several new items, including my mime based on Edward and his contact lenses, and Rob's 'A Shit, a Shower, a Shave and a Shag' song, with the intention of including three or four of them, along with a tranche of tried and trusted material, in our performances.

The other two noticed that I was in buoyant mood, which unexpectedly became superheated to the state of hyper-buoyancy when I found in my JCR pigeonhole, after we'd finished rehearsing, a reply from the BBC to my letter of application for the post of 'Producer, Light Entertainment, Radio', inviting me to an interview.

"Brilliant, man!" Alex enthused.

"Remember us when you're famous!" said Rob.

We sat on the bed. Melanie, having had a shower before I'd arrived, was in her flimsy dressing gown which delightfully kept falling open to expose her breasts, and I had on just my Peak Experiences tee-shirt and a pair of underpants.

I showed her the letter from the BBC.

"Hey! That's great! Well done! You'd be perfect for it, wouldn't you? Are you confident about it?"

"Confident I'll make an impression," I said.

"Course you will."

"Trouble is, I don't think they're looking for impressionists."

"Twit!" She reread the letter. "Your interview's the day before my birthday. I know – we could spend the day in London together – go out and celebrate after you've wowed them!"

"Buy you a proper ring," I said.

"Oh Phil! Really? That would be wonderful!"

"Yeah, really."

"I think we should drink to that," she said excitedly, getting up. "I've got some cheapo vino. Fancy some?"

From the bottom of her wardrobe she extracted a bottle of red, removing a pair of lilac knickers that had become draped around the neck. I wielded the corkscrew, and poured a generous quantity of putative wine into each of two mugs she held out. We both grimaced as we swallowed a mouthful.

"There goes my teeth enamel," I remarked, while Melanie muttered, "Not quite yer actual Châteauneuf-du-Pape, but it'll do." Resuming her place next to me on the bed, she swallowed another mouthful and coughed.

"Phil," she said, now putting on a serious tone, "I hope you don't mind, but I think it's time I should tell you some things I've kept quiet about until now."

"Sounds heavy."

"It is in a way, and I'm afraid it doesn't put me in a very good light." She grabbed my hand. "I'm scared that in telling you what I'm going to tell you, you'll go off me, big time."

"Rubbish!" I took her hand. "I'm not going to go off you, sweetheart, how could I?"

"You haven't heard what I'm going to say."

"Don't be daft. Whatever you tell me, well, I'm not going to stop loving you."

"The thing is, when I was sixteen I behaved very, very, *very* stupidly."

"Join the club."

"No, seriously. This was truly stupid. You see, I got myself involved with a married man."

"Ah. Right. That does rank fairly high."

"He had a couple of children as well, one of which was, I think, about my age from what I could work out, though I never met them. I never met his wife either."

"Bloody hell! Who was he?"

"He was called Derek, and he was the leader of a Christian group..."

"You're joking!"

"...or sect really. They called themselves the 'Movement of the Spirit' Church, and he came and gave the sermon, the address, at an anniversary service of the Followers. It was meant to be Cliff Richard, which would have been great, but he couldn't do the date. This man Derek came instead, and he was a very impressive, persuasive preacher. This was six or seven months after Aberfan, which had rather destroyed my pretty simplistic Christianity, but it hadn't destroyed – well, it couldn't destroy – my 'moments'. Some deep spiritual reality. The Christianity that Followers was on about – all sin and repentance and the blood of the Lamb – didn't address that at all. Here he was, Derek, saying things about the power of the Holy Spirit which just seemed to me at the time to make a little bit of sense of what I'd experienced..."

Her voice had taken on a calm matter-of-factness, and I continued to listen. The room beginning to darken, she spoke of how this man Derek had fired her with his preaching; of how he'd spoken about being 'blessed by the gift of the Holy Spirit'; of how she'd heard with excitement his invitation to any who wished to come to a special service later in the week where there'd be the 'laying on of hands'; of how several of them, including Simon and her friend Anne as well as Melanie herself, had accepted the invitation; of how they'd gone to the centre somewhere in Kent where the 'Movement of the Spirit' was based; of how after lengthy extempore prayer over them, this Derek had laid his hands on each of their heads in turn and 'invoked the Holy Spirit'; of how she'd felt an intense heat flow through her body; of how she became convinced God had special work for her to do; of how Simon and the others had not gone to any further meetings, saying they found the man Derek 'creepy'.

She paused, breathing hard.

I managed to stay silent, waiting. I was still holding her hand, and after a minute or so, she resumed her account of how this Derek had been waiting on her route home after Followers one Sunday claiming he had a personal message to her from God; of how she'd felt special, and privileged, and humbled by this attention; of how she'd secretly gone to the centre alone; of how he'd laid hands on her again, saying that the gifts of the Holy Spirit were all for her; of how he'd told her he needed to give her some personal teaching and guidance; of how she'd returned a few days later, and then again, and then again; of how on the fourth or fifth visit to him, he said that true trust in God meant being completely naked before him; of how he'd insisted she undress straight away; of how he'd grown angry and accused her of defying God when she hesitated; of how...

And here Melanie stopped talking, and turned to press her head against my chest again as she started to sob.

"No need to say anything more if you don't want to," I said as her sobs continued.

"I must," she moaned in between more sobs. "I must say it."

Her sobbing eventually receded. Again she resumed the litany of awfulness: of how she'd slowly undressed in front of this Derek; of how he'd fondled her breasts; of how he'd undressed; of how he'd taken her virginity.

"I made myself believe I was being specially chosen by God," she whispered. "How stupid can you get?"

"That's ghastly," I said, thinking, perv! The man was a total perv! "How long did it go on for?"

"Several weeks. We had sex seven or eight times. I told myself I was being made special, because he was a man of God."

"Oh bollocks!" I burst out, angrily. "Man of God? He was a total, one hundred per cent proof, 24-carat, undiluted, transuranic, quintessential bastard! He was abusing you. And he could've got you pregnant."

"No, not pregnant." She shook her head slowly. "He did at least use a condom. Still abuse, you're right, though that particular word didn't occur to me at the time. I don't know what his intentions were in the long term – I guess to have sex with me until he tired of it and went off to find a prettier girl. I'm sure there was no intention to leave his wife for me. Or maybe he did want me as a long-term mistress, I don't know."

"He didn't just chuck you over?"

"No. What happened was that a few months earlier I'd started to keep a journal. It was meant to be a record of my spiritual life."

She told of how she'd taken to writing at great length about every meeting with this Derek; of how she'd described in detail what they'd done and how it made her feel; of how she wanted desperately to be brought closer to God because of it; of how she longed to be known as special 'in the sight of the Lord'; of how her mother, ever the nosey parker, had come across the journal hidden in a box at the bottom of Melanie's wardrobe; of how her mother had read the accounts; of how her parents had questioned her about the relationship, her mother hysterical, her father furious.

"With you?"

"No, not with me, with Derek. Daddy was brilliant!"

She continued, speaking of how, having got the address of the sect's headquarters, her father had left the house that evening; of how her father had returned grim-faced, announcing that that man would not be troubling her again; of how she'd been terrified that her father had actually killed him; of how she felt dreadful shame and remorse and misery and anguish; of how she was certain that she'd be damned for ever; of how she was terrified that the police would come and arrest her father; of how intense the relief had been when her mother told her that her father hadn't killed the man; of how she subsequently learned that her father, after confronting him, had then contacted every church and every religious group he could, denouncing him and the sect he led.

"Didn't he go to the police?"

"Apparently he did, but they said they couldn't do anything. I wasn't underage, and it'd be his word against mine, and impossible to prove anything criminal had taken place."

"That's a hell of a thing to go through, sweetheart. My God!"

"I'm afraid that's only half of it, Phil. There's a part two."

"Come on, let's have some more gut rot." I emptied the bottle into the two mugs. "Have you any more, if needed? Or rather, when needed? I should've brought some."

"There're a couple more bottles in the wardrobe. My secret stash."

"All that rot about me going off you, what was that about?"

"You still might, when you've heard part two."

Chapter 55

Melanie

Exeter: May 1997

I've never told anyone about my 'moments' except Phil when we were in the Lake District, and he didn't really get it. Not scientific enough for his taste. Ironically, I'm sure he's had his equivalent experiences – what he described to me the day we first met about being caught up in laughter at a Footlights revue, and the wonderful time at the Pembroke May Ball cabaret – if anything was an experience of transcendence, and one *shared* with the rest of us, that was it. It's sad that I won't be able to tell him about what happened to me at Trews Weir.

Although I didn't want to talk about the Trews Weir moment to anyone else, I did want to see Chloe and talk about meeting Phil, as well as catch up on what's happening in her life. She's been away, only got back on Thursday just in time to vote; we couldn't meet until last night when we had a drink at the Mill on the Exe. She looked stunning in tight blue jeans and a velvet jacket affair, hair casually gorgeous and tumbling down her back, make-up perfect. If I weren't completely hetero I'd fancy her like mad.

Inevitably the first thing we talked about was the election. Amazing! I was up half the night – up to the Portillo moment. After that I told her about Phil and me, and she stroked my arm and said how sorry she was that it hadn't worked out, and asked if we'd be keeping in contact, which strangely was something he and I hadn't talked about. I shrugged, saying that maybe we'd meet each other again by chance in another twenty-five years' time, when we're both in our seventies. Just saying "in our seventies" gave me a fleetingly peculiar feeling, like nostalgia for the future.

Chloe echoed, "In your seventies? Hmm. Do you think you'll still be with Simon?"

"Probably, unless one or other of us is pushing up the daisies."

"You're going to stay in the marriage?"

"Why not? I thought I was going to leave, but that was because of Phil. There's no point now, is there?"

"Isn't there?"

Chloe gazed at me, with those incredibly dark eyes of hers holding a very steady look. I asked what she was getting at.

She tilted her head to the side and now looked quizzical. "It's just that this seems to be fresh start time," she said gently. "I was simply wondering if you were going to take the plunge and become independent again."

"That's quite a question."

"It was meant to be more of a pondering than a question. After all, you don't have to leave a relationship only if there's someone else you're going to. You, one, anyone, might decide to leave because – well, I *will* ask a question. Does your relationship with Simon satisfy you?"

I looked down and fiddled with an empty ashtray.

"It's dull," I admitted eventually. "You know it's dull."

"Yes, I had gathered." She pointed at my empty glass. "Another? And shall we go inside?"

As we re-entered the bar, Chloe said, "Hello!" in that tone the police use on comedy programmes when they follow it up with, "What 'ave we 'ere?" And Chloe did add, "Look who's here!" She nodded in the direction of the fire, where someone was sitting by themselves on one of the sofas. I recognised Natasha from the revue. Chloe whispered in my ear, and pretty urgently too, I must say, "I know it's my round, but could you go and get them? Another Bacardi for me. I must go and say hello." She thrust her purse into my hand, and I headed for the bar while she headed for Natasha. It took ages for me to get served thanks to a loudmouth who kept changing his order, and when I finally got our drinks she was sitting next to Natasha on the sofa, deep in what looked like earnest conversation. I hovered for a few seconds not knowing quite what to do, then started walking noisily towards them. My clumping footsteps made them both look round, and Chloe mouthed "one minute" at me, while Natasha smiled briefly in my direction, in the way you do when you feel you ought to know someone but haven't an earthly who they are. I veered off to a table by the window where I could still see the weir, which is a more impressive affair than the Trews Weir version.

One minute? It must have been more like five when Chloe finally joined me. She looked triumphant and was clutching her diary.

"Well?" I said, and when she said "Well, what?" as she sat down, I commented in what I hoped was an arch tone, "You take a long time just to say 'hello'!"

"There are hellos and hellos," she said.

"Which particular sort of hello was that?" I asked.

"It was '*hello!*'" She drew the word out somewhat like Leslie Phillips, oozing with innuendo, and I had to laugh as she concluded by making a perfect O with her lips. I know I'm sometimes accused of pouting when it's just the resting position of my mouth, but hers were formed into the ultimate pout way beyond my abilities!

"She's been stood up," Chloe said.

"Oh, that's lousy."

"By Siobhan."

"Who's Siobhan?"

"No idea. Safe to say female."

"You're thinking you just might be a comfort in her affliction?"

"Could be," Chloe said, tapping her diary. "I have her phone number, and she has mine."

I asked what she was going to do – had they arranged to meet? Would she be phoning Natasha? Chloe wouldn't be drawn and reverted to our earlier topic.

"Dull," she said. "Your marriage to Simon is dull."

"'Fraid so."

"What are you going to do about it?"

"I don't know."

"Remember," she'd put her hand back on my arm, "I have a decent-sized spare room. Theoretically it's Richard's, my son – well, stepson really – but he's only visited once in the past year. If you decide the time has come to leave, it's there for you to use for however long you'd need to."

"Move in, you mean?"

She nodded, keeping her eyes on me as she took her lippy and little mirror from her bag, and only then did she take her eyes from mine.

"How did you and your ex separate?" I asked.

"It was a bit of a drawn-out process," she said, snapping shut the mirror. "We'd been spending more and more time apart doing different things, and then something came up – the possibility of taking a gîte for the best part of a year, bargain rate – which he was determined to take. He had in mind a concentrated spell of painting, 'the light, my dear, the exquisite light!' and I saw myself becoming chief cook and bottle washer. *Only* bottle washer. Plus I had the pharm course I was in the middle of, so I said no."

"Farm?"

"Pharmacy. I think I was the one to put into words what had been in the air for ages, that perhaps it'd be better if we went our separate ways. He agreed quite readily, but we dithered about it for some time, until one evening when we were both a bit drunk he came out with what seemed like the secret of the universe. 'Look,' he said, 'nobody lives for ever. Let's just get the fuck on with it!' and that was that: we got the fuck on with it, and separated! It's not a bad principle to live by!"

Get the fuck on with it – yes, exactly. That's what I need to do.

Chapter 56

Phil

Cambridge: May 1972

As I went to disinter another bottle of tooth enamel solvent from the medley of underwear occupying the floor of Melanie's wardrobe, she left the room saying she wouldn't be a minute. I assumed she'd simply gone to the toilet, but it was at least ten minutes before she returned. Meanwhile, I had enjoyed fingering her numerous knickers, a lacy black pair of which with her lingering aroma on them I'd liberated into the pocket of my coat.

"Yes please," she sighed, sitting down heavily on the bed. I poured us both a top-up. "My stupid mother," she added, having drunk some and coughed loudly.

"What about her?"

She emitted an impressively long and sonorous belch, flapping her hand in front of her mouth. "This wine! Um, yes, I suddenly realised I hadn't phoned home to tell them I'd got back all right, so I thought I ought to give them a ring and, well, you'll never believe this."

"Try me."

"Well, apparently – and not only apparently, but actually – I'm not really drunk, am I? – apparently Simon turned up half an hour after I'd left this morning, right 'out of the blue' my mother claimed. As if!"

"Oh God! What a pain that guy is."

"I'd thought there was something fishy when she'd got very agitated this morning when I said I was going for an early train to London to pick up something before coming on to Cambridge, and she tried her hardest to persuade me to stay on until after lunch. I didn't know what she was on about. Now I'm damned sure she'd been in touch with Simon to tell him I was back home for a few days, and told him to get down from Bristol to see me. Because I'm positive she knew he was going to turn up this morning, and I bet she would've invited him to stay for lunch!"

I made an exaggerated gesture of incomprehension. "What's she trying to achieve?"

“What she’s been trying to achieve ever since I stopped seeing him: to get us back together again.” She turned and looked at me ruefully. “I wonder if she’ll get the message when we’re married. You and me!”

“She’d better,” I said. “Lucky you left this morning when you did. You had no idea he might turn up?”

“Not an inkling. I assumed he was safe in Bristol gearing up for his finals and captivating this Olivia person he’s supposed to be getting it together with. Whatever’s happening or not happening there, he descended on the Mason household this morning only to find that this little bird,” she tapped her chest, “had flown.”

“Flap, flap,” I said.

“I’m afraid Simon now features rather heavily in part two. I need to tell you about part two.”

“Leave it for another time if you like?”

“I’d like to tell you now.”

“Okay. More lubricant?” I flourished the bottle.

“Good idea.” She hiccupped, and swept her hair out of her eyes and hooked it behind her ears, where it stayed lodged for all of five seconds. She automatically repeated the gesture at intervals, with the same result. “Well, the thing is, the following few weeks after I’d stopped seeing Derek, and my father had gone into action about him – well, that time was absolutely appalling. I was absolutely sick with feelings of guilt. Crying all the time. Couldn’t sleep. Sure I was damned. I’d let everyone down. I’d let Jesus down. I’d let God down. Everyone must hate me. I was in absolute despair. It was awful.”

I didn’t know what to say, so simply held her hand as the rest of her account followed: of how her father put her on a course of antidepressants; of how the drugs made her feel woozy and peculiar and scared; of how she’d refused to take them after the first couple of weeks; of how she was far too ill to return to school at the start of the autumn term; of how the leader of the Followers had come to see her.

“She was really nice and understanding,” she added. “Mrs Armitage. Felicity. It made me feel even more guilty for making nasty comments about her in the past.”

Again she resumed, speaking of how the only person she could talk to was Anne; of how Anne had tried to cheer her up but without much success; of how Simon had called round regularly to ask after her and she’d always refused to see him; of how she’d felt herself spiralling down and down; of how one Saturday, when her family went out for the day taking visitors to Greenwich Park, she stayed at home; of how, at her lowest point with everything bleak and dark and dreadful and lonely, she’d taken an overdose of paracetamol; of how Simon had called round shortly afterwards, while she was still conscious but groggy; of how he’d let himself into the house;

of how she later learned that her mother had previously contacted him to ask if he could keep a discreet eye on her while they were out, telling him where to find a key; of how on finding her he'd immediately made her sick by putting his fingers down her throat; of how he'd rung for an ambulance; of how, semi-conscious, she'd been rushed to hospital where she'd gone through the ghastliness of a stomach pump; of how everyone said that Simon's quick thinking and actions had saved her life and even prevented any long-term damage; of how after that everyone spoke of Simon as being her saviour.

"Jesus!"

"Strangely," she mused, "looking back, it was a turning point. I was kept in hospital a bit, then when I went back home I realised how relieved I was that I hadn't succeeded in killing myself. I remember lying in my bed, saying 'thank you, thank you' over and over again. I was incredibly grateful to be alive still, and I managed to focus again on my 'moments'. Everyone was so *lovely.* They really were. It shook me, in a good way. Anne came round and made me laugh – I didn't want to, but she can be hilarious. Finding I could still laugh was a revelation. Mikey was difficult. He tended to avoid me a lot for a while – I think I'd scared him, he broods a lot.

"When I went back to school – I'd missed two terms, and had to repeat a year – when I went back in, everyone cheered. It was amazing, and I burst into tears. The teachers were all very kind. Nobody seemed to blame me. Not many people knew the whole story, but I think everyone was aware that something awful had happened which had led me to take the overdose, and they were all on my side. It was like they formed a huge safety net that I'd fallen into."

She paused, made an expansive gesture with her hands, then continued. "Anyway, after that, the whole guilt thing started to evaporate – very slowly! I'm not like Anne, who doesn't do guilt at all. These days I'm back at a fairly average level! I do still go through low periods, as you've seen. That's what was happening during the Christmas holidays – you know, after I left you in the lurch outside the restaurant. I went down quite a long way, a sort of extended panic attack, and intense weariness, and incessant crying. That was on top of the whole Simon issue, too. I know my parents got quite concerned. My father wanted me to try another antidepressant. I didn't want to."

"How did you get through it?"

"Work, mainly. I'm lucky, I've always liked schoolwork and now university, and reading and thinking and learning. I can get quite obsessed by some particular topic, and when I do get depressed, it's a safe place for me to withdraw into. I've good friends like Anne and Sarah, who are great, and, please don't take this the wrong way, I'll always be really, really grateful to Simon. All through the time after I'd taken the overdose he was kind and supportive and patient, while I was pretty rotten to him."

I poured the rest of the wine into our two mugs. I raised mine. "To Simon," I said, surprising myself at how very benevolent I now felt towards him. Odd: if it weren't for him, I wouldn't right now be with Melanie because she wouldn't be alive for me to be with. It'd struck me before that the choices and decisions and actions of people we don't know shape much of our lives, whatever our own choices and decisions and actions might be and however much we think we're in control of our own destinies.

"To Simon," Melanie echoed, and we chinked mugs.

"He was terribly modest about it," she continued. "But he was dead chuffed that he was the one to ride to my rescue, and it seemed only right to say yes when he started asking me out. I did genuinely like him."

"But not...?"

"Not really as a boyfriend, let alone husband or life partner, no. That's when it started getting difficult, when it became obvious he was thinking along those lines. He had a strong ally in my mother. He still does."

"What about your dad?"

"He doesn't put any pressure on me. He never has. He made some remarks about we all do crazy things from time to time, and the trick is to treat them as learning experiences. If I'd decided that Simon was Mr Right, I'm sure he would've been pleased, but he believes in people living their own lives and getting on with it, and not being told by other people what to do."

She abruptly leaned down to pick up the two empty bottles from the floor. "Have we really drunk all this?" Her tone of voice had lightened to one of facetiousness. "No wonder I'm feeling like I'm feeling!"

"How *are* you feeling?"

She snuggled up to me. "I'm feeling I'm the luckiest girl alive! All that's behind me. I feel... I'm not sure... I feel relieved. That's it. Relieved! And Phil," she continued in a puzzled tone.

"Mmm?"

"Why aren't you seducing me? Have you gone off me?"

"Not in the slightest!"

"Prove it! If you think you can after all that wine!"

There followed a brief, enjoyable wrestle on the bed before I had to acknowledge that I was drunker than I'd realised, at which point Melanie gave a pout and quoted Shakespeare about drink provoking the desire but taking away the performance. I recognised it, having done *Macbeth* for O level English.

"Well, if you're not up for it," she said, getting off the bed, "I'll show you something instead."

"Already seen it!"

"Philip Ellis! You are so vulgar!"

"That's why you love me like you do."

"Sez you. But see what you think." She went to where the large flat cardboard container she'd brought back on the train was lying on the floor. She opened it, and slowly drew out a long, flowing item.

"I'm going to put the light on," she warned. "You won't be able to see it properly otherwise."

I winced as light flared into the room, and stared at what she was now holding up against her body. A fabulous ballgown. Long and satiny, a shimmering pale gold and white creation.

"What d'you think? It's my posh frock!"

"Yer what?"

"That's what my mother would call it. 'Posh frock'."

"Well, I call it gorgeous! Put it on!"

"Better not. It's very much handle with care, and it'd take some time to get it on. You like it?"

"It's stunning! You'll look fantastic. Where d'you get it?"

"In London. I'd been up and found it a couple of days after I'd returned home, but it needed a little bit of an alteration. It's what I went to pick up this morning, before coming on here. I've got shoes to go with it, and some dead sexy undies."

She hung the ballgown, aka 'posh frock', on the wardrobe door. "How about these?" she continued, pulling open the top drawer of her chest of drawers and taking out two long, slender, creamy-white items. Gloves. When she pulled them on they covered her arms almost to her elbows.

"These were originally my great-grandmother's. Aren't they fab?" she cried.

"Groovy!"

"I'm going to get my hair done posh as well. Amirah's good at that. Three May Balls!" She clapped her hands in excitement, then gently peeled off the gloves and replaced them in the drawer. "My great-grandmother was quite a character by all accounts. She did something scandalous – no one's quite sure what – at a ball she went to when everyone was celebrating Queen Victoria's Diamond Jubilee. Whatever it was she did, she got thrown out! She was an angel, you know."

"Doesn't sound like it!"

"Oh, she was. Literally. That was her name, you see: Mary Anne Angel. Which means," Melanie looked archly at me, "that you should treat me with due reverence, because I," she preened herself, "am descended from the angels!"

"My," I said, thinking quickly, "how you've descended!"

After Melanie had persuaded me to agree that the angelic nature of her ancestor had incontrovertibly been transmitted unaltered down the generations to her – her threat of withholding her favours if I didn't agree struck me as a totally convincing argument, accompanied as it was with the offer of my being on the receiving end of a judo throw – she went to make coffee.

I switched on the desk lamp, switched off the main light, removed my Peak Experiences tee-shirt and underpants, and sat naked on the bed.

"Oh I see," she said, returning and putting the mugs of coffee on a little table. "It's like that, is it?"

Allowing her dressing gown to fall to the floor, she stood before me wearing nothing but a sultry look. "Remind me," she said, her voice equally sultry. "*Am* I descended from the angels?"

It happened that where she was standing, the glow from the desk lamp behind her created an aura surrounding her body, with her hair as a glowing halo.

"Without a doubt," I said.

"How's the desire coming along now?"

"Mounting rapidly. As you can see."

"So it is. Let's find out about the performance."

She joined me on the bed. We let the coffee go cold.

Chapter 57

Melanie

Exeter: May 1997

Well, here I am. Chloe's spare room. Clothes put away in wardrobe and chest of drawers; books on shelves; toiletries in bathroom; desk things neatly arrayed on this table; Buddha and crucifix on window sill; bits and pieces distributed among various drawers and surfaces. The vast bulk of my belongings are still at the house, and will have to stay there until I work out how and where I'm going to live more permanently.

It's been both easy and not easy, the last two or three weeks. Easy in that I've felt and still feel comfortable and confident that this is what I've needed to do – although I can't say that the inner serenity has persisted all this time at the same level of profundity; and telling Simon was one of the most difficult things I've ever had to do.

It was only last Sunday afternoon that I found the opportunity to say my piece. He'd been working in the garden, and when he came back in and we were having tea, I took the plunge, saying I had something to say that I knew would upset him. He immediately looked alarmed and said he'd been worrying about me recently. Was I going down with ME again? No, it's not that, I'm fine as far as that's concerned, but the time has come that I need to live my own life much more independently. Puzzled look – what did I mean by that? I mean, I feel I need to move out of the marriage. Stunned look, puffing out his cheeks and expelling breath in short bursts – move out of the marriage? What, leave me? I'm really sorry to hurt you, Simon, I feel stifled, we're only partly living. We're happy, aren't we? Happy together? We have a nice house, nice friends, I've got a job I enjoy and you're getting back to doing things you like doing. Yes, it's all very *nice*, I agree, stressing the word in a way that is meant to convey my intense dislike of it. Honestly though, we're not exactly flourishing, are we? As people. You're good at your job, I know; and you enjoy your chess, and you're involved with the cathedral; and I'm getting back to my academic studies, and I do the adult literacy, and I'm getting to more concerts, all of which is good, but what happens between us, between you and me?

We're good together, aren't we? he persists. We've made a go of it, haven't we? We have a good life, we've had some lovely holidays, we've good friends, and we love each other, don't we? I sigh and say yes we love each other as friends, but there's never been any passion, any romance has there? He protests that we've been married for nearly twenty-five years; perhaps we've gone 'a bit stale'.

Thanks to the residual serenity I don't explode at his depiction of our relationship as simply 'a bit stale'. It sounds too much like food that's exceeded its best before date. It's always been 'a bit stale', I counter; and our love life has been non-existent. I don't think that's true, he says in a voice which comes as close to petulant as he'll do. You know it has, I say – when did we last make love? Seriously, when did you last see me naked and get an erection?

He puffs out his cheeks again at that and looks embarrassed. That's never really been our way, has it? he says. What is our way, do you think? We're more affectionate, aren't we? Yes, affectionate, I concede, and there's nothing wrong with being affectionate, I like affectionate, but it's not enough for a relationship like ours is supposed to be, man and wife. We're friend and friend, that's about it, isn't it? I'm sorry, our marriage doesn't give me what I need and I honestly don't think it gives you what you need either, though you might not know it.

He goes quiet at this, apart from more puffing of his cheeks, and shakes his head very slowly like someone trying to free themselves from being entangled in masses of spiders' webs; then he asks in a flat voice if I'm saying I want to leave the marriage because I've got someone else, and I'm relieved to be able to be honest in saying that no, it's not because there's someone else, it's because I need to breathe, I need to get out of the rut that I'm in and you're in and we're both in. Where do you propose going, he asks. I tell him that Chloe has offered me her spare room, I'll probably move in with her for a while, and see how things pan out.

He gets up and paces about, fingers through hair making it stick up, more pacing, starts to speak, falls silent, leaves the room, and I hear him doing something upstairs, and he returns after several minutes with our wedding album. Look, he says, stabbing a finger at a photo of our coming out of the church, Anne and Jeremy just behind us with best man Kenny, all of us smiling, me in my lovely dress, looking happy, and I really was happy that day; there, he said, as though he'd produced a conclusive piece of evidence, that's us. That's us then, I say; it's still us now, he says, just twenty-whatever years older. He's breathing heavily. Keep calm, I tell myself, don't argue with him, don't push the river, it's huge for him to cope with, for anyone to cope with. Things change, I say, we change, life changes. I don't understand you, he says, and inside I say no, that's the problem, you've never understood me, and I've never really understood you. I'm going out, he says, I must clear my head, I must think about this, and I think you ought to think about it very carefully too. When he returns after an hour, an hour and a half, he seems to expect me to have changed my mind, but I haven't, and we go through it all again. And again.

We went through it again several times over the next few days, saying the same things using slightly different words. When I told him that I was getting myself a car he immediately said that's not a good idea; and I said I'm definitely getting one; he told me not to be silly, it was a waste of money to get another car, we can't afford it in any case, and I'm 'not behaving responsibly'.

"Don't you tell me whether I can have a car or not!" I protested.

"We can't afford it," he insisted doggedly.

"*We* might not be able to," I said, "but *I* can. Don't worry, I'm not expecting *you* to put a penny towards it. I've still got the money from my father."

"You've always said you were keeping that for a rainy day."

"Simon," I said, knowing he doesn't like vulgarity, "right now it's pissing down."

He made no comment when I went out last Saturday and arrived back in my 1100, though I did catch him looking under the bonnet on Sunday afternoon. Big relief when this morning finally arrived. I was afraid he would mount one last campaign of pleading to try to persuade me not to move out, or switch into his super-helpful mode and offer to pack my car and bring anything else I needed in his, which I would have found difficult, but I'd already told him that Chloe would be coming round with her car to help and he'd nodded and said that's nice, and that he'd be going out for the morning.

Chloe turned up and we were both sombre as we loaded up the two cars, leaving masses behind, and drove here and offloaded, then she had to go to work – which was good because I didn't want even her around to begin with. A right old mix of feelings keeps sweeping through me: relief, disbelief, excitement, serenity – and terror. I hadn't realised beforehand that terror lies on the far side of freedom. Terror that I'm on my own. Terror of what the future might hold.

It's now about seven thirty. Chloe should be back about eight, and we'll have a meal together. Sweet of her, since if it weren't for me coming today she'd be out with Natasha. Or possibly in with Natasha.

I need a shower. Followed by a glass of something.

Chapter 58

Phil

Cambridge: June 1972

The ancient staircase being too narrow for us to descend arm in arm, I preceded Melanie from Gerry's set of rooms down to Old Court where we encountered Mr Scrimshaw, standing as ever outside the porters' lodge, gazing on the scene before him of the college pullulating with ballgowns and penguin suits, the look on his face betraying the internal conflict he was presumably experiencing between, on the one hand, avuncular pride in being a part of the tradition of Pembroke College mounting an impressive May Ball every two or three years, and, on the other hand, grief and horror at the desecration being wreaked upon the holy lawns of the college's various courts by innumerable revellers below the rank of 'don' who had been revelling or were currently revelling or were about to revel in the marquees erected on and adorning said holy lawns.

"Evening Scrimmers! Quite a sight, eh?"

"Good evening, sir. Indeed it is. Good evening, miss." He doffed his bowler to Melanie. Rumour had it that he bought a new bowler hat every year the college mounted a May Ball, and certainly the specimen he was currently sporting looked pristine in its bowler-hattedness. His suit, too, straining at the buttons, had the air about it of having been recently dry-cleaned. A white rosebud adorned the jacket lapel. "You, sir," he continued in a tone which, for him, counted as bantering, "if I may say so, have scrubbed up well, very unlike your usual self. Would you not agree, miss?"

Melanie laughed, leaving it unclear as to whether she would or would not agree.

I fingered my blue velvet bow tie which completed the perfection of the frilly-fronted dress shirt I wore beneath the immaculate dinner jacket. I had even undergone the purgatory of a haircut, albeit at Melanie's insistence. "What about Miss Mason?" I queried. "Would you say she's scrubbed up well?"

Melanie gave a twirl. She looked fabulous, stunning, gorgeous, in her off-the-shoulder gown of shimmering, satiny gold and pure white, and her hair in a complicated braid with delicate wisps curling down over her cheeks.

"It's not my place to say, sir," Mr Scrimshaw asserted, giving me a wink. "I am but a humble servant of the college."

"Oh, come on, Mr Scrimshaw," protested Melanie as I packed a megaton of scepticism into a brief burst of laughter at his use of the word 'humble'. "You must at least like the dress?"

"I don't think it would suit me, miss! Not my size. If you press me, I will concede it is of exceptional attractiveness, and," he put his hand to his mouth and gave a little head-porterly cough, "you do it full justice, miss." He concluded by making a slight bow.

"Gallantly spoken!" I came close to clapping him on the back, but even in bantering mode to clap the back of Mr Scrimshaw would have been one bridge of familiarity too far, and I had to be satisfied with an embryonic back-clapping gesture. "Come on," I turned to Melanie, "let's see if we can find the others. Cheerio, Scrimmers! Behave yourself tonight!"

"Sir." He courteously raised his bowler once more. "Miss."

The ball was well under way. We had with us a printed programme of when and where various events were taking place: live bands, discos, food, entertainments. Air Raid Precautions were due to perform at midnight.

"Undiluted privilege," Melanie remarked as we made our way to where a college band, The Edyveans, with Tristan as vocalist, was scheduled to be playing.

"True. But now we're here..."

"Oh, I'm going to enjoy it, don't you worry!"

We started to immerse ourselves in the evening's hedonism, knowing that once ARP's performance was over, immersion could be complete.

Half an hour before our performance was due to start, Alex, Rob and I, with our glamorous entourage, gathered at the Old Reader. Gerry, again sporting his scarlet slash of a cummerbund reminiscent of a clumsy disembowelling, let us in. Our earlier preparations had been comprehensive, with the minimal set consisting of our screen, a couple of chairs, and three tables with various small props on them, all in place, hidden behind the stage curtains – the first time we'd had a curtain; and with the space for the audience, far too intimate to be referred to as an auditorium, set out cafe-style. Maybe seventy or eighty could be accommodated at the tables, with other scattered chairs around, and room for standees against the walls. As the place started to fill up, a lively atmosphere developed. Alex, Rob and I were lurking on the stage behind the curtains, keeping tabs on the mounting audience numbers by peering through holes. "Full house," said Rob with ten minutes still to go. Yet more people came cramming in.

At midnight, Gerry doused the house lights, brought up the stage lights, and pulled on the cord opening the curtains. A moment later a huge cheer went up as I strode out to centre-stage to start the entertainment with a fast-paced monologue as a commentator on a football match between two Welsh teams with all the players on both sides and all the officials named Evans. It was the sketch that I'd written and performed for the Footlights audition in my first term.

It went well, as did the next two items; all three were of material we'd performed before and had confidence in. The laughs came freely, and each sketch elicited sustained applause at its conclusion. We were starting to fly.

There followed, with numerical inevitability, the fourth item. This, a newly written ragbag of a sketch, went under the novel and inspiring title of, simply, 'Sketch'. It started with Alex and me pacing about the stage exchanging surrealistic comments, and being interrupted by Rob popping up as the genie of the cornflake, or genie of the bucket, or genie of whatever had just been mentioned. It was not a massively funny or coherent item, more a series of semi-comic lines haphazardly strung together, and was getting barely enough laughs to justify its inclusion when there came a bit of business which, stupidly, fortuitously, we hadn't fully rehearsed. It entailed Alex proclaiming he was hungry, tipping cornflakes from a cereal box into a bowl, then taking up a bottle of milk and pouring it into the box rather than the bowl and eating the cereal from there.

In the interests of milk and cornflakes conservation, we hadn't rehearsed the tipping-milk-into-the-box part of the routine, and the moment Alex did so the utterly predictable but nevertheless unpredicted outcome occurred: milk immediately started pouring from the bottom of the box. He continued to stride about the stage, munching cornflakes and delivering lines, clearly totally unaware of what was happening. This led to yells of laughter from the audience.

I grabbed another bowl and silly-walked after him, trying to catch the milk, until Alex, clearly puzzled as to why I hadn't uttered the lines I should have been uttering, looked round to see me following him like a bizarre hunchbacked shadow, and with milk spraying all over the place from his cereal box. Although had all this unintentional slapstick been deliberately scripted it would have been yawningly unfunny, the look of dawning comprehension that spread across Alex's face resulted in the audience laughter going through the roof.

As we finished the sketch and left the stage, a storm of applause broke out, and following that we could do no wrong. For the rest of the performance the laughter became total and continuous, punctuated by frequent peaks obliging us to pause, or Rob, if a song were in progress, to play a short instrumental passage before it became possible for him to resume singing. 'A Shit, a Shower, a Shave and a Shag' made strong men weep, and after boisterous chants demanding an encore Rob obliged, with the entire audience roaring the chorus. "The natives are going wild!" Rob panted, sweating profusely, as he left the stage.

As I then performed a solo sketch, an elaborate riff on quantum mechanics explained by a television cook, I had the sense of being outside time and having control over it; I could make it slow down to allow a finer and finer discrimination of when to speak and when to pause, when to move and when to stay still; I'd become a circus ringmaster, with the passing seconds and minutes as performing animals responding to my every command.

I could focus on one individual in the audience to see them laughing slowly, clapping slowly, like a film slowed down to a thousandth of its proper speed. I could pick out Melanie captured as in a photograph in mid-laugh, her eyes wide and bright and glistening with tears; or Ewan throwing his head back infinitely slowly, his mouth a rictus of extreme mirth; or Edward clutching his midriff in mid-gasp. Watching from the wings as Rob and Alex performed 'Russian Roulette' and waiting for the moment to fire the starting pistol, I was sure I could see every twitch of their facial expressions, every firing of their neuronal pathways, with each of them in turn spinning the barrel of the replica gun, putting it to his temple and squeezing the trigger.

The entire Old Reader was transformed into huge, pulsing waves of laughter bouncing off the walls and ceiling, waves which Alex, Rob and I were generating and simultaneously surfing; all one hundred plus people laughing synchronously, such that we were not so many separate entities but had become a single, greater, entity. I caught Alex's eye as he came off stage after one sketch, and could read in it something of the same sense, the same desire to *remember this, we will remember this for ever!* The forty minutes of what would normally have been a half-hour cabaret engendered in me what I could only think of afterwards as love, and a reckoning of how could hate possibly exist between people who could laugh together like this? Performers and audience alike, with no discrimination between or among us, had been caught up in the most overwhelming and intense love-in.

"It was weird, it was wonderful," I said to Melanie a little later, as we dug into a plateful of cold roast duck (I wondered if Mr Scrimshaw had had a say in the menu) and all the trimmings. "It was like being on a different plane of existence for a while, and seeing everything from a different angle, but being a part of it at the same time, totally immersed in it."

"Like that time you told me about, seeing the Footlights in Edinburgh?"

"Yeah, only this time I was on the stage, not in the audience. In a way, no distinction between the two."

"Mmm," she said. "You know what I think that's about?"

"What?"

"Possible sublimity," she said. "That's what it is, Phil. Possible sublimity."

Chapter 59

Emhalt: December 1969

The letter box clattered. Melanie instantly stopped playing her flute, and her father at the piano played a concluding couple of chords, leaving William Gluck's *Blessed Spirits* frozen in mid-dance. Orpheus would have to postpone his search for Eurydice.

Father and daughter looked at each other.

"Well, angel, are you going to go and see?"

Unable to speak, Melanie nodded and left the room. There was a scatter of envelopes on the front doormat, most of which would contain Christmas cards, but would the longed-for letter be among them this time? The last three mornings she had been disappointed, and her anxiety was mounting.

Her hands shook as she scooped up the post and rapidly flicked through it. She gave an involuntary gasp as her fumbling revealed a long white envelope with a transparent window showing her name and address on the letter within, the top left of the envelope being decorated with a heraldic shield, the arms, she knew, of Girton College, Cambridge.

She looked at it blankly. If she didn't open it, both the possibility that she had been offered a place and the possibility that she had been turned down remained equally likely. If she did open it, one possibility would vanish, the other become a certainty. The responsibility to cause one or other possibility to become certainty felt overwhelming.

Her father was standing in the dining room doorway.

"Shall I, angel?" he asked as she continued to fiddle with the envelope.

"Please." She handed it to him. "I can't do it."

He smiled, nodded, and retreated into the dining room. Melanie followed him. He usually tore letters open unceremoniously, but not this time. He had lowered the flap of the bureau and was scrabbling around in a cubbyhole. He turned back towards her, brandishing the letter opener the family called 'the silver sword' after Melanie's favourite children's book.

Delicately he inserted the silver sword inside the envelope's flap and slit it open. He drew out the contents of a single sheet, unfolded it, and read it. Melanie was having difficulty breathing.

Her father sighed, shook his head, looked up, and spoke in a serious tone. "Well, my angel," he said, "it would seem that I now have a daughter...who's going to Cambridge University!"

With a squeal, Melanie flung herself on him.

"What's more," he continued, gasping, "with a scholarship! How about that!" He waved the letter gleefully in the air.

"What?" She pulled back, stared at her father, leaped up to snatch the letter from his hand and gazed at it. She could barely read it, her vision had become blurred with tears. She could just about make out the words "delighted to offer you..." and "scholarship..." and "many congratulations..."

"Well *done* Melanie," her father was saying. "Wonderful! Thoroughly deserved! I am *so* proud of you, darling!" He went to the door and shouted, "Joyce! Joyce! Here a minute if you can! We have some news from the realms of glory!"

Melanie was now dancing crazily round the room, her little cross on its chain flying all over the place, her hair whirling about. A scholarship! Her dreadful stupidity was at last behind her. She'd come through. She was going to Cambridge! She had been awarded a scholarship! So lucky! So lucky!

Chapter 60

Melanie

Exeter: July 1997

I don't mind that Simon sent me a birthday card, but I could have done without the dozen red roses which arrived with the message "To my darling wife on her birthday, forever young in my heart." Oh dear.

Chloe, when she got back from work and saw it, did a very good imitation of someone throwing up.

"It's very sweet of him," I said.

"Way OTT, wouldn't you say?"

"That's the trouble," I admitted.

"Never mind! You're about to have a great girlie evening. I'd better get going in the kitchen."

"I'll be your sous-chef."

"Oooh, honey," Chloe said suggestively. "That means you're under me!"

Chloe being Chloe she'd done all the necessary preparation for my birthday girlie evening before going to work, which meant there wasn't really any sous-cheffing left for me to do. I laid the table, opened a bottle and poured two glasses.

We were both putting on our posh frocks when the door buzzer sounded. I came out of my room in time to hear Chloe say into the entrance phone, "Okay, Simon, come on up." She pressed the button to let him in, and we dashed back to our rooms to put on dressing gowns, so when he reached the top of the stairs he was confronted by me in my boring old towelling affair and Chloe in her amazing kimono with red dragons.

"Something smells good," he said.

"We're having a little dinner party," I said as we went into the main room. "Thanks for your card, by the way, and the roses."

Saying, "Happy birthday!" he handed me a shoebox-sized parcel he'd been awkwardly clutching. The wrapping paper had little teddy bears on it.

A handbag. A handbag of the sort that his mother, or my mother for that matter, would have had in the 1950s. A sensible size with a sensible clasp in the sensible colour of navy blue. I deliberately avoided catching Chloe's eye.

"Thank you," I said, trying to sound delighted. "That's very kind."

"I thought you'd like a new one."

I nodded. "And this *is* a new one. Thank you Simon. It's really nice." I kissed him on the cheek.

Chloe, having given me a quick look to check I was all right, said she really ought to finish dressing and get back into the kitchen.

"Nice place," Simon said when she'd gone.

"Yes. It is. It's lovely."

"You and Chloe are getting on all right?"

"Yes. Yes, we are. It's working out well."

"I see." There was a pause, then, "How long do you think you'll stay here?"

"I can't say. Why d'you ask?"

"Because I'm missing you," he said.

I found it difficult to know what to say. I could feel his misery radiating fiercely.

"I'm sorry," I said.

"Are you sure you won't come back?" He held up his hands in apology. "I shouldn't have asked."

"That's all right."

We made awkward small talk until Chloe came to the rescue, calling out, "Sorry to interrupt, but they'll be here soon."

Simon took his leave.

As ever, Chloe looked stunning. She positively shimmered in a satiny short-sleeved blouse, as iridescent as the head of a drake and much the same colour. It was loose-fitting, with wide half-sleeves and this wonderful plunging cowl neckline. Irresistible! She'd bought a new lippy for the occasion. I've no idea what daft name it's got, but she claims it's the exact colour of a ripe peach just before it falls from the tree. Not sure about that, but it did look absolutely right on her, along with her new eyeshadow – now, if I try to glam myself up I look like a complete tart, while she brings it off effortlessly (I guess it's an effortlessness that takes a lot of effort to achieve). Having said that, I reckon I looked pretty good for forty-seven in the dress I got from the Gandy Street boutique. As it's rather glittery I put glitter on my cheeks, checked in the mirror, reckoned it made me look disturbingly like Marc Bolan of sacred memory circa 1975, so wiped off the glitter and reverted to looking like me again – though a bit more sophisticated than usual, with the velvet choker Chloe has given me as a birthday present.

Rita gave me a sweet watercolour seascape she'd found in the little arty shop in Topsham, and Charlotte, looking very smart in a bright flouncy affair and much more upbeat than I've seen her recently, gave me a mug with a picture of a woman in 1950s clothes, clutching her face in horror, and with the line "Oh my God! I should have listened *to* Mother, not *with* Mother!" More frivolous than I associate with Charlotte.

"A contribution," she added. From a voluminous bag she took out four bottles of wine.

"My word, these are...they are, they look good," Rita sighed, peering short-sightedly at the labels.

"Oh yes," Charlotte said airily. "Jimmy only goes to the most exclusive wine merchants dealing with the most exclusive wines. I'm not absolutely sure, but I think that one is at least fifty pounds a bottle, and much the same for the others."

Chloe and I both gaped in comical surprise. Rita just looked puzzled.

"*How* much?" we demanded.

"Jimmy is financing this?" Chloe added.

"In a manner of speaking," Charlotte nodded. "Not that he knows it. You see, I'm not convinced it's his wine in any case. 'With all my worldly goods I thee endow'," she quoted, adding, "that's what he said, and he didn't add, 'excluding my wine cellar'. Not that his cellar amounted to much when we first got married, but I take 'worldly goods' to include everything subsequent to the wedding as well, don't you? Added to which," she continued, "he's made it clear he doesn't want me, and I take it that he doesn't want the wine either. He's not been back for it."

I thought Rita might disapprove of Charlotte's wine grab, but not a bit of it, though she did say hesitatingly, "I'm not sure Paddy would, that is, he might think, he's very, I would say...what would he say?"

"Render unto Caesar that which is Caesar's?" I suggested.

"And unto Charlotte that which was Jimmy's?" Chloe added.

It was a terrific evening. The food was wonderful, and the wine marvellous, but most of all it was spending time with such lovely friends. The only sour note sounded when Simon rang.

We could hear Chloe say, "Oh, hello Simon," out in the little passageway where the phone is, emphasising his name so we couldn't mistake who she was talking to. She reappeared at this point, looked at me and indicated the receiver in her hand. I shook my head. She returned to the passageway. "No, I'm afraid not...that's not possible...no, not this evening...what did you just say?...hang on."

We saw her go past the sitting room entrance, and a moment later heard her opening then closing the bathroom door. As we waited for her to return, we refilled our glasses and Rita told Charlotte and me about a jilted woman seeking revenge who some years ago had given to neighbours her lover's entire stock of vintage wine. Charlotte looked thoughtful.

Chloe rejoined us in the sitting room, also looking thoughtful.

"Okay?" I asked.

"It's all right, he's all right. Just a little tired and emotional."

"Are you sure?"

"Positive."

"What was he saying? What did he want?"

"Not a lot. He kept repeating himself. He asked if you would ring him tomorrow, but I said that's up to you. He's okay. He'll be okay."

"Thanks," I said, topping up our glasses again, and not wanting to delve any further.

"Men!" said Charlotte. She'd been knocking back the red and was getting pretty tipsy. "We're better off without them! Take Jimmy."

"No thanks," said Chloe.

"Very wise. D'you know why you're wise? I'll give you at least ten reasons why you're wise." She started enumerating what she saw as Jimmy's faults. "For a start he's got that silly beard which makes him look like a pantomime pirate. Then there's his laugh which is *so* embarrassing. And his utter lack of dress sense. His puerile sense of pathetic humour. His inability to aim straight in the bathroom..."

She'd paused for more wine. Chloe and I exchanged delighted smiles, and Rita had covered her mouth with her hand.

"The disgusting hairs he leaves in the soap," Charlotte resumed. "His ludicrous attempts to be regarded as an expert on wine. The way he calls me 'Charlie' which he knows I loathe. His uselessness at the simplest DIY. His hopeless sense of direction. The way he picks his nose in company. His pig-headedness and refusal ever to listen to good advice. And his complete ignorance of how to satisfy a woman when...well, you know..." She coloured up at this point, saying, "Perhaps I'd better not say anything more."

"Don't stop now," Chloe gasped, putting her hand on Charlotte's arm. "You can't leave us guessing, can she?" She appealed to Rita and me.

I cried, "No! Go on! Go on!" while Rita feebly waved her hand in encouragement.

"Well, it's when you're having marital relations," Charlotte said.

Chloe shrieked with laughter.

"All right, making love. All right! Sex! I tell you, with him it's like having a tree falling on top of you, one in urgent need of pruning."

When we'd finally recovered, we drank a toast: "Girl Power!"

Chapter 61

Phil

Cambridge: June 1972

The other two May Balls for which ARP had been booked were at Darwin and Emmanuel. The first, at which we had two slots, was a low-key, civilised affair characterised by string quartets rather than rock and pop groups, presumably thought to be more in keeping with the greater maturity of the graduate-only nature of the college's members. Whether our performances raised or lowered the maturity quotient is debatable, but we were still well received, despite at times inducing deep mystification in the minds of the high proportion of overseas students in the audience whose understanding of the British undergraduate sense of humour was still, like the cabaret itself, sketchy.

By the time we were due to perform at Emmanuel, however, we were all knackered. We were on late, or, to put it another way, early, as it was after three thirty by the time we were able to get going. A heavy rock band called Complete Tosserz, justifiably unknown before or since, were true to their name and refused to leave the stage but just kept on playing. We were moved to a small room near the toilets, and began performing to an audience of about a dozen random bon viveurs who happened to have crashed out in there for recuperative rather than entertainment purposes. The number eventually swelled to around twenty, with some of them even managing to remain conscious as we went through our paces. The best laugh came when one bon viveur whose *viveur-ing* had been exceptionally *bon* suddenly and violently vomited during a sketch by Rob. "Aha! A discerning critic!" Rob ad-libbed.

After this final efflorescence of ARP at the May Balls we went our several ways: Rob back to Selwyn Gardens, Alex accompanying Sarah back to Newnham, while Melanie and I took a taxi out to Girton.

"You were fine! It was great!" Melanie insisted in the taxi as I commented not for the first time that our performance had only just about been good enough.

"We earned our fee," I agreed.

She yawned. "You can take me out for a meal with it!" A moment later she was asleep.

I had to wake her a few minutes later at Girton. I paid off the taxi, and Melanie, for the last time that academic year, sneaked me into the all-women's college and up to her room. We had not made love for several days, but were both too exhausted to remedy the matter.

I became aware of a noise which resolved into a thumping on the door accompanied by a voice calling out some meaningless syllables.

"Melanie! Are you there? Phone!" I recognised Amirah's voice as the syllables coalesced into meaning.

Melanie dragged herself from the bed. I closed my eyes again as she spoke with Amirah.

"Phil?" She'd come back into the room. "It's my father on the phone." She sounded worried. "I might be some time." She disappeared again.

After a few minutes I decided tea was in order. Passing Melanie at the payphone I heard her ask, "He's going to be all right, isn't he?"

I made the tea, assuming something had happened to her brother, but when she returned to the room she said straight away that Simon had been in an accident. "It's really serious. He could've been killed."

"God! What happened?"

"He was hit by a lorry when he was on his bike. A pedal came off or broke or something, and he lost control and went in front of the lorry which hit him. He came off and hit his head and the lorry went over him and trapped him."

"Fuckin' Ada!"

"Daddy phoned the hospital this morning. Simon's conscious, but he's got a fractured skull, and they're doing all the tests and things. His leg's a mess. He's likely to lose it. Something to do with how he got trapped. Oh Phil!" She started weeping. I rocked her in my arms until she was up to saying more.

The accident, it emerged, had happened in Bristol, where Simon would be kept while all the tests were being done. I didn't like to ask how her father had known about the accident, but she volunteered that they'd found out when her mother had rung Simon's parents to let them know Melanie would be back that weekend. "Forever scheming," sighed Melanie, "but on this occasion, well, I'm glad she did, otherwise it might've been some time before I'd found out."

She'd already planned to return home the next day, Sunday, and her father would collect her in the morning. No, she said in response to my cautious query, she wouldn't be going straight on to Bristol to see Simon. Not yet. Strictly family only. She'd go when she could.

"You don't mind, darling, do you?" she asked.

"Not at all," I said, wondering how much I did.

"It feels only right to visit when I can." She was now pulling distractedly at her hair. "I'm just frightened that there'll be permanent brain damage. I need to see him for myself, when I'm allowed to."

"Yeah, sure," I said, feeling resentful at the prospect that for the foreseeable future bloody Simon would continue to loom large in our relationship.

Chapter 62

Melanie

Exeter: July 1997

When Chloe got in this evening I asked her what Simon had said last night.

"Nothing really," she said, taking out her lipstick and going into the bathroom to use the mirror. "He just wanted to talk to you."

I followed her in. "Come on, it must've been more than that – you came in here so we couldn't hear what you were saying."

"It wasn't anything important."

I grabbed her lipstick and swung her round until we were face to face. "Come *on*. What was he saying?"

She took a moment or two before nodding slowly. "He was a little… discourteous, that's all."

She gave her winning smile, but I refused to be won. "That doesn't sound like Simon."

"I'm afraid it was. Like I told you, he was…tired and emotional."

"You mean drunk? That's not like him either. What are you not telling me?"

"I'm sure he didn't mean what he said," Chloe talked over me, which is not like *her*.

"Why, what was he saying about me?"

"Oh honey, no! Not you! Not at all. It's me. He was talking about me. He doesn't think I'm good for you."

"What! Why? Just because you're letting me stay here?"

"No, it's more personal than that." She sighed, shaking her head slowly. "I'll have to come clean, won't I? Look, why don't you go and open a bottle of plonk? I'll just…"

She pulled her hands from me and brushed away a tear.

"It's because I'm gay," she said a few minutes later. She'd changed into her red dragons, and we were out on the balcony.

"What's that got to do with anything?" I said. "And I didn't know he knew. He certainly didn't know a few months ago, when he thought you might get it together with Phil."

"He saw me with Natasha a couple of weeks ago at the cinema, well, outside the cinema, we'd just come out and he was behind us. We were – how shall I put it? – being affectionate. It would've been obvious we were more than just a couple of good friends having a night out. Last night he asked me outright if I'm a lesbian."

"You're joking! What did you say?"

She shrugged. "I said 'I'm gay, yes'. What else would I say? I suppose I could have said it's none of his business, which is true, but I'm not going to prevaricate. He said he thought that must be the case. I asked him what he was getting at, and he said he'd prefer it if you," she pointed at me, her kimono sleeve fluttering in the slight breeze, "weren't living here."

"What? Why?"

"My very words. Apparently he doesn't think living with 'a lesbian' is good for you. He said I must be a…he didn't say *bad* influence. Something like that. 'Adverse influence', that was it."

I felt mortified. "Oh Chloe, I am *so* sorry! What a thing to say! You're the complete opposite."

She smiled at this. "I do my best! Not in his eyes, apparently, and I guess he wants you to phone him so he can urge you to abandon this den of deviancy!"

"I jolly well will phone him now, and I'll tell him not to be idiotic."

"It is idiotic, you're right. It probably won't do any good to have a go at him, though. It never does."

"It still upsets me," I said. "I'm upset Simon's like that. He shouldn't have hurt you."

"I'm not that hurt," Chloe said. "More exasperated. Not to say surprised. I would have expected it from Rita's husband, but not Simon."

I'm surprised as well. Simon's never expressed any strong opinion one way or the other about the issue, and I've always assumed his view was that of the liberal consensus that being gay isn't deviant or wrong, just another way of being human. It seems I was mistaken.

I rang him but got the answerphone. I didn't leave a message.

I got through to him when he'd returned from chess, and I was still shaking. He started off very brightly, saying how nice it was to hear my voice, hoping I'd had a good time yesterday evening, and what had I been up to today? I didn't answer but went straight into asking why he'd rung yesterday evening as he'd seen me only two or three hours earlier.

"I…wanted to hear your voice," he said, the brightness having gone from his own. "I was feeling a bit down. I'd been thinking of your other birthdays. This was the only one we'd not spent together for years. Since before we were married."

"What did you say to Chloe last night? About me being here."

He made his puffing sound. “Nothing in particular. I just asked if you could ring me today. Which you have!”

“She’s just told me that you said she’s a bad influence on me.”

“I didn’t!”

“Sorry. An ‘adverse influence’. She’s an adverse influence, you said. Didn’t you?”

“Did I?”

“That’s what she says. I believe her.”

“I might have. ‘Adverse’ doesn’t mean ‘bad’.”

“It certainly doesn’t mean good, does it? It’s because she’s gay. Isn’t it?”

“She *is* a lesbian. She admitted it.”

“So what? What has the fact that she’s gay got to do with anything?”

“I only realised recently. I saw her with that black woman who was in the revue.”

“You’ve never been anti-gay before.”

“I’m not anti-gay now!” he protested.

“Well, you’re doing a jolly convincing imitation of it. If it’s not because she’s gay, why on earth d’you think Chloe’s a bad influence on me?”

“Because you’re living with her.”

“So what?” I repeated.

“Other people might think you’re gay as well. *I* know you’re not, but other people might get the wrong idea.”

I did my own version of cheek-puffing. “Simon! You’re talking nonsense! First, I’m not ‘living with’ Chloe, I’m lodging with her. Second, if other people think I’m gay simply because Chloe is gay, they’re idiots. Thirdly, as you say, I’m not gay. But if I were, what’s that got to do with anything? Whether I’m gay or straight is my business, nobody else’s. Claiming that someone being gay makes them a bad or ‘adverse’ influence is downright ludicrous. You’re insulting Chloe, and Chloe is a *very* dear friend.”

“You must admit it’s not natural. Being a lesbian.”

“Oh, please! Get real! We’re in the twentieth century, almost the twenty-first. You claim you’re not anti-gay?”

“Well, I don’t like it, Melanie!” He suddenly became vehement. “I’d rather you weren’t living with her.”

“Lodging.”

“All right, lodging. I don’t want you lodging there anymore. I think you should come back here. Where you belong.”

I rang off, shaking. Where has this anti-gay stuff sprung from? I suppose as long as the issue didn’t impact directly on his own life he’s never given it much thought, but as soon as he thinks that it does impact, out pops the prejudice. Honestly, does he really think he can order me back like some Victorian paterfamilias? Spouting the equivalent of *never darken my door again* – only the other way round?

Chapter 63

Phil

Cambridge: June 1972

"Keep finding myself wondering how the sod arranged the whole accident in order to make Melanie feel sorry for him," I said. "Crazy thinking I know, and obviously he didn't. All the same he might as well have, because that's what in effect has happened."

Alex expelled a meditative jet of aromatic smoke and narrowed his eyes. Sunday afternoon, and we were sitting outside in the small garden of our penal colony supposedly enjoying the sunny weather, whereas in fact I was experiencing a marked absence of anything remotely approaching enjoyment but rather a marked presence of despondency. Melanie had left Cambridge in the morning with her father after a quick goodbye phone call to me.

"One gets all sorts of doubts and fantasies," Alex said in reply to my somewhat paranoid comment, fiddling with his pipe. "I'd say the trick is to recognise them as such and not allow them to take you over. Detach yourself from them and observe them objectively. Not," he added apologetically, "that I'm particularly expert in doing so myself. It's more that I've fallen into the trap more than once myself, seeing deliberate machinations taking place when in fact it's plain bad luck. It's only been afterwards that I've been able to look objectively at something that's happened and realise I'd misinterpreted it."

"Hello, you two!" Edward's voice cut in. "Lazing on a sunny afternoon!" he half-sang.

"Kinky," said Alex.

Edward was leaning out of my window, waving his squash racket at Alex. "A final thrashing?"

"Kinkier," said Alex, getting to his feet. "You're on."

Edward turned to me. "I'm surprised to see you here, Philippe, and not with the fragrant Melanie but with the less than fragrant Alex. At least, he will be *après*-squash. How is she?"

"His belovèd has departed to the foreign climes of London," Alex said, clambering back into the house through the window.

"Ah. That explains why you're looking like a turkey on Christmas Eve."

"A bit pissed off," I admitted moodily. "Sometimes wish I'd been one of my father's unsuccessful sperms."

"You were," said Edward, a microsecond ahead of Alex.

Melanie rang just after nine and cheered me up with the suggestion that she could come down to Devon to stay with me in the summer, or maybe we could head off to France or Italy for a while. "Ah, the food! How gorgeous!" she laughed. I asked if that was all she ever thought about, and she said no, there was something else almost as good as eating, but as she was on the phone she wasn't going to spell it out. She was sure I could guess. Even as she said it I started to feel tingles.

The topic of Simon was being sedulously avoided until not talking about it became more intrusive than talking about it would be, so I eventually asked if she had any further news. She sighed.

"That's sweet of you to ask," she said. "I rang his mother earlier. Good news and bad news. They're saying there shouldn't be any major permanent brain damage. He'll remain in Bristol a bit longer, then be transferred down here. The bad news is that he's had to have his right leg amputated at the knee."

"Nasty. That's rough. Sorry to hear it. He'll be fitted with a – what's it called? A false leg?"

"A prosthetic. Yes, in time. He'll have to have masses of physio to train him in using it. Anyway," there was a shift in the tone of her voice, a defensiveness entering it, "he can have visitors, so I'm going to go to Bristol tomorrow to see him. His mother says he'd like to see me. I won't stay long."

I'd been expecting something like this, but still had the curious sensation of a mass of cold porridge being tipped into my stomach. I didn't want her to go to Bristol, I didn't want her to see Simon, I didn't want her to spend time thinking about him. Unreasonable not-wants, maybe; but they were feelings, not rational thoughts, and no more amenable to alteration or elimination by the application of reason than would be a dislike of tomatoes or volleyball or Gary Glitter.

"Are you going on your own, or with what's-her-name, Anne, is it?" I asked. "Or someone?"

"I'll go on my own. Anne's still in Birmingham. Her term hasn't ended yet, and I might go on to see her afterwards."

"Ah, right."

There was an uncomfortable silence. "You don't mind, do you, Phil?" she asked, slightly sharply. "I hope you don't."

"Hope it goes well."

"I'm sorry if you do mind, but it's what I want to do, and what I think is the right thing to do as well. It doesn't take anything away from you, does it?"

"Guess not."

"I would've come home today in any case. I haven't cancelled something you and me were going to do together in order to go and see Simon, have I?"

"True."

"Well, then." She spoke with a tone of finality.

The other Selwyn Gardeners were out or away, which was just as well. I didn't want company. I opened a can of beer, slumped in the chair, and thought uneasily about Melanie, and her involvement with Simon. Not just Simon. If it hadn't been for the eruption into her life of the slimeball Reverend Derek who'd deceived her and shagged her, her depression and overdose attempt, Simon finding her just in time – if it hadn't been for that sequence of events, then he, Simon, wouldn't now be a significant factor in her life, or at least no more a factor than any of her other friends. But he *was* a significant factor, and one that was qualitatively different from others, not least because she'd felt obliged to go out with him. Simon had only been successful in taking Melanie out because of the actions of the slimeball Rev. No slimeball would have meant no Melanie-and-Simon.

Then the unpleasant realisation struck me that, in a way, the same could be said about me and Melanie. It was another example of how actions and decisions and choices made by other people, people you know, people you don't know, complete strangers, shape your life and constrain your own options and decisions and choices. After all, if it weren't for the slimeball, Melanie would not have taken that overdose, would not have gone into a long period of depression, would not have lost a school year, would have applied to Cambridge a year before she actually did apply, would have come up to Girton a year earlier, would probably have made different friends from the ones she did make, would probably therefore not have known about Gerry's party, would not have seen me perform with Air Raid Precautions, would not have been at the bar where I literally bumped into her.

In other words, I would not have met Melanie and got off with her if it hadn't been for the actions of someone who was and is and ever shall be a complete stranger to me, namely, viz. and to wit, the slimeball. I could not, would not, ever have had the possibility of being with Melanie, of kissing Melanie, of making love with Melanie, had it not been for him – and, moreover, I wouldn't even have known that those possibilities had been denied me.

For Melanie's sake I wished that that complete pervy bastard had never set foot in the church or wherever it was that Melanie's Bible class had gathered, and/or that she hadn't been taken in by him; and/or that her parents had been a damned sight more on the ball and had prevented Melanie's naïve enthusiasm leading her to disaster (and where *was* her interfering mother at that time, lamentably failing for once to interfere?); and/or that she'd never been involved in the whole dubious enterprise of religion in the first place...but without all those factors, the overwhelming probability was that I wouldn't have met Melanie. A whole range of people unknown to me – the slimeball, the Bible class leaders, Simon, Melanie's parents – had all fed into my life, opening up some possibilities and closing down others, every bit as much as or more than my own decisions and choices.

If, I wondered, I were to be briefly granted the power to go back in time and make one change, would I use it to prevent Melanie ever meeting the slimeball? That would have sent her life in a direction different from the one it did take, a direction in which I wouldn't feature. Hence would have caused my life to go in a direction, one without Melanie, different from the one that it's gone in ever since Gerry's party. Would I sacrifice my ever knowing Melanie, for the good of Melanie herself? For the sake of Melanie's happiness?

The obvious answer was that I should make that sacrifice if it were possible, but then again perhaps her being with me, with the requirement that she'd have to go through that ghastliness first, would be the best happiness outcome for her. That, I realised even as I thought it, must be just my ego talking.

Thank God, therefore – were that non-existent Being to exist – that such a question could only ever be hypothetical.

Chapter 64

Melanie

Exeter: August 1997

I've just been to see a cottage, and if all goes well I'll be moving into it very soon! Spot of luck running into Tredders in Smiths at the beginning of the week. He was almost unrecognisable in a sober business suit and a trilby, and I only realised it was him when he apologised for having almost walked into me.

When I said, "Hello, Tredders!" he looked at me quite baffled for a moment, then stepped back and swept off his hat. "Dear lady! How delightful to encounter the muse of young Philip, albeit in the emporium of drugs, medicaments and toiletries. You are, I trust, faring well?"

"I'm fine, thanks. How about you?"

"Busy, busy. Of the buying and selling of houses there is no end, let alone apartments, flats, cottages, mansions, maisonettes and sundry shacks."

I'd forgotten he's an estate agent, and on a complete impulse I told him I was thinking of looking for somewhere to rent, and wondered if he had anything suitable on the books? I went to his office with him, and he dug out the details of this sweet little terraced cottage in Alphington.

"I must warn you," Tredders said, "although it's ideal for one occupant, two people, however compatible, would perhaps feel somewhat cabined, cribbed, confined." He looked enquiringly at me.

"Just me," I said, and was grateful that he maintained a professional detachment and didn't enquire further. It's only part-furnished, which is what I would want; the rent's not bad; and it's available immediately.

Inevitably, and it was my fault, Phil did come up in conversation, after we'd agreed a viewing. I asked whether he had any more theatricals planned, and Tredders the estate agent gave way to Tredders the impresario as he exclaimed, "Indeed, dear lady, indeed! We have the promise of a magnificent pantomime, the script of which, as you will know, young Phil is at this very moment labouring over in true dramaturgical fashion."

I said, "A pantomime? Great!" though pantomimes have never been my favourite form of entertainment. Tredders looked at me with amazement.

"You mean you didn't know? He hasn't told you?"

"I'm afraid I haven't been in contact with Phil since he moved back to Kent."

He almost exploded at this. "Dear lady! You are his muse! He needs you for inspiration! This could spell catastrophe!" and he flung his arms out, adopting a dramatic posture of despair. "I am deeply sorry, dear lady, to be apprised that Phil's muse has deserted him!"

"I'm not the one doing the deserting," I started to protest.

He waved his arms wildly and announced, "Just a form of words dear lady, just a form of words! No offence intended! I had no idea! A rift? Very sad. That does explain why some of the lines he's been writing are on the dark side. Immensely funny, but dark."

Chloe's not at work today, so she came along to see the place. "I expect it'll be ghastly," she'd said jokily when I'd told her about it, "and you'll simply *have* to keep on living with me!"

"I will miss being with you," I said. "But you must be wanting your flat to yourself again, now you and Natasha are well established."

"That's not why you're moving out, is it? Please don't think I want you to. Yes, we're serious, Tasha and me, but that's no reason for you to leave."

"It's not that," I said. "It's just that it feels right. The next phase. Me as me."

"You're getting the fuck on with it?"

"Certainly am!"

The cottage is dead right. I knew it as soon as I saw it. It's down a little private lane, not fronting the road itself. Two bedrooms; one main room downstairs, fairly decent size, with a wood-burning stove; and a single-storey extension out the back where the kitchen and bathroom are. It has a small garden at the front with a log-store and an apple tree and various large tubs for flowers, and a much bigger back garden which I'd really like to get stuck into, with an outhouse and a decrepit gazebo.

The one problem is that the whole cottage inside is shabby and needs redecorating, especially the main room. I could live with it, at least for a while, but it's not ideal.

"The owner," Tredders announced, consulting a folder of notes, "is perfectly happy for the tenant to redecorate to their own taste, which I am confident in your case is exquisite."

"Hers is," I said, pointing at Chloe. "Mine isn't."

"The good news, dear ladies both, is that he is willing to pay for the requisite paint and materials if the tenant takes responsibility for the actual decorating."

"That's taking a risk!"

"He could arrange for it to be done professionally," Tredders added, "but I fear that would be reflected in the rent, especially as it would probably entail at least one more month of non-occupancy with no rental income. I could however make a small hint to the owner, a 'hint-ette' shall we say, that a reduced rent for the rest of this year as compensation for you doing the work would be in order? He's a reasonable man."

Chloe clapped her hands. "I don't know about you," she said, "but I've always fancied myself as a painter and decorator!"

Chapter 65

Phil

Cambridge: June 1972

"Two-two! Hey, I've got a two-two!" I yelped. "Wow! Phew! That's not bad! How about you, Rob? Can you see?"

Rob turned to face me, beaming like a slice of melon as he gave a double thumbs up. "Two-one," I saw, rather than heard, him say.

I gave a return thumbs up. "Well done! Fantastic!"

We were part of the unruly, noisy, shoving and pushing scrummage outside the Senate House as innumerable undergraduates sought visual reassurance from the postings on the notice boards that they were indeed destined soon to lose the prefix 'under-' from their current status. Our success now confirmed, we pushed our way out of the seething mass and headed for the Whim for a celebratory coffee.

We chinked cups. "What now?" I asked.

"PhD, here I come!" Rob said jovially. I knew he was on a promise from one of the London institutions to join a research programme on neurotransmitters, provided he gained either a first or an upper second. I'd expected him to get a first, but he seemed highly pleased with the degree he'd achieved, and he'd be set up for the next few years.

"Great! When will you let Natalie know?"

"I'll tell her tonight. We have things to discuss! We might have news of a different variety to tell you all tomorrow!" He tapped his finger against the side of his nose. "You might want to start saving your pennies for an electric toaster or a fondue set or half a dozen solid gold serviette rings with matching solid gold serviettes." His words didn't surprise me and I mirrored his nose-tapping. He and Natalie had been going out together for years, and it'd been the general assumption by all who knew them that they'd get spliced once Rob had graduated.

"What about you?" Rob asked. "More specifically, you and Melanie? Plans? You two look great together."

"We're doing all right," I said, crossing mental fingers. "No big plans.

She's still got another year to go here." I was thankful I'd stuck to the agreement Melanie and I had made that we wouldn't tell anyone else of our intention to get married until we'd told both sets of parents sometime during the summer. I was feeling uneasy about things, and would remain so until the Bloody Simon Factor had been eliminated.

"Hey," said Rob, "just remembered. Natalie was saying the other day that we could provide a cabaret for her firm's annual jamboree in September. She's organising it. It'll be in one of their super-flash London offices. There'll be a bob or two in it for us."

We left the Whim in high spirits, Rob heading into college while I went to see about hiring a gown and hood for graduation day.

I'd hoped Melanie would ring immediately after six o'clock, when the cheaper rate kicked in, but the hour came, went and receded rapidly into the past without her calling, with a false alarm at about six thirty when the phone rang for Tristan, who failed to respond to loud shouts up the stairs – he was either out of the house or, if in the house, out of his head.

I didn't feel like eating. Several times I left my room and slowly approached the phone, telling myself that if it hadn't rung by the time I'd counted to a hundred I'd do the ringing. What if her mother answered? I retreated each time.

I cracked at ten o'clock. Against expectations, it was Dr Mason who answered.

"Hello, young man. I take it you're after Melanie?"

"In a manner of speaking. Is she there?"

"Bad news for you, I'm afraid. She's away for a few days."

"Oh. Ah." For a second time cold porridge settled in the stomach. "I thought she was only going for the day, yesterday?"

"You mean to visit what's-his-face in Bristol? Change of plan, apparently. She's gone on from there to stay with her friend in somewhere else for a few days. Manchester? Newcastle?"

"Anne? In Birmingham?"

"That sounds about right. She spoke to her mother. She tried ringing you as well, to let you know, but no one there."

"When will she get back?"

"Hang on."

The sounds of shouting came distantly down the phone, then Melanie's father was back on the line. "Friday, apparently. She and this friend are going to travel back down together."

"Right, thanks, good," I said. "Appreciate that. I'll phone again Saturday, or maybe she'll ring me. You haven't got a number for her in Birmingham, by any chance?"

More non-telephonic shouting.

"Apparently not. Or so her mother says."
"Her mother says. Right. Well, thanks. Sorry to disturb you."
"Not at all, young man. Sorry about that. Good to talk to you."
"Bollocks!" I said loudly, clumping back to my room.

Chapter 66

Melanie

Exeter: September 1997

Yesterday afternoon was not exactly the easiest couple of hours of my life, nor, obviously, of Simon's. Ever since the paterfamilias conversation our relationship had been even more tense, but whenever we'd spoken on the phone we'd stuck to strictly practical matters. I arranged to go round yesterday, and when I got there he was in an ominously hyper-cheerful mood suggesting he had hopes I was coming to say I wanted to return.

He gave me a kiss, said in his jocular voice for me to "go on through, I think you know the way!" and we went into the sitting room, where he still had a number of birthday cards on display – the one I'd sent him in the centre of a line of them on the mantlepiece. The room was over-tidy. Not a thing out of place, and a faint tang of furniture polish hung in the air. Furniture polish? Since when did we use furniture polish?

He brought in a tray of tea things, including my Marc Bolan mug and a chocolate cake, sat on the settee opposite me, ran his fingers through his hair, puffed out his cheeks, said, "Shall I be mother?" and poured the tea.

"This is nice," he said. "I'm glad you're here. How are you? You're looking well."

We exchanged mundane comments before he asked in a hopeful tone, "Is it something in particular you want to talk about?"

I took a deep breath and plunged in. "I'm afraid there's no easy way to say this. I've been thinking a lot about you and me, and how to move on from the current situation, and I realise we probably want very different things. I might be wrong, but I expect you'd like us to be back together again and resume married life."

"You know that," he said, nodding a lot.

"The thing is," I had to say, "that's not what I want. I'm sorry, Simon, but as I told you before I've felt stale and dull over many years. Restricted. Claustrophobic. I'm not blaming you, I'm not blaming myself, it's nobody's fault. Simply, that's how it's been."

"That was your ME," he said, "your feelings of what you said. It did restrict you. You're over that now for the most part."

"The ME didn't help, I know," I said. "But what I'm talking about goes back to long before that. It's always been there, in our marriage. I've never really been the person you thought you were marrying, that's the problem."

"You're exactly the person I thought I was marrying," he protested. "I never wanted to be with anyone else. I knew that even before we started going out together."

"No," I said, "the person you thought you were marrying was a good little Christian girl from Followers who'd got herself into a mess because of Derek the horrible dragon, and you were the knight in shining armour who'd come along to rescue her. You thought that like every good fairy tale it had to end with a wedding and happy ever after. Which, after your accident, it did. The wedding bit. However, I was never simply a good little Christian girl from Followers. Far from it. Nobody is ever *simply* anything. I'm me, me!"

"I know you're you!"

"Do you? Do you actually know who I am? I don't think you do, Simon. I think we should always have been just good *friends*, very good friends. Not husband and wife, not life partners."

"Look, Melanie. Darling," he was at maximum cheek-puffing and invisible-candle-blowing-out, "I get it that for now you don't want to move back here. I understand. You want your own 'personal space' for a while, and as it's evidently working out with Chloe – and I know I was out of order, what I said about her – why don't you continue to stay there for as long as you need, and when you're ready..."

"No, Simon, sorry," I had to interrupt. "It's not a matter of staying a bit longer at Chloe's and then everything'll be all right. For a start, I'm going to be moving out of there very soon. I've found a place to rent. Secondly, and I'm sorry that this will upset you, I need to move on in life more than just living apart from you. I'm sorry Simon, in due course I'll be looking to get a divorce."

I don't think I understood the term 'a deafening silence' before, but that's what happened: Simon sat frozen for some time, then slowly put a hand to his forehead and pressed it. I think his eyes were closed. I looked away and contemplated Marc Bolan.

"Why did you marry me?" he eventually said petulantly.

I tried to keep my tone of voice neutral as I said, "Because I felt I ought to."

He blinked several times, frowned, started to say something, stopped, stood up, and walked about, limping a lot.

"Ought to?" he finally demanded, leaning on the back of the settee and staring at me. "What do you mean, you felt you *ought* to?"

"Because I was grateful to you." This was the nub of the matter for me.

I'd married Simon out of gratitude, topped up with pity. Not out of love. It had been, I still think, right at the time. What I hadn't realised until recently is that 'what is right' can change.

"Grateful? Why?" Simon demanded.

"For all the support you gave me when I was at my lowest. When I took the overdose. You literally saved my life, didn't you?"

He shrugged. "In a way."

"No, seriously, you did. Then when you had your accident and it was all so awful for you, I wanted to be there for you in the same way."

"Out of gratitude!" He started limping round the room again, after a circuit coming to the mantlepiece and leaning against it, in the process knocking off two or three birthday cards. "You didn't really want to marry me? You did it out of *gratitude?*" He made it sound like some appalling evil.

"Simon! You said over and over again that the only way you'd get through it all would be if I stuck by you. You pleaded with me!"

"I did not!" he said heatedly.

"You did! After we married it was the same. You needed me. You said you couldn't live without me."

"I wanted to be with you. I loved you. Love you."

"You said you needed me. You made that pretty clear. Don't get me wrong – I think the way you battled to adjust to losing your leg, and the times your prosthetic kept going wrong, all those horrible infections – it was brilliant how you kept going. You wouldn't give up. It was impressive. I was there for you all the time. You *needed* me, and I was there—"

"Out of *gratitude!*" This time it was with bitterness. He banged his fist on the mantlepiece. "You've done all right out of me, though, haven't you?" He raised his voice more than I'd heard him do before. His face was going red.

"In what way?"

"How long have you been out of work because of your ME? I've been the only breadwinner for the past few years. *And* I paid the deposit on our first house because you were doing your PhD!"

"No you didn't!" I jumped up and faced him. "You paid half! Daddy paid the other half."

He flung his arm out angrily. I was still holding my tea, and his hand hit the mug, sending it flying. I cried out, tea splashed on Simon, the mug fell onto the tile surround and shattered. We looked at each other, aghast.

I bent down to pick up the three or four larger pieces of the broken mug and put them on the mantlepiece.

"I'm sorry," Simon sounded abashed. "I didn't mean to do that. I wasn't trying to hit you."

"I know. That's not you."

"Are you all right?"

"Perfectly. You?"

"Nothing to worry about. No big deal. I'm sorry it's that mug. I know it means a lot to you."

"There are more important things."

Simon limped back to the settee. "Would you like some fresh tea?"

"I'll make it," I said, heading for the kitchen, needing a breather more than I needed the tea.

"Why divorce?" he demanded when I returned. "What's the point?"

"I need to be independent," I said. "My own person."

"We could still stay married, and you be independent. When – all right, I should say if – the time comes when you might want to return, well..." his voice died completely.

I shook my head. "I'm really sorry."

He poured the tea. "What are you going to do about money? What your father left you won't last for ever you know, and I can't run two houses."

"I'm not asking you to! I know I'll need to get some sort of income. It's not urgent right now."

"It'll become urgent much sooner than you expect!"

"Maybe. I can deal with it."

"How do you propose to divorce me? On what grounds?"

"I was thinking we'd wait until two years of separation are up, and go for a no-fault divorce."

"No-fault? Well, it's certainly not *my* fault! I must say, Melanie, I think you're being incredibly selfish!"

After that we went round in circles a few times, with Simon trying to raise all sorts of practical objections and me discounting them. In the same way that he thinks that Mikey could be released from his psychosis by simple statements of rational fact, he also seems to believe that someone's emotional and existential life is amenable to logic, if only he could hit on the killer argument. When finally I rose to go – he wasn't going to make any move to end the conversation – I said something about him needing to get himself a solicitor. He surprised me by saying he already had one.

"Can I ask who?"

"No one local. I've simply talked over things with a friend from my Bristol days who's a solicitor. I'll tell them what you've told me."

That was it. Not easy, but apart from not doing it at all I can't see how I could have avoided upsetting him. He's called me selfish, which hurts, mainly because it's true. I *am* being selfish. Totally selfish. I feel I have to be, or I'll go under.

He's basically a nice man. The trouble is that too much niceness is toxic, like too much oxygen or too much water, and over the years our marriage has been overdosed with niceness. A constricting, confining niceness which, I'm sure, contributed to making me ill. If I were to return to Simon, or even stay married while continuing to live apart from him, I would die.

Chapter 67

Phil

Cambridge: June 1972

"Have I heard correctly that you intend to join the list of our distinguished alumni who have trod the boards, sir?" Mr Scrimshaw enquired, as he continued to sort through a mound of substantial keys and hang them on hooks, "Or will you be getting a proper job?"

"Proper job?" I echoed, appalled. "My God, Scrimmers, you sound just like my parents!"

"Having never met your parents, sir, it is somewhat difficult for me to comment on the matter. If what you say is correct, they are evidently people of sound mind and rational judgement."

"Are you implying that I'm not?"

"Without training in psychology or psychiatry, sir, I am not in a position to judge."

"The BBC are interested in me," I informed him mildly. "They've invited me to an interview. I could soon be working for them."

"In exactly what capacity, sir?" he enquired, adding, "Many are called but few are chosen. Sir." I had no idea what he meant. "However," he went on, "I will concede that some of your predecessors have distinguished themselves. Mr Cook, now, he's made a name for himself, along with that Mr Dudley Moore. Though Mr Moore," Mr Scrimshaw paused and sniffed disparagingly, "was an Oxford man. Still," he smiled his pachydermous smile, "we shouldn't hold that against him too much, should we? Then there's been Mr Idle and Mr Brooke-Taylor. Most amusing young gentlemen. Not forgetting Mr May. We mustn't forget Mr May, must we?"

"Mustn't we?" I replied, unable to think of any comedian of that name. "Afraid we already have. Who is he?"

"Mr *Peter* May!" Mr Scrimshaw sounded shocked. "Finest post-war batsman England has produced. Magnificent on drive."

"Ah," I said. "Not a comedian. A cricketer. You had me stumped there. Stumped," I repeated as Mr Scrimshaw failed to react. "Cricketer.

Stumped. It's a joke, Scrimmers, a joke."

Mr Scrimshaw turned, put down the key he was holding, placed both hands on the counter and stared at me. "I had spotted that, sir," he said gravely, nodding slowly, "and if I may say so, sir…" emphasising the 'sir', "…it was bloody awful. No offence intended." There was a fractional pause before he added, "Sir."

"None taken, Scrimmers. Now, if I could have the key, please?"

Scrimmers passed over the key to the Old Reader, where I was going to store some cabaret bits and pieces for a couple of weeks after I had moved out of Selwyn Gardens.

Back at SG a letter awaited me. As I recognised Melanie's handwriting on the envelope, an unspecified anxiety lunged at me. I went into my room, slit open the envelope, took out the two sheets of paper and turned straight to the end: "I'm sure you'll understand," I read, "and we can work this through for what's best. We can talk soon. I'll be back home late Friday – I'll give you a ring on Saturday. Take care. Love, Melanie." My anxiety became supercharged – what sort of valediction was "Love, Melanie"? Not "love you lots and lots", not "x x x x x", not "longing to be with you". Just "Take care. Love, Melanie."

I returned to the start of the letter. It was dated simply 'Tues'.

Dear Phil,

How are you? I hope you're all right. I think you should know your result by now – I'm so sorry you can't let me know straight away. I'm thinking of you, hoping you did as well as you wanted to. Or even better! I'm sure you did.

I'm writing this from Anne's room in Birmingham as I decided to come on to see her for a couple of days after seeing Simon in Bristol. I did try ringing you at Selwyn G yesterday but got no reply. I couldn't even leave a message.

I visited Simon yesterday. I got there just after lunch and was able to stay for about an hour, which was good timing as his parents had been in during the morning. He was in goodish spirits and really pleased to see me, so I'm pleased I decided to go. His speech was slightly slurred, but I'm not sure if this is because of his head injury or a side effect of the medication he's on. He gets tired very easily. He doesn't really remember much about the accident, which is quite common, and all he wants is to get home asap, but he's going to be in there a while yet. There's all the post-op things to do with his leg amputation to be gone through.

He said he's been thinking a lot about me and about us – that is about him and me, though that does mean about me and you as well. I don't want to sound big-headed about this, but he is really completely in love with me still and is really upset that I'm with you and has begged me to think again, saying how much he needs me now and will need me in the future. He hasn't actually said in so many words that he was there for me for a long time when things were so awful for me, but that was sort of in the air, and it's quite true. And I feel that somehow I need to be there for him now in return.

I put the letter down on the bed. I could feel myself trembling. I went out to the toilet where there was only a meagre dribbling. I came back, sat on the bed and picked up the letter again.

I thought about this all the time as I went on to Birmingham, and talked about it with Anne all evening, and I lay awake all night thinking about it. He's right, Phil. I can't get away from the fact that he's right – he does need me. The accident isn't going to be something that he'll get over in a few weeks – it's got lifelong consequences. I know there will be lots of other people giving him support, but because of how he feels about me, me being there for him is, I think, crucial. I know that sounds egotistical, but I think that's how it is.

I think that we (you and me) have to step back from our thoughts about getting married. I love you, Phil, you do know that, don't you? I really love you. But I think it's only right, morally the proper thing to do, for me to be there for Simon. It's tearing at me to write this and I'm all shaky, but I can't bear the look of anguish on his face when he talks about losing me.

I can't write anything more now. I'm exhausted. I'm so sorry that this will hurt you and upset you. I'm sure you'll understand, and we can work this through for what's best. We can talk soon. I'll be back home late Friday – I'll give you a ring on Saturday.

Take care.
Love, Melanie.

Fuckin' Ada! Fuckin', bleedin', soddin' Ada!

Chapter 68

Melanie

Exeter: October 1997

I don't know how Chloe does it! She came round yesterday to help with redecorating the cottage, and even when dressed in old painting clothes and with her hair pinned up and hidden under a sort of Australian outback hat without the corks, she still looks glamorous.

"Do you like my dyke dungarees?" she asked gaily, coming down from the bedroom.

"Give us a twirl!"

She twirled. "Can't be a dyke without dungarees," she said. "Well-known fact."

"Very becoming," I said, and dammit, on her they were, the blue denim enhanced by numerous coloured blobs, streaks and splashes of dried paint as though by design.

I've been here just over a week now, and it's absolutely perfect for me – snug, cosy, welcoming, and it's *my* space. Heaven knows when it was last redecorated, so we were rectifying that.

We quickly got into the swing of it in the downstairs room, her rollering the walls, me tackling the ceiling up the stepladder I'd found in the outhouse. It was making my neck ache, so when the post came I was ready to take a break.

I held up one of the envelopes for Chloe to see. "From Phil," I said.

"Are you going to open it?"

It was a welcome-to-your-new-home card (a pretty, thatched cottage with climbing roses and a cat) along with a handwritten letter.

Hi Mel!

Hope you don't mind me sending you this (I know it's a bit twee – all right, a lot twee), but my spy in Exeter (Tredders) tells me you've moved into a cottage (good choice!).

Apologies if I'm about to put my foot in it – would I be right in deducing that you and Simon are no longer, as it were, 'Melanie-and-Simon'? There's been a parting of the ways? If that's the case, I do hope it hasn't been too traumatic for you (I'd like to hope it hasn't been traumatic at all, but that might be a hope too far) and that things are moving on, you're settling in well and flourishing and all that jazz. Must be a difficult time all round.

Are you able to get on with what you want to get on with (I'm thinking especially of your hopes of returning to some sort of university work)? I do hope things work out, Mel. I do.

You might like to know that I'm going to be back in Exeter for a few days leading up to Christmas, and then again in early Jan. I'm writing a pantomime (Aladdin Trouble) for Tredders, and I'll also be playing the part of Widow Twanky (please note the 'T' of 'Twanky').

Would you like to meet up? I'd like to, but I'd fully understand if you didn't want to. You won't be obliged to come and watch the panto – it's a rather groanworthy affair.

Take care, with love,
Phil xxx

PS In case you're wondering, when I come down to Devon I hope I'll be able to stay with Charlotte – haven't asked her yet. Ellisian Fields has a tenant in it now.

PPS I was with Lem (Melanie) the other day, visiting a place in deepest Kent that's interested in stocking some of her jewellery, and we passed a large-ish mansion place a few miles outside Maidstone called Five Elms. Isn't that where your brother lives now? How is he these days? I wonder if he remembers meeting me back in Cambridge.

PPPS There is no PPPS

I handed Chloe the card and letter in exchange for a mug of coffee. She glanced at the former, then read the latter impassively, asking at the end, "How do you feel about it, honey?"

"Slightly disconcerted," I had to admit. "I'd assumed he'd want to cut off all communication, and besides which, I'm not at all convinced it'd work if we attempted to move into the 'just good friends' category."

"I wonder what his agenda is."

"He might not have an agenda."

"We *all* have an agenda, honey. Remember, you don't have to go along with his if it doesn't fit yours."

"I know," I said. "I just don't want to not go along with something just to be contrary."

We resumed painting. Five minutes later Mummy rang. Her opening salvo was a curt, "What's all this about you and Simon?"

"What's all what about me and Simon?" I said as Chloe discreetly withdrew.

"That's what I'm asking you. I've just rung you at your home and he said you're not there, and something about ringing this number. Why aren't you at home? Where are you?"

I'd been putting off telling Mummy about leaving Simon, but I couldn't duck it any longer. She responded acerbically to my explanation, saying nothing I did surprised her however silly it was, and adding that, "you've never tried with him, have you?"

"What's that supposed to mean, Mummy?"

"You've never behaved like a normal person in a normal marriage, have you? The way you are with him. The way you pout. Simon would have made you happy if you'd let him. Now what precisely is your future going to be?" I could imagine her glowering at the phone. "You can't expect Simon to keep you, you know, if you do leave him. You'll have to live in the real world, no more lounging around like a Victorian lady with a fit of the vapours," which has always been her charming and supportive way of referring to ME.

"I don't expect him to keep me," I told her sharply. "I don't want him to. I've got the money Daddy left me to tide me over."

"Hmph! Your father didn't leave you that money to 'tide you over' leaving your husband."

"Mummy, I am *not* going to argue about it," I repeated.

"You said. I think it's shameful how you're treating Simon. While we're at it, when are you going to visit your brother again? You've neglected him as well."

I winced at this, because there's some substance to that particular accusation. I haven't been able to get to see Mikey for ages, now that I'm taking on things like TALC and starting music lessons and mentoring a couple of students, and I'm cautious about not overdoing things. I don't want to trigger a relapse.

I didn't tell her this, just said that I hope to get up to see him very soon.

"Make sure you do. I can't get along there on my own nowadays, as you know. Not easily."

"I know, Mummy. I know. Is that why you were ringing me? About Mikey?"

"No, it's about Felicity Armitage. I thought you should know. She died yesterday of a heart attack. She was someone else who was very good to you in your stupidity, wasn't she?"

Felicity Armitage – the Followers' Madam Skull. She hadn't come to mind for years, and I was surprised that I felt tearful straight away. Mummy was right: when push came to shove she'd turned out not to be the old bag Anne and I had thought her; she'd never said anything along the lines of how sinful I must be to try to take my own life or how I must ask Jesus to forgive me. On the contrary, she'd been very solicitous, and had made it clear I'd always be welcome back at Followers if I wished, no pressure. Remorseful, perhaps, at her part in introducing the Rev Derek to me.

"Could you let me know when the funeral will be?" I said. "I'd like to go."

"Two or three weeks I expect. I'm surprised you're not too busy to think of going to a funeral."

"It could work for me to get to see Mikey on the same trip."

"Don't forget, Melanie, I'll be at your Aunty Laura's for my usual visit, first week in November, so I won't be able to go with you if it's then."

"That would be a pity," I said, thinking the opposite.

"What about Simon? Wouldn't he want to go to the funeral?"

"I doubt it. He didn't know her. Only who she was."

"He still might want to go." She tutted and gave a sigh. "I think you're doing the wrong thing, Melanie."

"What? Going to a funeral?"

"Leaving Simon. You're very foolish."

"I'm going now, Mummy," I said as calmly as I could. "I'm in the middle of decorating. Thanks for ringing. Bye."

She started to say something else. I rang off.

"Like that, was it?" Chloe said, smiling, hands over her ears, returning to the room as my long yell of frustration still seemed to be bouncing off the walls.

"My mother's just had a go at me for leaving Simon."

"I thought that might be it."

"I think she already knew. I think Simon must have told her, but she pretended she didn't know. That doesn't bother me actually so much as Mikey – she accused me of neglecting him."

"That's a bit rich!"

"Actually, she has a point. I haven't been to see him for ages. I couldn't get to see him much when my ME was at its worst, but I don't have that excuse now. Anyway, I *want* to see him. He's weird, but he's my big brother and I love him. Trouble is, finding the time at the moment."

Chloe pointed at Phil's letter. "I take it Phil was right about your brother being in Kent?"

"Near Maidstone, yes. Bit of a distance for my mother to go, but it's a very good place for him. Why?"

"Phil's down in Kent as well?"

"Yes," I said, puzzled for a moment. Then I realised what she was getting at. "What a good idea," I said.

Chapter 69

Cambridge: October 1970

"Thanks, Daddy, that's wonderful," Melanie said.

"You're going to be all right?" her father asked.

"Don't worry! I'll soon make friends here, and once term properly starts I'll be flying. It's really exciting. There's always Sarah at Newnham if there are problems, she knows the ropes already. There aren't going to be any problems."

"Well, if you want to come home for a weekend at any time, you're always welcome. Your mother would be pleased to see you, and obviously so would I. Mikey too."

"Daddy! I'll be fine! University life won't be university life if I keep coming home. You'll see me at Christmas!"

"Make sure you give us a ring from time to time in any case, you know how your mother worries. Right, darling, I'll be off."

"I'll see you out."

"I'll find my own way. You get on with your unpacking and your 'university life'! You'll soon forget your poor old parents! Oh, and here's a little something, angel." He tossed an envelope onto the bed. "Expensive time to start with. Let me know if you need a top-up."

"Oh Daddy, you are sweet! Thank you."

Father and daughter kissed each other goodbye, then Melanie watched as he walked down the corridor. He turned at the top of the stairs and waved.

"Love to Mikey!" she shouted. He raised a hand in acknowledgement, blew her a final kiss, turned and was gone, but she continued waving even when he was out of sight.

Returning to her room, she sat on the bed marvelling. "I'm here," she murmured. "I'm actually, really here. Melanie Mason, scholar!" She opened the envelope her father had tossed onto the bed. A card with a Raphael angel on it, and inside was the handwritten message:

Our darling daughter. We know you'll work hard, but do enjoy your Cambridge career as well! Remember: you're descended from the angels! Much love, M & D xx

With the card was a sheaf of five-pound notes.

She picked up her shoulder bag and ferreted around in it, taking out a number of good luck cards, including one from Simon. Where could she put them? Did she want to put them anywhere? She didn't really want people who came to her room to see them – no, more specifically, she didn't want people to pick up Simon's, read the inscription ("all my love xxxx") and ask, "Is he your boyfriend? What does he do? How long have you been going out together? Is it serious..." No, please not that.

She put the other cards along with the angel card on a shelf over the radiator. Simon's she put back in her bag, feeling a twinge of guilt, and took out the little framed photo of her and Mikey, taken several years ago, and put it prominently on the dressing table.

It was lucky she'd been assigned a decent-sized room as she'd brought up a massive amount, her father insisting that it was no problem to load the car including the roof rack. What to unpack first? Clothes? Records? Books? Food?

She'd just started removing books from one box when someone knocked on the open door, and a slender girl, dressed in denim jeans and a denim jacket, looked in. She had very long brown hair cut with a dead straight fringe, and a red *bindi* on her forehead.

"Hiya!" she said. "I'm Amirah. Your neighbour but one," pointing, "in that direction."

"Hi Amirah! I'm Melanie."

"Hi Melanie! There's a sort of kitchen-y place down the corridor. I was going to make some tea. Would you like some? Proper Indian tea!"

"Great," said Melanie. "I've got some cake somewhere Mummy...my mother gave me."

"Me too," Amirah laughed. "Mothers!"

"Mothers!" Melanie echoed. She found a box with food in it and followed Amirah down the corridor.

Chapter 70

Melanie

Exeter: October 1997

I saw Sam in the High Street yesterday afternoon. She's very identifiable even from a distance, the combination of her petite-ness with that strikingly long hennaed hair in pigtails. I very nearly called out, wanting to ask did she know how Phil is; but I stopped myself in time. She's very protective of her 'coz', and although I'm sure Phil would have told her why he and I have split, she might have reverted to a dislike of me. Not that that ought to worry me, but I didn't want to find out if someone who's important to Phil feels that way in case it reflects something of his feelings. As though she's a proxy for him.

Coming on top of the heavy hint Chloe had made when we were painting, it did result in a decision to phone Phil, so this morning I made some tea and returned to bed with the phone.

He answered at first ring, and I could hear the sound of crunching toast as he said, "Hi Mel! This is unexpected. But nice."

"Hello, you. What are you up to? Having breakfast?"

"Yep. Very leisurely at the moment. Gearing up for a day's do-it-yourself-ing at Lem's. She's there already."

"Can we talk? Is that all right?"

"Sure."

"Is, um…are you on your own?"

"Yep. Ros isn't here, if that's what you mean. She's at the salon then she's going to Lem's to help with arranging a window display. She's good like that."

"That all sounds very industrious. What will you be doing?"

"Men's stuff," he said in a gruff voice. "Drilling and hammering and putting shelves up, followed by taking shelves down and putting them up again only this time in the right place, and shoving Polyfilla in the holes I've drilled in the wrong place. That sort of thing. As per normal."

"Sounds exciting!"

"Can't say I like doing it, but I'll like having done it. When I've done it. It's for Lem, which makes it all worthwhile. Anyway, how are you? I was sorry to hear about you and Simon. Difficult time for you."

"I'm okay. Thanks for your card and letter by the way. That was sweet of you."

"Well, you know," he said, but didn't complete what it was I was supposed to know. "How's it working out in the cottage?"

"It's lovely. It's really lovely. Chloe and I were decorating yesterday. It's looking fab downstairs. We'll tackle upstairs some time."

"That's great." I heard him crunch more toast.

"Look," I said, "I've rung hoping you could do me a favour. A rather big favour. But it sounds like you've got your hands full."

The crunching stopped. "Not necessarily. Ask away. What is it?"

"It's about Mikey. You asked how he is. Mikey."

"Oh God, has something happened?" He sounded genuinely worried.

"No, nothing's happened. He's okay. He's doing okay. At least, he was the last time I saw him. That's the trouble – I haven't been able to get to see him recently because I've been busy and I think it'll be another two or three weeks before I can realistically visit, and..."

"Would you like me to go and say hi?" Phil broke in. "Is that what you'd like?"

I felt immensely relieved. "How would you feel about it?"

"Fine," he said. "Can go on Thursday. I'll be going into Maidstone to collect some display cabinets for Lem. I can go see him afterwards."

"Are you sure?"

"Positive. If you think it'll do any good."

"I'm sure it would. That would be great. Just as a stopgap. I might be going to a funeral in two or three weeks, when I could get to see him as well."

"Anyone I know?"

"Mrs Armitage. She ran the girl Followers."

"Ah, I take it you want to dance on her grave?"

I laughed despite myself. "Don't be rotten. She turned out to be one of the good guys when it all went wrong for me. If you can see Mikey before then, especially if it turns out I can't get up for the funeral, that'd be great."

"Thursday, as I said."

"He does remember you, you know," I said. "He hasn't actually mentioned you on recent visits, but every now and again he's asked about you – he asks if you're still dead."

It was some time before we could continue the conversation. As at that morning in the Cafe Leofric when we had our first coffee together, helpless laughter seemed to release something between us. There was a loud clunk as, I assume, he put down his phone, but I could still hear his choking laughs in between repeating, "Asks if I'm still dead!" I was laughing so hard that I wet myself, which made me laugh even harder as I rolled out of bed to go and grab a towel.

"That's superb!" Phil finally picked up his phone again. "Am I still dead! Classic! Hey Mel, it's great talking to you, and I'll visit Mikey with pleasure."

"Pleasure? I think that's expecting too much," I said. "He's much weirder now than when you saw him."

"Don't worry, I can manage. You'd better give me the address. I'm not exactly sure where I was when I spotted the place."

I gave him the details, and asked if he could take Mikey some cigarettes, adding, "Give him my love."

"Your love. Will do," Phil said. I'm probably imagining it, but I thought he sounded wistful.

Chapter 71

Phil

Cambridge: June 1972

The cafe nearest the station already had a smattering of customers. I bought a coffee of the non-instant variety and a bacon roll, and sat with a copy of *The Times*. No doubt I should have been deeply interested in all the news, but the only subject which held any interest for me was nothing to do with national or international developments, but Melanie. Me and Melanie.

Saturday morning. She should have arrived back at her home sometime last night, and was due to ring me this morning, but I'd decided I wanted to talk with her face to face. I'd get myself to Charing Cross, then phone her and suggest that either she come up to central London, or we meet somewhere near where she lived.

Two or three stops down the line a large influx of passengers filled the carriage to standing room only, a knock-on effect, according to a barely audible announcement, delivered in Mandarin or possibly Ancient Babylonian through an antediluvian PA system with a built-in echo, of some previous service having been rerouted via Penge and Kuala Lumpur.

Sitting next to me now was a young woman with severely drawn-back dark crinkly hair who spent several minutes as the train got under way again feverishly checking and rechecking the contents of her shoulder bag, while uttering tiny sounds of exasperation, and occasionally knocking me with her elbow. Eventually she gave up, sent a quick "sorry" in roughly my direction, and leaned back in her seat, muttering to herself. Occupied though I was with thoughts of Melanie and worries about how the meeting with her would go, I still was aware that she wore a shortish tight black skirt, displaying rather sexy legs in black stockings or, more likely I suppose, tights.

The conductor appeared, checking tickets. Sexy Legs told him she'd mislaid her purse with her ticket and all her money, though she had a good idea where she had left it. A surreal conversation developed. No, she hadn't got a ticket because as she'd said she'd mislaid her purse. No, she had no means of identification, all that sort of thing was in her purse. No, as she'd just explained, she'd left her purse somewhere. No, her driving licence was in her purse. Yes, it was a large purse, more of a wallet really, but she used the term as a generic rather than specific description and hadn't expected to be quizzed on her usage of the English language. No, surprisingly, and presumably unlike her fellow passengers, she tended not to carry ID with her when travelling on the train in the British Isles. No, if she hadn't lost her purse, she wouldn't need any identification, would she? Because she'd be in possession of her ticket, thus rendering any form of identification otiose.

As well as being impressed by her level of developing sarcasm, I was struck by her use of the word 'otiose' which I'd not come across before. I filed it away in my memory to look up later and use whenever possible.

Eventually the conductor grumpily conceded that she was unlikely to be a deliberate fare dodger, and took her name, Rosamunde Deveaux, and her address. He checked more tickets, and moved on.

"Moron," I heard Rosamunde 'Sexy Legs' Deveaux mutter.

"Hard luck," I said.

She shifted in her seat and her right leg briefly pressed against my left leg.

"Anyone would think I deliberately lost my purse – sorry, *wallet* – simply to con British Rail out of a quid or two. God, some people."

"Some people," I agreed, and returned to pondering on Melanie and me.

As the train approached King's Cross, Sexy Legs spoke to me again. "Look, I'm very sorry to bother you," she said in a low voice, "and feel free to say no, but I realise I literally don't have a penny on me. Is there any chance you could lend me something, just enough for a phone call to some friends to sort things out? I'll repay you."

I wasn't really able to afford to subsidise purse-losing strangers, but that was counterbalanced by this particular stranger's legs and her use of the word otiose. I dug out a couple of notes and some coins, and after an unconvincing and unsuccessful attempt to refuse accepting more than required for a phone call she took my name and address, promising to send repayment when she got back home.

At King's Cross, she flashed me a quick smile of thanks and disappeared, her tight skirt and sexy legs being my last view of her. I headed for the tube station.

At Charing Cross, I found a phone box and rang Melanie's number. Inevitably her mother answered, purporting at first to have difficulty in placing who I was, and deliberately, I was sure, misconstruing me. "There's no one here called Phil," she maintained. "I'm afraid you must have the wrong number."

"No, Mrs Mason, I'm not *phoning* someone called Phil. I *am* someone called Phil. Phil Ellis. Cambridge. We have spoken before."

"Oh. Indeed. Yes, I think I remember." She sighed theatrically. I could imagine her – though I'd never met her – sweeping the back of her hand across her forehead in a weary what-is-the-world-coming-to? gesture. "You'll be wanting to speak with Melanie, will you?" she lamented. "She's still in bed. She didn't get back until late last night. Very late. I'm afraid."

She broke off as I heard Melanie's voice asking who it was. A few seconds later, after a brief off-phone conversation, Melanie was on the line, preceded by her saying irritably, "I'm perfectly capable of deciding for myself, *thank* you Mummy."

"Phil? Is that you?" she asked, sounding tense.

"Hi sweetheart!" I said, injecting a lightness into my voice I did not feel.

"I was going to ring you later. I've only just got up."

"Well, I've beaten you to it, and you wouldn't have got hold of me in any case, if you'd rung SG."

"Why ever not? Where are you? Are you all right? Phil, are you all right?"

"Fine, I'm fine. I'm here in London. At Charing Cross. Caught an early train."

"Oh. Oh, I see. Oh. What are you doing in London?"

"We need to talk about your letter."

"Yes, we do. I'm sorry. It must've been hard for you, I'm sorry. Bad timing I think, by me. Um, it's difficult to talk on the phone," she added, followed by a muffled, "Go *away*, Mummy!"

"That's why I've come to see you."

"No privacy!" she said. "But you're right," the tension in her voice lessening, "we need to talk properly."

We arranged to meet in a small park called the Tarn near where she lived. "There's a sort of summer house affair," she said, "just a little way down the path on the right. I'll be around there." She told me which station to come to.

"I'll be carrying a copy of *The Times* and wearing a red carnation," I said.

Chapter 72

Melanie

Exeter: October 1997

A letter from Phil came this morning, along with a photocopy of a poem. I took them with some coffee out to the gazebo and lit the ancient paraffin stove left by the owner.

The visit seems to have gone all right. "I gave him the fags," Phil wrote, "then he launched straight into something about shitting himself to death. He wanted to know how many times I'd been dead. I said, 'just the once, and that's still in the future'."

There's some stuff about rock guitarists they started talking about, then he got on to the poem. "Apparently he attends some day-centre place in Maidstone a couple of times a week, and he's been doing some writing. Poems and things. He showed me an exercise book with some of them in, and the staff photocopied one of them for me to send you. It's not yer actual Wordsworth, but to my non-poetic mind it's got something."

After one or two further comments, he wrote, "You said you might be visiting him in a couple of weeks' time or so when you come for a funeral. Let me know the date if you do come, and if you like I could visit him with you – if that's okay by you."

He's right about the poem: it's not great poetry, but I find it very moving all the same. I'd forgotten that years ago when he was a teenager or in his early twenties, Mikey wrote reams of poems and would-be song lyrics, usually very dark and depressing. Mummy hated them, and I can't blame her. Whenever she found any lying around she burned them in case visitors read them. Didn't stop him; he just wrote more.

The poem is rather carelessly photocopied at an angle on a single sheet of paper, with the black border you get when you haven't put down the cover of the photocopier.

'A Form of Death'

When I tell you that I'm dead
you laugh at me. You say
how can I be dead
when I walk
and talk,
eat
and excrete,
and smoke cigarettes?
You say
these actions are not the actions
of a dead man.

I cannot deny
that there is a walking
and a talking,
an eating
and excreting
somewhere in my vicinity,
but they have no causal connection
with myself.

They are chance events
without structure, without pattern,
without purpose, unwilled,
spontaneous, random;
actions without an actor,
fleeting occurrences
unlinked to what precedes or follows,
deriving from no inner unity.

I lack that inner unity,
for I am dead
and have been all my life.

The vocabulary surprises me, for a start, and the structure of some of the lines: "there is a walking/and a talking…somewhere in my vicinity" – a real disconnect between him and his behaviour. My main feeling is sadness: it's the line "I lack that inner unity" which particularly gets me, because I was at much the same place around the time of my OD attempt when everything seemed to be disintegrating around me – or rather, disintegrating *inside* me – and I felt I couldn't endure it and the only way to escape it was through oblivion. It turned out to be a fairly short-lived experience for me, whereas for Mikey his sense of 'being dead' is a chronic condition.

Another thing that occurs to me is that Mikey's delusion of being dead is in effect the shadow side of my 'moments' or 'possible sublimities', my feeling intensely alive, with everything both within and without cohering, like segments of an orange being brought back together. The bedrock awareness of my experiences, of the super-unity of all things, is of *something being there*, whereas for Mikey it must be more a case of *nothing being there*. This raises the question of whether my 'moments' are any more authentic than his, and perhaps I'm the deluded one. It's a question that strictly speaking can't be answered, as there's no independent criterion by which to judge them.

I also wonder if there are many people who haven't had an experience, a 'moment', of some sort – not necessarily an awareness of 'presence', more something which involves self-transcendence: sublime music (like choral evensong), prolonged helpless laughter with others, seeing the sky on a clear night away from light pollution, and wonderful sex too, totally self-transcending at times. As well as these things, there are tiny, so-called ordinary things which have an element of raising you to a greater awareness of being connected, like a good coffee with a friend, or watching a heron on the weir, or seeing a spider lurking by its web. They're also fragments of sublimity.

I know it's easy to focus just on the good things; the trouble is the existence of all the dreadful things that happen in the world as well, such as Aberfan or Princess Di's horrible death, along with Mikey's experiences. There's plenty that would seem to counter the assumption that my 'moments' affirm an underlying goodness of being. Yet I think you have to be true to your own experience – how I perceive something is how I perceive it, whatever anyone else might think or say, and my 'moments' are, I believe, self-authenticating, like knowing when I'm looking at a tree that I *am* looking at a tree.

All that doesn't diminish one jot the anguish of Mikey's situation. What can I do about it? Not a lot I'm afraid, but I can and must visit, to be there for him – whatever that means, and sometimes I think it simply means taking him cigarettes and listening to him, so that I can be, as it were, not *something there* but *someone there.*

Chapter 73

Cambridge: October 1971

"I thought we could have a nice candlelit dinner for two," said Simon.

"I did let you know about the party," said Melanie.

"I don't want to go to a party," said Simon. "Apart from you I won't know anyone."

"You'll know Sarah."

"All right, apart from you and Sarah."

"You've met Amirah."

"Who?"

"Amirah. Along the corridor. We've had tea with her a couple of times."

"I can't say I *know* her. I'm not up for long, either, so we don't have much opportunity to spend time together, just the two of us."

Melanie did not want to say bluntly that that was the whole point, she didn't *want* to spend time with Simon, just the two of them.

He'd written to her announcing he would be coming up again to see her without asking whether it would be convenient; but as it happened the day before the letter arrived she'd been invited to this party in St John's. She had written back telling him she intended going to it, but he'd come nevertheless. Now he was making a fuss.

"Well," Melanie said after they had each reiterated their positions on the matter, "this isn't getting us very far. I'm going to go to the party whether with you or without you. Amirah and I are going to meet Sarah at Newnham, and we'll go on together. It's up to you whether you come or not."

"I don't like parties."

"In that case, Simon, don't come. It's as simple as that. You can see me in the morning."

"Why don't you come round when the party's finished?"

"Who knows what time it'll finish! These aren't the sort of things where parents come with cars at half past ten to collect their defenceless offspring. I'll see you in the morning. All right?"

Simon made no further objection. Melanie went to make a conciliatory cup of tea, accompanied by some chocolate biscuits. They sat together in tense amiability, drinking tea, eating biscuits, and saying little.

Chapter 74

Melanie

Exeter: October 1997

Yesterday evening I received an admonition. I ought to be outraged by it, if it weren't so…bonkers. As it is, I'm feeling a mixture of amusement and sadness that such attitudes still exist today.

I'm not sure many people would cast Patrick, the Roth of God, in the role of the Angel Gabriel, or me as the Virgin Mary; nevertheless he clearly saw himself as God's messenger, and he equally clearly expected that once the message had been delivered I would bow my meek and humble head, and sing some equivalent of the Magnificat. Not a chance.

Unlike Gabriel's arrival, I did at least have early warning that he was coming as he rang in the morning to say he wanted to see me that evening to "discuss matters".

"What matters?" I asked.

"Important matters."

"About what?"

"I'd prefer not to discuss it on the phone. Shall I come round at seven?"

"Seven thirty," I said, "unless you want to catch me in the bath."

There was quite a pause. Was he conjuring up the possible delights of seeing me lolling about in the bath? Or at least in a saucy bathrobe? Perhaps, but he denied himself the opportunity and said, "Very well. Seven thirty."

He checked to make sure he knew where to find me, and left me wondering what on earth it was all about. Though I now see Rita quite regularly at TALC, I've only seen Patrick at two or three concerts since the meal they came to, and a few times at choral evensong.

He turned up on the absolute dot of seven thirty, and had to duck to come through the door as he's well over six feet and the door frame isn't. Actually he would have been all right if he had banged his head as he still had on a cycling helmet, as well as a yellow high-vis jacket. He took them off as I made us some coffee. He got down to business straight away by leaning forward in the cane chair which creaks a lot, clasping his hands and looking earnestly at me.

"I only became aware on Wednesday that you and Simon have separated," he began, his voice not booming as much as usual. "That you've left him."

He paused, presumably expecting me to nod or say, "that's right". I sat still and said nothing.

He frowned, and continued, "I was talking with him at the chess club, hoping to fix a date for you both to come for a meal, and he told me."

Another pause. I still didn't say anything.

"I'm very distressed by the news," he was shifting in his chair and making it creak, "and I've wrestled in prayer about it, and the Lord gave me understanding that the Spirit guided Simon to reveal the situation to me so that I might do the Lord's work of bringing about reconciliation." More chair creaking. "'He healeth the broken in heart, and bindeth up their wounds', Psalm 147:3."

"Has Simon asked you to come and talk with me?"

"No, but he knows I was intending to. I rang him to get your phone number and address."

"What did he say? Go ahead and visit?"

"He sought to dissuade me at first," he admitted. "But as I told him, 'the Spirit of the Lord is upon me', Luke 4:18."

"So you've come even though Simon told you not to?"

"It is the Lord's wish."

He stretched out his legs and I had to stop myself giggling when I saw that he still had on his yellow reflective cycle clips, which made me think of *The Great Escape*, when they had earth from the tunnels they were digging hidden in their trouser legs. "We are taught by holy scripture that what God has joined together, let no man put asunder," adding, as I guessed he would, "Mark 10:9."

He paused at this and again was clearly expecting some sort of response, and again I disappointed him, though I could have pointed out that it isn't necessarily always God who does the joining together.

"I also have reason to believe," he continued, "that you are conducting an illicit relationship."

Time to be more forthcoming. "Patrick," I said, staring at him hard, "what relationships I might have or not have are none of your business."

"They are the business of the Lord," he insisted, "and I believe you have been having a clandestine affair with Philip Ellis. You may remember I saw the two of you together in Leofric's a few months ago, and you were clearly involved with each other. I also happen to have seen the two of you together on occasions, clearly very intimate, walking along by the river."

"That's because we *are* very intimate," I said. "We're intimate friends. We go back a long way. The nature of our relationship is as we choose it to be, not what other people might think it should or shouldn't be."

"Melanie, scripture is very clear about the sanctity of marriage. The Lord will be grieved by your disobedience."

My yelp of, "What!" made him jerk back as though I had slapped him, and he spilt some coffee. That didn't stop him. He wiped his trousers, noticed he still had his cycle clips on, and removed them (disappointingly, no earth started trickling out) while saying, "Disobedience, Melanie. As St Paul wrote, 'Wives, submit yourselves unto your own husbands.'"

"Colossians 3:18." I said, beating him to the draw. "You do realise," I said, back to being calm and collected, "St Paul probably didn't write that."

"What do you mean? It's in the Bible."

"Lots of things are in the Bible, Patrick. That doesn't guarantee their validity." I gave him a quick rundown of the letters attributed to Paul, which ones scholars accept as genuine, which ones they agree are written in his name but are not by him, and which ones, including Colossians, scholars disagree about. He squirmed a bit as I talked, trying to interrupt, but I didn't let him until I'd said what I wanted to say. He countered that, nevertheless, the letter to the Colossians is in the Bible and is accepted as being the word of God. "That doesn't mean it *is* the 'word of God'," I said. "Don't forget that the compilation of the New Testament took a couple of centuries," and I subjected him to another mini-lecture on the sociological and political factors that helped shape the creation of the New Testament, after which he said, "I know you're very clever, and could no doubt out-argue me. 'The foolishness of God is wiser than men', 1 Corinthians 1:25."

I quoted back at him, "'Judge not, that you be not judged', Matthew 7:1. I know my Bible too, Patrick, and it's unedifying to rip texts out of context, ignoring the sociopolitical culture of their origin and whatever agenda the original biblical authors might have had, and use them for point-scoring, which is what I've just done. Or for trying to browbeat someone else who has different views from you, which is what you're doing. You can't use texts from the Bible, or from the scriptures of other religions, like chess pieces, manoeuvring them to try to outwit the opponent."

He leaned forward again and for a split second I thought he was going to launch himself at me, but all he did was to point at, nearly touching, my cross. "Why do you wear that?" he demanded.

Phil has asked me exactly the same question, and I've often played through what answer would truly express my belief. "Because Jesus died challenging the political and religious powers that be," I told him. "He refused to conform just to save his skin. He remained true to the deep insight he had about the nature of ultimate reality, and how humans could and should behave. I can't possibly hope to emulate him, but he remains the inspiration of how we all could be."

"Jesus died..." he said, and I swear the colour was rising on his face, "... to save you from your sins. He was the Lamb of God, sacrificed so that you might have eternal life. It's your choice whether or not you accept him as your saviour, but the consequences of rejecting him are dire. Eternal damnation, and I urge you—"

"You can urge as much as you like," I interrupted, "but from now on you will kindly keep your urges to yourself."

The cane chair emitted a great deal of creaking. "I see the Lord has hardened your heart as he hardened the heart of Pharaoh," he said, sparing me the reference.

"Nonsense!" I said. "You're making assumptions about me when you barely know me. Even if you knew me well, you've no right to try to subject me to your particular belief system. I've no objection to you believing what you believe, but I do object strongly to you thinking you have the right to impose it on other people." He started to say something else, but I'd stood up, and I said, "I don't think there's anything to be gained by continuing this."

After breathing heavily for several seconds, he said, "Very well," and stiffly thanked me for my time, adding that he'd pray for me. He reattached his cycle clips, wriggled into his high-vis jacket, ducked at the very last second as he went through the door, put on his helmet, and safely regained his bicycle which he'd padlocked to a railing. I didn't say anything about not trusting in the security of the Lord.

I actually find it all quite sweet as well as annoying. After all, he's acted according to his lights. He didn't balk at doing what he believed he'd been called to do. At the end of the day, he hasn't exactly harmed me – unlike the not-really-a-Reverend Derek – and I'd say his intentions were good. Moreover, it's a lousy night out there, wet and windy, and he'd cycled from the other side of the city and it will have been quite a slog getting back, and he's not the youngest of men; he could just as well have spent the evening curled up in front of a nice warm fire with a cup of cocoa and a nice evangelical text to read. Good for him, in a way.

Still a cheek. And slightly bonkers.

Chapter 75

Phil

Emhalt: June 1972

Finding the little park called the Tarn is easy. Out of the station, up the cul-de-sac to a main road and there it is on the other side, its wrought-iron gates standing open. Delaying the inevitable, I pause briefly at an information board detailing the various wildlife species the Tarn is home to and the attraction of an ice-well.

Trees, bushes, some grassy areas, all surrounding the eponymous water where a number of ducks and moorhens are in evidence, along with a cohort of Canada geese. I can see on the right a wooden structure mostly hidden by vegetation, which must be the summer house.

There's no sign of her. I'm early, so leave and head for a cafe near the station to have a cup of surprisingly decent coffee. When I return fifteen or twenty minutes later, I see her immediately, down on her haunches at the water's edge where a flotilla of hopeful waterfowl has gathered. She's wearing jeans and a pale green top. The way she's hunched over has caused her hair to flop forward in a honey-coloured curtain hiding her profile. I stop and gaze at her, consciously trying to imprint the scene on my memory while at the same time trying to control my breathing. My mouth is dry. I feel sick.

A squirrel scampers down a nearby tree and approaches her, presumably expecting easy food. It's attracted Melanie's attention. She looks round and sees me. Slowly, she stands up, and a second or two later we have our arms round each other, holding one another tightly, her head pressed against my chest as I kiss her hair. Neither of us has said anything.

At a slight movement on her part we separate and, each holding both hands of the other, look intently into one another's eyes. That supremely desirable face burns into me.

"Oh Phil," she says, with a sad smile, "it's lovely to see you. It really is. How are you?"

"Worried. Puzzled. Alarmed. Hoping. You name it."

"Thank you for coming down. That's sweet of you. I'd been wondering if I could get back to Cambridge to see you before your graduation. Oh!" She opens her eyes wide then screws them shut. "I never asked!" Opening her eyes again she looks at me enquiringly, tilting her head to one side. "Should I ask?"

"Two-two," I say.

"Oh, brilliant! Well done." She kisses me on the lips. "Are you okay with that?"

"Relieved. How about you? What did you get for your Part I? Do you know yet?"

"Um," she hesitates. "I sort of got a, um, a first."

"Brillianter!"

"A starred first!"

"Brilliantest!" I take the opportunity to kiss her in return. The restrained nature of the kisses we've exchanged is agonising.

"We need to talk, don't we?" she says. "Let's walk on a bit."

I put my arm round her waist as we walk along the path but she doesn't reciprocate. The squirrel briefly acts as vanguard before it suddenly turns aside, scampers up a tree, along a branch and acrobatically leaps onto the branch of an adjoining tree. "They can be very tame," Melanie says. "I used to come in here a lot when I was revising for A levels. My home's just up the road." She points vaguely.

There's a wooden bridge, looking recently renovated, over a narrower part of the pond, though as there seems to be a slight current in the water it can't be a fully closed-in pond. There's no sign where any stream enters or leaves.

We stop at the halfway point on the bridge and lean against the rail, looking over the body of water. There are a couple of young women with small children on the far side, and an elderly couple sitting on a bench, tossing food to a mass gathering of hopeful ducks. I no longer have my arm around her waist.

I can understand why this is a favourite place of Melanie's, why she'd come here when revising, with its quiet water, meandering paths, ducks and moorhens, squirrels, the rustic benches, the dappled shade. An oasis in suburbia. Then with perfect timing comes the sound of a train – invisible behind a boundary of trees – which shatters the tranquillity, and moments later we can hear it draw into the station I'd arrived at. It's on a main line to the capital – straight to London Bridge and Charing Cross.

"Hope you don't mind me coming," I said. "I don't think I can cope with telephone calls."

She didn't respond directly, saying, "I saw Simon again yesterday," as she picked at something on the bridge's wooden rail.

"Again? You saw him on when? Tuesday? Wednesday?"

"And yesterday. Anne drove me there from Birmingham – you know I went to see her? – and she drove me back here afterwards. I was able to stay with Simon quite a while this time, and talk. He's in a fragile state."

"Hardly surprising."

"The thing is…" she'd stopped scraping at the wooden rail and examined her fingernails, now clogged with dirt, "The thing is, what I put in the letter to you, I feel even more strongly is right, I'm sure it's right."

"What is?" I was trying to control a rising sense of panic.

"Well, he knows we were planning to get married, you and me…"

"You told him before even *I* knew about it!"

"…and it's really gone deep into him. He's really despondent about it. He tries to sound cheerful, that's what he does, but actually he's, well, devastated."

"Well, I'm sorry, that's how the cookie…"

"No, wait. You can't just dismiss it."

"I'm not!"

"He almost died, you know. He could've died. He's at such a low ebb, there was nothing else I could do."

"Do? Do what?"

"I told him that it was no longer…" she takes a deep breath, "no longer going to happen. You and me. Getting married."

Chapter 76

Melanie

Emhalt: November 1997

I've just been talking with Phil on the phone. He rang me here at Mummy's, though Mummy herself is away at Aunty Laura's. I'm here because of Mrs A's funeral, which took place this afternoon, and I'll go to see Mikey tomorrow.

The funeral was very traditional. I didn't know the minister, and the only person I recognised was the leader of the boys' class, Mr Griffen. He used to have a huge black beard, but he's pretty well bald now, and his beard is a wispy shadow of its former self, and totally grey. There was no one else there I knew – at least, not that I'm aware of. Not that I did any mingling, but stayed at the back of the church and didn't go to the wake afterwards.

I was just getting some food when Phil called on my mobile. I told him I was at Mummy's, that she was away, and that I'd just been to the funeral.

"Mrs Thing, the Followers person? How was it?"

"Felicity Armitage. It was fine. I'm glad I went – she'd been very kind to me."

"Hence going to the funeral. Well, this is good timing – I was ringing to find out if you've fixed when to visit Mikey again, and I guess you've either just been or..."

"I'm going tomorrow."

"Even better timing. What d'you reckon if I tagged along? I could easily be free to come and say hi to him."

I remembered that when, months ago, Phil had explained how his daughter had come to be named Melanie, he said he'd had a "nanosecond choice" whether or not to tell his wife about me. I now had a nanosecond choice. Yes, do come; or no, stay away. If only I could discover how one response would pan out, then come back to this point and find what the other response would lead to, and only then make the final choice between them. But the coin had to fall one way or the other now.

"That'd be good," I said, and immediately felt relieved I'd made that choice.

"Hey, great! You driving? Meet you there. What time?"

"I've come by train. Too much of a fag to drive."

"In that case, I can pick you up – where? Maidstone station? What time?"

We only stopped talking when the credit on his phone ran out.

Chapter 77

Cambridge: October 1971

"It's great!" Melanie said to Sarah.

"You're not wishing Simon had come after all?"

Melanie shook her head. "Not really."

"Are you two all right?"

"Yes, yes," Melanie said, feeling, "no, no." It had never been 'all right'.

"I just wondered."

The party in St John's was well under way, and Melanie was longing to dance, but so far she had stood around, drinking and talking with Amirah and Sarah, and one or two other friends. At the far end of the room a free-standing folding screen, decorated with three caricatures and the legend 'Air Raid Precautions', marked off one corner.

"Any idea what that's for?" she asked Sarah.

"There's going to be a cabaret," Sarah said. "Friends of Gerry, the Pembroke half of the celebrations."

"Oh," said Melanie. "Are they any good?"

"I don't know," said Sarah. "Probably just a lot of puerile undergraduate humour."

It was about twenty minutes later when the music was turned off and the party-giver called Gerry, dressed in a dinner jacket and a scarlet cummerbund, called for quiet. "In a few minutes there'll be a cabaret," he announced. "Could those of you who can, grab a chair, and the rest of you make yourselves comfortable on the floor."

There was a lot of shuffling around. More drinks were being bought at the bar, chairs dragged out of a side room, coats commandeered as temporary floor cushions. It took several minutes for people to organise themselves.

Gerry clapped his hands for more silence, and the hubbub marginally subsided. "Cabaret time! We bring you Alex, Rob and Phil, who together are the Air Raid Precautions! I thenk yew!" There was a smattering of cheers and whistles as the three performers launched into an exuberant opening number.

Chapter 78

Melanie

Exeter: November 1997

Phil met me at Maidstone station. There was a moment of awkwardness as we stood facing each other – do we hug? Do we kiss? Do we simply say "Hi!" and leave it at that? A bit like 'scissors, paper, stone' only with both players playing for a draw. Simultaneously we both chose 'hug'.

It took about half an hour to get to the Five Elms. Phil came in with me to say hello to Mikey in the smoking room, and gave him a magazine on rock music.

"Who do you think's the best ever guitarist?" Mikey asked him.

"You asked me that last time. Toss up between Hendrix and Clapton."

"Yeah," said Mikey. "What do you reckon on Peter Green?" They talked about musicians I hadn't heard of until Phil asked, "What about Marc Bolan?" and grinned at me.

"Rubbish," Mikey said flatly. "My sis liked him. Didn't you?"

"That's girls for you," Phil sighed as I nodded. "No taste." Mikey sniggered. It was strange, but lovely, to see Mikey having what you might call a fairly normal conversation.

"He's all right, sis," Mikey said after Phil went to sit in the car to let me have time alone with him. "I like him. What's happened to old…?" He gave an exaggerated puffing out of his cheeks.

"Simon?" I said, and explained that I'd left him. He took it how I thought he would, with indifference, then announced, "I haven't shitted myself this week."

As we drove away afterwards I told Phil I was desperate for caffeine. We pulled in at a farm-shop-cum-cafe with a huge sign announcing 'Organic Fruit & Veg Sold Here!'

"Of *course* it's bloody organic!" Phil fumed as we got out.

"It doesn't have to be," I said.

"Yes it does! By definition! Everything that grows is organic! There's no such thing as an *in*organic carrot or cauliflower. An inorganic carrot would be made of concrete or galvanised iron or glass. Neither does 'organic' mean 'good' or 'healthy' as everyone seems to think. The smallpox virus is organic. CS gas is organic. Bubonic plague is organic. Fly agaric—"

"I think you've made your point awfully well," I interrupted.

"Well, I should know, being a whizz at organic chemistry!"

"A whizz? That's not what I've heard. Now let's go and have a nice organic cup of organic tea and a nice organic slice of organic carrot cake!"

On the wall by the counter was a corkboard covered in business cards and small adverts for counsellors, therapists, yoga classes, gurus, spirit guides, courses in tantric sex, courses in miracles, shamanism, dowsing, astral projection, massage, past-life regression, positive thinking, chanting and numerous other human potential possibilities. As we waited to be served Phil pointed to a card advertising 'Psychic Crystal Therapy'.

"Therapy for psychic crystals?" he asked.

"Or crystal therapy for psychics?" I added.

We both laughed, Phil fluttering his eyelashes at me, and we held each other's gaze until the woman behind the counter broke the spell by asking what we'd like.

"Mikey's really important to you, isn't he?" Phil said as we sat opposite each other on rather uncomfortable bench seats at a scrubbed wooden table with a wildly undulating surface.

"Very," I said.

"You're his lifeline to sanity. You're bound up with him."

"Yes," I said. "It's just me and my mother now who care and can visit."

"You've trusted me to visit," Phil said. "That means a lot to me."

While we were tucking into large Chelsea buns, almost but not quite as good as Fitzbillies' best of ancient memory, Phil's phone rang. He listened for a few seconds, then slapped the table hard with his hand, leaped up and shouted, "Yes! Yes!" making me jump and everyone else in the place stare at him. He started punching the air and shouting into the phone, "How many?" and "Which ones?" and "When?" Pacing about he nearly collided with a trolley stacked with returned trays, raised an apologetic hand to an approaching member of staff, and retreated to our table, still talking into the phone. "Okay, okay, okay," he was saying as he sat down. "That's great, Tredders! Great! Well done! I'll send the others asap. Cheers. Cheers. Thanks again, Tredders. That was Tredders," he told me, putting his phone away.

"I gathered! What was that all about?"

"Deliberately not told you till now, in case it all went tits up – as it still conceivably might." He slapped the table again and shook his hand. "Really must stop doing that. Tredders knows someone who knows someone who's a producer at the Beeb. Radio. There's a new sketch show being developed called *Mind the Boggles*, and they're looking for writers. Tredders has called in a favour or two and got some of my material submitted, and the producer person likes it!"

"Phil, that's wonderful!"

"They want to see some more!"

"Fantastic!"

"It's not definitely accepted at this stage, but Tredders says it's exactly the sort of stuff they're looking for."

"That's wonderful. Come on," I stood up, "I want to give you a hug."

We had a hug. A long hug. A very long hug. We drew apart, with our arms still round each other.

"Want to tell you something else, Mel," he said, looking straight into my eyes.

I felt myself tremble. "About the sketches?"

"No, something else. A helluva sight more important, too. Been wondering how to – no time like the present, and all that."

"What is it?"

"Siddown!" We sat. "It's about Ros and me."

The room seemed to go quiet. I couldn't breathe.

"What it is, is that...well, it's...oh hell," he broke off. "Help me out."

"I don't know how to. You and Ros. What about you and Ros?"

"It's not going to work between us," he said in a rush. "That's it."

It's difficult to say what went through my head when he said that. I'm not sure anything did. I looked at him as he stared down at the table.

Finally I said, "Can you explain?"

"What is there to explain?" He looked up and shrugged. "We've both realised that as a marriage our relationship won't get going again. We haven't rowed, but a few weeks ago she came into my study and said, 'It isn't working, is it?' and I rather agreed. That's really all there is to say."

"What are you going to do?"

"Well, in the long term, we'll be going for a divorce. The two-year thing."

I almost cried out, "Snap!" but didn't: too frivolous. Nor did I say that I was sorry to hear it hasn't worked out for him and Ros, because even as he was telling me I was conscious of not being sorry but relieved, and excited, and scared.

"Feel a bit of a failure, to be honest," Phil was saying, "and so does she. We've agreed to work together to make a success of our failure! Don't think either of us is looking forward to sorting out a whole load of things we should have sorted out years ago – at least there's fewer complications with the girls this time round, now they're that much older. Still consequences, of course."

"All that sort of thing is daunting, but it will get done," I said.

"We're getting help from this Relate therapist we've been seeing. She's very good, but it's been painful at times. The last couple of sessions we've spent talking through how to do it sensibly. Actual practicalities."

"Is it working?"

"Yeah, think so. The plan is for me to move out and rent a little place while we're still dealing with this and that, various long-term arrangements about her business and the girls' futures and stuff. Lem and Amy know and are being very understanding. But you still can't get away from the feeling of being a failure. At least, I can't."

"I don't think you're a failure."

"Thanks for the vote of confidence! Yeah, we'll get through it, and the next phase of my life will begin, and the next phase of Ros's, too."

"Has Ros..." I started, then thought better of it, both wanting and not wanting to be inquisitive.

"Come on," he said. "Has Ros what?"

"I was wondering, do you think she's got another relationship in the offing?"

"No. Sure she hasn't. Don't think she'll have any trouble getting together with someone else if she wanted to, mind, but there's no one on the horizon at present."

We both fell silent, almost certainly thinking about much the same thing. He was the one to break it.

"Whereas you?" he said.

"Whereas me?"

"Have you anyone lined up?"

"I don't believe you just said that!"

"Badly expressed, sorry."

"How would you express it?"

"I wouldn't. Scrub that. I still want to check something with you, though."

"Which is what?"

"Lem asked me a few days ago about my cottage. My uncle's cottage. Ellisian Fields."

"What about it?"

"She asked if I had any thoughts of returning to it. She was suggesting it might be a good idea. Not that she wants to get rid of her old man, but she knows how happy I'd been there. When she asked I knew immediately that's what I'd like to do."

I tried to stay in the present. I tried not to think of what he might be implying in case I'd got it wrong.

"You know there's another tenant in it at the moment?" he asked. "It's a limited tenancy, lasts until end of Feb. Now, the point is, I could get Tredders to give notice to quit."

"Why don't you? As that's what you'd like to do."

"Want to know how you'd feel about it, if I did."

I needed to know something: had he and Ros decided to separate for good before or after he'd learned that I'd left Simon?

"Only found out from Tredders three or four weeks ago about you and Simon," he said. "It came as a total surprise. Ros and I had already agreed some time before then that we'd separate and get divorced. Why?"

"I don't want to be the cause of you two not making it."

"No, you aren't, you weren't. Ros and I are going our separate ways in any case. So, Mel, what would you think about me coming back to Devon?"

I took a deep breath. "It'd be wonderful. I'd love it if you moved back."

He sniffed a few times, looking sheepish, and when he spoke again there was a tremor in his voice. "Christ, Mel," he said. "That's fantastic."

Chapter 79

Phil

Emhalt: June 1972

That bloody gong again. Blotting out everything else. I see a couple of geese lumberingly taking off from the surface of the pond, but can hear nothing except for Melanie saying she'd told Simon our wedding is off. Off.

"Postponed, you mean?" I say.

She slowly shakes her head. "Not just postponed. The point is, I have to be there for him properly. That's what I've come to realise over the past two or three days. I thought that if we just put things on hold for a year or two, you and me, that would work. I know it won't. It has to be more than that. It has to be the whole thing. Hundred per cent commitment."

"Fuckin' Ada!"

"I'm so sorry Phil, I am so sorry!" She turns and presses her face against me. "I hate doing this."

"Then don't! You don't have to!"

"I know it's right. It's right that I stick by him fully, and and and that means that you and me…oh Phil!"

"Jesus wept!"

"I can't continue with our relationship. Not as it's been."

I hammer my fist on the wooden rail of the bridge several times. "Don't be crazy!" I finally say, breathing heavily. "Mel, for God's sake! What do you mean, you 'know it's right'? You can't possibly know it's right!"

"I do. I can't prove it, but it's what I feel."

"Which is what?" I yelp. "What is it you feel?"

"I feel oddly at peace when I think that that's what I need to do. And I know that if I were to turn away from him to be with you, I'd feel…well, I'd feel guilty."

"Guilty? Guilty! Why on earth would you feel guilty?"

"Because I'd be going against what I feel I'm called to do."

"Sorry, don't get it." I hammer on the rail again. My fist hurts, but not as much as my heart. "If you were to feel guilty, that would be just a feeling."

"Feelings are important," she says. "Ultimately important. Feelings tell you. They have to be a guide."

"Do you love him?" I ask angrily.

She's silent for several seconds, then come her heartbreaking words. "Not like I love you, Phil. Phil, look at me, Phil. Phil, I love you," she emphasises each word. "I love you so much."

"Why the hell are you doing this? Are you saying 'I love you Phil, but now piss off'? Because that's what it sounds like from where I'm standing."

"No! I don't mean that! The relationship we had, that has to end, but I hope we—"

"Don't bloody say you hope we can still be good friends!" I shout.

"Can't we?"

"How? How can we after what we had? After what we *have*, for God's sake, which you're chucking away." I put my hands to my head and grip it hard, storm off the bridge, thump a tree, then return to her. She has on her face her pouty look.

"Look, Mel, sweetheart, darling." I've forced myself to quieten down. I put my hands on her shoulders and stare into her eyes. They're glistening with tears. "At the very least take your time over this. Wait until Simon's back on his feet, and back home, and everything's stabilised and he's got going again. Even then – well, *of course* give him support and all that, but not at this crazy cost of chucking away what we've got."

She gives the slightest of nods, and covers my hands with hers. "Phil, love is not just the wonderful romantic feelings we have for someone – what I have for you, and I do, honestly I do – and wanting to be with you and everything like that. There's also love which is tied up with doing the right thing. Love is what you *do*, not just what you feel. 'Love your neighbour as yourself' – even an arch-atheist like you must have heard that one." There's a teasing tone to her voice as she says that, but I don't smile. "It doesn't mean you ought to have lovey-dovey romantic feelings or sexy feelings towards your neighbour, it means treat them fairly, treat everyone fairly, do what is right for other people, even if it's at your own expense, against your own best interests, against what you really want to do for yourself. I know it might sound crazy, but I have to love Simon in that way. I couldn't live with myself, let alone with you, if I didn't act on it. Do what is right. Be there for him. Fully there. It's not easy. It goes against what I *want* to do. What I want and what I should do – well, often they don't coincide. Often they're complete opposites."

I'm a chemical retort with anger and bewilderment and sadness boiling away inside me, boiling and merging and splitting and recombining, synthesising a mass of hyper-complex organic end products with multiple toxic properties. I look round at the rest of the Tarn. The mothers and children, along with the elderly couple, have all disappeared. I can't blame them. Loony at large.

"I'm sorry if I'm not making much sense to you," she says. "It's difficult to put it into words, but I'm not being arbitrary about it. It's part of how I see things."

She removes my hands from her shoulders, takes me by the elbow and leads me over the bridge to the bench where the elderly couple had been sitting. A metal plaque screwed into the back tells us it was presented in memory of some local but long-dead aficionado of sitting in parks and, presumably, duck-feeding. Much good did it do him. We sit there, incongruously holding hands, sporadically talking, repeating ourselves, saying nothing for a long time, then resuming. More invisible trains in both directions come and go at irregular intervals. More squirrels are fooling about nearby, oblivious to what is happening in the world of humans. I feel emotionally eviscerated.

"Please don't hate me for this," she says after one long silence. She sounds appallingly miserable.

"Hate you? I could never hate you! God almighty, I love you! Haven't you got that? I love you!"

"I love you too, Phil. I don't suppose you believe me, but it's true. I think I'll love you for ever. I know I will."

I mutter ironically, "She says she'll love me for ever," and we fall silent again. Someone has stolen my future and substituted their own crappy version. I want mine back.

The afternoon has almost passed. I've had no lunch. I'm not remotely hungry.

"I ought to go soon," she says. "I'm meeting Anne in a bit."

"Anne!" I exclaim, suddenly energised. "Does she know? Have you told her? You must have! What does she think?"

"She thinks I'm an idiot," she admits. "She spent the entire journey back from Bristol trying to argue me out of it."

I spread my arms in an exaggerated gesture of *you see?* I say nothing.

"Phil," she says hesitantly, in a small voice. She sweeps back her unruly hair, but it tumbles forward again. "I can't bear it if we part on bad terms."

I'm too choked to say anything. I want to find some words, not of blame but of reassurance. All I can manage is a mumbled, "Yeah. Yeah."

We get up from the bench and return, hand in hand, to the wrought-iron gates, where we have a final restrained, innocent, unsexy kiss.

It's only as I'm walking away, heading for the station, that I realise what it is I want to say.

"Mel!"

She stops and turns round. I return to her.

"You know what the great Dave Allen says?"

"No. What does he say?"

"May your God go with you."

"And also with you," she whispers.

Chapter 80

Melanie

Exeter: November 1997

Curiously, in the past three or four weeks following the visit from Patrick, I've come to feel grateful that that encounter took place. I didn't allow him to impose his views on me and that seems to have had the effect of shifting a piece of shrapnel from my psyche that's been there since I was sixteen.

It'd be wrong to equate Patrick with Derek. Derek was, as Phil called him, 'a slimeball and a perv', whereas Patrick's middle name could well be 'rectitude'. Nevertheless, they have in common an overwhelming belief in their right to impose their views on other people, that they are incontrovertibly *correct* in their views, and that everyone who disagrees with them in any way is not only misguided but is sinful, Satan-inspired, condemned by God – and actually that's the second thing they have in common: a belief in a ghastly, retributive God who almost gleefully tots up your sins and is determined to punish you for them, ultimately by eternal damnation. Well, if they want to believe that for themselves, let them; it's attempting to impose such views on others – especially vulnerable teenagers as I was when Derek was around – that's objectionable. I know I was, as Mummy never tires of telling me, stupid in getting involved with Derek, but at that age I was still pretty vulnerable. I know I could have made other choices, but the bottom line is that Derek was using his power, and what you might call spiritual scare tactics, to get me to go along with his abusing me. What happened with Patrick has, it feels, neutralised that, even though sex wasn't involved (well, not sex with him. It's only just struck me that sex is a linking factor: Derek persuading me to have it, forcing me, actually, and Patrick attempting to persuade me not to have it). But, and this is the overwhelming difference, whereas I allowed Derek to dominate, I didn't allow Patrick to, and I didn't allow him to make me feel guilty for rejecting his view of things. That's the difference. If I could go back in time, I'd tell the sixteen-year-old me, "Don't give Derek power. You don't have to give him power. You are your own being." In standing up to Patrick, I was doing what I could have and should have done over thirty years ago.

The fact that I stood up to Patrick can't make what happened with Derek unhappen, but it does feel as though psychic shrapnel from that era is being eliminated or dissolved or whatever metaphor is best. Last night's mini-encounter with Patrick in the White Hart, with him acknowledging fault on his side, has strengthened that feeling.

Chloe and I were at an exhilarating performance of *Carmina Burana* in the cathedral in which Patrick was singing. He was superb. Afterwards she and I went for a drink and I told her about Mrs A's funeral and the fact that I'd visited Mikey, but deliberately didn't mention Phil at that stage, wanting to spring it on her when it'd have maximum effect. She, however, looked at me quizzically and said, "Nothing to write home about?" in a tone of voice that contradicted her words.

"What are you getting at?" I said.

She waved a hand airily. "Just wondered if anything more...*exciting* occurred?"

"What sort of exciting?"

"What sort would you like?"

"Well, yes," I said slowly. "I was going to tell you. Phil rang me when I was at my mother's place."

I expected her to produce her lippy and mirror at this point, but she simply gazed at me expectantly and said, "Did he now?"

"He came to visit Mikey with me."

"Did he now?"

"Afterwards we went to this place for a coffee, and he told me that he and his wife have decided their marriage isn't going to work after all."

"Did he now?"

"Will you stop saying that!"

"I'm sorry!" She smiled a smile that was more of a suppressed grin. "It's just that I'm so, so happy for you." Now she did go for her lippy and mirror, but smiling too much to do anything with them.

I stared at her. Something was dawning on me. "You know this already, don't you?" I said.

"Maybe," she admitted.

"Meaning that you do! Come on, Chloe, how? What's going on?"

"All right, confession time!" She put away her lippy. "A few weeks ago Phil rang me."

"Did he now?"

"Don't you start! He wanted to know how I thought you were, and if you'd want to get back together with him. He told me about the decision he and his wife had made."

"What did you tell him?"

"I said I thought you were doing amazingly well, but I couldn't say one way or another about getting back together, it wasn't really my call. I did say that I personally thought it'd be lovely to see the two of you reunited. I'm sorry honey, I know it was a bit of a risk saying that."

"No," I said, and I could feel the tears coming. "You encouraged him. I'm so glad you did. Did he know I'd be at my mother's when he rang?"

Chloe nodded. "He'd asked if I'd let him know when you'd be up for the funeral. Which I did. Next confession: he rang me again on Sunday evening, incredibly excited, to tell me the news that you two are an item again!"

As we were sitting opposite each other at a table, we couldn't exactly hug, but we both leaned forward and she put her arms round my neck and I put mine round hers. "It's so exciting!" she whispered. I was too choked up to say anything.

We came out of our semi-clinch with tears in our eyes and smiling like anything. Looking over my shoulder she made a movement with her head to indicate something. "The superstar's here."

I looked round. Patrick Roth was standing at the bar, and I could see Rita and three or four others heading for a distant table. I stood up.

"I must go and say thank you to him for the concert," I said. "Right now I'm in love with the entire universe."

"Don't go snogging him," Chloe warned.

Patrick had just given his order when I got to him. "Good evening, Melanie," he said in his grave manner.

"I just wanted to say it was fabulous," I said. "The concert."

"Thank you. You're very kind," he said. "The Lord has been very gracious to me. I'm glad you enjoyed it."

"Wonderful. You're a star."

"I wouldn't say that, but again, thank you. May I get you a drink?"

"No, thanks, that's okay. I'm with Chloe. She thought it was great as well."

His drinks had arrived, and I was turning to go while he was paying when he suddenly said, "Melanie. Just a moment if you will. I must take this opportunity to say something to you. It's been on my mind."

"No preaching!" I warned him.

"Quite the opposite. I have come to realise I owe you an apology. When I called round three or four weeks ago, I fear I spoke out of turn."

"Oh."

"You graciously heard me out until I went a little too far. A lot too far if I'm honest. You quite rightly put a stop to it. Wrestling with it afterwards, the Lord showed me that my pride was getting in the way – your knowledge and understanding is quite formidable and I don't like to be bested."

"Especially by a woman?"

"Especially by a woman!" he agreed gravely. "Which is unworthy, and I apologise unreservedly. Since then I've been wondering about the best way to make amends for my clumsiness and, frankly, rudeness."

"You just have," I said. "Thank you. That's very gracious of you. And I do mean *gracious*."

"It's very gracious of *you*," he said, offering his hand.

"Your new best friend?" Chloe smiled as I rejoined her.

Chapter 81

Cambridge: October 1971

Melanie could barely catch her breath before the next spasm hit, she was laughing so hard. Amirah beside her was laughing equally hard along with the rest of the audience. As one sketch gave way to another, with an occasional witty song providing variety, the laughter had swelled, died down, then swelled again, punctuated by increasingly enthusiastic applause at the end of each item. She hadn't laughed like this for years, if ever.

The waves of laughter felt utterly liberating, and when the performer with long dark hair and a tall angular body seemed to look straight at her during one sketch and briefly grin, it felt like an electric shock. She knew it had only been part of his performance, and not really personal to her; all the same it thrilled her. Simon had not quite vanished from her consciousness, but he seemed far distant, and her resentment towards him for his stubbornness and intransigent attitude towards party-going had evaporated. He was such a sobersides, but right now that was irrelevant. He wasn't there and she was utterly enjoying herself.

The cabaret came to an end. There was loud and sustained cheering, good-natured catcalls, prolonged applause. Melanie herself clapped until her hands hurt, and was one of the last to stop clapping.

There was a general movement towards the bar, which Melanie joined. As she pushed through the crowd, Melanie noticed the long-haired performer, the one called Phil, appear from the side room into which he and his fellow performers had retreated, and also head for the bar. She wanted to tell him how much she'd enjoyed his performance. He'd had a way of fluttering his eyelashes which had had a peculiar effect on her. Perhaps he would flutter them at her.

She changed direction as he changed direction, and contrived to arrive at the bar just before him. She knew he was somewhere behind her; recognised his voice as he said, "Thanks, glad you liked it!" to someone; wondered how she could get to talk with him.

Luck took a hand. She was jolted forward by a movement in the crowd; she turned, and there he was. Right behind her. As he fluttered his eyelashes and grinned, she had the strange sensation of an inner deliquescence.

"Sorry!" he said. "Just trying to get a drink!"

"Oh hi!" she said. "You deserve one! You were great! That was really funny! I haven't laughed like that for ages 'n' ages!"

Chapter 82

Melanie

Exeter: December 1997

Yesterday Phil took me to Wistman's Wood.

He's down staying at Charlotte's in order to do some serious pantomime rehearsals. "Won't stay with you," he'd said when he'd told me about the arrangement. "Far too big a distraction."

"You saying something about my size?" I'd said.

"Far too slim and svelte a distraction," he'd amended.

He's been working hard with Tredders, and stayed on for an extra day.

It's crazy – I've lived down here over a year and I've been out on Dartmoor just twice before yesterday. When I let on to Phil my ignorance he was incredulous, and said he'd take me to Wistman's Wood, "as a start of your education." I asked what was so special about it, and he said, "You'll see," then added a sentence I never would have expected from him: "If anywhere is my spiritual home, it's there."

"I thought you didn't believe in that sort of thing, O rational scientist!"

"Hey, don't get me wrong! Don't believe six impossible things before breakfast, it's true, but somewhere like Wistman's you can feel the specialness. You're in contact with something deep and mysterious that stretches way back in time."

"There's hope for you yet," I said.

Parking at Two Bridges about half ten, we had a short walk to the wood. To be honest, it doesn't look anything special as you're approaching it, just a ragged stretch of woodland above the river. As we got nearer though, I started to understand what Phil meant – all the curiously shaped trees are oaks but nothing like as tall and spreading and grand as you associate with oak, and they're growing among great granite boulders. What's amazing is the moss and lichen simply dripping from the branches. It also covers most of the boulders as a thick, green, spongy cushion.

We entered the wood, careful not only to make sure we didn't slip between boulders and twist an ankle, but also, as Phil insisted, not to scrape the lichen and moss off them. All the trees are incredibly gnarled, and some of the branches are completely covered in the moss, with lichen hanging down in great fronds like untrimmed green beards. There are ferns growing in the forks of the trees, whose bark is all patchy and crumbly, and you have to duck all the time because the branches are low and twisty, constantly trying to grab you. Because the wood's growing on a slope you get the feeling it might all slide down into the river, only it's anchored in place by the boulders.

The sun was low and bright. You could see shafts of light picking out trees seemingly at random. Magical.

"Well?" Phil said. We'd sat down on a large, almost flat boulder.

"It's wonderful!"

"I'm not a great fan of Tolkien," he said, "but looking at these trees you can understand how he could imagine them to be animate creatures."

"They're amazing!"

"It's worth coming here on a misty day, 'cause as you approach the wood you can't see it for much of the time, then as you get nearer it starts to loom up at you, the individual trees coming into being all twisted and spooky, as though the mist were solidifying. Very *eldritch*."

"Great word."

"Now look up," he said.

I lay back and looked up. The sky was criss-crossed by an intricate tracery of branches and twigs with their coating of green hairiness, but what's odd is that somehow you can't quite tell how near or far away this incredible network is – for a few moments it seems to be way up in the sky, like a strange celestial phenomenon, then the perspective switches and it seems to be just an inch or two from your eyes.

"Don't you feel caught up in it?" he asked, and started to tell me the history of the place. I stopped him, saying I was really interested, but to leave it for another time. "I just want to lie here and absorb it," I said.

He stroked my hair, saying, "You'll only absorb what it wants you to absorb," surprising me again. Is he a closet animist?

We stayed silent for a while, then he said, "Penny for your thoughts."

"They're about spirituality, if you must know."

"Yeah? Tell me."

"You know I said on some occasion or other that spirituality has a people dimension?"

"Did you? I mean, yeah."

"Well, lying here, I was just thinking how it's much more than that. It doesn't involve only people, but includes lichen, rocks, trees, birds, animals, everything – you name it. Are you with me?"

"Think so, yeah."

"What I'm getting at is that spirituality isn't really about an individual's private connection with some metaphysical entity we call God. It's more something that expands and expands indefinitely outwards to include not only our connections with each other but ultimately with everything there is. Even to the farthest star. Which means that you, Philip Ellis, arch-atheist, like it or not, are as much caught up in spirituality as Jesus, Muhammad and the Buddha!"

"That sounds a bit cosmic," he said.

"Exactly," I said. "Now, you've had my thoughts; you owe me a penny, please!"

"Does this expanding circle include our connection with coffee?"

"Definitely!"

"That I can understand."

As we drank the coffee he'd brought, two or three sheep ventured into the wood and nibbled away at something, unbothered by our presence. Do sheep eat moss? There are so many things you never think about knowing.

It's quite a long wood, compared with its width at any rate, so after a while we went back up to the path and walked further on to near the other end, and scrambled down into it again. More sheep, but these ambled away at our approach. We sat down and cuddled up to each other, and I felt curiously protected – I don't mean by Phil so much as by the wood itself. Are there spirits of trees? Of places? I'm sure it's a 'thin' place, where, as they say, the distance between heaven and earth has collapsed; where the divine, the transcendent, is always more accessible; where a 'moment' has a greater probability of occurring.

What of other places? 'My' other places? I can quite believe that Loch Lomond is a thin place – it's a location that has its own mysteriousness, its own metaphorical as well as quite literal depths. But Silver Street in Cambridge? Hardly an obvious candidate for being a thin place, yet my 'moment' there was as profound as at Loch Lomond; and how about Trews Weir here in Exeter? More likely to be a thin place than Silver Street, granted, but nothing like as likely as Loch Lomond or Wistman's Wood. Perhaps the arrow of causality is the other way round, and it's not that a thin place makes an experience of transcendence more likely, but that such a 'moment' confers or creates thinness onto the place where it occurs.

We talked of the coming few months, how in the spring he would be moving back into Ellisian Fields, and how he's looking forward to getting back there and reclaiming Erwin ("if he'll condescend to return"). Getting some hens, too. I talked about developing my university work, and more involvement with adult literacy, and my worries about Mikey's future.

"What about us?" he asked.

"I'm looking forward to spending a lot more time with you," I said. "And doing loads of things with you as well."

"I was thinking on slightly different lines."

"What lines?"

"Was wondering more about you and your place," he said. "D'you plan to stay there?"

"I wasn't thinking of moving. Why?"

"It's just that there's easily room in my cottage for you as well. To move in. If you'd like to."

"Is that what you'd like?" I asked. "Would you like me to move in with you?"

"Yes," he said, doing his eyelash-fluttering. "Love it. Will you?"

Even as he asked I realised what my answer had to be. I didn't need to think. I sat up, looked at him, and said, "No."

Chapter 83

Phil

Teignford, Devon: January 1997

I've just finished reading the stuff I wrote in 1973 about the whole Melanie imbroglio, just before Ros and I got married. I think I convinced myself at the time of writing that it was an attempt to put it all behind me, trying to write her out of my system, as it were, before I got on to the next phase of my life. I'm not sure how successful I was in that – or whether that was the real motive. I suspect the real motive had more to do with the exact opposite, namely (viz. and to wit, as I regularly used to say) a refusal to let it go – otherwise why call my daughter 'Melanie'?

I found the memoir, a sort of quasi-journal, in Mum and Dad's attic, where I'd been rummaging through the boxes of old sketches for the Red Nose Day revue I've been roped into doing, and with it were a number of Melanie-related items. Cards and letters, including one from her friend, Anne, who'd told me about Melanie getting engaged to Simon, and adding that although she'd never met me, she was sorry it hadn't worked out between Melanie and me. When I got that letter, the news of Melanie's engagement twisted the heart all right, but by then I was married to Ros. And it's somewhat painful to reread it now.

There are the articles from *The Guardian* about the 'Movement of the Spirit' scandal, with the slimeball Derek Cranbrook (who, it was revealed at his trial, had never been a proper 'Reverend' in the first place – complete charlatan) being done for having sex with a series of underage girls. Bastard. Serves him right. There's also the review I cut out of *The Times* of Melanie's book *Transcending Gender.* Dr Mason, the reviewer opined, "has made a major contribution to the subject". I'd felt proud on her behalf, although I remember it plunged me into a hell of a melancholic 'what if' mood which lasted ages; and rereading it now triggers the annoying and frankly pointless feeling of 'if only'. There are a few other items – including photos from the Lake District and Cambridge, the empty wine bottle from the Varsity, and a pair of her black lacy knickers. All rather *otiose.*

So long ago, all that. I do wonder if there is a parallel Phil in a parallel universe who's still with his parallel Melanie, and what they're up to. Lucky parallel bugger. In this universe I'm going to Charlotte and Jimmy's little soirée, as Charlotte calls it, with Sam, as she's on her own for the weekend. No idea who else is going to be there; I'll have to check with Jimmy.

As for the scripts, reading through them I've laughed out loud quite a lot, though some of it is dire in the extreme. Utter drivel. Astonishing what some people laugh at. Between us, though, Alex, Rob and I had our moments. We did several more cabarets after Cambridge days, but it had faded out after about a year, what with Rob PhD-ing as well as getting married and settling in north London, me getting married and moving to darkest Kent, and Alex also plunging further into academia – ironically at Exeter just as I was moving away from Devon. My hopes of working for the BBC had already evaporated at an agonisingly awful interview a few weeks after Melanie and I had split: the four-man interviewing panel did not expend much of their valuable time on me, no doubt wisely, as I'd probably come across as more depressed than Spike Milligan on a bad day but nothing like as funny.

However, that was then and this is now. It'll be fun to tread the boards again.

Chapter 84

Melanie

Exeter: December 1997

Phil's head jerked back when I said I wouldn't move in with him. "Oh," he said in a small voice. "Oh, I see. Um, why not? Isn't that what we...um..."

He looked so mournful I would have fallen in love with him then and there if I hadn't already done so twenty-five years ago. I managed to keep my composure and said teasingly, "Why would I want to live with you?"

"Thought that was where we were heading. If you don't want to..."

"What I do want," I told him gently, "is for me to continue living on my own while Simon and I are still married, but once we're divorced, and I guess when you and Ros are divorced as well, I utterly and absolutely want to be with you full-time."

He brightened up. "That's more like it!" Then he frowned. "Hang on, you're talking about another two years plus!"

"During which we'll spend a lot of time together, do a lot together, including making lots of love," I assured him, "and after that we'll be together properly."

He was silent for ages, staring into the wood then looking up through the branches and twigs, so that I got worried in case he was going to say that wasn't good enough. I knew I wouldn't budge.

"You might have gone off me by then," he muttered.

"No chance. I haven't gone off you for over twenty-five years, so another two years isn't going to do it. You might go off me. You might decide to hitch up with Charlotte instead!"

"You cannot be serious!" he said in a McEnroe voice.

"Idiot. I love you."

We didn't say much more for a while as we were too occupied in kissing each other, then he admitted that what I'd said sounded like a good idea – we both needed to clear the decks of our marriages.

He picked up his backpack and started rummaging in it, saying, "You might call me a sentimental old fool..."

"You're a sentimental old fool," I obliged. "Now tell me why I'm calling you that."

"I've got something for you." He held out a tiny box just long enough for me to read on the lid in flowing gold script: "Melanie Ellis Jeweller". He opened it, saying, "Very sorry, but I couldn't find another key ring. You'll have to make do with this."

A real ring. A beautiful ring. Delicate gems of red and green. "A Lem special," he said. "Now, as a mere male I'm probably mortally offending you by this symbolically patriarchal and patronising action of mine in offering you a ring. Just say the word and I'll take it back to Lem, get a refund, and allow *you* to buy *me* some leather bondage gear instead."

"As far as rings are concerned," I said, "I'm prepared to be regularly offended. The same goes for flowers and chocolate. Don't you dare take it back! On the other hand, if you're going to be patriarchal and patronising, you can jolly well do it properly. On your bended knee, slave!"

"I've already done that in Cambridge!" he protested.

"Bended knee!"

He got down on one knee, there in Wistman's Wood as he had done twenty-five plus years ago first in my room at Girton and then in the Varsity, yelped and leaped up again as evidently something dug into his knee, knelt down again but this time on a patch of wet moss, said "Oh fuck!" loudly to which I said, "Later, darling, later," got up again, and squatted on his haunches in front of me in a rather lavatorial pose, and said, "Melanie Mason," (I didn't correct the wrong surname. To him I want still to be *Mason*), "this can't be an engagement ring because we're already married...to other people! Instead, this can be an eternity ring. Will you," he asked solemnly, "do me the honour of becoming my eternity?"

I simply said, "I already am." I couldn't think of anything more original or profound or witty.

He put the ring on my finger in the time-honoured fashion. It fits perfectly.

Digging into his backpack again, he pulled out a small bottle of fizz and a couple of plastic glasses, and witnessed by the spirits of Wistman's Wood, disguised as moss and lichen and fern, and in the presence of bleary-eyed sheep and circling crows, we drank a toast: "to us!"

Epilogue

Exeter: Saturday 15th July 2000

"That's brilliant!" Anne exclaimed, her voice shrill down the phone. "It's all happening today?"

"Even as we speak," said Melanie. "They've nearly finished loading the van."

"Fantastic! Is Phil there?"

"He's at our cottage."

"Waiting to carry you over the threshold?"

"Ha! He'd better not. I don't want him to rick his back!"

"I think it's dead lovely," said Anne. "Moving in with the man of your dreams."

The two friends talked a little longer until, a removal man indicating he wanted a word with her, Melanie ended the phone call, telling Anne she hoped that before long she and Jeremy would come and visit.

"Okay, sweetie!" Anne chirruped. "That'd be nice. In the meantime, have fun! Lorra lorra love!"

Melanie's divorce from Simon had been straightforward. The decree absolute had come through at the beginning of the year, Simon having left Exeter the previous autumn. He was now down in Cornwall to be more on hand for a major development in the original transport project. His solicitor had turned out to be Olivia, Christian Union Olivia. The last few times Melanie and Simon had spoken, her name had regularly cropped up, and not solely in her role as his solicitor, though precisely what the relationship between her and Simon was Melanie had not inquired too closely. Whatever it might be, she hoped it would work out well for Simon.

In the first week of 1999 Melanie's mother had died suddenly of a brain haemorrhage, leaving Melanie and Mikey half-shares in her sizeable estate. Mikey's share had been put in trust.

Phil's divorce from Ros had taken longer than expected, thanks to complications concerning Ros's business into which Phil's parents had once put some money to enable her to open another salon. An agreement had finally been reached and the money released. This, combined with Melanie's legacy, had enabled them to buy the Ellisian Fields cottage from Sam, who had just inherited it from her father.

Today, Melanie's fiftieth birthday, sees the culmination of the process of her and Phil being together.

The removal man told her the van was packed, and would set off for Teignford after lunch. As Melanie wandered around the cottage where she had lived for the past three years, James Tredwell in his guise of a letting agent arrived. He called her formally "Ms Mason" – she had reverted to her maiden name – and went quickly round the cottage, making a few notes, complimenting her on the state of the property, announcing himself satisfied that there was nothing that counted as damage above only ordinary wear and tear, signing a form, requesting her signature, receiving the keys from her, then asking her to wait a moment while he went to his car.

On his return, he had put on a wildly flamboyant harlequin jacket and was carrying a huge bouquet of flowers. Mr James Tredwell the sober businessman had been replaced by Tredders, the outrageous impresario. "My dear lady!" he announced grandly. "This is a great day for Philip and his muse! I cannot let it pass unremarked!" With a deep bow he handed her the bouquet. The scent was overpowering, and the attached card read, "Melanie & Philip! Phil & his Muse. Two hearts that beat as one! The world is your stage! Your loyal and devoted Tredders!"

"Wonderful! Thank you! You are so sweet!" Melanie said, and kissed him. He made another deep bow.

Melanie had already loaded her car with items not going in the van, including her computer and some academic files, among which were her burgeoning notes on the visions and music of Hildegard of Bingen. She gathered the few remaining items and left the cottage, Tredders locking it behind them. A few minutes later he was waving her off, calling out, "Kindly inform him that from now on I fully expect scripts of superlative genius to emanate from his pen!"

Phil was outside waiting with Charlotte when Melanie drew up at Ellisian Fields. Smiling as he opened the driver's door, he looked tired, having been working hard over the previous few months: in addition to his private tutoring, sketches were being written for the next series of *Mind the Boggles*, as well as new material for another Tredders revue, and a five-minute film script informally commissioned by the Honourable Tristan Edyvean, one-time occupant of a room in the Selwyn Gardens set-up, now chair of a government-backed enquiry into the social and psychological ill-effects of recreational drug use.

Melanie had noticed in the last few months that Phil's hair was definitely getting greyer, but still considerably more abundant than that of Alex or Rob, who had visited earlier in the year. Their cabaret from scratch, performed in the village hall, had been shambolically hilarious.

"Hi!" Phil said.

"Hi!"

"When's the van arriving?"

"About two. Have you got the bubbly?"

"Charlotte's brought it."

"How sweet."

The van's contents were transferred to the cottage without too much fuss. Phil had drawn up a schedule for where everything was to go which worked remarkably well, though the second bedroom ended up more cluttered than ever. Erwin, in the main bedroom, was thrusting his nose repeatedly into one of Phil's unwashed tee-shirts, and purring loudly before curling up on the contents of a half-emptied suitcase of Melanie's clothes. Charlotte, arranging the flowers from Tredders in a number of vase substitutes such as a large milk jug and a cylindrical pottery wine cooler, and (re)organising the kitchen on Melanie's behalf despite her protests that Phil's way of doing things was fine by her, kept up a running commentary on recent village gossip, the main item of which, however, did not have to be revealed, concerning as it did Charlotte herself: she had recently remarried after an acrimonious divorce from Jimmy followed by a whirlwind romance with a therapist she had been recommended. "He calls himself a body worker," she'd confided to Melanie and Chloe as they'd polished off the last of Jimmy's former wine cellar when she'd told them the news. "Quite frankly, he can work my body any day," and she had sniggered in a way that had become increasingly noticeable in her since Jimmy had left.

Phil's cousin, henna-haired Sam, arrived at her childhood home with a present of a wheelbarrow and a set of garden tools. "I'd love to come and help you get the garden in order," she told Melanie. "He's hopeless at it! Aren't you, coz?" Phil had agreed.

As arranged, Chloe and Natasha dropped in for half an hour on their way to a 'Wimmin Together' event at some allegedly sacred site out on Dartmoor, followed by Rita with a gift of scented candles. "Patrick sends... from him...he wants to wish...sends his good wishes," she sighed. "With love from Patrick & Rita" in the accompanying card was in just the one handwriting.

A candle was lit, the bubbly cracked open, toasts were drunk; then all the visitors in turn hugged and kissed Melanie and Phil.

*

They'd gone. Melanie and Phil had the cottage to themselves. Phil closed the front door, locked it, and turned to Melanie, taking both her hands in his. He kissed her. "Happy birthday, sweetheart!"

"What a lovely birthday! Fifty not out." She smiled mischievously. "What's happened to my present?"

"In hand," Phil said, "or rather, on foot. You know that posh place in Cathedral Close that sells shoes and handbags and stuff like that? They've got a poster in the window advertising 'Fabulous Women's Shoes'. I was thinking of getting you a pair, seeing as how you're—"

"A fabulous woman?" Melanie laughed. "That'd be wonderful!"

"Meanwhile, you've got me," said Phil, fluttering his eyelashes. "What more could you possibly want?"

"You really are a conceited sod, aren't you?" she laughed again.

"With much to be conceited about."

"Prove it!"

So he did.

Lightning Source UK Ltd.
Milton Keynes UK
UKHW030756250920
370505UK00002B/18

9 781781 329917